*In memory of Margaret C. Brauer (1917–1996) –
always encouraging, always sure my latest work was
the best thing I'd ever written. Thanks, Mum.*

Damsel in Distress

A Daisy Dalrymple Mystery

CAROLA DUNN

Constable • London

CONSTABLE

First published in the US in 1997 by St Martin's Press, New York

First published in Great Britain in 2010 by Robinson,
an imprint of Constable & Robinson Ltd

Reprinted in 2015 by Constable

5 7 9 10 8 6

A CIP catalogue record for this book
is available from the British Library.

ISBN 978-1-84901-331-4

Printed and bound in Great Britain by
CPI Group (UK) Ltd, Croydon CR0 4YY

Papers used by Constable are from well-managed forests
and other responsible sources

MIX
Paper from
responsible sources
FSC® C104740

Constable
is an imprint of
Little, Brown Book Group
Carmelite House
50 Victoria Embankment
London EC4Y 0DZ

An Hachette UK Company
www.hachette.co.uk

www.littlebrown.co.uk

CHAPTER 1

Phillip strained his ears. Yes, there it was, that sinister knocking noise again.

The aging engine of his Swift two-seater made a deuce of a racket going up the steepish hill, and odd squeaks and rattles from chassis and body were inevitable. He worked the old bus pretty hard. For every joint oiled, for every bolt tightened, another loosened. But the knocking was new, different, and bally sinister.

Safely over the crest of the Surrey Downs, he pulled off the 'B' road into a convenient gateway. A cow looked at him over the five-barred gate and mooed.

'I'll be gone long before milking time,' he assured her, jumping out.

Taking off his blazer, he dropped it on the seat and rolled up his sleeves before he opened up the bonnet. As he peered into the oily depths, the hum of a well-tuned engine approached along the road. He glanced round to see a scarlet Aston Martin zip past, stop, reverse, and come to a halt beside him.

'Say, are you stuck?' enquired the girl behind the wheel, putting back her dust-veil to reveal a pretty face surrounded by blond curls. 'Can I give you a ride?'

'Thanks awfully, but I'm not exactly stuck.'

'Oh.' The American girl – Phillip was sure she must be American – looked enquiringly at the Swift. 'You have the hood up.'

'The hood?' He glanced at the hood, folded down on this mild, dry spring day. Ah, but she was American, she probably called it the roof. 'You mean the bonnet? Something's knocking in the engine,' he explained, 'but if a few minutes' tinkering with my own tools won't solve it, I'll drive on to the next garage and borrow their tools.'

'You fix your own automobile? Gee, that's real smart.'

'Nothing much to boast about,' Phillip said modestly. On a closer inspection those curls were gold, not mere blond, and her face was the prettiest he'd seen in years, not smothered in powder and paint, either, like most these days. 'I like messing about with motor-cars,' he confessed, glad that he hadn't yet got around to crawling underneath and getting oil on his face. 'Just wish I could spend more time at it.'

'I've always wanted to take a whack at it.' She was a girl in a million! 'But Poppa won't let me. He says it's not ladylike. Real set on me acting ladylike, Poppa is. Why, it took me years to talk him into letting me drive. Now I test automobiles for him, just motoring around to check out how they feel to an amateur driver.'

'Is that what you're doing with this beauty? Don't see many of them on the roads.'

'It runs swell. Poppa's thinking of investing a few bucks so they can raise production. That's what we're doing in England, looking for up-and-coming auto manufacturers for Poppa to invest in. I guess you can tell I'm not English?' she asked wistfully.

'I think your accent's absolutely ripping.'

'Honest Injun? And there I was wanting to learn to talk like a proper English lady. I just love England, the quaint little villages and the history and flowers everywhere.'

She waved her hand at the verge and hedge-bank. Phillip suddenly noticed the April profusion of primroses, violets, celandines, and stitchwort, hitherto unobserved.

'But gee,' the girl continued, sounding quite regretful, 'I mustn't keep you from your tinkering. The truth is, I'm kinda lost. The signposts all point to places I don't want to go. Can you direct me to the main London road?'

Phillip opened his mouth to say, 'Second to the right and straight on till morning,' or whatever the directions were, when he was struck by a brain-wave. At least, he rather thought it might be a brain-wave. The Honourable Phillip Petrie was not sufficiently acquainted with the bally things to be quite sure at first sight. In fact, he was all too accustomed to being regarded by family and friends alike as a bit of a chump.

Still, it did look awfully like a brain-wave. 'It's rather complicated,' he lied, 'from here to the London road. If you're not in a frightful hurry, if you wouldn't mind waiting a few minutes, you could follow me.'

The girl's dazzling smile made him blink. 'What a swell idea,' she exclaimed.

Much heartened, Phillip produced the second part of his inspiration. 'I don't know about you,' he said recklessly, 'but I'm getting jolly peckish. It's nearly tea-time and there's a frightfully good little tea-shop in Purley. Would you ... Do you think you might consider joining me for tea?'

'Golly gee, I'd love to,' said the wonderful girl. 'We don't have anything like the English afternoon tea, but when I get home I'm surely going to keep it up. I'm Gloria Arbuckle, by the way.' She held out her hand.

'Phillip Petrie.' Shaking hands, he frowned. 'You shouldn't accept invitations from strangers, you know, Miss Arbuckle. Come to that, your father shouldn't let you drive around the countryside alone. What if you broke down?'

'I'm supposed to take Poppa's assistant with me,' she admitted, 'but he was busy, and on the first fine day in ages, I wanted to get out of that smoky city. As for the invitation, it's not like you asked me to go drinking and dancing in some speakeasy. You don't even have speakeasies over here.'

'No,' said Phillip, rocked by another brain-wave, 'but we have jolly good dance floors, perfectly respectable, and I'd be most frightfully bucked if, one of these days, you'd go dancing with me?'

'We'll see,' she said, but she smiled.

'What-ho, old thing.'

At this unceremonious greeting, Daisy looked up in annoyance from her second-hand Underwood. She had assumed the footsteps in the hall were someone calling on Lucy, who shared the 'bijou' residence with her.

'Oh, it's you, Phillip. What do you want? I told Mrs. Potter I can't see anyone. I'm busy.'

'She said you were just writing,' Phillip said defensively, dropping his grey Homburg hat on the desk.

'*Just* writing! I'll have to have a word with her.'

'Well, perhaps I put the "just" in. No need to rag the poor old dear.'

'For heaven's sake, Phillip, writing is how I make my living and I've two articles due. I keep forgetting to allow for how long the post takes to New York. The American magazine pays jolly well and I don't want to risk losing the work by being late. So unless you've got something urgent to say . . .'

'Not exactly urgent, but it won't take a minute, honestly.' With a diffident gesture, Phillip smoothed his sleek, fair hair. His conventionally good-looking face bore such an appealing look that Daisy gave in.

'All right,' she sighed. 'Let's hear it.'

Perching his loose-limbed frame on the corner of her desk, he swung a long leg clad in pin-stripe trousering and contemplated the well-polished tip of his shoe. She swivelled her chair to face him.

'Well,' he said, a faint flush creeping up his cheeks, 'it's like this. Er . . .'

'Phillip, get a move on!'

'Yes, well, dash it, this is a bit difficult, old bean.'

'Is it *necessary*?'

'I should ruddy well think so. A proper cad I'd look if I didn't . . . You see, the thing is . . . I say, Daisy, you know I've proposed to you once or twice?'

'At least half a dozen times.'

'That many?' he said, rather aghast.

'And I've turned you down just as many. I know you only ask because you feel Gervaise would expect you to take care of me.' Daisy's brother, killed in the Great War, had been Phillip's best pal since childhood, growing up on a neighboring estate. 'Which is rubbish, so out with it. You've found someone else, haven't you? Someone you really want to marry?'

'By Jove, how did you guess?' Phillip's patent relief almost made Daisy laugh.

She managed to control herself. 'Who is it? Someone I know? One of the latest crop of debs?'

'As a matter of fact, she's American. You like Americans, don't you?' he asked anxiously.

'I've met some charming Americans. The one who especially springs to mind is Mr. Thorwald, my editor.' Daisy looked longingly at the half-typed sheet of paper in the typewriter. 'Tell me about her,' she said, resigned.

'Her name's Gloria – Gloria Arbuckle. She's a poppet.'

Daisy had expected a 'stunner,' an 'angel,' or a 'jolly good sport.' The old-fashioned word Phillip chose to describe his beloved impressed her even more than the glow in his blue eyes. Unlike others she could name, he wasn't given to falling for pretty girls, so perhaps he really had found his true love. She hoped so.

'Miss Arbuckle is here with her family?' she asked.

'Her father. Her mother died a couple of years ago, and she's an only child. Mr. Arbuckle's a millionaire. I know what people will think, Daisy,' he said earnestly, 'but you don't believe I care about the shekels, do you?'

'Of course not, old dear, not when I haven't a bean and you've been proposing to me regularly once a month for ever. I take it Miss Arbuckle's convinced of your unmercenary nature, but what about her father?'

'He's a good sort and he seems to rather like me. In fact, Gloria says he's taken to me in a big way, but he doesn't know yet that I want to marry her.'

'Does he know your father's a lord?' Daisy asked. Republicans though they were, quite a lot of Americans seemed to consider a title for their daughters well worth the price of purchase.

'Yes, but I don't think he has a frightfully high opinion of the peerage. Besides, I've explained it all, that I'm a younger son with no chance of inheriting the title, and I'll never be more than an "Hon." or have more than a small allowance.' He grimaced. 'My people haven't met them yet.'

'Aha! You're expecting a ragging from ... What is it, Mrs. Potter?'

Breathing heavily, the stout charwoman beamed as she set a tray of tea-things on the desk. 'The kettle were just on the boil, miss, so I thought I'd bring up a nice cuppa for you and the gentleman. No biscuits,' she added regretfully. 'We finished 'em up for elevenses, miss, remember?'

'Yes,' Daisy said guiltily. Though no slimming diet could possibly make her rounded figure fashionably boyish, she really ought to make an effort. At least, Lucy said so. Frequently. 'Thank you, Mrs. Potter.'

'I'll pour,' Phillip offered, leaving his perch and pulling the other chair up to the desk. 'The typewriter's in your way.'

'This is *not* turning into a tea-party! One cup, and off you go. Happy as I am to hear your news, I've work to do.'

'You'll be free this weekend, won't you?' he asked hopefully, passing her a steaming cup. 'I want you to meet Gloria and Arbuckle, and ... well, actually, I hoped you'd go with me when I take them to meet my people. Lend your support, and all that.'

'You're going to brace up and bite the bullet? I could spare a couple of hours, if you really think my presence would help. Are Lord and Lady Petrie coming up to town specially to meet them?'

'Lord no! The Arbuckles are staying in Great Malvern,

at the Abbey Hotel. Gloria wanted to get out of town – she adores the English countryside – so I persuaded Arbuckle that Malvern's convenient for his business doings in Oxford and Coventry and Birmingham.'

'Hardly! And apart from the Malvern Hills, the countryside isn't anything special.'

'It's easy to drive to both the Cotswolds and the Welsh mountains,' Phillip argued, 'and none of those cities is more than fifty miles away. Not to mention the concerts and tennis and golf . . .'

'You needn't go on,' said Daisy, laughing. 'I've read the adverts. "Healthiest of health resorts, lowest death rate in the kingdom, purest water in the world."'

'I threw all that guff at him, but the clincher was the Morgan Motor Company being in the town. Arbuckle's looking to invest in British motor manufacturers to diversify his holdings. He made his packet by selling out his railway stocks – railroad, they call it – and going into automobiles, in America, at just the right moment.'

'Stocks and shares, just your line.'

Shaking his head, Phillip pulled a face. 'I can't stand the perishing City much longer. I'm an absolute duffer at it. If Gloria will marry me, I hope her father will find me a job in the technical end of the motor-car business, but I'm going to tell the pater I'm getting out anyway.'

'You've always hated it,' Daisy sympathized. 'Like me and stenography.'

'I'd rather be a common-or-garden hired motor mechanic, greasy overalls and all, and what's more, I'd make more money at it. I'd even rather sell second-hand cars. If that don't suit the pater's notions of consequence, he can jolly well cough up the ready to set up my own business. I know a fellow who's dying to go into partnership, and . . .'

'Not now, Phillip. I can't make it to Malvern this weekend, but if you can wait till next, I'll come along to hold your hand.'

'Will you? You're a real brick, Daisy!'

'I owe Mother a visit. She's feeling neglected, as she never hesitates to let me know.'

'I'll pop in and see her. I'm buzzing down on Saturday anyway – I've been home every weekend since Gloria left town. There's a chappie staying at the hotel,' he added darkly, 'who's been making a dead set at her. I get down as much as I can.'

'Your parents must be a bit surprised by the sudden excess of filial devotion, and the Arbuckles that you haven't yet introduced them. You've only just plucked up the nerve?'

Phillip was indignant. 'Not at all. It's only last week I began to think I had a real chance with Gloria, and then I had to talk to you first. The mater . . . All right,' he said hastily, standing up as she thrust his hat at him, 'I've talked. I'm going. You'll like her, Daisy. She's got golden curls and the bluest eyes you ever saw, and . . .'

'Toodle-oo, Phillip,' said Daisy, cutting short the rhapsody.

'Oh, right-ho, pip-pip. And you honestly don't mind?'

'I honestly don't mind a bit.'

Phillip went off at last with an air of enormous relief.

Her fingers resting on the typewriter keys, Daisy pondered a moment before taking up her interrupted train of thought. So Gloria had golden curls and blue eyes, did she? And no doubt a million-dollar wardrobe. Well, her own eyes were blue, but her shingled hair was an intermediate brown and her wardrobe mostly last year's, if not older, and bought at Selfridge's Bargain Basement.

Not that she was jealous. Phillip was an honorary brother. He had never even pretended to be in love with her. She was just afraid the dear old ass might have fallen for a pretty face without considering what was behind it.

But he had described Gloria as a poppet, not a stunner. Daisy could only hope she was going to like the American girl.

Occasional gateways in the hedges revealed Bredon Hill on the horizon to the right; the Malvern Hills loomed ahead. From a cloudless sky the sun shone down on drought-parched fields and orchards, rotten luck for the farmers but perfect for a fellow in love.

"'It's three o'clock in the morning,'" Phillip warbled merrily, if inaccurately and off-key, as he tootled along the narrow, winding lane across the Severn plain. "'We've danced the whole night through.'"

Nearly home. He'd have a quick wash and brush-up, change his clothes, and then drive into Great Malvern, stopping at Violet's for a box of chocs. After tea with the Arbuckles at the Abbey Hotel, he and Gloria would stroll by the swan pool in Priory Park. Later they might go to the pictures, if there was anything decent showing, or dance at the Winter Gardens ballroom to the music of Billy Gammon's All-Star Players.

Dancing, he hoped. If there was any bliss greater than doing the Charleston, tango, or fox-trot with Gloria, it was waltzing with Gloria.

Lost in a dream, he zipped round a bend – and jammed on his brakes. A large motor-car, though pulled into a gateway, blocked half the lane.

'By Jove!' Phillip muttered. 'It's a good job I overhauled the brakes the other day. What the deuce . . . Oh!' His irritation with the idiot who'd stopped in such a spot vanished as he recognized Arbuckle's vast blue Studebaker touring car.

Arbuckle, sitting in the back seat, turned and waved. And there was Gloria, perched on the top bar of the gate, slim, silk-clad ankles very much in evidence, golden hair outshining the stubble of the hayfield behind her.

'Phil . . . Mr. Petrie,' she cried, 'aren't you just an angel? A regular White Knight rushing to the rescue!' She started to climb down.

Phillip leapt from the Swift, squeezed between Studebaker and hedge, and arrived just in time to catch her as she jumped the last two bars.

'Careful,' he said breathlessly, his arms about her waist. She gazed up at him, eyes blue as the sky, rosy lips parted. Overhead a lark poured out a burst of melody, and the air was full of the fragrance of wild roses.

Mr. Arbuckle coughed. Phillip and Gloria sprang apart.

'Waal now,' said her father, a short, spare man with a long face lengthened by a receding hairline, 'if this isn't quite a coincidence.'

'You've broken down, sir?' Phillip asked, at last noticing the Studebaker's bonnet open on both sides. 'I'll have a look, shall I?'

'It's mighty kind of you to offer, young fella, but I guess it's not something that can be fixed on the spot. Me, I'm the financial wizard, don't pretend to understand the mechanical stuff, but Crawford, my technical man, was driving us. Say, you've met him.'

'Yes, you introduced us.' He hadn't pursued the acquaintance, not having taken to the American engineer, despite his enviably extensive knowledge of motor-cars' design and manufacture.

'Crawford knows autos if anyone does. He went off with some broken part or other to hike to the nearest garage.'

'I might as well have a dekko.' Phillip already had his aged tweed jacket off. He tossed it into the Studebaker and rolled up his sleeves. He wasn't about to pass up a good excuse to examine an unfamiliar engine.

Gloria came and stood beside him. 'Mr. Crawford said something about the radiator,' she said uncertainly. 'Didn't he, Poppa?'

'Beats me, honey.'

'That's it.' Phillip pointed. 'Look, the hose is gone. It must have split. I think I have a spare in my tool-box which just might fit. Let's give it a try?'

'Atta-boy!' said Mr. Arbuckle with a nod of approval. 'That's what I like to hear. Be Prepared. It's a wunnerful motto, yes sirree, and not just for Boy Scouts.'

'Yes, sir.' Phillip grinned at him. He was growing quite fond of the old bird.

He fetched a couple of lengths of different-sized hose, a knife, spanner, and screwdriver from the tool-kit attached to the Swift's running board. As he bent over the Studebaker, a brown Ford motor-van with FARRIS, BUTCHERS painted on the side panel came along the lane and stopped.

A burly man, shabbily dressed, stepped down. Touching

his cap to Arbuckle and Gloria, he addressed Phillip, 'Wotcher, cock. Need an 'and?'

'No, thanks. It's just a matter of getting a new radiator hose clamped in.'

The man leaned with meaty hands on the Studebaker's nose. 'Yer'll need water to fill 'er up, gov'nor,' he pointed out.

'True,' Phillip agreed. 'I'll buzz over to the nearest farm in my bus.' Gesturing with the screwdriver towards the Swift, he turned his head slightly. From the corner of his eye he caught a sudden motion.

Arbuckle cried out. Phillip swung round. Heavy boots thudded on the dry, packed earth of the lane as four men masked with handkerchiefs rushed around the front of the van.

Two dived over the side of the Studebaker reaching for Arbuckle. One grabbed Gloria. The fourth swung a crowbar at Phillip.

He ducked the blow.

'Gloria!' he shouted, and went for her attacker with the screwdriver.

The van's driver caught him from behind and wrenched the screwdriver from his grasp. A second swing of the crowbar caught him on the side of the head.

Exploding stars blinded him. His ears rang. Distantly aware of a heavy, sweetish odour, he sank into darkness.

CHAPTER 2

Chloroform! The word came to Phillip in the instant of rousing. Then the explosive roar of the big guns inside his head claimed all his attention.

After a while, he grew almost used to the internal shelling. He was lying curled up on his side, he realized. His wrists were tied behind his back and his shoulders ached dully. The dark red inside his eyelids suggested a dim light. Cautiously he opened his eyes.

A narrow sunbeam streaked, flickering, across dusty, uneven floorboards, then zigzagged upwards, climbing, gleaming on beige silk stockings ... Gloria! Ye gods, how could he have forgotten? The devils had bagged her too!

'Miss Arbuckle?' he whispered. 'Gloria?'

She did not move. Praying her stillness was just the effect of the chloroform he had smelled, that they hadn't hurt her, Phillip raised his head. The pain sent him spiraling back down into the dark.

He roused again – five minutes, half an hour, half a day later, he had no way of knowing – to feel a drop land on his cheek. The detonations inside his skull had diminished to mere hammer-strokes. Some seemed to come from a distance, *tock-tock-tock*, like a woodpecker. And that angry chattering scold sound like a squirrel. Was he in a wood?

The air he breathed had a damp feel, a woodsy, mildewy smell, but the surface he lay on was too hard for leaf-mould and there was a faint odour of paraffin. He remembered floorboards, warped and split, with cracks between. And Gloria!

Opening his eyes as another drop plopped onto his cheek, he turned his head and looked up into Gloria's face. There was just enough light left to see her heavenly blue eyes red and swollen with tears.

'Don't cry, Glow-worm. We'll get out of this somehow.'

'Oh, Ph-Phillip, I was afraid you were d-dead,' she sobbed, positively raining on him.

'Well, I'm not. So be a good girl and dry your eyes and blow your nose and let's put our heads together.'

'I c-can't reach my handkerchief. I couldn't even wipe the blood off your poor head.'

Her hands were tied in front of her. Phillip seethed at the sight of the cord cutting into her slender wrists. He gritted his teeth – an outburst would help neither of them.

'Perhaps you can reach mine,' he said calmly, 'if you think you can use it when you've got it. In my shirt pocket.' His jacket, he supposed, must still be in the Studebaker where he had dropped it . . . how long ago?

While Gloria, kneeling beside him, fumbled for his handkerchief, Phillip studied what he could see of their surroundings. The low ceiling, sloping downward on two sides, was rough, discoloured plaster, speckled with mildew, between ancient, sagging beams. In one corner, a dark brown stain looked like the result of a leak in the roof above.

The stain ran down the wall. On the floor at the bottom lay a few chunks and a small heap of crumbled plaster.

A hole? Phillip silently cursed the confounded bonds about his wrists. Not that a way into the attic seemed frightfully useful, always supposing he could have reached it, but it irked him that he couldn't even investigate properly.

'I have it!' With two fingers Gloria triumphantly fished the handkerchief out and shook it open.

'Well done.'

She promptly dropped it on the floor. 'Darn. Now it's too dirty to use to clean your head.' Groping, she picked it up between finger and thumb. This time when she shook it, a cloud of dust flew.

Phillip held his breath till the dust settled. The way he felt, a sneeze might take off the top of his head. 'You'd have had to use spit, anyway, Glow-worm. I expect I look a frightful mess, but on the whole I'd rather you didn't touch it.'

'Poor honey, it must be real sore. Does your head ache badly?'

In spite of their situation, Phillip revelled in her solicitude. 'Not as bad as it was,' he assured her, awkwardly rolling over and sitting up. The bursting shells promptly returned full force and his sight blurred. For a ghastly moment he thought he was going to be sick. Then the pain diminished again to a dull throb. 'But it does still ache rather, and I don't want to find out how tender it is where I got whacked. How do you feel?'

'I was sure woozy when I woke up, but I'm okay now. Do you know what it was they used?'

'Chloroform, by the smell. I was put out with it once

when I broke my arm and had to have it set. I wish they'd used that on me instead of a crowbar!'

'Oh, Phillip, why did they hit you and drug me and bring us here? What are they going to do with us? What do they want?' She bit her lip, but a sob escaped. 'What have they done with Poppa?'

She sat beside him, nestled against his side. Had Phillip possessed a fortune, he would have given every penny to be able to put his arms around her now. But Arbuckle was the one with the fortune.

'Ransom!' he said. 'They won't hurt your father because he'll have to be free to cough up the dollars.'

'Do you think so?'

'I bet that's what it's all about. They're always doing it in America, aren't they? Speakeasies and gangsters and kidnappings, you read about them all the time.'

'You make it sound terrible, and it's not. Most places aren't like that at all. Ordinary people don't have a thing to do with gangsters.'

'But you're not ordinary, Glow-worm,' Phillip pointed out gently. 'Apart from being the sweetest, prettiest . . . Yes, well, I won't go into all that now. But apart from that, it's no secret your poppa's simply rolling in the stuff. He's practically a walking target for hoodlums.'

'But we aren't in the States. And the guy who drove the butcher's van sure sounded English to me. He was one of them, wasn't he? I figure the rest were hiding in the back of the van.'

'Probably. Yes, he was definitely English, a Cockney actually, though the number plate was local. They must have stolen it, or the van.'

'Cockneys are from London? You all sound just plain British to me.'

'And all Americans sound American to me. I didn't hear the other men speak, did you? They could have been Yanks.'

For once Gloria didn't tick him off for his use of the slang term for her countrymen and threaten playfully to call him a Limey. As an effort to distract her, the scheme was a dismal failure.

'I hope they're not,' she said with a shiver. 'Some of those gangsters don't think twice about spraying bullets around.'

'They won't do that. Your father will want proof of your safety before he'll hand over a farthing. A dime.'

'Oh Phillip, I'm glad you're here. I'm scared, but I'd be even more scared without you.'

She needed him, not like Daisy, who tended to regard his efforts to protect her as an irritating intrusion. But what was a fellow to do, when all he wanted was to shield his sweetheart against the world and he couldn't even hold her little hand to comfort her?

He bent his head and kissed her forehead. It wasn't quite the circumstances he had imagined for their first kiss.

It didn't help morale that the light was fading fast. The small, square window, in the centre of one wall of the small, square room, was barricaded with heavy boards, nailed in place. The streak of sunshine which had earlier squeezed between the planks was long gone. Outside, the long summer evening might linger. Inside, it would very soon be dark.

Time was a-wasting. He didn't think more than a few minutes had passed since he came to, but what an absolute ass he was, sitting here chatting!

'Glow-worm, you've tried the door?'

'Yes. There's no keyhole but it won't budge. I guess it's barred on the other side.'

'Oh well, not much chance they'd forget it. Before the light goes you'd better see if you can untie my hands.'

'I tried before, when you were unconscious. The knots are too tight. But I guess I could try to cut the rope with a bit of broken glass. There's some over there under the window.' She struggled to her feet, crossed to the window, and crouched down. 'I didn't dare try as long as you might wake up and move any moment. I was afraid of cutting a vein and killing you.'

Phillip joined her. Among the scraps and splinters of the broken window-panes were three or four largish shards. 'Can you pick up a piece without cutting yourself?'

'Yes, but I can't get a real good grip on it. I won't be able to see too well, either. Gee, I wish I really was a glow-worm.'

'I'll turn around, so you have all the light there is. Hack away, and don't mind my groans when you stab me.'

Stab him she did, and nick him, and slice him. After an 'Oh, Phillip, I'm sorry,' at the first sign of blood, she sawed away in silence and he managed neither to groan nor to twitch. It might have been worse if his hands had not been pretty well numbed by cut-off circulation.

In the quiet, Phillip heard voices. They seemed to come from below, through gaps between the shrunken floorboards.

'Hear that?' Phillip whispered. 'Hold on a jiffy I want to see if I can hear what they're saying.' He lay down and pressed his ear to one of the wider cracks. The smell of paraffin grew stronger.

'. . . still out?' someone asked.

'Out to the wide, last time we 'ad a butcher's.' Butcher's hook – look; it was Cockney rhyming slang. Not a Yankee, nor a local man, but another Londoner. 'That chloroform's powerful stuff.'

'You *sure* you didn't clobber the bloke too 'ard, Jimmy?' The third voice, also Cockney, held the anxious note of an oft-repeated query.

'Not bloody likely. D'ya fink I wants to dangle? Pity I didn't 'ave me sandbag 'andy but we wasn't supposed to need anyfing else, just the chloro. Anyways, I got it down to a fine art, 'asn't I, so not to worry, cock.'

'Better start worryin'.' That was the first voice again, the van driver's, Phillip was almost sure. 'The Yank's mad as fire 'bout you bringing the young cove along too.'

'Us! 'Oo was it said 'e talked like a nob, and 'oo found 'is card-case in the two-seater? 'E's a Hon, you says, and what that means is, 'is pa's a lord.'

'Did I tell ya to grab 'im for ransom along wiv the girl?' the driver demanded aggrievedly. 'Did I? Like bloody 'ell, I did! The Yank's right, most nobs's dough's tied up in land and big 'ouses and art and such. They ain't got the ready, not quick, any'ow, not like Mr. Moneybags. Yer want ter 'ang around a few weeks while 'is bloody lordship sells a few of 'is fancy pitchers?'

'Weeks? Gorblimey, no.'

'Right, then.'

'So whatta we do?' asked the anxious voice. 'We can't just let 'im go. "E'll 'op it to the rozzers straight orf.'

'We'll 'ave to keep 'im till the ransom's paid and we let the girl go.'

"E's no use,' the driver said carelessly. 'Just get in the way.

The Yank says, you're ter get rid of 'im – for keeps. Rub 'im out, pronto.'

A long silence followed this announcement.

Phillip shuddered. Nothing in four years of appalling trench warfare had affected him quite like that apparently casual order to murder him in cold blood. Shells and shrapnel, poison gas, machine-gun bullets, even a sniper's fire, were impersonal. One didn't know the name of the man one bayonetted face to face, and anyway it was a case of kill or be killed. But Phillip was no threat to these men, no mortal threat at least, though he'd gladly see them rot in gaol for the rest of their lives for what they were doing to Gloria.

'I dunno . . .' said one, hesitantly.

'Not me,' the crowbar-wielder affirmed. 'I don't swing for nobody.'

'Yer'll all be assessories anyways,' the driver advised them. ''E don't care who does it, but summun's gonna 'ave ter or the deal's orf, 'E reckons no one won't miss 'im for a while, the way 'e's always 'opping about, 'ere today and gone termorra. If ya wants yer share o' the goods, don't cross the Yank. Ya'd better pick cards or summat.'

'Us? What abaht you?'

'Me, I'm orf back to the Smoke. The old man saw my face, it ain't safe for me round these parts. Done my bit, I 'ave, all I were brung in for, and bin paid my bit f'rit. Them as wants ter scoop the pool 'as to work 'arder. Enjoy yerselves among the clod'oppers, mates. Bright lights, 'ere I come!'

His blithe voice grew fainter as he spoke, and a moment later, Phillip heard a door slam shut. He sat up.

'Have they gone?' Gloria asked softly. 'What did they say?'

He thanked heaven she had not listened. 'One of them has left. The rest are still here, or only stepped out for a moment. They're after ransom, as we guessed. They were talking about letting you go when it's paid.'

'Poppa will pay, just soon as ever he can.'

'Of course.' Not soon enough for Phillip, however. He wasn't going to go without a fight, though. 'Gloria, are you almost through the rope?' he asked urgently.

'It's awful slow work, honey,' she apologized. 'There's one strand about ready to part, but I can't see properly any longer and . . . and it's hard to hold the glass steady now it's slippery.'

'Slippery' Have I bled all over it? Try another piece.'

'I . . . It won't help for more than a minute. I . . . I'm bleeding, too.' She held out her hands. The last light was just enough to show the blood welling in slow drops from her fingertips.

'Oh, Glow-worm!'

She came to him, looping her bound wrists over his head and pressing herself to him as her soft lips brushed his.

'I'm okay as long as you're with me. Oh, here they come.' At the sound of boots clomping upstairs, she removed her arms from around his neck, but she stayed close. 'We'll ask them to untie us. Why shouldn't they? We can't get out of here.'

'You might as well ask.' Phillip was desperately trying to formulate a plan.

There were four men, he thought, if they all came, but the doorway was too narrow for more than one to enter at a time. Still, it was the only way out, and if he got past the first, the rest would be waiting.

It looked hopeless, yet he could not just let them lead him away like a lamb to the slaughter, or, worse, do away with him right there in front of Gloria. Now was the time to discover whether tennis and squash had kept him as fit as he hoped, not the moment to remember that a gentleman does not brawl in the presence of a lady.

Even without the use of his hands, surely he might at least give them something to remember him by.

With a creak and a thud, the bar was withdrawn. The door swung open. On the threshold stood a brawny figure silhouetted against the flickering light of a paraffin lamp.

Phillip's head took the brute in the stomach. He went over backwards, cannoning into the man behind. Together they tumbled down the stairs.

Struggling to regain his balance, Phillip caught just a glimpse of shadowy shapes closing in on either side of him on the tiny landing. He kicked out desperately as they grabbed his arms, as the sweet, sickly smell of chloroform wafted to his nostrils.

A damp pad clamped across his face. He couldn't breathe. His head hurt like hell. He didn't care.

He drifted dizzily into nothingness.

CHAPTER 3

What was that place Roman Catholics went to after death if they weren't bad enough for Hell nor good enough to go straight to Heaven? Pur-something, Phillip thought dizzily. By Jove, they were right. He was damp and chilly, his head and his shoulders ached, his hands managed to be both sore and numb at the same time, altogether deucedly uncomfortable. Definitely not Paradise, but not the burning, fiery furnace, either.

Somewhere a cuckoo called. The air smelled of wild roses, like a promise of Paradise to come.

Something warm and wet slithered across his face. Startled, Phillip opened his eyes, and looked up into the grinning muzzle of a liver-spotted spaniel.

'Pepper, heel!'

The dog gave a short, sharp, self-satisfied bark and bent its head to lick Phillip's cheek again.

Ye gods, was he alive?

He lay in long, dew-soaked grass under a hawthorn hedge wreathed with pink roses. Above his head, a spider's web spangled with dewdrops sparkled in the slanting rays of the early morning sun. An insect crawled invisibly up his neck, a maddening tickle. He couldn't brush it off. His hands were still tied.

He was alive!

'Pepper? What have you found there?' called the fussy, schoolmasterish voice.

'Help!' croaked Phillip.

The dog wagged its stumpy tail approvingly and uttered another bark.

Boots swished through the grass. A stocky man in his midforties, wearing tweed knickbockers, a deerstalker, and pince-nez, stood over Phillip. He looked vaguely familiar.

'A tramp,' he said, displeased, tapping his cane on his hand in a thoroughly schoolmasterly fashion.

'Help,' Phillip croaked again.

'My good man, if you're hungry you may go up to the kitchen and tell them I said to give you bread and cheese. Then be on your way. Our local magistrates are hard on vagrants.'

By the time he finished, Phillip had both cleared his throat and recognized him. 'I say, Lord Dalrymple,' he said, 'I must look like the most frightful vagabond, but I'm Phillip Petrie. I'm afraid I'm in a bit of a spot.'

Daisy's cousin – second or third, and once or twice removed – hitched the pince-nez lower on his nose and stared down at Phillip over the top.

''Pon my soul! Petrie? So you are. My dear fellow, give me your hand and let me help you up. No, wait a moment.' Leaning down, he pushed his eye-glasses back up and peered through them. 'That is, if I am not mistaken, the larva of *Calothysanis amata* on your neck. The Blood Vein moth's caterpillar, you know.'

'Would you mind removing it?' Phillip asked with what patience he could muster. 'I've lost enough blood lately, as a matter of fact.'

'Dear me no, it feeds on dock leaves, not blood. None of our native moths and butterflies is a blood-sucker – though some do, admittedly, feed on the juices of decaying meat – and I rather doubt whether even any tropical . . .'

'*Please*,' begged Phillip, who felt not unlike a piece of decaying meat himself. He was also suddenly aware of his own juices, long pent up, suddenly demanding egress.

'Yes, yes, let me rid you of it. There. Not a rare species, alas. But you don't want a lecture on the *Lepidoptera*. Your hand, my dear fellow.'

'I can't. My hands are tied behind my back.'

'Good gracious! Well, happily I always carry a pocket-knife, to collect the leaves fed upon by any larva I wish to try to hatch. If you will roll over, I shall see what I can do.'

Clucking in horror over the dried blood on Phillip's head and hands, Lord Dalrymple efficiently severed the cords. Phillip's hands stung like blazes as the circulation was restored, but his bladder insisted on more immediate attention. He clambered shakily to his feet and, with a word of apology, pissed long and satisfyingly into the hedge.

During this exercise, Lord Dalrymple politely turned his back, moved away a few paces, and hummed a verse of the Eton Boating Song. Phillip, amused, recalled Daisy telling him her cousin had taught at a very minor prep school before unexpectedly inheriting Fairacres and the viscountcy from her father.

Fairacres, presumably, was where Phillip now found himself. He had been dumped not ten miles from the site of the kidnapping, considerably less from his own home, and alive. At least half alive, he amended, as he struggled with smarting, tingling fingertips to button his fly.

He took a few steps towards Dalrymple and found himself staggering. The bright morning blurred before his eyes, poppies, ox-eye daisies, and purple knapweed swirling in a vast kaleidoscope with the blue sky and green hedges. He sat down and buried his head between his knees.

'I'm awfully sorry,' he gasped, 'but I seem to be a bit wonky. I'll be all right in a minute.'

'You *have* been in the wars.' A comforting hand patted Phillip's shoulder. 'You just sit here, old chap. I'll pop down to my gamekeeper's cottage and between the two of us we'll carry you up to the house.'

'Gad no,' said Phillip, revolted, 'I'll be able to walk in a minute.' He raised his head. The blood red poppies, as always, reminded him of Flanders, but at least they kept still now.

'Sure? Then I shall send him along to lend you a hand while I go ahead to warn Geraldine to expect a guest.'

'I don't want to impose on Lady Dalrymple.'

'Nonsense! Fate has put me in Gervaise's place, and the least I can do is welcome his friends as if he were still with us. Carlin will be with you in a trice. I'll leave Pepper to keep you company.'

The spaniel, having drawn his master's notice to his find, had gone off after rabbits, but he rushed back when called. Told to stay, he sighed and lay down with his head on Phillip's ankle.

Phillip watched Dalrymple tramp off, noting that what he had taken for a cane was actually a butterfly net. He blessed the man's apparent lack of curiosity. Before he told anyone at all about the kidnapping, he had to try to get in touch with Gloria's father. The poor fellow must be quite frantic.

How Gloria was feeling, Phillip didn't want to think.

The few minutes before Carlin arrived did much to restore his strength. As the stalwart, grizzled gamekeeper approached, Phillip stood up with only a touch of giddiness. With a growl, his stomach reminded him he had not eaten since lunch yesterday, and then no more than a slice of cold pork pie in a pub on the drive down from London.

He had been saving every shilling to buy Gloria chocolates and take her dancing. The hollow in his stomach was nothing to the hollow in his heart.

'Well now, Master Phillip,' Carlin greeted him, 'what have 'e bin up to now?'

He spoke in just the tone of patient reproach he had used when Phillip and Gervaise got stuck up trees, or fell out of them or into streams, in early youth. Later he had taught the boys to shoot – and dug the shot out of Phillip's retriever pup when she rushed ahead and Gervaise accidentally peppered her.

'Does Lord Dalrymple shoot?' Phillip asked with curiosity as they set off.

'Nay, sir, not he. Nor hunt, leastways nowt but butterflies. He don't properly understand country life, if 'e'll excuse my boldness. He don't have much need for the likes of I, but he knows better than to turn off them as've served the Dalrymples time out o' mind.'

'I'm glad you're still here.' If Phillip had to be ignominiously helped up to the house, he'd as soon it was by Carlin as anyone.

All the same, he was pleased to find he needed little help. The combined effects of the blow to the head and the chloroform were wearing off, and his hunger would soon be satisfied, he trusted. Climbing a stile was an effort; he accepted Carlin's hand to steady him. Otherwise he walked slowly but under his own steam, across a hayfield, already cut, through a plum orchard (scene of many a raid in the old days), and into the park.

The rear façade of the house rose above gardens and a balustraded terrace. Fairacres, though too large to be called a manor, was no vast ducal mansion. The formality of its classical symmetry was offset by the patchwork appearance found in many local buildings. Pinkish sandstone, amber Cotswold limestone, pale grey stone from who knew where, placed at random blended into an attractive whole.

It was once Phillip's home from home. The War had kept him away for four years. Since the death of Daisy and Gervaise's father four years ago, in the great 'flu epidemic of '19, he had called only two or three times, for politeness' sake. He still thought of Edgar Dalrymple, ex-schoolmaster, and his wife Geraldine as intruders.

He could not blame Daisy or her mother for not accepting their offer of a home.

Dash it all, he had promised Daisy to drop in and see the Dowager Lady Dalrymple at the Dower House. Not a chance, not for the foreseeable future, not while Gloria suffered in the hands of those vile brutes.

The swine had added insult to injury by pinching his wallet and all his change, as he discovered when he felt for a shilling for Carlin. Thank heaven they had not dumped him in the middle of nowhere!

'I must make a telephone call,' he said to the butler, new since Daisy's time, who met him in the marble-floored front hall with its twin semi-circular staircases. 'At Once.'

'Certainly, sir.' The butler, no doubt forewarned by Lord Dalrymple, was not visibly perturbed by the arrival of a guest in his shirtsleeves, filthy and encrusted with dried blood. 'If you will be so good as to . . .'

But Lady Dalrymple came hurrying down the stairs, followed by her husband.

An angular woman, an inch or two taller than his lordship, she looked Phillip up and down po-faced, but she said civilly enough, 'Mr. Petrie, I am so sorry to hear you have had an accident. Edgar was not certain whether we ought to send for the doctor?'

'No, thank you, Lady Dalrymple. I'm much better already.'

'At least you must have some sort of dressing on your head.'

'And hands, dear,' said Lord Dalrymple.

'And hands. Let me see them.'

Reduced to a schoolboy, Phillip obediently held out his hands, himself examining them for the first time. They looked far worse than they felt. 'I'm afraid I'm rather a mess,' he apologized.

Lady Dalrymple was too polite to agree, but she said, 'I shall see to the dressings when you have bathed. Lowecroft, have Mr. Petrie shown to the Blue Bedroom, and a bath drawn immediately.' She glanced doubtfully from Phillip to her considerably shorter husband. 'I suppose you have a change of clothes at Malvern Grange, or in your motor, if it was not too badly damaged to retrieve your luggage?'

So she assumed he had pranged his car. Wondering for a moment what had become of the dearly loved Swift, Phillip seized his chance. 'At home, yes, but I don't want to worry the mater by sending for clothes. Any old thing will do for the present. But if you don't mind, before I take a bath I'll make a 'phone call.'

'Yes, of course. Your parents will be worrying. Lowecroft, show Mr. Petrie to the telephone.'

Phillip didn't explain that his parents, far from requiring notice of his visits, expected him when they saw him. His eldest brother, with wife and children, and his youngest sister all lived at Malvern Grange. One more in the house was neither here nor there. He had no intention of ringing them up.

The butler ushered him into Lord Dalrymple's den. The deep leather chairs and red Turkey carpet were unchanged since the old days. Phillip had a vague, uncomfortable sense of being in a museum, though any major changes might have disturbed him equally.

'The instrument, sir.' Lowecroft crossed to the knee-hole desk, where the telephone still stood. Gravely he took a handkerchief from his pocket and spread it over the chair. 'No offence, sir, but her ladyship is particular. Will that be all?'

'Yes, thank you, and I *would* like a bath as soon as I'm finished.'

Phillip knew the Abbey Hotel's telephone number by heart. He had spent enough 'phoning there in the past few weeks to condemn him to lunch daily at the A.B.C. instead of the Piccadilly Grill. Lifting the earpiece, he waited impatiently for the operator to answer.

The hotel's number was engaged. 'Will you ring back later?' the girl asked him.

'No, I'll hold on. Please put me through as soon as you can. It's urgent.'

'If it's an emergency, sir, I can ask the other party to get off the line.'

'N-no . . .'

He was tempted, but the instinct which had stopped him blabbing the whole story to the Dalrymples took over. Claim an emergency and people would require explanations. It was up to Arbuckle and the police to decide whether the kidnapping should be broadcast or kept quiet.

Which raised another question: Should he notify the police while he waited to get hold of Arbuckle? And if so, who?

He didn't have much faith in the local bobby's ability to do much more than move on a tramp or catch boys scrumping cherries. Call in the county force and his father would have the news within the hour, whereas if Arbuckle notified them, Phillip might manage to keep his own name out of things.

The best man for the job would be Daisy's friend, Detective Chief Inspector Alec Fletcher of Scotland Yard. Not that Phillip approved of the friendship. Daisy had a genius for picking the wrong sort. Just look at that conchie she'd been engaged to! Agreed, the Friends' Ambulances' work was not to be sneezed at, and the fellow had the grace to get himself blown up by a mine, just like any soldier, but it was the principle of the thing.

And now Daisy had taken up with a middle-class copper, a widower with a child at that. Still, he was no conscientious objector – he'd been an officer in the Royal Flying Corps – and there was no denying the man knew his stuff. Clever was the word, he'd even gone to one of those new provincial universities where they only took swots. He wasn't a bad chap, either, when he wasn't fixing one with an eye like an eagle's, sharp as a bayonet, enough to convince a fellow of his own guilt.

But Phillip had a feeling there were all sorts of obstacles to bringing in Scotland Yard. Was it worth a try?

'Hullo, caller, I'm connecting you now.'

The hotel receptionist was not at all keen to fetch Mr. Arbuckle to the telephone. 'It's only just after eight,' she said crisply. 'We don't disturb our guests so early unless they request a call the night before.'

Phillip glanced at the brass clock on the mantelpiece. Five past eight it was. He was dashed lucky Dalrymple was an early riser or he might still be lying under that hedge.

But nothing was more certain than that, if Arbuckle had slept at all with his daughter in peril, he would want to be roused for news of her. That was assuming he was actually there. Phillip had assured Gloria her father must be safe. It had seemed logical at the time, but kidnappers might not be logical.

There was only one way to find out. 'I promise you,' Phillip asserted, 'Mr. Arbuckle won't kick up a dust if you wake him, but he'll very likely have you shot out on your ear if you don't.'

'I'll take a message and give it to him when he comes down.'

'No soap. Just tell him my name and he'll come running.'

The woman put up a fight but eventually was persuaded to send a page-boy for the American.

'Petrie?' The tense, slightly breathless voice came over the wire so soon, either Arbuckle had run downstairs in his dressing-gown or he had been already dressed. 'Is she okay? Where in all tarnation are you?' He sounded worried, but not as frantic as Phillip had expected.

'She *was* all right when I last saw her. At least, not hurt. Sir, I'd have given anything to . . .'

'Not on the telephone. There's no knowing who's got an ear to the wire. She's not with you?'

'No.' Phillip swallowed the lump in his throat. 'I don't know where she is.'

'Then just tell me where *you* are.'

'At Fairacres. Lord Dalrymple's place. I expect his chauffeur would run me into Great Malvern.'

'This here lord, what have you told him?'

'Nothing. He didn't ask any questions, though, believe me, a few would have been justified.'

'Can he be trusted?'

'Of course!' The idea of the kindly but stuffy ex-schoolmaster getting mixed up in any shady business, let alone kidnapping, boggled Phillip's imagination.

'You know the guy? He won't spill the beans?' Arbuckle persisted.

'Oh, that!' Discretion must go with schoolmastering, he thought vaguely. Not upsetting the parents and all that. And he hadn't mentioned Phillip's bonds to his wife. 'No, I should think he's pretty good at keeping mum.'

'Then I'll come to you. How do I get to this place?'

Phillip gave directions. 'I'll tell them to expect you.'

'Don't tell 'em why,' Arbuckle said sharply. 'Okay, I'll be right over.'

A click as the line disconnected left Phillip with his mouth open, about to ask what he should say. He had to give his host – and still more his hostess – some explanation for the imminent arrival of an American businessman at an ungodly hour of the morning. Hanging up, he cudgelled his brains for some story to satisfy the Dalrymples without saying more than Arbuckle would like.

Come to think of it, all this secrecy twaddle was dashed queer. Shouldn't they be rousing the countryside to hunt for Gloria? Yet he himself had instinctively held his tongue when he could already have had search parties sent out.

His head was too muzzy still to work out his own reasons. Heaving himself to his feet, he returned to the front hall, where a youthful footman awaited him.

'Lor,' gasped the stripling, all agog at the sight of the battered gentleman. 'Your motor must be smashed all to bits.' Recollecting himself, he straightened into rigidity. 'If you'll please to come this way, sir, your bath'll be ready by now.'

'Look here,' Phillip said, following him up the stairs, 'an American gentleman by the name of Arbuckle is going to be popping in to see me in about half an hour. We don't want to disturb anyone, so just park him somewhere out of the way and drop me the word, will you?'

The footman glanced back, a conspiratorial gleam in his eye. 'You can count on me, sir,' he whispered. 'I'll tip you the wink.'

What the deuce did he think was going on? Phillip wondered.

Wallowing in the bath was bliss but, regretfully, he made it a quick wallow. He didn't want Arbuckle to arrive and be left fuming and fretting. When he got out, he hurried, wrapped in a borrowed dressing-gown of startling buttercup hue, to the assigned bedroom. Clean clothes awaited him there, laid out on the bed and emitting a pungent odour of mothballs.

The grey flannel bags and white shirt could have belonged to anyone, but he recognized the lightweight blue and grey herring-bone tweed jacket. It was Gervaise's, no doubt resurrected from a trunk in boxroom or attic. Phillip's soul revolted against donning his dead friend's clothes.

He forced himself to be practical. He was no good to Gloria lounging about in a bright yellow dressing-gown. His nose revolting against the stink of naphtha, he dressed.

Adjusting the navy, grey-striped tie in the looking glass, he regarded his reflection and winced. The clothes hung loose, exposing wrists and a good deal of sock. Gervaise, though taller than the present Lord Dalrymple, had been somewhat shorter and broader than Phillip. Phillip liked to consider himself a natty dresser, except when delving into motor-engines, of course. At present he looked, and smelt, like an overgrown orphan clothed by the Salvation Army.

A shock of damp blond hair usually confined by pomade didn't improve the picture. Nor did the trickle of blood seeping from his head wound. The hot water of the bath must have started it up again. Luckily someone had thought to provide a large white handkerchief. Clamping it to his head with one hand, the other holding a hairbrush, Phillip endeavoured to subdue his rebellious locks.

The young footman, Ernest, brought his cleaned shoes. 'Brilliantine, that's what you wants,' he observed sagely.

'Can you get me some?'

'Yes, sir, but her ladyship's waiting to bandage you up. Looks like you need that worser nor hair stuff,' he added, kneeling to tie the shoelaces so that Phillip didn't have to let go the red-stained handkerchief. 'She's in her sitting room, an' not to worry, the Yankee gent didn't turn up yet.'

Phillip wasn't sure whether he was glad or sorry that Arbuckle hadn't yet arrived. On the one hand, he was impatient to set about rescuing Gloria. On the other, he was beginning to think he must be an absolute duffer not to have rescued her while he was actually with her. A cleverer chap would surely have found a way. How was he to explain his failure to her father?

CHAPTER 4

Lady Dalrymple liberally bedaubed Phillip's wounds with boracic ointment, as she had very likely done in her time for hundreds of scrubby schoolboys. Though she accepted with reluctance his refusal to have sticking plaster on any but the worst cuts on his hands, she insisted on bandaging his head. By the time she finished, not much hair was visible to be pomaded.

'Oh dear,' she said, looking him up and down, 'I'm afraid you will have to miss Church.'

'I'm afraid so,' Phillip said without regret. 'I say, a fellow, an American chappie, is going to drop by here this morning to have a word with me. It's fearful cheek, I know. I hope you don't mind awfully.'

Obviously a bit put out, she muttered something about 'rackety young people nowadays.'

Aloud, however, she said with conscious graciousness, 'Not at all. You must consider Fairacres your home from home until you feel well enough to return to the Grange.'

'Thanks awfully,' said Phillip, deciding instantly that he was feeling pretty rocky. He wasn't going home to face his parents' interrogation.

'This American was responsible for your accident, I take it? Disgraceful! Foreigners should not be allowed to drive in this country. I understand many of them are accustomed to motoring on the wrong side of the road.'

Phillip murmured a vague agreement.

'I hope he means to make proper amends.' She stood up. 'Have you breakfasted, Mr. Petrie?'

'As a matter of fact, I'm most frightfully hungry.' Weak with hunger, he thought, as he rose with a huge effort to his feet.

Once again she eyed him askance, from bandaged crown to exposed ankles, sniffed with wrinkled nose, and blenched. 'Fortunately our only guests this weekend are my brother and his family. But perhaps you are too shaken up to come down?'

'I do feel a bit grim.' This time Phillip's agreement was wholehearted. He was only too delighted to cater to her sense of decorum by breakfasting in his room. 'Could you possibly have Mr. Arbuckle shown up when he arrives?' he requested.

'Certainly. Perhaps seeing your condition will persuade him he ought not to drive in England. And I shall send up your breakfast immediately.'

Phillip thanked her and returned to the bedroom. The bed looked immensely inviting. Turning his back on temptation, he sank into an easy chair by the window.

The glorious morning sun, shining on the formal gardens below and the park with its oaks and chestnuts, only reminded him of the tiny gloomy room where his beloved was imprisoned. How terrified she must be, all alone. He wished he were still there to comfort her, and, given enough time, to work out how to escape.

He had botched it, he thought wretchedly, and the worst of it was, Gloria was the one to suffer for his bungling.

Before he could worry himself into a decline, Ernest brought up his breakfast. 'Cook says she hopes as how you still likes your eggs done four minutes,' he announced, setting his tray on a small folding table, 'and coffee to drink.'

'Tell her, yes.' The eggs in their eggcups nestled under knitted cosies beside a full toast-rack, butter and marmalade dishes, and a small plate. Phillip peeked under the silver cover over the large plate. 'Bacon, sausages, kidneys, absolutely ripping! Mr. Arbuckle's still not here?' He slathered butter on a piece of toast.

'No, sir. I won't have to tip you the wink on the quiet, like,' the footman added regretfully. 'Her ladyship said to bring the gentleman straight up here when he arrives.'

'Yes, do, please,' said Phillip, topping the first egg. 'Perfect! My compliments to Cook. When Mr. Arbuckle gets here, you might ask him if he's eaten this morning.'

'Righty-oh. I mean, very good, sir. Will there be anything else, sir?'

Phillip mumbled his thanks through a mouthful of egg. The very taste of it made him feel better.

Surely the kidnappers would feed Gloria? It was in no way to their advantage to let her go hungry. The thought took the edge off his appetite; nonetheless, when Ernest ushered in Arbuckle a few minutes later, both eggs, most of the toast, and half the plateful had vanished.

Pushing back his chair, Phillip jumped up. If he had thought the American sounded too little concerned, the sight of him was enough to confound that impression. The man's long face was pale and hollow-cheeked, with dark pouches under his bloodshot eyes. He looked as if he hadn't slept a wink, and had aged ten years overnight.

Phillip's bandaged head gave him a shock. 'Jeez, they sure ...' He stopped, glancing at the footman who was fetching a second chair. He held up the jacket folded over his arm. 'Here's your coat.'

'Thanks.' Phillip slung it over the back of his chair and held out his hand.

Arbuckle shook hands without appearing to notice the sticking plasters. In a low voice he asked, 'You haven't told anyone?'

'Not a soul. Come and sit down, sir. You don't mind if I finish my breakfast?' he went on, as Arbuckle slumped onto the chair the footman moved to the table. 'Will you join me?'

'Coffee, thanks. I'm not hungry, son.'

Behind him, Ernest shook his head slightly: the American gent had not breakfasted.

'You must eat, sir, to keep up your strength.' Phillip nodded to the young footman, who winked and slipped out.

The moment the latch clicked behind him, Arbuckle leant forward, saying eagerly, 'Okay give me the low-down. You said she's all right? She's not hurt?'

'Only her hands.' Phillip displayed his own. 'She's a real sport. You see, her hands were tied in front and mine behind me. I couldn't do much of anything but Miss Arbuckle found some broken glass and had a go at the cords around mine. It was getting dark, and we both got a bit sliced up.'

'Getting dark? This was last night?' He frowned as Phillip nodded. 'She freed your hands and you escaped?'

'By Jove, no!' cried Phillip, outraged. 'You can't imagine I'm the sort of blighter who'd toddle off and leave her there!'

'Pardon me.' Arbuckle leant his elbows on the table and sank his head in his hands. 'I'm half out of my mind with worry. How about you start at the beginning and just tell me what happened?'

'Right-ho. They knocked me out – you saw that?'

'Yep,' the American said wearily. 'That is, I saw you attacked with a crowbar. I figure they only had enough chloroform prepared for me and Gloria. I ought to ask, how's your head?'

Gingerly, Phillip pressed the tender spot. 'Sore, but it seems to have stopped aching. I woke up with a heck of a headache. We were shut up in ...' He stopped as Ernest entered with another trayful.

'Fresh coffee, sir,' the footman said cheerfully, unloading, 'and another cup an' saucer. More toast. An' I took the liberty of bringing a spot of breakfast for the gentleman.' He set down a plate in front of Arbuckle and whisked away the cover.

'Good man!' Phillip approved.

'Thanks,' said Arbuckle with more politeness than enthusiasm. He grimaced but picked up knife and fork. 'Okay, I guess you're right, I better eat.'

Ernest reluctantly departed, looking about to burst with curiosity. Phillip took up his story.

'We woke up in a small room with the door and window barred. With my hands tied there wasn't a damn thing I could do. Actually, I don't know that I could have done much anyway, but if Miss Arbuckle had managed to free my hands, I'd have had more of a chance when they came for me.'

'Came for you?'

'Four of 'em. I got past the first two,' Phillip said with pardonable pride. 'You see, I overheard them talking. They'd been told to ... er ... rub me out. I can't understand it.' He shook his head, puzzled anew at his continued existence.

'That you're still alive? Don't question it, son, just thank the good Lord.' Having cut up his bacon, Arbuckle put down his knife and shifted his fork to his right hand. 'But who told them to bump you off? They didn't mention a name?'

'Not exactly. They all sounded English, and they just called him "the Yank."'

Arbuckle groaned. 'I knew it. This business never smelled to me like a homegrown Limey plot. Much more the kinda thing they do back home.'

'You have enemies in America?'

'Enemies! Who needs enemies? All it takes is a few bucks in your pocket and half the world feels entitled to a share.'

'They referred to you as "Mr. Moneybags." It was because the Yank didn't think my father could come up with much cash on short notice that he told them to get rid of me. And that's why I went for them when they came for me.'

'Nothing to lose.' Arbuckle nodded. 'Still, you've got guts, one against four and your hands tied.'

'Well, by my reckoning I wouldn't be any use to Gloria – Miss Arbuckle – dead, so I might as well give it a try. But it was nearly dark and I didn't see the second pair of men till too late. They bagged me with chloroform. I couldn't believe it when I woke up this morning under a hedge. And what luck to find myself here at Fairacres!'

'So this Lord Dalrymple took you in?'

'I must say it was jolly decent of him. I was a frightful mess.'

'How well do you know him?'

'Not well. He's my father's neighbour, of course, but he's only a distant cousin of the people who used to live here when I was growing up.' Phillip started to attempt to tackle the intricacies of entails, primogeniture, and inheritance through the male line.

Arbuckle was not interested. 'Never mind all that baloney. You told me on the 'phone he wouldn't spill the beans, but if you don't know him that well . . . I hoped I could maybe ask his advice as well as yours.'

'*My* advice?' Phillip was staggered. No one ever asked his advice.

'Sure thing. I'm a stranger in England. I've learnt a bit about the way business works over here, but I don't pretend to unnerstand the rest. And with my girl in trouble, I don't pretend to be able to think straight.'

'I don't expect I can, either. I . . . I'm dashed keen on Miss Arbuckle, you know. The police are the people to advise you.'

'No!' Arbuckle dropped his fork, his shoulders sagging. 'If I contact the police, they'll kill Gloria.'

Phillip opened his mouth, and closed it again. The silence lengthened.

'K-kill her?' he stammered at last. 'What makes you think so?'

'When I came round from the chloroform, there was a note saying so beside me in the auto.'

'They left you in the car?' He clung to irrelevant details to avoid the enormity of the threat to the girl he loved. 'There in the lane?'

'No, not there, or Crawford would have found me pretty quick. I guess they fixed the radiator with your bit of hose. They drove it back to the hotel and parked it with the top up in an out-of-the-way corner, under that big old tree out front.'

'The cedar? Yes, no one would go near it there. But Crawford must have returned to Great Malvern when he found the Studebaker gone?'

'That poor guy! I feel real badly about him. He walked miles to a garage, and when he got there he found he'd left his note-case behind.'

'They pinched mine,' Phillip said, still aggrieved. Arbuckle stuck his hand into his pocket. 'Here, you'd better take this.' He brought out a fistful of notes.

'I wasn't angling for money!'

'No, no, but you'll need a few bucks – quids – and you don't want to have to ask your folks. You can pay me back later. Now where was I?'

'Crawford left his wallet behind.'

'That's so, and I guess it took him a while to talk the garage man into driving him back to the Studebaker.'

'And it wasn't there when they got there.'

'Crawford thought he must have mistaken the spot. All these lanes of yours look pretty much alike.'

'It's quite easy for a stranger to get lost,' Phillip agreed, refilling their coffee cups.

'They motored around awhile, till the mechanic figured he'd been had for a sucker. To cut a long story short, Crawford ended up hoofing it dam near all the way back to Great Malvern, except for a short ride on a hay-wagon. He was beat and he was kinda mad, though in general he's a real cool customer.'

'He must have thought you had abandoned him, having somehow replaced the hose.'

'You'd think a guy oughta know after ten years that's not how I treat my employees,' said Arbuckle, rather querulous. 'Waal, he spotted the Studebaker there under the tree, but what with one thing and another he just went on up to his room to nurse his blisters and his grievances.'

'Leaving you to wake up in your own time.' The subject of the threat to Gloria could no longer be postponed. 'What exactly did the note say?'

'That they have my daughter. I'm to wait for further instructions on how to pay to get her back, and how much, and if I contact the cops, I'll never see her again alive.'

'They talked about killing me, but they didn't,' Phillip pointed out hopefully. 'None of them wanted to get mixed up in murder.'

'Your crooks just don't have itchy trigger-fingers like ours do, and the boss, the man they call the Yank, wasn't there, was he? He'll rub out my girl himself if I don't do what he says.'

'I don't see why. He'd have nothing to gain by it.'

'As a warning. Next time he pulled the same trick, someone would remember Gloria dying and pay up. It works. It happens all the time in the States, and the result is I'm not going to the police.'

'Our police are pretty good on the whole,' Phillip contended. 'At least, Scotland Yard is.'

'I've the greatest respect for your Scotland Yard, son. A swell bunch of guys, I hear, not dumb stiffs or on the take like half ours at home. But I'm not prepared to risk Gloria's life.' Arbuckle's gaze at once pleaded and demanded. 'Are you?'

'No,' said Phillip unhappily. By no means convinced that the proper authorities were not the best people to deal with the situation, he was all too aware of his inability to present persuasive arguments. 'Of course not. Only . . .'

'Swear you won't go to the police.'

'You have my word as a gentleman.'

'I guess that'll do. Now, maybe you can advise me what to say when people ask where Gloria is. We've gotten kinda buddy-buddy with some of the folks at the Abbey Hotel, see. They're sure to ask. The last thing I want is for anyone to think there's something fishy going on, or next thing we know some busybody will be starting rumours that'll get to the ears of the police.'

'Oh . . . er . . .' Phillip looked for inspiration to one of the plaster cupids on the ceiling. He was racked by a sudden vision of Arbuckle disenchanted with him and turning for advice to that bounder at the hotel, Major Purvis, who had his eye on Gloria.

'The best I can come up with is to say she wasn't feeling too good so I sent her to Lunnon to see one of those classy Harley Street doctors. Only no one would believe I let her go alone.'

'I should rather think not! Besides the Harley Street johnnies aren't on call at the weekend like one's local medico. Can't you just tell people she's gone to stay with friends for a few days?'

'But they'll want to know who, and where, and why I haven't gone too. Wise me up. Give me some plausible answers, something that won't make 'em raise their eyebrows. Your English swells have a way of raising their eyebrows, and I never can be sure what's going to get 'em going.'

'By Jove, sir, if anyone asks such infernally impertinent questions, you jolly well raise your eyebrows at *them*. Not at all the thing.'

Arbuckle was surprised into a snort of laughter. 'Attaboy,' he said, standing up. 'I figured you'd come through with the goods. Waal, I'd better be getting back to the hotel.'

'Would you like me to come with you?'

'I don't say I wouldn't appreciate your company, son, but that surely would raise eyebrows, you calling on me when Gloria's gone off visiting.' His knowing look made Phillip blush. 'No, you'll have to steer clear of the hotel. Better not come into town, either, because I'll be damned if Gloria would have accepted an invitation from anyone but royalty knowing you'd be in this part of the country. I'll be able to get hold of you here?'

'For the present.' Phillip was suddenly overwhelmed by a wave of fatigue. He really was too rocky to face his family's inevitable questions if he went home. No earthly use raising his eyebrows at *them*! 'I'll ring you up before I leave. You will keep me in the picture, let me know at once if there's anything I can do? Anything at all!'

'Sure thing. Just be careful what you say on the 'phone.' Arbuckle wrote down the Dalrymples' telephone number. Shaking Phillip's hand, he said, 'I reckon my girl's found her a mighty fine guy, yes sirree. Now don't you go tearing your hair. I'll pay whatever they ask. Gloria's going to be okay.'

If so, Phillip thought miserably, escorting his visitor down to the hall, why was her father so haggard?

For want of anything more helpful to do, he trudged back up to the bedroom. How he wished he were the clever sort of chap who always knew the answers, who had a plan at his fingertips to meet any situation! Someone like Bulldog Drummond, who not only knew just what to do but had the devil's own luck. Perhaps if he sat down, closed his eyes, and concentrated . . .

Or lay down. His bones ached and the bed looked awfully inviting. One could think just as well prone as sitting up, he assured himself, as he hung his jacket on the back of a chair, kicked off his shoes, and stretched out on top of the bedspread.

Sleep hit too fast to be resisted.

When Phillip woke up, he knew precisely what to do. The notion buzzing around in his brain was an absolute corker, he decide examining it from every angle.

What did Bulldog Drummond do when his back was to the wall? He called in his friends. Phillip would consult Daisy.

Daisy not only had brains, she was quick-witted. She was forever getting mixed up in shady business and finding her way out in one piece, even helping the police, he gathered. He didn't approve. He had done his best to dissuade her from letting herself be drawn into murder investigations, so he'd look an absolute ass calling her in now, but this was different.

This was Gloria in danger. Besides, if it came to taking any risks, he would keep Daisy well out of the way. Even Gervaise could not have faulted him for asking her advice.

Nor could Arbuckle object. Phillip would make Daisy swear not to contact the police, and he trusted her if he trusted anyone in the world.

Sitting up, he swung his legs off the bed and reached for his shoes. He must wire her at once, begging her to hop on a train this very afternoon. Surely she didn't slave over her blasted articles on Sunday afternoons?

As he tied his shoes, Ernest arrived. 'Oh, you're awake at last, sir,' he said. 'Her ladyship wants to know – wishes to enquire, that is – will you be coming down to dinner?'

'To dinner! What time is it?'

'Half past six, sir. The dressing-bell will ring in half an hour.'

'Ye gods, I've slept the whole day away!' said Phillip, shocked.

'Yes, sir.'

'I must send a telegram immediately.'

'Yes, sir. Dinner, sir?' the footman ventured to enquire as Phillip sped past him.

'I'm abso-bally-lutely ravenous,' Phillip called back over his shoulder, well on his way to the stairs. Dash it, he thought, bounding down, how could he have wasted so much time? Daisy might not be able to come till tomorrow now.

If only she had a telephone, he'd be able to persuade her of the urgency of his plea without blowing the gaff to any inquisitive operator. A wire was going to take some thought.

CHAPTER 5

Alec opened the passenger door of the Austin Chummy. Daisy stepped out onto the pavement. A whiff of petrol fumes ceded to the lingering smell of his aromatic pipe tobacco and the fragrance of the roses in the front garden.

'It's been a lovely evening,' she said, not wanting it to end. 'Will you come in for a nightcap? Only South African sherry, I'm afraid, unless Lucy's splurged on Spanish "cognac."'

'I'd better not.'

'Binkie might have left some whisky, or there's always coffee, or cocoa.'

Alec laughed. 'Fear of South African sherry couldn't stop me, though I'd hesitate to drink Lord Gerald's Scotch. Unfortunately, crooks don't cease operations over the weekend. It's early to rise for me tomorrow. If anything is certain in this life it's that the stack of paper on my desk will have grown since I last scowled upon it.'

'My stacks of paper are all ready to be posted,' Daisy said with satisfaction as he escorted her up the short path to the front door. She stopped on the step, fumbling in her evening bag for the key by the light from the street lamp.

'Well done. The best I can say is that there are a couple of cases I can close and send down to Files.'

Key in hand, Daisy paused. 'Alec, I don't suppose you could get away next weekend for a day or two?' Was she being frightfully presumptuous? She had ragged Phillip about being slow to introduce Miss Arbuckle to his parents, and she had known Alec much longer. These days a girl didn't have to wait for a man to make all the running, she reminded herself. 'I'm going down to Fairacres, to Mother at the Dower House, and I'd like awfully for you to meet her.'

Without warning, she found herself enveloped in an ardent embrace. The key clinked on the step as she put her arms around his neck and kissed him back with great enthusiasm.

'Gosh!' she said shakily when at last forced to come up for air, 'can all coppers kiss like that?'

'I hope you have no intention of trying to find out.' He let her go and stepped back, running a hand through his thick, dark hair. 'Daisy, that was shockingly ungentlemanly of me,' he said ruefully.

'What rot! You can't say that without implying that I was unladylike.'

'In that case, I withdraw the apology.' He smiled. 'Do you mean you won't withdraw the invitation?'

'Of course not, idiot,' Daisy said lovingly. 'Can you accept?'

'I have a few days' leave due. I can't . . .'

'. . . promise – I know. A second Jack the Ripper might be on the prowl at this very moment.' Her involuntary shiver led Alec to put his arm around her shoulders. She looked up at him. 'But you'll try?'

'That I can promise. You'd better give me the name of the nearest hotel so that I can ring up and book a room.'

'There are lots of hotels in Great Malvern, but the inn in the village is nearer, and I'm told it's quite comfortable. The Wedge and Beetle at Morton Green.'

'The Wedge and Beetle it shall be. I'll try to get away for lunch one day this week, too.' He bent his head.

This time Daisy was prepared to be kissed. To her frustration, a motor-car promptly pulled up behind the Austin and she heard Lucy's penetrating soprano.

Alec's lips brushed hers. 'I really must be off,' he said regretfully. 'Lunch on Tuesday, if I can make it?'

'Spiffing. Wire me if you can't.'

She watched him walk down the path, a broad-shouldered figure in the lamplight, with a spring in his step despite the lateness of the hour. He paused at the gate to exchange goodnights with Lucy and Binkie, turned to wave to Daisy, then was eclipsed as the other two approached.

'What-ho, Daisy,' said Lord Gerald Bincombe, a large, taciturn ex-rugger Blue.

'Solved any mysteries tonight, darling?' Lucy asked sardonically.

'No, darling, but you can help me solve one. I've dropped my dratted key.'

'Aha!' Lucy sounded amused. 'I wonder what made you do that?'

Feeling herself blush, an outdated affliction she was mortifyingly prone to, Daisy stooped to search. She said crossly, 'Give us a hand, do.'

'Hullo, here it is.' Binkie bent down, retrieved the key from the path, and presented it to Daisy with a slight bow.

'Thanks.' She opened the door and flipped the electric light switch. A yellow envelope lay on the mat inside. 'Oh, there's a telegram. For me,' she added, picking it up and dropping it on the hall table while she took off her hat and gloves.

They all went down to the semi-basement kitchen for cocoa. Sitting at the kitchen table, Daisy opened the telegram.

'Who's it from?' Lucy asked, pouring milk into a saucepan with the utmost care to avoid splashes on the hipwaisted yellow silk georgette clinging to her slender figure.

'Phillip. How odd! "Urgent emergency,"' Daisy read. '"Come pronto Fairacres not Dower House need you now please." With his name, it's one word over the twelve – the "please" was an afterthought.'

'Urgent, emergency, pronto, now; he's certainly keen to get you there in a hurry.'

'But why? I suppose it's too late to telephone from a box to find out.'

Binkie consulted his wrist-watch. 'Nearly midnight.'

'Too late, and you don't know where he is,' said Lucy.

A horrid possibility crossed Daisy's mind. 'Oh Lucy, you don't suppose Mother's fallen seriously ill? Why should he say to go to Fairacres not the Dower House? He hardly knows Edgar and Geraldine.'

'Surely not, darling. You would have heard from your cousin, or maybe a doctor, not Phillip. You know what an ass he is. No one would leave it to him to contact you. Mysteriouser and mysteriouser – just your line – but I shouldn't worry about the dowager.'

'No, I expect you're right.' Could it be that the Arbuckles had met his family by chance with disastrous results? Daisy debated whether to tell Lucy and Binkie about Gloria. Not her tale to tell, she decided.

'Drive you down tonight, if you want,' Binkie offered gruffly. 'Back in time to toddle to the office.'

'You're an angel, but Phillip can't possibly expect me to leave at this time of night, not to mention what Edgar and Geraldine would say if I turned up on their doorstep at dawn. I'll take the first train in the morning. Where's the Bradshaw's, Lucy?'

'You used it last. Oh drat! The milk's boiling over.'

Binkie coped manfully with the emergency, and Lucy made cocoa with what was left of the milk Daisy took her three-quarters of a cupful up to her den to look for the railway timetable, more to give the other two a spot of privacy than because she was in a hurry to find the best train.

On her way upstairs, she wondered what on earth had put the wind up Phillip. He was by nature on the phlegmatic side, not easily excited to more than a bit of minor bluster or a temperate enthusiasm.

Why had he not been more explicit, if not to avoid worrying her? Lucy was right, of course, about Phillip being the last person anyone would ask to get in touch with her if her mother was ill. All the same, Daisy could not help being anxious. She could not imagine why he should tell her to go to Fairacres rather than the Dower House, or even Malvern Grange, if the Dowager Lady Dalrymple were not involved.

Unless he didn't want her ladyship to *get* involved – which suggested a row with his family over Gloria. The question then became, did Daisy want to get involved? To be present at their meeting, to help smooth the way and prevent a row was one thing. Landing in the middle when he was already hock deep in the soup was quite another.

Sitting down at her desk, she reread the telegram. 'Urgent emergency' sounded positively desperate. She had better go, but she'd really give it him in the neck if all he wanted was his hand held!

The train service to Malvern was excellent, the Victorian spa enjoying a renaissance since the Armistice. Reading, Oxford, the long, slow pull up into the Cotswolds and the rush down the steep slope into the Vale of Evesham, with Bredon Hill dominating the plain to the south. A brief stop in Worcester, then over the Severn and Daisy was in her home country.

At the ripe old age of twenty-five, one ought to be blasé, but she still felt some of the excitement of the end-of-term return from school.

The rich, red soil, orchards, hop-fields, and market gardens, streams and pastures, woods crowning the low rises, and always the Malvern Hills to the west – this was home. She had climbed the hills, walked and ridden through the woods and fields, cycled along the twisting lanes, through the villages of brick and stone and half-timbered cottages.

Puffing and sighing, the train drew into Great Malvern station. The porter who opened the compartment door for Daisy greeted her by name.

'Morning, Miss Dalrymple. Mind the wet paint.'

The pillars and elaborate brackets holding up the roof over the platform had just been repainted red and blue; their fanciful wreaths of ironwork leaves and flowers were glossy green, yellow, and white; men were scrubbing the patina of soot from the walls of the long building, patterned with vari-coloured stone. Daisy stepped down to the platform with an involuntary sense of civic pride in the uniquely decorative station.

'What-ho, Daisy!' Phillip loped along the platform towards her. 'I hoped you'd be on this train, old dear.'

'I had to get up frightfully early to ... Gosh, Phil, what have you done to your head?' she exclaimed as he took off his tweed cap, revealing an encircling bandage.

Hastily he clapped the cap back on his head. 'You should have seen me yesterday. I looked like a ruddy native in a turban.'

'What happened? What's going on? I hope you have a jolly good reason for dragging me all this way!'

'I can't tell you here.' He glanced furtively over his shoulder, then turned to her porter. 'Is this all your luggage?'

'Yes, I don't expect to stay long and anyway I have a few things at the Dower House. Phillip, Mother's not ill, is she?'

'Ill? Lady Dalrymple? By Jove, no. At least, not that I know of. Why?'

'For pity's sake,' Daisy said, exasperated, as she handed in her ticket, 'because your telegram was so urgent and so obscure I didn't know what else to think. Unless it's something to do with Miss Arbuckle?'

'Sshhh!' he hissed in an agony of apprehension, casting another rapid glance over his shoulder. 'I'll explain when we get there.'

Daisy sighed. They emerged onto the station forecourt and she looked around. 'Where's your car?'

'I don't know,' Phillip said gloomily. 'Please, Daisy, don't ask questions, just wait till we get to Fairacres.'

A green Vauxhall pulled up in front of them. Daisy recognized the chauffeur. Bill Truscott had worked for her father before the War, returned when demobbed, married a parlourmaid, and stayed on with the new viscount. He grinned at her, jumping out and tipping his peaked cap.

'Hello, Bill. How's Mrs. Truscott?'

'Morning, Miss Daisy.' He opened the car's back door for her. 'The wife's doing fine, still helping up at the house now and then. Three nippers we've got now, and his lordship's moved us into the lodge.'

'Good for you. The flat over the garages wasn't designed for a family. Edgar seems to be doing quite well,' she added to Phillip, stepping up onto the running board as the chauffeur went to open the boot for her bag.

'Considering he wasn't brought up to it, and his head is full of moths and butterflies.'

Laughing, Daisy conceded, 'He still has Father's bailiff, who knows what he's about. I doubt Edgar has to do much but approve his plans.'

'Lady Dalrymple acts as if she's still married to a housemaster,' Phillip grumbled, 'and the rest of the world is made up of small boys.'

Daisy laughed again. 'I know what you mean. She's never actually ordered me to wash off my powder and lipstick, but she looks as if she'd like to. Only Scarlet Women paint.'

'She forbade me to drive this morning because of my head.' Phillip joined Daisy in the back seat after tipping the porter. 'It's perfectly all right now.'

Bill took his place behind the steering wheel and pressed the self-starter. The Vauxhall proceeded in stately fashion out onto Avenue Road and turned down the hill away from the town.

The back of the chauffeur's head before her, Daisy managed to subdue her rampant curiosity but for one low-voiced question. 'Does Geraldine ... do she and Edgar know why you called me down here?'

'Actually,' Phillip said sheepishly, 'as a matter of fact, you see I spent last night there and I'm afraid I rather left them with the impression that I was going home. I didn't actually say so, mind.'

'They aren't expecting me? And they think they've rid themselves of you? Phil, you hopeless ass, I can't just march in as if I still lived there. We'd better go to the Dower House if you don't want to go home yet.'

'No, I can't stay at your mater's. You'll think up a story to tell your cousins, old bean. I know you can if you'll just put your mind to it. After all, isn't that what writers do for a living?'

Reluctantly flattered by his confidence, Daisy bit back a vigorous protest and a reminder that she wrote factual articles, not fiction. She put her mind to it.

The final details fell into place as they rolled past the Dower House, a charming red-brick Georgian residence set in its own gardens at the edge of the park.

'You promised to call on Mother,' she said.

'I haven't had half a chance!'

'No, that's the basis for our story. You asked Bill to stop while you popped in to say hullo and ...'

'He knows I did nothing of the sort.'

'No one is at all likely to ask him, and if they do, he won't mind telling such a little fib for me. I'll ask him.' She leaned forward. 'Bill, you remember stopping at the Dower House on your way to the station, to let Mr. Petrie call on my mother?'

'If you say so, miss.' He flashed a grin over his shoulder. 'Won't be the first taradiddle I've told for you or poor Mr. Gervaise. Quite like the old days.'

Coming to the lodge, they turned in through the open gates and proceeded up the elm avenue, while Daisy rapidly explained the rest to Phillip.

'Mother asked you to pick me up at the station, because her car wouldn't start.'

'*She* won't fib for you.'

'She hardly speaks to Edgar and Geraldine. She still resents their getting Fairacres. Listen, we're nearly there. When we got back to the Dower House, you were deadbeat . . .'

'Oh, I say, a feeble sort of chap that makes me out!'

'Do you or do you not want to go on staying at Fairacres?' Daisy snapped, thoroughly peeved. 'If you want me to make up a farrago of lies for you, just let me get on with it. You were feeling pretty rotten because of your head so I insisted on you coming back here, Mother being what she is. Like it or lump it, it's too late to change,' she added, as the Vauxhall drew up before the front door.

Coming back to Fairacres now it was no longer home was too painful for her to have much sympathy with Phillip's chagrin. Memories, which might have been exorcised had she gone on living there, haunted every nook and cranny.

She had no time to dwell on the spectres. Geraldine, looking disconcerted and somehow dowdy despite her smart tailored costume, was coming down the steps beneath the pillared portico.

'Hello, Daisy,' she said. 'I didn't know you were down here. I'm always happy to see you, naturally, but if you have come to call, I'm afraid I'm on my way out. I have an appointment in Worcester and I've just been waiting for Truscott to return with the motor.' She frowned at the chauffeur as he opened the door for Daisy.

'You mustn't blame him for taking longer than intended.' Daisy stepped down and brushed cheeks with her cousin's wife. Glancing back, she saw Phillip leaning heavily against the Vauxhall, with one hand pressed rather theatrically to his bandaged head. He was going along with her story. She just hoped he wouldn't overdo it and groan.

Geraldine greeted the tale with annoyance visibly repressed. 'Of course you must stay, Mr. Petrie.' She spoke to the butler who stood on the threshold, then turned back to Daisy. 'You'll have to excuse me, though, and Edgar is out after butterflies. Will you do the honours? Make yourself at home. You know Edgar and I wish you would look upon Fairacres as a second home.'

'Thanks, Geraldine. I'll try to make Phillip comfortable,' Daisy said diplomatically. 'I expect a spot of brandy will buck him up.'

'Spirits? I hardly think . . .' The arrival of a footman to help Phillip into the house mercifully cut her short. 'Well, dear, I'll have to leave it to you. Worcester, Truscott.'

Daisy and Phillip settled in the formal drawing-room since Daisy was reluctant to make herself sufficiently at home to use the family sitting room. The drawing-room's furnishings, an eclectic mix of the best of the past two centuries, hadn't changed a bit. It gave Daisy an eerie feeling, as if her father or Gervaise might walk in at any moment.

Phillip refused with loathing to put his legs up on an elegant Regency sofa but condescended to raise his feet onto the footstool solicitously provided by the footman. Luckily his face was tanned enough from sporting weekends to conceal the absence of invalidish pallor.

'Coffee, miss?' inquired the butler, who had followed them in.

'Yes, please.'

'Ernest, coffee.'

'Right away, Mr. Lowecroft.' Passing Daisy, he whispered, 'I'll bring the brandy, too, miss.'

'Thank you, Ernest,' said Daisy, noting for future need his willingness to brave her ladyship's disapproval, though she did not intend to let Phillip drink a drop. She wanted a straight explanation from him, unclouded by a spirituous haze.

He would not say a word until the young footman had departed, returned with brandy, coffee, and strawberry tartlets, and left again. Then he kicked away the footstool.

'Right-ho,' he said, accepting the cup of coffee Daisy handed him and absently helping himself to two tarts. 'Here we go.'

CHAPTER 6

Before Phillip's story had progressed far, Daisy whipped a notebook and pencil from her handbag. In her own peculiar brand of Pitman's shorthand, indecipherable to anyone else, she made notes as he spoke. It allowed her to listen to the terrifying tale without interrupting.

'So that's it,' he said at last. 'Arbuckle's gone up to town to see about getting hold of the ransom money. He insists Gloria's in no danger as long as he pays up and doesn't involve the police, but he's not acting as if he believes it. He's like a cat on hot bricks.'

'Having met – if that's the right word – the villains, do you believe it?'

'Well, they kindly didn't do me in, but then there's the Yank . . .'

'One does read awful stories about American kidnappers taking the ransom and leaving a body,' Daisy admitted.

'Don't!' Phillip shuddered, his face pale in spite of the tan. 'In any case, Gloria's alone and frightened and in their power. I *can't* sit back and do nothing. That's why I wired for you.'

'I can't see what you expect me to do, old dear. The police are the ones to tackle it – not the locals, Scotland Yard.

I should think a foreigner being involved would be a good enough excuse for them to butt in. You can trust Alec to investigate without letting the world know.' She put down her coffee cup and rose. 'I'll ring him up right away.'

'No!' He jumped up and grabbed her arm. 'I gave Arbuckle my word not to contact the coppers. He won't like it that I've brought you in.'

'Are you afraid he won't let his daughter marry you? He may not *have* a daughter if she's not found.'

'It's too big a risk, Daisy. He showed me the letter. The slightest whiff of the police and the Yank will kill her.'

Sighing, Daisy sat down and took another strawberry tartlet. Breakfast had been a cup of tea and a slice of toast, snatched on the run.

'All right, let's see what, if anything, we can do without them. I have half a hundred questions.' Ruminatively munching, she studied her notebook. 'But first, I'd say the cottage they took you to must be quite nearby, within a few miles.'

'Why?'

'Simply because they dropped you off here after snatching you not far away. It would make less than no sense to bring you back to the same area from a distance. Was the van plain, or did it have a tradesman's name on it?'

'It had a butcher's name painted on the side.'

'What name? Was it a local firm? We might be able to trace it?'

'No address. The name began with P, I think. Potter, Parslow, Paget . . . Ah, I have it: Ferris, or maybe Farris.'

'Never heard of him,' Daisy said, disappointed. 'Not local, then, though the police might be able to trace it.'

'No! Besides, they could easily paint over the words.'

'I suppose so. It was a long shot at best. You said the van driver sounded Cockney.'

'Yes, definitely, and so were the others.'

Daisy perked up. He hadn't mentioned the accents of the other men before. 'All of them?' she asked eagerly.

'All those I heard talking.' Phillip was puzzled. 'What difference does it make?'

'For a start, Londoners don't understand the countryside. Imagine being used to the East End, all the back-to-back buildings, people swarming everywhere. A few streets away you're in a completely different district where no one will recognize you.'

'By Jove, so they may have thought they'd taken me a long way!'

'Quite possibly. Besides, this must seem like a desert to them. I shouldn't be surprised if they left you under that hedge half expecting you'd never be found. They may have regarded it as a compromise between disobeying the Yank and actually doing you in.'

'They didn't sound at all keen on actually doing me in. The one who hit me boasted of his skill at knocking people out without killing them.'

'It's the Yank we really have to worry about, but the others may lead us to him, or to Gloria. Even if they've laid in supplies, you can bet they'll be popping into the nearest village for cigarettes or a pint. With Cockney accents they'll stand out like a sore thumb.'

'Won't they realize that?' Phillip suggested dubiously.

'I doubt it. We had lots of Cockneys in the military hospitals in Malvern during the War. If they paid any attention at all to how people spoke, they tended to think they were normal and everyone else talked "funny." Whereas country people notice like a shot when they hear an accent that's not local.'

Phillip grinned. 'Anyone from more than ten miles off is a furriner.'

'Exactly. Of course, the Yank might warn the men.'

'He may not even have noticed their accents. Gloria said we all sound plain British to her.'

'That's a point! I suppose their boss really is an American, by the way? It could be just a nickname, we have no way of knowing.'

'He wants the ransom half in pounds, half in dollars. Arbuckle showed me the note.'

Frowning, she refilled their cups and helped herself to yet another tart 'He's probably American, then, unless he's an Englishman planning to do a flit. It's more of an American sort of crime. I wonder if it's just for money, or does Mr. Arbuckle have enemies?'

'He said not. Daisy, what's the point of all these questions? I want to *do* something, not sit here chatting and scoffing pastries.'

'If I've learnt anything from Alec,' Daisy said severely, 'it's the importance of seemingly unimportant details. I've already dragged a whole lot of helpful stuff out of you that you didn't bother to mention. There could be more.'

'Oh, right-ho,' he said, abashed. 'If it's helping you decide what to do, fire away.'

'I still think the best thing to do is to tell Alec everything, but don't worry I won't without Mr. Arbuckle's permission. I must say I'm rather surprised you didn't telephone the police as soon as you reached the house, even before you spoke to him. You didn't know about the threat in the first note until he arrived.'

'I didn't want to bring the local force in unnecessarily. The Chief Constable's a pal of the pater's.'

'Aha,' said Daisy understandingly.

'As a matter of fact, I thought of trying to get hold of Fletcher, but then I got through to Arbuckle and he told me not to breathe a word to a soul.'

'You haven't told anyone at all but me?' She raised her eyebrows as he shook his head. 'Not even Edgar and Geraldine, I gather. You must have said something to them, after turning up under a hedge trussed like a chicken!'

'Dalrymple didn't seem interested in the least in how I got there.'

'As you said, his head is full of butterflies. Anyway, I expect it's a relief not to have to know what everyone is up to all the time as he did with his schoolboys. Geraldine's another kettle of fish.'

'She didn't see me trussed up, and all Dalrymple told her was that I'd had an accident. She assumed I'd cracked up the old bus, and that Arbuckle had caused the crash and came to set things right. Her brother and his family were here for the weekend, but luckily they left last night. I didn't even see them.'

'I wonder what happened to your car. If the police find it abandoned, they're going to want an explanation.'

'Oh lord!'

'Well, we'll cross that bridge when we come to it. So you and I and Arbuckle are the only people who know about the kidnapping, besides the villains?'

'He told his assistant. The poor fellow was driving them and ended up tramping all over the countryside when the Studebaker disappeared. But he didn't tell him I'm involved, in case word might get back to the kidnappers.'

'They know you're involved,' Daisy pointed out.

'They don't know I survived, nor that I'm going to pull out all the stops to find Gloria.'

Ernest stuck his head around the door. 'Telephone call for you, sir.'

'Mr. Arbuckle?'

'No, sir, a lady as won't give her name.'

'Fenella,' Phillip groaned, and hurried out.

'More coffee, miss?'

'No, thanks.'

He came in and started to clear up the coffee-things. 'Cook wants to know, miss, will you and Mr. Petrie be here for luncheon?'

'Yes,' Daisy said absently, her thoughts on the sudden introduction of Phillip's young sister into the affair. Fenella knew he was at Fairacres, if no more.

'Very good, miss.'

Daisy suddenly woke up to the fact that she was no longer at home at Fairacres. 'Here' for lunch, the footman had said, not 'in.' 'Oh, Ernest!' she said as the door closed. He reappeared. 'We haven't exactly been invited to lunch.'

He gave her a friendly if unfootmanly grin. 'Not to worry, miss. Her ladyship's lunching out and there's no knowing when his lordship'll turn up. 'Sides, you're family, miss. Luncheon for two it is.'

She smiled at him. 'Thanks!'

Abandoning for the moment the puzzle of Fenella, Daisy

turned over in her mind all she had learnt from Phillip and tried to decide how to approach the problem of Gloria's whereabouts.

They could go from village to village enquiring in shops and pubs as to whether any Cockneys had been sighted – heard, rather. If only one or two villages were so distinguished, that would narrow down the search area. Two would be better, in fact, since one could presume the kidnappers were hiding somewhere in between.

It would be much easier, however, if they could narrow the search before they set out. If only Phillip had some sort of clue as to where they had taken him. She gathered he'd been completely unconscious both coming and going, but she'd better make sure.

What else had she not asked him? Alec would probably come up with dozens more questions. How she wished he was here!

Phillip came back, looking disgruntled. 'Sisters!' he said bitterly.

'How much does she know?'

'Only that I'm here and don't want the parents to know. I had to get hold of some clothes from home somehow. She cycled over with a bag yesterday evening.'

'Jolly decent of her. And now she's let the cat out of the bag?'

'What? Oh! No, but she's been thinking and she's decided I must be in trouble, so she wants to help. I managed to put her off, but I bet she'll go on pestering. Dash it, girls shouldn't be allowed to think!'

Torn between umbrage and amusement, Daisy plumped for the latter. Laughing, she observed, 'And there I was believing you brought me all the way from London to think for you!'

'I did. I say, old thing, don't fool about,' he pleaded, adding humbly, 'I know I'm not much brainier than Fenella. You are. I need you. Gloria needs you.'

'I know, old dear, I know. I was teasing. If Fenella 'phones again, we'll think of a way to put her off. Phil, you have absolutely no idea where you were taken, where Gloria is?'

'Not the foggiest.'

'You didn't see or hear anything at all, coming or going, even something you don't believe is significant?'

'I was out for the count both ways. It could have been any wood in the county, or outside it.'

'Wood? For pity's sake, you know you were in a wood?'

'It was only an impression,' Phillip said defensively. 'I heard what sounded like a woodpecker, and then a squirrel. You know how they sort of chatter when they get annoyed? They might have both been in the only tree around.' He knit his brows in thought. 'There was something else, though, which gave me the same impression. What was it?'

'Imagine yourself back there,' Daisy suggested.

He closed his eyes. 'It makes my head ache. I've got it! The sunbeam flickered as if it was shining through fluttering leaves – that still could be just one tree, close to the cottage, though, couldn't it?'

'Yes. Nothing else?'

'The air seemed to be sort of damp,' he said doubtfully. 'Sort of mouldy – not rotten, just the way woods are. Sort of *green*. I might have imagined it.'

'I know what you mean. It's not a smell you get from one tree. If it seemed damp after weeks of drought, you're

probably right about the woods. Anyway, it gives us somewhere to start.'

'I don't see how. There are dozens of woods and copses
and spinneys within a few miles.'

'Not many with an isolated, dilapidated, deserted cottage
in the middle. Good, we don't have to search all the fields
and commons and riverbanks – you didn't hear running
water?'

'No.'

'It cuts down the area enormously, and both of us know
the local countryside like the backs of our hands. All the
same, as you say, there are dozens of woods. It would take us
centuries to explore them all.'

Phillip slumped. 'We're only guessing they're not more
than a few miles off, anyway. It's hopeless, isn't it?'

Daisy had never seen him so downhearted. His usually
equable temperament took the rough with the smooth,
occasionally a bit ruffled but without a stumble. Even the
dreadful years in the trenches of Flanders had left little
apparent mark on Phillip, unlike so many more sensitive
spirits who still suffered years later.

It must be true love. She remembered how her heart
had hurt when Michael's ambulance unit left for the front,
knowing his noncombatant status was no protection against
stray bullets, poison gas, or landmines. Then there had been
the awful time when Alec was in danger, and later his little
girl. Daisy had been able to help both Alec and Belinda,
though. Half the pain was the helplessness of wanting desperately to do something when there was nothing to be done.

Phillip must be given something to do, however useless.
And you never could tell, it might prove useful after all.

'Buck up, old thing,' she said. 'We're not going to give up so easily.'

'What can we do?'

'The first thing is to go round the villages making enquiries about Cockneys, or other conspicuous strangers. Or Americans, come to think of it, though I doubt he'd risk letting anyone hear an American accent near the hiding place. Still, with luck we'll be able to pinpoint a smallish area to search. I suppose it's no good asking Fenella to help?'

'The mater would want to know where she kept disappearing to. What's more, she'd tell. She's not much more than a child, in spite of that broken engagement.'

'My mother's going to be a problem, too,' Daisy reflected. 'She's bound to find out I'm here and she'll want to know why I don't stay at the Dower House, and if I do *she'll* want to know where *I* keep disappearing to. Nor can you stay there without a risk of her catching the wrong sow by the ear.'

For once Phillip was quick on the uptake. 'You mean she'd think we were engaged?' he cried, aghast.

'Or on the brink.' She continued the dispiriting list: 'You can't go home without all sorts of explanations. Neither of us can stay at Fairacres without ... Phillip, I've got an absolutely spiffing idea!'

'What? What is it? Tell me!'

'Not yet Just be quiet and let me work it all out. There may be an insuperable flaw I haven't seen yet. Hush.'

CHAPTER 7

Edgar arrived in the dining room after the green pea soup, just as Daisy and Phillip started on lamb cutlets with parsleyed new potatoes and salad. He apologized for his lateness.

'Very bad form when we have guests,' he said with a severity directed at himself.

'Soup, my lord?' enquired the butler.

'Yes, Lowecroft, if it's still hot.' Gazing at Daisy and Phillip with a puzzled air, he went on, 'Please, carry on, don't wait for me. Odd, Geraldine's not here to entertain you?'

'She's lunching with a friend in Worcester, I believe, Cousin Edgar.'

'I rather thought I should be lunching alone. She must have omitted to tell me you were expected, Daisy. And your mother . . . ? Ah!' He rubbed his hands together as Ernest set a bowl before him. 'There's nothing like a soup made with new peas from one's own gardens. It pains me to admit that school food, though of course nutritious, was not always toothsome.'

Daisy had decided to tackle Edgar first. Geraldine would find it difficult to express her inevitable disapproval openly if her husband had already succumbed. Now he had given her a perfect opening.

'There are so many things I miss about living in the

country,' she said, trying to sound wistful. 'The fruit and vegetables are one, of course. By the time they've been carted up to Covent Garden and sold to greengrocers and carted off again to the shops, they're always a bit battered.'

'My dear, I can very easily send you up a hamper of whatever's in season now and then. I wish you had mentioned the matter sooner,' Edgar reproached her.

'How frightfully kind of you, Cousin Edgar,' said Daisy, filled with guilt. 'Lucy and I would enjoy fresh stuff no end. That's another thing I miss,' she ploughed on gamely for Phillip's sake. 'Lucy often invites me for country weekends at her parents', and I hate not being able to reciprocate. I'm afraid Mother's not really in a position to entertain a crowd of young people.'

Edgar blenched, but equally game – perhaps also equally guilt-ridden, as a usurper, however legal – he squared his shoulders. 'You know, Daisy, Geraldine and I have frequently begged you to regard Fairacres as your home still. Naturally that must apply to inviting your friends to stay. A crowd?' he added with misgiving.

'Just in a manner of speaking,' she hastened to assure him. 'Half a dozen or so. I wouldn't dream of trying to arrange formal dances or anything like that. Tennis and golf and bicycling and hiking...'

'Hiking?'

'Oh, it's a rather slangy term for tramping, going for long country walks. Gosh, Cousin Edgar, do you really mean I may invite a few people down?'

It was only fair to allow him a chance to back out. For a moment it was touch and go and Phillip's face took on a painfully anxious expression. Daisy had forbidden him to put his oar in, for fear of mucking things up. To her relief Edgar turned up trumps – to use another slang term and mix the odd metaphor.

'Certainly,' he said bravely. 'Er, which weekend were you thinking of? We shall have to consult Geraldine, I'm afraid . . . that is, of course.'

'No time like the present. I don't want to disrupt Cousin Geraldine's plans for weekend guests, or put her out in any way. I'll make all the arrangements and sort out menus with Cook and so on. Tomorrow?'

Edgar's jaw dropped. 'T-tomorrow? Oh well, I suppose it's best to get it over with. I mean, yes, by all means, why not tomorrow? As far as I know Geraldine has no particular plans for the next few days. Though she doesn't always let me know in advance . . .'

'Oh, if she's giving a luncheon or dinner party or anything, we'll clear out of the way with a picnic, won't we, Phillip?'

'By Jove, yes! Don't want to get in the way, dash it all. Awfully good of you, Lord Dalrymple, and all that'

Daisy gave her cousin's hand a consoling pat. 'Now, don't you worry about a thing. I shall see to everything. I dare say you'll hardly notice we're here.'

The utter disbelief in Edgar's eyes almost made her giggle, but she meant what she said. His unwanted guests were going to be invited solely to spend every minute of daylight scouring the countryside.

A gooseberry fool followed the cutlets. In spite of her persuasive exertions, Daisy thoroughly enjoyed the meal. At home she and Lucy subsisted largely on eggs, cheese, and sardines, for lack of both money and cooking skills. Her father had been fond of good food, and the prospect of several days of his cook's creations was almost enough in itself to reconcile her to the ignoble wiles she had used on Edgar.

Phillip's patent relief removed the last qualms.

Magnanimous in victory, she listened with every appearance of interest to Edgar's lepidopteran blather. As pleased as any big game hunter, he had captured several caterpillars of *Pyronia tithonus*, the Gatekeeper butterfly. This afternoon he would prepare and finish a tank in which to keep and study them until they pupated and hatched, when he intended to release them.

'I'm glad you don't spend your time massacring inoffensive creatures for the sake of displaying their remains,' Daisy told him.

'It is their life-cycles that interest me,' he said a trifle pompously, then added with a disarming honesty, 'Besides, I have never had the good fortune to come across a rare butterfly. The most casual collector can easily procure a specimen of the Gatekeeper.'

Daisy pondered the irony of his snaring Gatekeepers on the very day he had proved himself so inadequate a gatekeeper. She had stormed the gates of Fairacres without firing a shot.

She had to remind herself not to triumph too soon. Geraldine was a harder nut to crack than her defenseless husband, who was accustomed to facing the simpler stratagems of small boys. Daisy's interview with her mother was bound to be difficult, too. To fortify herself for the battles ahead, she gratefully accepted a second helping of gooseberry fool.

'When will Lady Dalrymple be back?' Daisy asked the butler as they left the dining room.

'Her ladyship expected to return for tea, miss, at half past four.'

'Not till tea-time?' exclaimed Phillip, agitated.

Daisy gave him a warning glance. He was a pretty hopeless conspirator, especially as he was the one who insisted on secrecy.

'It *is* awkward, Cousin Geraldine not knowing yet that Cousin Edgar has invited us to stay,' she said. 'Lowecroft, I expect you heard Lord Dalrymple ask me to invite a few people to come to Fairacres tomorrow for a few days? I'll let you know the exact numbers as soon as I can, but perhaps you would like to begin preparations.'

'Very good, miss.' The butler's stolid face gave no hint of whether he had noticed and appreciated her brilliant wangling. 'I shall speak to the housekeeper.'

'Thanks. Mrs. Warden is still here, isn't she? I'll have a word with her later.'

Conveniently, Edgar had asked them to excuse him if he took his postprandial coffee in his conservatory-insectarium. Daisy and Phillip went out to the terrace for theirs.

'We can't wait till tea-time,' Phillip fretted as soon as they were alone. 'Tom Pearson and Binkie will have to arrange with their offices to be gone for a few days.'

Tommy Pearson was a solicitor in his family's firm. Binkie did something obscure (to Daisy) with stocks and shares in the City, like Phillip but with somewhat more success. All three, having gone straight from school into the Army, were in junior positions.

'Did you telephone your office?' Daisy asked.

'I rang up first thing this morning and said I couldn't come in this week. They can give me the sack if they want,

I don't care. But Tom and Binkie won't want to risk their jobs.'

'Lucy will have to notify clients, too,' Daisy pointed out dryly, 'and you're jolly lucky I'm free at the moment. You're right, though, we must notify them right away. We can't wait for Geraldine's say-so. Anyway, however livid she is with Edgar, she's far too proper to rescind his invitation.' *I hope*, she added to herself.

Phillip's resolve wavered, his highly developed sense of social fitness momentarily coming to the fore. 'It's not at all the thing, inveigling an unwilling hostess into putting us up.'

'It's for Gloria,' she reminded him. 'Come on, let's decide how much we can safely say to the others to persuade them to come. Then you can wire Lucy and telephone the others while I go and deal with Mother.'

'Right-ho.'

'And you'd better ring up Fenella. Tell her it's a house-party and we're having a treasure-hunt. That will explain us haring about the countryside.'

'She'll want to join in,' Phillip objected.

'Say she wouldn't enjoy it; everyone's older than she is.'

'Oh, right-ho.'

Half an hour later, Daisy wended her way across the park along the footpath leading directly to the Dower House. The afternoon sun was hot enough to make her regret that parasols, and even broad-brimmed straw hats, were out of fashion. She could practically feel the freckles appearing on her nose as she walked.

In the green patches beneath the clumps of frees, pale amber Jersey cows clustered in the shade, their tails swishing against the flies. Elsewhere the grass was parched to a golden brown. The only moisture it had received for weeks must be dew at dawn, evaporating before it soaked in except where protected from the sun. Even the air smelled dry, Most years the park stayed lushly green all summer, Daisy could not recall ever seeing it dried up so early.

Her footsteps kicked up puffs of dust. The sight lent weight to the scanty evidence that Phillip had really been confined in the midst of woodland.

Which still left a lot of ground to be covered. Even if enquiries pinpointed a general area, Daisy had little hope of finding Gloria Arbuckle before her father paid the ransom. The crooks surely wouldn't want to hang around for longer than necessary. But the searchers just might strike it lucky, and the quest would be worth the effort just to stop Phillip sinking into despair.

It might even be quite amusing, rather like the treasure-hunts so popular among young people at house-parties.

She came to the gate in the high, neatly-trimmed beech hedge around the Dower House. The garden inside was equally neat and flourishing. One thing the Dowager Lady Dalrymple hadn't grumbled about for some time was the young Welsh gardener Daisy had foisted on her. Owen Morgan was a hard worker who knew his stuff.

Seeing him up a ladder picking cherries, she begged a handful and asked after his family before going on into the house.

Her mother was in the sitting room, seated at the satinwood Sheraton bureau, writing a letter. Daisy regarded her oblivious back with fondness mingled with anticipated exasperation.

A short, plumpish woman in her mid-fifties, the

dowager viscountess was never happy without something to moan about. In her eyes, the charming and very comfortable Dower House was utterly inadequate. Its mere five bedrooms – not counting servants' quarters – made guests other than family out of the question. Even her elder daughter Violet's family could only be squeezed in with the greatest difficulty. It would be unbearably cramped if her younger daughter came to live with her, yet she strongly objected to Daisy's working to support herself in London.

Both daughters neglected her terribly, their rare visits always much too short. What she would say when she discovered Daisy was in Worcestershire but staying with the enemy up at the big house remained to be seen.

'Hello, Mother.'

Lady Dalrymple started and swung round. 'Good gracious, Daisy, what a horrid shock you gave me! I suppose it's too much to expect you to give me a few hours' notice if you mean to come down.'

Daisy kissed her. 'I hoped it would be a nice surprise.'

'Of course I'm always glad to see you, dear, but I have the Waddells and Miss Reid coming to dinner and bridge tonight.'

'I shan't upset your numbers, or put you out in any way. Edgar and Geraldine have invited me and several friends to stay for a few days.'

'Indeed! So now the encroaching parvenus are attempting to alienate my children from me? How *could* you accept?'

'It was very kind of them. One can't refuse all their olive branches, Mother. I'll be able to pop in to see you now and then without upsetting your bridge evenings or your other engagements.'

'If only you would learn to play bridge, Daisy. It's very awkward not being able to call on you to make up a table.'

Having sedulously avoided learning the game, Daisy had no intention of starting now. 'I'd never meet your high standards,' she said. 'I think my mind works the wrong way.'

'You take after your father. He never did play well.' This, by an inevitable progression, called to mind another of the late viscount's faults. 'It's a great pity he didn't leave you better provided for, so that you would have no excuse to work.'

Though she knew it was pointless, in defense of her father Daisy trotted out the old arguments. 'You know he always assumed Gervaise would inherit Fairacres and give me a home and an allowance. And he was too shattered after Gervaise . . . afterwards to get around to making a new will at once. He was still comparatively young and healthy. He thought he had plenty of time.'

'I can't think why he went and succumbed to the 'flu,' the dowager fretted, as if her husband had deliberately died to inconvenience her. 'If you only had the sense to get married, like Violet . . .'

'As a matter of fact,' Daisy said cautiously, 'there's a man I want you to meet.'

Her mother brightened. 'Who is he?' she asked eagerly. 'He'll be at your house-party, at Fairacres?'

'No, actually . . .'

'I knew it. He's unsuitable!' she lamented. 'Since you will insist on working, you're bound to mingle with *hoi polloi*. What is he? Some scruffy, penniless intellectual? A wealthy upstart with pretensions? Oh, Daisy, not a *foreigner*?'

In comparison, a middle-class police detective just might come as a pleasant surprise, Daisy hoped. Let Mother worry for a few days. 'You'll find out when you meet him,' she said. 'I was going to write and ask if this coming weekend would be convenient.'

'Let me look in my diary. For you, yes, but I really cannot have a stranger staying in the house, especially if he's not one of us. Besides, it's quite impossible to entertain properly with only three indoor servants.'

'He's booking at the Wedge and Beetle.'

'Well, at least he has the decency not to thrust himself in where he's not wanted.'

'Mother! I don't expect miracles of cordiality, but unless you promise to be polite, I shan't bring him. We'll get married quietly in a Registry Office and ...'

'My daughter marry in a Registry Office? Over my dead body!'

'You wouldn't know about it until afterwards,' Daisy pointed out. 'Do be reasonable, Mother.'

'Naturally I shall be polite,' the dowager sniffed. 'I trust I am never otherwise. I can only hope seeing the bounder among well-bred people of your own class will make you see sense.'

Daisy bit her tongue to hold back a futile retort. 'Yes, well, I'd better be getting back,' she said. 'I'll drop by again tomorrow. Oh, by the way, Phillip Petrie sends his best regards.'

'Phillip? Is he at Fairacres? You'd do well to marry Phillip,' her mother lamented. 'The Petries are an excellent family.

'Phillip may be neither scruffy nor an intellectual but he hasn't a bean, and anyway, he's in love with someone else. Cheerio, Mother. See you tomorrow.'

Phillip was in love, Daisy reflected as she made her way back across the park, and he believed his beloved was in danger. Daisy could not help wondering whether he had unwittingly exaggerated Miss Arbuckle's peril, or altogether misunderstood the situation. On this peaceful June day, the notion of a band of murderous thugs marauding about the countryside was awfully hard to credit.

Still, he was afraid for his Gloria, and for some reason he had chosen Daisy to come to the rescue. She, in turn, wanted nothing more than to lay the burden on Alec's broad and admirably competent shoulders. That expedient being ruled out, she'd have to do her best without him.

She had set things in motion. With any luck, reinforcements would arrive tomorrow. In the meantime, she needed to prepare a plan of campaign.

'Maps,' she said aloud. Her father had kept two inch to the mile Ordnance Survey maps of the county in the desk in his den. To judge by the lack of change in the parts of the house she had seen, they were very likely still in the same drawer. Ferreting them out would keep poor old Phillip occupied for a while.

Half-way back to the house, she saw him coming to meet her, very long-faced.

'Tom can't get away till noon tomorrow,' he reported. 'Some beastly court case. And Binkie was out seeing a client when I rang up. I sent him a wire.'

'That will give us time to make plans,' Daisy consoled him. 'We need maps, and bicycles, and as I said, there may be places easier to explore on horseback. You told them all to bring riding togs, as well as asking Lucy to bring me some more clothes?'

'Yes, and I said to motor down, not take the train, so we'll have their cars, too.'

'Good. But I've no idea what, if anything, Edgar has in the stables, so you'll have to check, and if there's nothing suitable, arrange to hire a couple of hacks when and if we need them. Or you could beg, borrow, or steal them from your people. Now that we're a duly constituted house-party, it won't matter if they know you're here. Is Geraldine back yet?'

'I saw the Vauxhall drive up. That's why I ducked out the back way to meet you,' Phillip admitted sheepishly. 'At least I don't have to worry about the mater. She's taking Fenella up to town for a few days.'

Daisy laughed. 'Ready to face any dragon for your damsel in distress,' she said, 'but not Cousin Geraldine or your mother? Tut, tut!'

CHAPTER 8

As predicted, Cousin Geraldine was outraged to discover, on her return from a pleasant jaunt to Worcester, that her husband had committed her to a house-party. Daisy had made Phillip stay with her to share the brunt of her lady-ship's displeasure. However, Geraldine was scrupulously, if stiffly, polite to them.

Later, Daisy squirmed when she overheard Geraldine berating Edgar for inviting a horde of rackety modern young people. Her guilt faded when she realized Edgar was not humbly excusing himself but burbling rhapsodically and with magnificent irrelevance about the hatching of a Dingy Skipper.

Erynnis tages, she gathered as she moved out of earshot, though not actually rare was usually found on chalky soils. She must remember to congratulate him at a suitable moment.

She managed to keep Phillip busy enough that evening to stop him brooding. Binkie rang up to say he and Lucy would arrive at Fairacres by tea-time the next day. Daisy was glad the reticent young man had 'phoned – not Lucy, who would have demanded explanations.

Shortly before they went to bed, Mr. Arbuckle telephoned to speak to Phillip. His arrangements for the ransom money were under way, Phillip reported in a whisper in the hallway outside Daisy's bedroom. Though he would not have the cash till the end of the week, he'd leave his secretary, who had stayed in London all along, to deal with that end of things. He himself hoped to be back in Malvern by Wednesday evening to receive any further messages from the kidnappers.

'The end of the week!' Phillip repeated in anguish. 'Suppose the brutes demand the money sooner? They might think he wasn't going to pay up and take it out on Gloria.'

'Bosh,' Daisy said in a heartening voice, thinking fast and furiously. 'They'll allow more time. Once she's dead, their chance of striking it rich is gone. They wouldn't be so stupid.'

'They might hurt her.'

For the first time a shiver of real apprehension ran down Daisy's spine. A glimpse of what it might be like to be utterly in the power of evil men flashed through her mind.

'The Yank's not stupid,' she argued. 'He guessed your father wouldn't be able to produce a large amount of cash on demand. He must realize it takes time to convert even securities into cash, especially as the certificates or what-not are in America, I presume.'

'Oh yes, I hadn't thought of that.'

'Besides, since they threatened dire revenge if he contacts the police, they must be watching him. They know he's doing what he can.'

'Of course,' Phillip said gratefully.

Bidding him good-night, Daisy could only hope she was right.

Tuesday! The thought brought a surge of drowsy happiness as warm as the sunbeam on Daisy's face. Tuesday lunch, Alec had said. If he could get away, to be sure, but it was no use anticipating bad luck.

Unlike many people, she had always enjoyed being awakened by the morning sun. Vi and Gervaise had been more than glad to let her have this east-facing bedroom. She had arranged the bed specially to catch the rays as often as possible, and it had not been moved.

Moved? she thought, sleepily confused.

Oh yes, years had passed and this room was no longer her own.

This room had nothing to do with Alec, in place or time. He was in London and she was back at Fairacres, where nothing had changed. She opened her eyes to see the sun pouring in at the open window between the pulled-back blue chintz curtains printed with meadow flowers, butter-cups, ox-eye daisies, poppies, faded now. More faded than she remembered, but otherwise unchanged.

Perhaps Edgar and Geraldine could not afford to change things. She hadn't considered the possibility before, though these days everyone complained about death duties.

Edgar and Geraldine: still half dozing, she wondered what she was doing in their house, in her old bedroom, when she was supposed to be going out to lunch in town with Alec?

Suddenly remembering, Daisy sat bolt upright. Phillip's girl was being held by kidnappers. She shook her head in dis-belief. Surely a dream . . . but it couldn't be, or she wouldn't be at Fairacres when she badly wanted to be in London.

She'd have to 'phone Alec. The trouble was, if she rang him at home, she would interrupt the bustle of his prep-arations for work and Belinda's for school. Resenting the disturbance, his mother would see it as further proof of Daisy's unsuitability for her son. Mrs. Fletcher no more approved mixing the classes than did the Dowager Lady Dalrymple.

Yet Daisy hated to telephone Alec at Scotland Yard. He was a busy man. She didn't want to disrupt his work or try his patience – or embarrass him before his colleagues and subordinates.

While she wondered which was the lesser of two evils, a maid brought her early morning tea. Sipping it, she decided to ring up Alec's home. If he did not answer the 'phone himself, she wouldn't ask for him, just leave a brief message.

In the event, Belinda answered. 'Sorry, Miss Dalrymple, Daddy's already left,' she reported.

'Oh bother! He hasn't been called out of town, has he?'

'No. He said he had lots of work to do and he wanted to get an early start because of meeting you for lunch. So its no use me taking a message, is it? Because you'll see him first.'

'I can't make it. I'll try to get hold of him at work, but just in case, will you tell him I'll 'phone this evening to explain?'

'All right.' Her voice faded momentarily: 'Coming, Gran. I've got to go, Miss Dalrymple. 'Bye.'

''Bye, darling. See you soon.'

Daisy held down the earpiece hook for a moment, realized Alec was probably en route from St. John's Wood to Whitehall, and reluctantly hung up. She went to join the others for breakfast.

Her telephone call to Scotland Yard later was equally fruitless. Alec and his sergeant, Tom Tring, had both been called out, though not, she was glad to hear, to the farthest ends of the kingdom. The police operator didn't know how long they would be gone. Would she like to speak to another officer?

'No, thanks,' Daisy said hastily.

Very likely Alec was going to have to call off lunch anyway, a not unusual occurrence. He wouldn't arrive in Chelsea to find her missing.

All the same, she wished she had at least heard his voice. Though she had promised not to mention the kidnapping, she felt the very sound might give her confidence and encouragement in the task she had taken on.

The maps she and Phillip consulted last night had pointed out the magnitude of that task. Where was Gloria Arbuckle?

'She's not here? Where is she?' Alec demanded of Daisy's cool, faintly antagonistic house-mate. Though the tall, elegant Miss Fotheringay had softened towards him a trifle recently, she could not be described as approving. 'Will she be back soon? We were to go out to lunch.'

'She won't be back for lunch.' Nothing so homely as a frown marred the smooth, expertly made-up face, framed by a sleek, dark bob, yet the amber eyes held a shade of anxiety. She appeared to come to a decision. 'Actually, she's at Fairacres. Perhaps you'd better come in for a minute, Mr. Fletcher.' With a languid gesture she waved him past her into the narrow hall, made narrower by a pair of large suitcases.

'At Fairacres? With her mother?'

'No, not at the Dower House, at Fairacres itself. Her old

home. Here, read this.' Miss Fotheringay picked up a yellow telegram from the hall table and handed it to him. 'See what you make of it.'

'"Urgent emergency,"' Alec read with alarm. '"Come Fairacres house-party pronto Binkie too bring riding togs and Daisy's clothes." Signed "Daisy," but that's an odd way to word it if she wrote it. Why not *my* clothes"?'

'The combination of an urgent emergency with a house-party isn't exactly normal either, would you say?' drawled Miss Fotheringay. 'I'll be damned if I can make head or tail of the business.'

Alec tried not to wince too obviously at her language. He was all for women working if they chose to, but he was old-fashioned enough not to care for their swearing. 'An urgent house-party does seem to be something of a contradiction in terms,' he agreed dryly.

'The first two words echo the wire Phillip Petrie sent her, which took her haring down there in the first place, so I suspect he wrote or dictated it.'

'Petrie? She went because he sent for her?' Alec firmly squashed a pang of jealousy. Daisy had often enough described the young man as an amiable ass. Socially he was of her class; intellectually a definite also-ran. 'Judging by the baggage, you too are obeying the summons. You haven't telephoned for an explanation?'

'Binkie rang up last night to say we'd go. He spoke to Daisy, but the old dear's the strong, silent type. He didn't ask any questions. I tried 'phoning this morning, but the butler said both Daisy and Phillip were out and he didn't know when they'd be back. I've been too busy to keep buzzing down to the telephone box. I haven't the foggiest what clothes Daisy wants so I've just guessed.' She waved at the bags. 'Too, too maddening!'

'You don't know anything about this emergency, I take it?' He ran his hand through his hair as she shook her head with a rueful moue. 'At least it appears to be Petrie's problem, not Daisy's.'

'To start with, anyway. Knowing Daisy, whatever it is, she's taken it to heart. But where Binkie and I come in, I simply can't imagine. Of course, it may be some sort of lark, in which case I'll kill both of them. I've had to put off half a dozen clients.'

'You're leaving now?' Alec took in her motoring dustcoat, fashionable as well as practical, and the veiled hat sitting on the hall table.

'As soon as Binkie arrives with the Alvis. His wire asked him to drive, not go down by train. Curiouser and curiouser, is it not?'

'It is. Dash it, I wish I could go with you, but I can't get away for at least a couple of days, quite possibly not till the weekend. Will you tell Daisy I'll telephone this evening? Lateish. I'll be working late.'

'Right-oh, Chief Inspector. Heaven knows what it's all about, but to tell the truth I'm quite glad to know you're hovering in the background.'

'Even coppers have their uses,' Alec said mildly, recalling past battles. 'Don't let Daisy get into too much trouble if you can help it. I shan't hold you responsible, though. I know only too well how impossible it is to stop her once she has the bit between her teeth!'

'Riding togs,' he brooded as he returned down the path to his little yellow Austin Seven. Of course all Daisy's set rode horses, practically from birth. Was it too late for him to learn?

Daisy might like to teach him, and Belinda.

What had she got herself into this time? What on earth sort of trouble could Phillip Petrie have landed himself in which would require not only her help but that of their mutual friends to extricate him?

And why disguise it as a house-party?

As the hour of the house-party's assembly approached, Geraldine asserted her right as nominal hostess and waited in the drawing-room to greet her guests. Daisy and Phillip couldn't very well hang about in the front hall to waylay them.

'They're bound to demand explanations right away,' Daisy said in a low voice.

'Don't I know it! I'd have had a hard time with Tom yesterday if he hadn't been called away from the 'phone just in the nick. Lady Dalrymple's going to wonder what the deuce is going on.'

'We'll just have to stand behind her and shake our heads madly. Lowecroft will think we're potty, but it's just too bad.'

'He already does,' Phillip averred.

Geraldine called for their attention. 'Since I find myself giving a house-party,' she said a trifle acidly, 'suppose you tell me something about my guests? Who are the Pearsons?'

'Madge was Lady Margaret Allinston,' Daisy informed her. 'She doesn't use her title because Tommy doesn't have one. She was at school with Lucy and me, but a year older, so we didn't know her awfully well. Then quite by chance she VAD'ed in the same military hospital in Malvern where I worked in the office, so I saw a lot of her.'

'You worked in a hospital office? Mrs. Pearson was with a Voluntary Aid Detachment?' Geraldine seemed surprised, as if she had not realized many of today's bright young things had actually done their bit during the War.

'And Lucy was a Land Girl. She didn't mind the work so much, but she claims wearing that hideous uniform nearly killed her. She still has nightmares about finding herself on a dance floor in it.'

'I was VAD.'

'You can swap stories with Madge, then. She met Tommy in the hospital – he was pretty crocked up.'

'Pearson was in our outfit,' Phillip put in, 'with Gervaise and me. He finished up a major.'

'His family are Pearson, Pearson, Watts & Pearson, one of the top solicitors' firms in London, old-established and frightfully respectable.' Daisy paused, suddenly wondering whether Tommy was too respectable and too legally-minded to be dragged into a scheme which involved concealing a crime from the police.

Geraldine interrupted her fruitless speculation. 'I'm glad to learn you have friends in respectable professions,' she said austerely. 'You were at school with Miss Fotheringay, were you not? And now you share lodgings, in *Chelsea*.' Her tone of voice equated residence in that district with the worst excesses of Bohemia.

'Yes. She's a photographer. Her grandfather is the Earl of Haverhill.' A good splodge of blue blood nicely balanced out the artistic profession, Daisy hoped. She was about to move on to Binkie's pedigree when voices and footsteps approached the drawing-room.

Lowecroft appeared on the threshold. 'Mr. and Mrs. Pearson, my lady.'

Geraldine rose and moved towards the door. Daisy and Phillip hung back behind her. They shook their heads vigorously and Daisy put a finger to her lips as Madge and Tommy entered the room.

Tommy, bespectacled, brown-haired, and stocky, looked startled and rather bewildered. Madge, whose froth of blond curls and effervescent manner often misled people into taking her for a bubble-head, was quicker on the uptake. She deftly steered her husband through conventional greetings.

'Explain later,' Daisy hissed at the first opportunity.

She and Phillip went through the same pantomime when Lucy and Binkie arrived, a few minutes later. They both caught on at once.

Lowecroft's face simply grew stiffer and more wooden. 'Tea, my lady?' he enquired.

'Yes, on the terrace, please, and inform Lord Dalrymple that our guests are here.'

Edgar's presence at afternoon tea to some extent relieved the frustration of the delay in clarifying matters. He discoursed with his usual knowledgeable enthusiasm on the annual migration from Africa of *Vanessa cardui*, the Painted Lady butterfly. Since Geraldine kept casting sidelong, scandalized glances at Lucy's skillfully painted face, everyone but she and Edgar was in a state of barely repressed hilarity.

Even Phillip relaxed, once he realized what the joke was. Daisy was glad to see his lips twitch. His anxiety returned soon enough when Edgar and Geraldine went into the house. The four newcomers sat up and looked expectant.

'Right-oh,' said Lucy, 'this Painted Lady is simply dying to hear what's up. Let's have it. Oh, before I forget, darling, your tame copper's going to 'phone this evening.'

Phillip blenched. 'Chief Inspector Fletcher? You haven't told him what's happened, have you?'

'I don't *know* what's happened. He popped round to take Daisy out to lunch and found her gone – frightfully bad form, darling,' she added in a severe aside to Daisy.

'I tried to get hold of him.'

'Well, I was on the point of leaving, too, and it seemed only decent to show him the wire. I think it rather put the wind up him. Anyway, he's going to ring up tonight to make sure everything's all right.'

Turning to Daisy, Phillip said urgently, 'You won't tell him?'

'I still think it would be best, but I promised.'

'Gosh, this gets more and more mysterious.' Madge's eyes sparkled with excitement. 'Too, too divine. Do tell.'

'First,' said Daisy, 'what we tell you must go no further. Absolute secrecy is essential.'

Tommy frowned. 'I don't like the sound of this,' he said bluntly, taking off his horn-rimmed glasses and polishing them with his handkerchief. 'I hope I know you both well enough to be sure you wouldn't do anything you believed morally wrong, but I have to consider the legal aspect, too, don't y'know. You must admit keeping secrets from the police sounds downright fishy.'

'What piffle, darling!' Madge's merry laugh rang out. 'It was just the other day you were grumbling like billy-o about some nosy policeman who wanted information you regarded as confidential. Don't be an old stick-in-the-mud.'

'That was a matter of privileged communication between client and solicitor, my pet, not to be confused with aiding and abetting, let alone committing . . .'

'This is a matter of life and death!' burst forth from Phillip.

'It could be,' Daisy confirmed with more caution. 'At least I can promise you we're trying to foil a crime, not commit one. I can't say more unless I have your word to keep mum. If you don't feel able to give it, Tommy, then we must apologize for dragging you all the way here for nothing.'

'Count me in,' Binkie said tersely.

'I'm with you.' Lucy covered a delicate yawn with a well-manicured hand. 'As long as it isn't too frightfully fatiguing.'

'I'll help as much as I can.' Madge's rosy cheeks grew pinker. 'I can't ride a horse, though, I'm afraid. You see, I'm preggy.'

'Darling, how marvellous,' cried Daisy, jumping up to kiss her.

'Congratulations, darling,' Lucy said dryly, 'or do you prefer condolences?'

'Actually, we're rather pleased,' Madge admitted, 'aren't we, pet?'

Daisy and Lucy both turned to look at Tommy. He was quite pink-faced himself, self-consciously proud.

'Time to bring another little solicitor into the world,' he said half mockingly, then sighed. 'Right-ho, I'll rally round.

Can't let the side down, don't y'know. Unless your scheme is actually criminal, I'll lend a hand.'

'Spiffing!' said Daisy, and got down to brass tacks.

Dinner was over and the long Summer Time evening waned. Swifts swooped over the gardens, wreaking devastation on the clouds of midges. All her plans laid and approved by the others, Daisy was glad to relax at last. In the twilight on the terrace, chaffing about indifferent subjects since her cousins were there, she could almost pretend nothing had changed since she was a girl.

Lowecroft came out of the house. 'Telephone call for Miss Dalrymple. A Mr. Fletcher, miss.'

'The Drinker!' cried Edgar. Before Daisy could object to his casting utterly unwarranted aspersions on Alec, he seized his butterfly net, never far from his side, and dashed down the steps to the lawn. The spaniel, Pepper, loped after him. '*Philudoria potatoria*,' came floating back.

Daisy hurried in to the telephone. 'Alec?'

'Hello, Daisy.' He sounded tired. 'I hope I'm not interrupting anything.'

'Oh no. We were just sitting out on the terrace. I'm glad you rang. I'm so sorry I didn't manage to let you know in time about lunch.'

'You tried. I take it I wasn't abandoned for a common or garden house-party?'

'As though I would!'

'You're not in trouble, are you?'

'No, honestly.'

'Petrie is?'

She hesitated. 'Not exactly,' she said. Strictly speaking it was the Arbuckles who were in the soup.

'Daisy, I know how far you'll go to help someone you've taken under your wing. Don't go and land yourself in a hole trying to pull him out.'

'It's nothing like that.'

'What is it? Why don't you tell me? Perhaps I can advise, if not help.'

'I'd like to tell you, Alec, but I can't.'

'Can't, or won't?'

'Mustn't. Don't worry, I shan't do anything stupid.' Time to change the subject. 'It feels frightfully peculiar staying at Fairacres as a guest.' She went on to describe the eerie effect of the changed residents and the unchanged furnishings. 'I'll show you around this weekend,' she finished. 'I'm sure Edgar won't mind. You can come, can't you?'

'You still want me to?'

'Of course! I just wish you were here now,' Daisy said with fervour.

'I'll be there. The Super's promised to cope without me even if a second Guy Fawkes blows up the Houses of Parliament. Belinda sends her love.'

'Give her mine. Good-night, Alec.'

'Good-night, love. Sweet dreams.'

Daisy held the earpiece to her ear for several moments after the click of Alec hanging up came over the wire. He had called her 'love,' even though she could tell from his voice that he was hurt by her refusal to confide in him.

If Gloria was not free – rescued or ransomed – by the weekend, she would insist on telling him everything.

CHAPTER 9

The first phase of Daisy's plan was for her and Phillip to enquire after strangers in the villages where they were known and could therefore expect people to talk to them. She had decided they would be less conspicuous – in case the kidnappers were on the watch – if they bicycled rather than motored. She and Binkie were to circle around Fairacres, Phillip and Lucy around Malvern Grange, where he was better known. All four were to meet for a picnic lunch in a copse on the boundary between the two.

Though Madge's doctor had banned only horseback riding, Tommy absolutely forbade her to bicycle. Daisy therefore sent them in their Lagonda to investigate some villages rather further out, beyond convenient cycling distance.

At that distance, she hoped, they were unlikely to be connected with the Fairacres party, should the villains be aware of Mr. Arbuckle's visit to Phillip. Strangers themselves, they would be regarded with some suspicion if they made direct enquiries, but they could ask whether many visitors came that way.

'Don't ask about deserted cottages, though,' Daisy said. 'It's a pity, but that's the sort of thing which might get back to the kidnappers.'

Tommy nodded. '"Someone's interested in that old place you're staying," that sort of thing. We'll steer clear.'

They all set off. As soon as the others were out of earshot, Daisy confided to Binkie, 'I rather doubt this search is any use, but I can't think what else to do.'

'Pretty hopeless,' he confirmed tersely.

Having hoped for encouragement, Daisy consoled herself with a reminder of his generally pessimistic outlook on life.

'Still,' she said, as much to herself as to him, 'I can't really believe Miss Arbuckle is in danger of anything worse than a few days of discomfort.'

'Regular brutes, these American gangsters,' said Binkie. 'Wouldn't put anything past 'em.'

Daisy turned her head to glare at him. She wobbled as her bicycle wheel went over a stone, and thereafter concentrated on where she was going.

It was a beautiful morning for a ride. Garlands of pale pink roses and yellow honeysuckle in the hedges perfumed the air. Foxgloves, campion red and white, and yellow toadflax flourished on banks and verges. A cock pheasant scurried down the road ahead of them for a few yards before diving beneath a gate. Small birds warbled, whistled, and twittered.

Impossible to envisage a girl locked up in a dingy room and in fear of her life!

Ahead of Daisy and Binkie a tower, stone horizontally striped with red brick, protruded above a knot of green trees. Like many local villages, Morton Green was dominated by its church, built on a slight rise. The village straggled around its namesake green. Cottages of brick with lichened tile roofs, whitewashed stucco with slate, red sandstone, yellow Cotswold stone, or half-timbering, mingled higgledy-piggledy.

The largest building was the Wedge and Beetle Inn, foursquare, whitewashed, with scarlet geraniums in window-boxes. Daisy decided to tackle it first. The bar was not open yet, but she had an excuse for enquiries.

She and Binkie leant their bikes against the wall and stepped through the open door out of the sunshine into the dimness of the lobby.

'Hullo, there!' Binkie called.

Mrs. Dennie, the landlord's wife, came bustling through from the back. 'Why, if it's not Miss Dalrymple.' She gave Binkie a curious look. 'Come down for a visit, have you, miss? What can I do for you?'

'Good-morning, Mrs. Dennie. A friend of mine mentioned that he hoped to stay here. I just wondered whether you had room for him, whether he'd made a reservation.'

'We've got a couple of fishermen – anglers they likes to be called, bless their hearts – and a young pair, honeymooners by our reckoning, the way they spoon, if you'll pardon the expression. The other room, well, there's casuals dropping in. The odd commercial, like, and the touring season's well under way already this year, what with the weather we've been having.'

'Isn't it marvellous?'

'Not for the farmers, miss, but it don't hurt our business, I must say.'

'People like to get out of town when it's hot Do you have many Londoners?'

'Can't say we do, miss, not being a beauty spot like some. Mostly from Birmingham way. No, I don't believe as we've had a Londoner in the house, nor yet in the bar even.'

'Nor many foreigners, I expect.'

Mrs. Dennie laughed heartily at the notion of foreigners patronising her modest establishment 'This friend of yours, miss,' she went on, 'what's the name? I'll check and see if he's booked.'

'Fletcher, for this weekend.'

Alec had a room reserved for both Friday and Saturday nights. 'Seeing he's a friend of yourn, miss,' said Mrs. Dennie, 'I'll move him to the back corner room. It's bigger and quieter, not being over the public bar.'

Daisy thanked her, enquired after her family, and preceded Binkie back out into the sunshine. He hadn't said a word after his halloo. An inarticulate companion was useful in the circumstances, Daisy decided. Pessimist he might be, but at least he didn't lengthen the already-chatty interrogation.

Mrs. Dennie's chatter was nothing to what Daisy met with in the tiny, overflowing shop they called at next. POST OFFICE, NEWSAGENT, TOBACCONIST, AND SWEETS proclaimed the sign over the door. Miss Hibbert had once sold pennyworths of dolly-mixture and bull's-eyes to Daisy and Gervaise. Older and greyer now, she happened to have seen one of Daisy's articles in *Town and Country*, and she was dying to hear about her writing career. In exchange, she passed on a vast quantity of village gossip.

Interrupted by two or three customers, half an hour passed before Daisy and Binkie escaped with the information they sought: neither Cockneys nor Americans had bought tobacco or newspapers from Miss Hibbert, not recently. There had been a touring couple last year, or was it the year before, who might have been American. Gentlemen from London staying at Fairacres occasionally popped in for cigarettes. And East Enders came down from London for the hop-picking in August, of course, though not, Miss Hibbert thought, in such swarms as went to Kent.

Dismayed, Daisy wondered if she had been too optimistic in believing the kidnappers would not know the country. She had forgotten the hop-pickers. It dawned on her, too, that some of the Cockneys among the wounded soldiers in the Malvern hospitals during and after the War might well have roamed the countryside while convalescing.

'Blast!' she said, mounting her bicycle.

'You didn't expect anything so close to where Phillip was dumped,' Binkie reminded her.

She decided not to reveal her fresh qualms. 'No, but one always hopes,' she said vaguely. 'It would have been so convenient. Do you think we ought to try the general store, too? They could have gone in for supplies.'

'Might as well,' grunted Binkie.

The general store, which purveyed flour and baking-pans, cheese and mousetraps with equal enthusiasm, provided as little information at almost as great a length. The day was already growing hot when Daisy and Binkie rode out of Morton Green. They were glad to plunge into the green shade of Bellman's Wood, just beyond the village.

'Don't we explore?' Binkie asked as they pedalled along the lane.

'No, not here. I know every inch of this wood. It belongs to one of the Fairacres farms, actually. There are plenty of squirrels and woodpeckers but no buildings, deserted or otherwise. At least, there could be something recently built, but what Phillip described sounded like an ancient cottage.'

All too soon they left the shade of the trees. A motor-car passed them, raising clouds of dust. By the time they had pursued their fruitless enquiries in the next two villages, Daisy felt as if she had cycled across the Sahara, and the afternoon was yet to come.

Meeting the others for their picnic by the stream in Boundary Copse, she dismounted on leaden legs.

'I'm out of form,' she confessed ruefully to a maddeningly cool-looking Lucy. 'Maybe one never forgets how to ride a bicycle, having once learnt, but it must use different muscles from walking, and mine are telling me they're out of practice.'

'We got here half an hour ago, darling, and I've had my feet in the water. Try it, it helps. No luck, I take it?'

'No. You?' Daisy asked, taking off her shoes.

'Not a bite. Phillip's frightfully pipped, the poor old fish.'

Daisy glanced at Phillip, who was helping Binkie unpack the picnic from the bicycle bags. She sighed. Much as her thighs cried out for the afternoon off, she couldn't let him down. Sitting on the grassy bank with her feet dangling in the lukewarm stream, she dipped her hankie in the water and wiped her face.

Ginger-beer and sandwiches revived her somewhat, but better still was the thin layer of clouds which came up to cover the sky. It was still hot, but at least the sun would not blaze down on her head. A breeze rose as they left the shelter of the copse, cooling if not cool. With renewed vigour she and Binkie set off for the next village on their list.

The afternoon's circuit was wider flung than the morning's. There were more villages, and Daisy was less well known if recognized at all. This proved a mixed blessing.

Each interview was shorter, because less encumbered with gossip. On the other hand, it was more difficult to find an opening for her questions, and they had to purchase something at each stop as an excuse to ask. The saddlebags emptied of food were soon packed with cigarettes and pipe tobacco, fast-melting chocolate bars, and miscellaneous odds and ends.

Of useful information they collected none.

Daisy flagged before they finished the list. 'It's teatime,' she pointed out to Binkie, 'and very likely the shops in the next place will be closed before we get there anyway.'

'You want to head back to Fairacres?'

'If we don't,' she said frankly, 'you may have to carry me home, and my bike too.'

Binkie grinned. 'Dashed if I don't think we've done our duty for the day. Wouldn't be surprised if Lucy's dragged Phil home by now.'

They were the first back, but only by a few minutes. Geraldine had people to tea on the terrace. The weary searchers, four of them far too grimy to join the party, collapsed on the grass under a wide-spreading chestnut. Ernest, obviously bemused by the curious habits of the gentry who exhausted themselves for fun, brought them tea.

All reported equal lack of results. Five pairs of eyes turned to Daisy.

'It's hopeless, isn't it?' Phillip blurted out.

Daisy rallied herself. 'Not at all, old dear. We've barely scratched the surface. Only I think tomorrow we'd better each go out on our own – is that grammatical? You know what I mean. We'll cover much more ground that way, and it'll be ground where Phil and I have no advantage. Tommy and Madge will go together, of course. You made it about half-way round your circle?'

'Just about,' Tommy confirmed, 'but Madge is finding it pretty tiring even by car don't y'know. I think she ought to stay behind tomorrow.'

'Oh no,' cried Madge, 'I'll be perfectly all right after a night's sleep. You must admit, Tommy, people talk more to me than to you, and I want to do my bit.'

'You can,' Daisy said quickly, 'without stirring a step. I've been thinking,' she lied, 'we ought to have someone here to sort of coordinate things. Each of us will ring up periodically, so if someone finds out something the others can all be told right away. We'll work out some kind of code.'

'Good tactics,' said Tommy with a grateful glance. 'Definitely the best use of available troops.'

'I hate to be a wet blanket,' Lucy drawled, 'but while people talk to Tommy, if less readily than to Madge, is anyone going to say a word to Binkie? Did you open your mouth to anyone but Daisy today, darling?'

'No,' Binkie confessed, blushing.

Daisy hurried to rescue the embarrassed young man. 'In any case, Lucy, you don't look at all the sort who'd be buzzing about on a bicycle without a man at your side. Binkie had better escort you. His moment will come when we find Miss Arbuckle and have to storm the castle, if we decide that's the best thing to do. Pass the cake, Madge, I'm starving.'

Well fortified with Victoria sponge and Shrewsbury biscuits, Daisy spent the next couple of hours poring over maps and plotting new courses for the morrow. Knowing what had been covered today, she was dismayed to see how long it was going to take to survey even a ten-mile-radius circle. Before she went up to bathe and change, she cornered Phillip.

'You know, old thing,' she said, 'we'll find Gloria, but I'm dead certain the police could find her sooner. I do wish you'd let me consult Alec.'

Phillip stubbornly shook his head. 'They'd find out.'

'With the local chaps, I expect so, but Alec will know how to keep things hushed up.'

'Fletcher's a good chap,' he said unexpectedly. 'If I hadn't given Arbuckle my word, I'd consider putting it to him as a hyp . . . hypno . . . what's the dashed word I want?'

'Hypothetical case?'

'That's it. But I can't. You'd have to persuade Arbuckle. He should be in touch,' Phillip added, his brow creased with worry. 'You don't suppose he's having trouble collecting the money?'

'It just takes time,' Daisy soothed him. 'He'd have let you know if there was any difficulty.'

Phillip accepted that, and Daisy went off to take her long-overdue bath.

After dinner she went over the next day's plans with the others. Then they joined her cousins in the drawing-room, the terrace being ruled out by Geraldine, who was sure it was about to rain. Somnolent after an excess of exercise, they were settling down to a quiet evening when Ernest appeared.

'Telephone, Mr. Petrie, sir.'

Phillip dashed off, to return a few moments later and beckon urgently to Daisy.

Joining him, she asked in a low voice, 'Mr. Arbuckle?'

'Yes. He's back in Malvern and he wants to come over. Is that all right? He's holding the line.' Phillip started back to the telephone in the front hall and Daisy followed.

'Can't we go there?' she proposed.

'He doesn't want anyone to see me with him while Gloria's supposed to be away visiting friends.'

'Oh yes, I forgot. He's right, people would talk. We must see him, and it's less conspicuous for him to come here.'

'It's frightful cheek to invite him.'

'I'll think of something to tell Geraldine.'

'She thinks he ran me off the road.'

'Right-oh, how's this: You discovered he has pull with a publisher – a big investment or something – so you invited him to meet me. That will give us an excuse to talk to him privately, too. Warn him,' she advised as Phillip picked up the telephone.

He spoke briefly to Arbuckle, then hung up. 'He'll be here in half an hour.'

'I'll ask Edgar if we can use his den. That will circumvent Geraldine nicely.'

As they reached the drawing-room, Edgar was saying, 'And then I spotted a Chinese character.'

Startled, Daisy wondered if a Chinaman had somehow got mixed up in the kidnapping. Could 'the Yank' be a deliberately misleading nickname? Didn't Chinese criminals favour the white slave trade rather than abductions for ransom?

'*Clix glaucata*, you know,' Edgar continued. 'At rest, with its wings folded, the adult moth looks remarkably like a bird dropping.'

'Really, Edgar!' exclaimed Geraldine.

Phillip chose that moment to announce, 'I say, that was Arbuckle on the 'phone. The American chappie, you remember, Lady Dalrymple?'

'Oh yes. Edgar, I wish you would not...'

'I discovered he's a publisher, or has influence in a publishing company, or something of the sort. Investments, what? So it seemed a good idea to introduce him to Daisy.'

'...discuss the revolting habits of your insects...'

'So I've asked him to pop over this evening. I hope you don't mind.'

'...in mixed company. By all means, Mr. Petrie. It's really most improper.'

'There's nothing improper about it,' Edgar argued. 'It's a matter of scientific observation.'

'Would you mind if we used your den, sir? Business matter, and all that.'

Edgar waved permission. 'Don't you see, dear, one must be able to describe the appearance accurately but in layman's language. And the Chinese Character looks like a bird dropping.' He repeated the phrase with a defiant air. 'Camouflage, you see.'

'Spiffing,' said Daisy, stifling a giggle as she caught Lucy's sardonic eye. 'We'll wait for him there so as not to disturb you all when he arrives.'

She hustled Phillip out before Geraldine's attention left the indecorous behaviour of moths and moved to the indecorous behaviour of a guest who invited a guest of his own.

They went to the den. Daisy, her legs still tired from bicycling, flopped into one of the vast leather-covered chairs. Phillip was too restless to relax. He went out again to pace the front hall.

Daisy's eyelids were drooping when he stuck his head back in a few minutes later to say, 'I'm going to walk down the drive to meet him.'

Shaking herself awake, Daisy set her mind to marshalling her arguments for calling in the police. Her thoughts on Alec, she started wondering if her mother was going to treat him with the sort of icy politeness which was in effect a form of insult. That reminded her that she'd promised to pop in to see the dowager today and hadn't.

'Oh blast!' she said aloud.

'Pardon me?'

The American voice sounded infinitely weary. Daisy looked round. Arbuckle was not at all what she had expected of an American millionaire, that is large, overfed, and exuding a slightly false bonhomie.

About her own height, he was lean to the point of boniness. She guessed he had lost weight recently, for his charcoal suit, though of unmistakable Savile Row cut, hung on him as on a scarecrow. His long, gaunt face had a greyish cast to match his receding hair.

Mr. Arbuckle, she realized with a rush of sympathy, had no faith in his daughter's safety.

His desolate eyes brought home to her with a jolt that she and her friends were not engaged for fun in a treasure-hunt with which she was already rather bored. Their efforts might mean the difference between life and death.

CHAPTER 10

'Well now,' said Arbuckle, shaking Daisy's hand, 'if this isn't mighty kind of you, ma'am. Petrie's explained to me what you're trying to do for my little girl. He tells me he has absolute faith in your discretion, yours and your friends'.' The doubt expressed by his choice of words was echoed in his tone.

'We've all promised not to let the cat out of the bag, Mr. Arbuckle, and we're frightfully careful with our enquiries. I think you'd better meet the others – but later, if you feel up to it. Do sit down, won't you?'

A sigh escaped him as he sank gratefully into one of the big chairs.

Phillip leant against the mantelpiece, one hand in his trouser pocket. Despite the casual pose, Daisy saw he still had the jim-jams.

'We really are careful, sir,' he said. 'Daisy – Miss Dalrymple – has worked it all out.'

'How do you mean?'

'I came up with ways to ask questions that sound like casual chit-chat. Local people aren't at all likely to gossip with Cockneys or Americans, anyway. They look on people from the other side of the Malvern Hills as practically foreigners.'

'You folks can honestly tell the difference?'

'With Cockneys, certainly, if not with Herefordshers.'

'Waal, I guess a Middle Westerner like me knows a Texan from a New Yorker, so why not? Say, Miss Dalrymple, you figure you guys have a real chance of finding Gloria?'

'A chance. The police would have a much better chance. Won't you let . . . ?'

'No dice,' said Arbuckle with grim determination.

'I was going to say, at least let me consult a friend of mine who's a detective at Scotland Yard. Mr. Fletcher's discreet and absolutely trustworthy.'

'Abso-bally-lutely,' Phillip confirmed. 'Besides, we could tell him it's a hypo . . . what was that word, Daisy?'

'Hypothetical.'

'It's no go.' Arbuckle was adamant. 'You just don't unnerstand how things are back home. Kidnapping's by way of getting to be big business, see, like bootlegging, and Detroit where I come from's one of the places it's biggest. There's lots of lucre floating around on account of the automobile business.'

He leant towards Daisy, hands on his knees, and asked her earnestly, 'Now why do folks buy an automobile when they've always been contented with a horse and buggy? Because they see other people enjoy owning one. And why do folks do just exactly what kidnappers tell 'em? Because they see what happens to other people's loved ones if they don't. A kidnapper not doing what he's threatened to is like an auto not doing what the manufacturer's promised it will. Bad for business.'

'Yes, I see that,' Daisy said slowly. She had a feeling there was a flaw in the argument somewhere, but she couldn't quite pinpoint it. Alec would have seen it.

'So, they tell me "no cops," no cops it is. After Gloria's safe, now that's a whole different ball game. You can call in your Scotland Yard buddy then. What I want,' Arbuckle snarled, 'is I want to see the sons of bitches put away in the hoosegow for life.'

'Oh, I say!' Phillip protested.

'If you'll pardon the expression, ma'am.'

Daisy indicated that she considered a certain amount of heat was justified in the circumstances. 'I hope you haven't had too much trouble coming up with the ransom money,' she said.

'The bank will have gotten it for me by Friday. I'll have to go to Lunnon to pick it up.'

'Don't want to leave anything to chance,' Phillip put in.

'That's right, son. It's a heck of a lot of dough, though it won't bankrupt me by a long ways, no sirree. Not that I wouldn't bankrupt myself for my girl, Miss Dalrymple,' he added earnestly. 'But it makes me think they know what they're up to and aren't going to demand delivery before I've had time to round up the cash.'

'That's a relief. We have at least a couple of days to go on searching for Gloria. Unless you want to call off the blood-hounds, Mr. Arbuckle?'

His brow wrinkled in thought. 'No, I guess it sounds like you can't do any harm. If you came through with the goods, if you found where she's at, why then I'd sure have to think again about bringing in the troopers.'

'We'll do our best,' Daisy promised. 'Would you like to come and meet the others now?'

'I surely would like to shake those folks by the hand.'

'You'll have to be careful what you say,' she warned.

'My cousins, Lord and Lady Dalrymple, think we're just a house-party.'

Arbuckle chuckled. 'Petrie tells me I'm to pose as the guy who ran him off the road, come to make amends.'

'I'm sorry, sir,' said Phillip, flushing. 'It seemed easiest since that's what Lady Dalrymple guessed.'

'That's okay, son. I figure I owe you a new auto if yours isn't found in one piece.'

Phillip's face darkened to crimson. He opened his mouth but nothing came out.

Daisy had never seen him at such a loss. 'Gosh, that's jolly generous of you, Mr. Arbuckle,' she said for him. 'Did Phillip explain that you're also posing as a partner in a firm of publishers dying to publish my work?'

'Sure thing.' Arbuckle grinned at her. 'Just tell me what magazine you want to write for, ma'am, and I'll buy it up.'

She laughed. 'How about the *Saturday Evening Post*?'

'Now that could be a mite difficult to purchase outright, but if shares are traded on Wall Street, I'll buy enough to have a say in the business.'

'I didn't mean it!'

'I did. No one can say Caleb P. Arbuckle ever forgot a favour, and you couldn't do me a bigger one than trying to help my Gloria.' His face sagged and his shoulders slumped. 'My poor little girl,' he said softly.

Daisy decided it was not the moment to argue about the *Saturday Evening Post* and wanting to sell one's work on its merits. 'Let's go to the drawing-room and we'll introduce you to the others,' she suggested.

His social savoir-faire once more in evidence, Phillip presented the American to Geraldine.

'How do you do, Mr. Arbuckle,' she said with a stiff nod.

'Howdy-do, Lady Dalrymple. It's real kind of you to let me do my little bit of business with my young friend here in your beautiful house. I want to apologize for gate-crashing, ma'am, and me not even in my tuxedo.'

Geraldine thawed slightly. 'What quaint terms you Americans use. Gate-crashing is self-explanatory, I suppose. A tuxedo is a dinner jacket?'

'Sure is. I've been in Lunnon and I didn't have time this evening to change.'

'Have you dined, Mr. Arbuckle?'

'Yes, I thank you, ma'am. I grabbed a bite on the train.'

At Daisy's side, Lucy murmured, 'Unorthodox vocabulary, darling, but acceptable manners.'

'I rather like him.'

'I was afraid he might turn out to be an absolute bounder. Too, too ghastly to discover we'd rescued some tawdry parvenu shopgirl.'

'Not likely. Phillip's no more likely to excuse vulgarity than you are.'

Lucy raised meticulously plucked eyebrows and turned an attentive gaze on Phillip, hovering anxiously nearby as Geraldine introduced Arbuckle to Edgar. 'Aha,' she said, 'so that's how it is? Don't tell me Phillip has found his soul-mate!'

'Found,' Daisy admitted, 'and lost.'

'That does add a certain piquancy to the situation.'

'Let's just hope he finds her again. Don't tell anyone else, darling. His people don't know yet.'

'My lips are sealed. By the way, that reminds me, Binkie says your tame 'tec is coming to stay in the village this weekend.' Lucy's tone was languid but her eyebrows rose again in a shrewdly enquiring look.

Daisy's cheeks grew hot. 'Yes, he's coming down.' She tried to sound casual. 'I'd promised to support Phil when he introduces the Arbuckles to his parents, and it seemed a good moment for Mother to meet Alec.'

'Cupid's been busy, I see.' Lucy sighed. 'Perhaps its about time I proposed to Binkie. The poor prune isn't likely to find the words to do the job. The best I can hope for is that your example will inspire him to utter, "What about it, old girl?"'

'Alec hasn't proposed.'

'He will. Isn't it going to be a bit awkward, his landing in the middle of all this? Our American friend won't be frightfully happy to see a full-blown Detective Chief Inspector on the doorstep.'

'With any luck it will all be over by the weekend,' Daisy said hopefully. 'Mr. Arbuckle's fetching the ransom from town on Friday. If we haven't found Gloria by then, it'll be too late.'

Phillip brought Arbuckle over to introduce him to Lucy. In a low voice, the American expressed his gratitude, sincere but not fulsome, for her assistance. Probably the sternest critic present, she appeared to continue to find his manners acceptable.

Daisy would have liked to regard it as a good omen for his reception by Phillip's parents. The Petries, however, were liable to be rather more exacting when informed that Caleb P. Arbuckle was to become a relation by marriage.

But that was jumping the gun. First catch your hare, as someone or other had said. Until Gloria was safe, there was no sense worrying about how Phillip's family would receive her and her father.

A few minutes later, after meeting the Pearsons and Binkie, Mr. Arbuckle sought Daisy out. 'Say, Miss Dalrymple,' he said, 'could we have a quiet word?'

'Of course.' Praying that he wasn't going to expect an optimistic estimate of their chances of finding Gloria, she led the way to a massive Victorian sofa relegated to an obscure corner of the room.

Sitting down beside her with an irresolute air, he hesitated a moment, then embarked upon a subject Daisy was sure was not on the top of his mind.

'Your cousin – Lord Dalrymple's your cousin, right? – he's a swell guy. I wasn't too sure at first. He kept talking about a red-necked footman, so I figured he was having trouble with a hayseed lackey. "Red-neck" is what Southerners call farm labourers, see, and I've heard a lot about the servant problem since I've been over here, though it's usually the ladies complaining.'

'Endlessly,' Daisy agreed, 'but I bet Edgar was talking about a moth, wasn't he?'

'Or a butterfly, I couldn't say for sure. Something that lays eggs that turn into caterpillars. He knew the Latin name right off. Me, I like a guy with a real good grasp of his subject, even if it's just bugs. That's one of the things I like about young Petrie.'

'Really?' Daisy didn't want to queer Phillip's pitch, but if Arbuckle was labouring under the delusion that he was a stock market wizard, it might be better to disillusion him before it was too late. 'Actually, I don't think he's frightfully keen on stocks and shares,' she said with caution.

'Jeez no! I wouldn't trust him to buy me a hundred bucks worth of blue chips! That's *my* line. It's carburetors and radiators I'm talking about. Petrie has a real good practical know-how when it comes to the innards of an automobile – considering all his disadvantages.'

'Disadvantages?' Daisy queried still more cautiously, wondering what a blue chip was.

'That swank family of his that thinks it's beneath a lord's son to meddle with mechanics,' said Arbuckle with considerable heat. 'Pardon me, ma'am, I guess I shouldn't talk that way to a lord's daughter.'

'No, it's all right. My mother feels the same way about my writing, or working at all. As a matter of fact, Phillip told me just the other day that he wants to leave the City and have a go at something to do with motors. Anything to do with motors.'

'Does he now? That's real interesting! I'm sure glad you told me that, Miss Dalrymple. Say, listen, I've been wanting to ask you something. I know you're a mighty good friend of young Phillip's and I hope you won't take offence if I've gotten hold of the wrong darned end of the stick.'

'Ask away,' said Daisy, dying of curiosity and throwing caution to the winds. 'I shan't take offence and I'll answer if I can.'

Arbuckle patted her hand. 'It's like this, see. It seems to me Petrie's taken a shine to my girl. You don't mind?' he asked anxiously.

'Phillip and I are *friends*,' she assured him, 'practically since our cradles.'

'Waal, that's a relief, I don't mind telling you. I wouldn't want Gloria pinching your boyfriend, specially now I've met you. Now, I've been a mite puzzled, not knowing just how things are done in your country, and not being able to ask the boy. Just let me ask you this: Him inviting Gloria and me to meet his folks this weekend, does that mean he's decided he wants to get hitched?'

'It does. You wouldn't mind your daughter marrying into a "swank" family?'

'Miss Dalrymple,' Arbuckle said passionately, 'if I get my girl back safe and sound, she can marry the local ditch-digger if that's what she wants.'

'Or the local motor mechanic?' Daisy asked. 'Phillip said he'd mentioned he's not in line for the title or estate, and a very modest allowance is all he can expect from his family.'

'Heck, if Honourable's good enough for Gloria, it's good enough for me, and even with the ransom paid, I've enough to support them in style. But it's my impression of the boy – correct me here if I'm wrong – that he'd rather earn his keep.'

'He told me he hoped you'd find him a technical job, if Miss Arbuckle accepted him.'

'If and when he marries Gloria, my notion is to make him my technical adviser.'

'That would suit Phillip down to the ground!' Daisy knit her brows, struck by a sudden thought 'But what about the chap who advises you now? He'd be out of a job. Could he have foreseen it?'

'Don't you worry about him, Miss Dalrymple. I'd never fire a trusted longtime employee for no fault of his own. Crawford's been with me ten years, and I've him to thank for a good part of what I own today. It'll be easy enough to find him something else to do for the same salary.'

Daisy pursued her thought. 'What about people you've sacked for good cause? Phillip told me you haven't any enemies, but I should think you must have made one or two.'

Arbuckle cast a shamefaced glance at Phillip, who was patiently submitting to one of Edgar's lectures on the far side of the room. A fortuitous lull in everyone else's conversations allowed his lordship's wistful words to float across. 'The other evening I nearly captured a small elephant. Pink, you know, with some yellow, and really quite pretty.'

Noticing Arbuckle's scandalized face, Daisy said, 'It's all right, Edgar isn't a dipsomaniac. I'm sure it's another moth or butterfly.'

'Oh, sure. By golly, he had me worried for a minute there. Though come to think of it, why shouldn't a lord be a lush same as any other guy? Well, like you were saying, ma'am I haven't got where I am without making an enemy or two. I guess I didn't want Petrie to think Gloria's poppa was the kinda guy to go round treading on people's toes for kicks.'

'Are you?' Daisy ventured to ask.

'I am not,' he said emphatically. 'But there's guys have it in for me because I fired 'em, like you guessed, or because I beat 'em to a bargain, or because I wouldn't invest and they went bust, or . . . heck, you get the picture.'

She nodded. 'I wondered why you were concerned about Miss Arbuckle's safety when you said American kidnappers know it's good business to keep their promises. No one would pay ransom if they killed their victims even when the families obey instructions to the letter. But if it's a matter of revenge . . .'

'If it's a matter of revenge,' said Arbuckle in a hollow voice, 'it's anyone's guess what they might do to my little girl.'

CHAPTER 11

'Be like a Turkish bath later,' Binkie observed gloomily, as the searchers gathered in the stable-yard after breakfast.

The sky was still overcast, but Geraldine's prophesied rain had not materialized. The air was muggy, already warm, without a hint of a breeze.

'You like Turkish baths, darling,' Lucy consoled Binkie. 'Just think how shiny my nose is going to get. It's hardly worth bothering to take face-powder.'

Truscott, wheeling out the last of the bicycles, hid a grin. 'I've dusted 'em off, Miss Daisy,' he said, 'and checked the brakes and tyres. You're all set. And I topped up the oil in the Lagonda, sir,' he added to Tommy. 'The level was down a tad. You want to keep an eye on it.'

Tommy thanked him, kissed Madge good-bye, and zoomed off down the avenue. The bicyclers set off at a more leisurely pace, Lucy and Binkie following the green Lagonda, Daisy and Phillip in opposite directions across the park.

Pedalling towards the Dower House, Daisy wondered whether she ought to have told the others what Arbuckle had said about the possibility of an enemy out for revenge. Their enthusiasm for the hunt had waned – except Phillip's, of course – at the prospect of another hot day's exertion on the off-chance of sparing a girl they didn't know a day or two of discomfort.

If they understood Gloria's peril, they'd be keen as mustard to find her. The trouble was, Daisy was afraid if she told the rest, Phillip would find out, and the poor prune was already in a state. She didn't want to send him into a tail-spin.

Coming to the Dower House back gate, she wheeled her bicycle through. Owen Morgan peered at her from among runner-beans twice his height, aglow with scarlet blossoms buzzing with bees. Hoe in hand, he emerged and touched his cap.

'Morning, miss. How is the treasure-hunt going?'

'Not too well,' she admitted with a grimace, amused that the cover story had spread as far as her mother's gardener.

She regarded the dark young Welshman appraisingly. He was on the skinny side, but wiry. Supposing they found Gloria and decided to rescue her, able-bodied men would be in short supply.

But for Daisy's intervention, Owen might have been tried for murder. She had arranged this job with her mother, too. A nice boy, he was eternally grateful. She might just temporarily shanghai him.

'Later on I might want to ask for your help, Owen,' she said.

He beamed. 'There's happy I'll be, look you, miss, to do aught I can for you.'

She smiled, nodded, and went on towards the house. Bill Truscott was another who might join the troops, she reflected, and perhaps the footman, Ernest, who had for some reason taken a fancy to Phillip.

But it was no use enlisting volunteers until they knew

where the enemy was bivouacked, if that was the proper military phraseology. Fuming at the waste of time, Daisy went into the house.

The Dowager Lady Dalrymple complained not only about her daughter's absence yesterday but the early hour of her presence today. Daisy apologized profusely and left as soon as she could, aware that the briefness of her visit was another cause for offence. She was not doing frightfully well at putting her mother in a good temper to meet Alec.

Perhaps it would be best to put him off this weekend, she thought as she rode on. Only he had such trouble getting away at all, she hated to postpone the introductions any longer. She had known him jolly nearly six months already. Who was she to rag Phillip for a few weeks' hesitancy before he plucked up the courage to present the Arbuckles to his family?

His devotion to Gloria was indubitable. Daisy was dying to find out what sort of girl inspired such feelings in her previously untouched friend.

She had plenty of time to consider the various charms which might appeal to Phillip, having decided to cycle straight to the farthest village on her list before the day grew any hotter. What was more, eyeing the sky, she suspected an afternoon thunderstorm was not out of the question. This way, when she was exhausted she would not face a long ride home with lightning flashing about her head.

The clouds darkened but still no rain fell as she worked her way back towards Fairacres. She telephoned two or three times to report her lack of success. Madge told her Tommy had learned of an American stopping to ask directions a week or two ago, but from the description of man and motor, it was Arbuckle himself. Phillip and the other two had had no better luck than Daisy.

A depressingly lonely picnic lunch, on top of a rise in the hope of catching any whisper of breeze, made Daisy wish she had not proposed solo searching. However, it also reminded her of how lonely Gloria must be feeling. She pedalled on, and approached the last village just when the prospect of the tea awaiting at Fairacres became unbearably enticing.

Little Baswell was one of the villages Daisy and Binkie had failed to reach the day before. The land roundabout belonged to an estate neighbouring Fairacres, well within reach of children on ponies or bicycles.

They had ridden that way quite often, the chief attraction being a favourite nursery-maid who had married the village blacksmith. Mrs. Barnard had always provided a slap-up tea for her former charges without expecting any notice. Surely she would provide Daisy with at least a cup of tea to cheer her on her way.

Freewheeling down a slight slope, Daisy noticed that the woodland on her right had gone to rack and ruin. Fallen trunks lay enmeshed in brambles and bracken; hazel and holly struggled with saplings for light and air under the tall oaks, ashes, sycamores, birches, and wild cherry trees. She remembered Cooper's Wood as a pheasant covert, well cared for at least to the eye of a passer-by. For some reason she had always gone around it, not cut across, still less explored, though it was an extensive wood, larger than most in the area.

Then she remembered why she had avoided it. Gervaise and Phillip had once taken her to spy on the aged crone, bent and wrinkled, who lived in the middle. They said she was a witch, who ate children for supper. She boiled them in her cauldron, picked the meat from the bones, and used the bones to tell fortunes and cast spells.

In fear and trembling, Daisy had told her sister. Vi, a year older than Gervaise, asked their nurse, who assured Daisy the woman was just a gamekeeper's widow, allowed to stay on in the cottage when her husband died. The boys retorted – not in Nurse's hearing – that the witch had used a spell to make the grown-ups believe she was an ordinary person. Though Violet was sceptical, she couldn't prove they were wrong. Daisy had swallowed the tale for long enough to make avoiding the wood a habit.

The old woman was probably long since dead. Judging by the condition of the wood, her cottage might well have been abandoned. Could it possibly be where Gloria was imprisoned?

Would the kidnappers have dumped Phillip so close to their hide-out?

Coasting to a halt as the lane levelled, one foot on the ground, Daisy tried to visualize the area as seen on the map. She intended to cycle home along a cart-track through the fields and then across the Fairacres park to the house. That way wasn't much more than a couple of miles. By road, with a motor-vehicle, from here to the spot where Edgar found Phillip must be more like six or seven miles. At least five, anyway.

Still not far, but she recalled what she had said to Phillip: To people used to the anonymity of the metropolis, a mile or two from home was another world. Five miles must be about the distance from fashionable Mayfair to the dock-side slums of Limehouse, with the whole City of London, business heart of the Empire, in between.

The Yank might have a different view of the matter, but having disobeyed his order, they were not likely to tell him.

Daisy peered into the gloomy thickets of the wood. The urge to explore warred with the urge to hurry to Fairacres or Mrs. Barnard's for tea. What a triumph if she returned to announce she had found Gloria!

A russet-furred squirrel chattered at her angrily from a branch overhanging the lane. Somewhere in the depths of the greenery a woodpecker hammered, paused, and hammered again.

Just what Phillip had heard in his captivity! Of course it meant nothing; every copse and spinney had its squirrels and its woodpeckers. All the same, the sounds crystallized Daisy's intentions. She'd go and have a look at the witch's hut.

The tangle of brambles and bushes looked impenetrable just here. She pushed her bike on a bit until she found an opening, but it was little more than a rabbit path, still no good for cycling.

'Blast!' said Daisy. On a bicycle she might have pretended to be looking for a short-cut, but even Cockneys must realize no one would choose to walk for pleasure in this heat, under those threatening clouds. If they saw Daisy poking about, they'd be suspicious – always supposing they were there.

She didn't know her way through the wood, so she could not march right along like someone on an errand. What she needed was a dog. Dogs had to be exercised whatever the weather. No one could suspect a dog-walker.

The Barnards had had a dog, a lurcher called Kitchener. He must be long dead, but dog people seldom go without.

Daisy hopped onto her bicycle and set off, again at a brisk

pace. She'd pop into the village shop and the pub with her questions, then kill two birds with one stone: Get a cup of tea and borrow a dog.

The all too familiar negative answers to her queries rather dampened her zeal, but she rode on to the smithy. Amid showers of sparks and the clang of iron on iron, Ted Barnard was forging a shoe for a vast, patient carthorse. Daisy waved to him. His grin white in his blackened face, he waved back with his hammer.

She wheeled her bike around the smithy and leant it against the back wall, out of the way. The Barnards' white-washed brick cottage was right next door, its tiny front garden ablaze with sweet williams, candytuft, tall blue delphiniums, and fragrant mignonette.

Mrs. Barnard stout and grey now but as motherly as ever, was delighted to see Daisy. So was Tuffet, a tousled, dun-coloured bundle of energy with bright brown eyes behind her shaggy forelock who danced around Daisy's feet, stumpy tail wagging madly.

'Go to your basket,' Mrs. Barnard ordered. 'She's got more bounce than I can cope with, Miss Daisy, and that's a fact. You just set yourself down for a nice cuppa, dear. The kettle's on the hob.'

Over seed-cake and an amazing assortment of homemade biscuits, Daisy told Mrs. Barnard about her writing career. 'And now I'm doing some articles on London museums for an American magazine,' she finished.

'Well I never, fancy that! Such a naughty little moppet as you was, too, always running after your poor, dear brother and always a heap of pinnies to be ironed, so quick as you dirtied 'em.'

Daisy laughed. 'Unlike Vi, who was always clean and tidy, and still is.' She looked down ruefully at her dusty blouse and skirt. 'One of the advantages of writing is that no one sees you a lot of the time. Mrs. Barnard, do you remember Gervaise frightening me half to death with a tale of a witch living in Cooper's Wood?'

'That I do, dear, being as how it was me sat up with you through your nightmares for a week after.'

'Is she still alive? Does anyone live in that cottage now?'

'Nay, the old 'oman died a few years sin' – ninety-four, she were! Mr. Feversham up at the big house being too old himself to care for shooting or much else nowadays, he's let the cottage moulder and the coverts grow wild.'

'I thought I might go and have a look at the place. It would be a good setting for a story. Only I'd rather like company. Do you think Tuffet would like to go for a walk with me?'

At the magic word, the dog bounded from her basket and came to sit at Daisy's feet, peering up hopefully through her fringe.

'It's my belief,' said Mrs. Barnard, laughing, 'as she'd love to go with you. Nor you needn't be bringing her every step of the way back if it's out of your way. Tell her to go home and she'll be on the doorstep in no time flat, begging for her dinner.'

Daisy stopped at the telephone booth by the pub, but it was out of order, so she rode on back to Cooper's Wood with Tuffet racing beside the bicycle, short legs at full stretch.

Finding the narrow path, Daisy lugged the bike a few paces in from the lane and hid it under a straggly laurel she was sure she'd recognize. The dog at her heels, she continued along the path until it forked.

Both branches led onward into the depths of the wood. Daisy hesitated but, nose to the ground, Tuffet forged ahead down the right-hand path, so she followed.

A jay screeched a general warning. The muted sounds of birdsong ceased abruptly. In the eerie quiet under the thick canopy of leaves a twig snapped like a pistol-shot beneath Daisy's sandal. She stopped, heart in mouth. Nothing came to her ears but the scuff of Tuffet's feet in the damp, crumbling leaf-mould.

The path gradually swung back on itself towards the lane. Loath to retrace her steps in the heavy stillness, Daisy kept an eye out for a side turning. Before she found one, a dense mass of holly barred the way.

Or rather, it barred Daisy's way. The dog scurried on, hot on the trail of a rabbit, squirrel, fox, or pheasant.

'Tuffet!' Daisy called reluctantly, in a low voice, to no effect. She tried to whistle, but her mouth was too dry.

So much for her camouflage. Presuming Tuffet would find her own way home, Daisy turned back. She soon came to another path leading the way she wanted to go – or did she? It led around the giant bole of a once-pollarded oak, wreathed with ivy, which had concealed it from the opposite direction.

She took it, telling herself firmly she had no reason for nerves as the chances that she had chosen to explore the right wood were practically nil. All the same, she walked carefully, avoiding stepping on dry twigs, like in the Red Indian games Gervaise and Phillip had occasionally let her join.

The path twisted and turned, but as far as she could tell continued inward. She had to duck under low branches, climb over a fallen tree-trunk, unhitch her skirt from grasping brambles, and stop now and then to wipe the sweat from her brow.

She must be mad!

Birds were twittering again, having, decided the intruder was harmless. Then came another jay's screech. A moment later, Daisy heard the patter of feet on the path behind her and Tuffet rejoined her with an ecstatic yip.

Heartened, Daisy pushed on. Around a last bend and they emerged into what must once have been a pleasant ride.

The abandoned bridleway had sprouted a forest of birch saplings, and blackthorn thickets, and masses of purple-pink rosebay willow-herb. Still, the going looked somewhat easier, and it seemed likely that the cottage would have been sited somewhere near the ride for accessibility. Tossing a mental coin, Daisy turned left.

She followed the path of least resistance. Within a few yards, her suspicions were aroused. The way was too wide and, though twisting around obstacles, too straight for fox or badger, or even deer. Though the ground was too dry and hard for footprints, here and there a plant appeared to have been crushed beneath a heavy boot. She spotted the odd broken branch, withered leaves brown against the green backdrop. In a blackthorn, among the swelling sloes, hung a scrap of blue cloth.

Daisy found she was holding her breath. She let it out silently and proceeded with stealthy tread.

Quickly tiring of this slow means of locomotion, Tuffet bounced ahead. To make use of the camouflage, Daisy ought to behave like a legitimate dog-walker, she realized, not skulk along like a poacher after pheasants. Besides, skulking was hard on tired legs. She tramped on at a more normal pace.

In any case, the way through the brush had probably been forced by someone genuinely walking a dog, she assured herself as Tuffet disappeared around a clump of gorse. Inhaling the coconutty fragrance of the yellow blooms, Daisy followed. Before her stood the witch's hut.

Beneath the branches of a towering sycamore, the cottage crouched like a cornered animal. Weeds sprouted from the sagging thatch roof. Whitewashed plaster had yellowed, peeled, and in places flaked away to show the wattle-and-daub walls beneath. The glass in the two small windows was broken. The door between was cracked and warped, its iron latch rusted.

Nothing could have looked more desolate, derelict, deserted. Daisy heaved a sigh, half disappointment, half relief. So much for her triumphant return with news of Gloria's whereabouts.

The dog had paused to snuffle at something in the small garden, where pink flowered convolvulus smothered overgrown currant and gooseberry bushes. Now she sat down for a brief scratch, before trotting off around the end of the cottage.

'Tuffet!' Daisy called in vain.

They had come quite a distance from the village, and Daisy was afraid the dog might not find her way home. She followed. No sign of Tuffet. Around the next corner, a thatched lean-to slumped against the cottage's back wall. Perhaps Tuffet had found a way into it.

As she went to investigate, Daisy glanced up. Above, in the gable of the end wall, she saw the window of an upstairs room. At least, she assumed it was a window. It was boarded up.

The boards should have been grey, weathered, splitting. Instead, they were the colour of newly sawed wood. Bright nail heads gleamed.

Daisy's heart began to thump. She backed away, turned, and hurried round the corner to the front, calling breathlessly for her camouflage. 'Tuffet, come! Come here, you naughty dog. Time to go home.'

The door swung open, smoothly, noiselessly, on well-oiled hinges. A large man in braces and a collarless shirt stood on the threshold, his baleful glare adorned with the fading remnant of a black eye.

'Just walking the dog!' Daisy squeaked. 'Have you seen her?'

He blinked. 'Nah.'

'Get on wiv it,' snapped an impatient voice behind him.

The big man stepped out, uncertainly. 'I dunno, she . . .'

'Too late, mate. She's seen yer now. We gotta stop 'er.' By then Daisy was half-way to the gorse bush marking the path. Feet pounded after her.

Tuffet appeared from nowhere, frisking about her ankles, barking joyfully. Daisy tripped, staggered a few steps trying to regain her balance, and fell headlong into a bed of nettles.

Hands like iron bands gripped her arms.

'Gotcha!'

CHAPTER 12

'Miss Arbuckle, I presume?' said Daisy gloomily as the bar thudded into place on the outside of the door behind her.

The grimy girl huddled on the lumpy mattress on the floor stared up at her wide-eyed. The room was too dark to make out the colour of her eyes, but her limp, unkempt hair was fair. No doubt gold and curly when shampooed, Daisy thought charitably.

Feeling rather limp herself, she stepped forward, saying, 'Do you mind if I join you?'

'Gee, sure, please do.' Miss Arbuckle moved over. 'Excuse me, I wasn't expecting...' And she burst into tears.

The straw-filled palliasse crackled as Daisy flopped down beside her and put an arm around her shaking shoulders. With the other hand she absently rubbed a particularly painful patch of nettle-rash on her leg.

When the sobs showed signs of giving way to sniffs, she offered her handkerchief.

'Here, take this. My name's Daisy Dalrymple.'

'I *am* Gloria Arbuckle. How did you know? Oh, I guess those guys downstairs told you.'

'Actually,' Daisy said in a low voice, 'I was looking for

you, and there can't be many girls locked up in tumbledown cottages in woods in this area. At least, I hope not!'

'Looking for me?' Gloria said in wonder, following Daisy's example in speaking softly. 'You? Wait a minute, though! Dalrymple? You must be Phillip's deceased friend's sister. Have they . . . have they found his body?'

As she started to dissolve in tears again, Daisy deduced that she was talking about Phillip's body, not Gervaise's. The last Gloria had seen of Phil, he was being dragged off to be murdered, Daisy recalled.

'He was so b-brave, trying to escape, and the one he hit was raising Cain, shouting about k-killing him.'

'He's alive,' Daisy said hastily. 'He's perfectly all right.'

The tears came anyway, but they were tears of relief. 'And Poppa?' Gloria sniffled a few minutes later. 'Phillip said they wouldn't harm him.'

'I met Mr. Arbuckle last night. He's right as rain except for worrying about you, and being a bit tired from running round collecting ransom money. He'll have it by tomorrow.'

'So they'll let me go soon, and you, too.' Gloria heaved a shuddering sigh. 'It's been horrible, but the worst was thinking Phillip was dead. Miss Dalrymple, I'm real sorry you've gotten mixed up in this.'

'Daisy, please. Formality seems too, too idiotic in the circs. Phillip involved me in the first place, but it was my own fault I was caught. I'm never going to hear the last of it.'

'Well, I can't help being glad you're here. You start imagining all sorts of dreadful things when you're alone.'

'They haven't mistreated you?' Daisy asked. 'I mean, apart from all this.' She waved her hand at the squalid room, noting a covered chamberpot in one corner; noting also that it was already darker than when she arrived. The sun wouldn't set for hours yet, so the clouds must be growing thicker. 'They haven't beaten you, or starved you, or anything like that?'

'No. They've even apologised for the food all being cold.' Gloria managed a shaky laugh. 'They don't dare light a fire because they're afraid the smoke would attract attention. What brought you here? Why did Phillip involve you?'

Already editing the story in her head to eliminate the upsetting parts, Daisy said, 'I'll explain later. Right now, while there's still some light, I'm going to see what I can do about getting us out of here. I refuse to wait for them to let us go. A friend of mine's coming down from town tomorrow.'

Stiffly, she hauled herself to her feet. The door she ignored, and a brief inspection eliminated the window, as a means of egress. Even with a hammer, no fear of making a noise, and all the time in the world, she doubted she could have knocked out the sturdy boards.

That left the possible hole in the ceiling Phillip had mentioned. Unable to make use of it because of his tied hands, he had not examined it closely.

She crossed to the corner where the stain ran down the wall – the worst stain, rather; none of the walls was exactly pristine.

Actually, at that point the wall and the ceiling were interchangeable. The rear wall of the cottage ran up vertically for three or four feet. Then the incline of the roof forced an inward slope to a horizontal portion of ceiling running down the centre, which met the opposite roof slope at the front.

On tiptoe, Daisy could touch the flat part. She did not need to. The crumbled plaster on the floor came from an indentation just level with the top of her head.

She reached up to feel the hollow, and jumped back hurriedly in a cloud of dingy white powder as a large chunk came loose. Landing with a thump on the floor, it broke into little pieces. Daisy held her breath, swinging round towards Gloria with her fingers to her lips.

No outcry below, no footsteps rushing up: the men must be in the other downstairs room.

'Gee!' said Gloria.

Breathing again, shallowly because of the dust lingering in the air, Daisy looked up to see a small patch of green. Leaves! Beautiful green sycamore leaves and a bunch of winged seeds . . .

'Oh blast!' said Daisy.

'What's the problem?'

'Is anyone likely to come up in the next few hours?'

'I guess they'll bring something to eat. Quite soon, because its going to get dark and they won't let me – us – have a lamp. Why?'

'They'll see the hole.'

'Can't we stuff your handkerchief into it?'

'We'll try,' Daisy said dubiously, studying the ragged edges of the opening, 'though I'm afraid it may be rather too large.'

'We could use my stockings, too. I gave up wearing them days ago.'

'All right, that might work. I'd have preferred to make the hole still larger while we have some light, but that would never do. We'll just have to wait until dark.'

They succeeded in fashioning a serviceable plug. It caught on the splintered spikes of broken, half-rotted laths and looked as if it would stay up for long enough.

'What good will a hole in the roof do us?' Gloria asked hesitantly.

'We'll work that out once we have one big enough to climb through,' Daisy told her with an assumed confidence she was far from feeling.

She could not sit here tamely, hoping for release, wondering whether the Yank would murder one or both of them. She had to try to escape. Resolutely she turned her mind from the possibility of a fall from the roof leading to a broken leg or a broken neck.

As the Austin Chummy reached the end of the elm avenue and Alec saw the house before him, he let out a long, low whistle. Knowing Daisy's father was a viscount had failed to prepare him for anything quite as impressive as Fairacres.

The entrance portico boasted four Ionic columns, and behind it rose a cupola, white against the slate grey overcast. On either side stretched four tiers of windows: a semi-basement rustic below, attics above, and between them two rows with pilasters. The balustrade running along the top of the façade was interrupted at regular intervals by classical statues, with a smaller cupola at each end.

Both in the course of his duties and as a student of history, taking tours on open days, Alec had visited grander mansions. Wentwater Court, where he first met Daisy, was considerably larger and more impressive, for instance. It was the fact of Daisy's having grown up here that he found a bit intimidating.

More than a bit, he acknowledged ruefully, drawing up before the portico. He must be mad to imagine she might consider marrying a middle-class, widowed copper with a child, a resident mother, and a semi-detached in St. John's Wood.

Yet she had invited him to meet *her* mother.

Wearily stepping down from the car, he glanced up at the relief on the pediment above the pillars. Just distinguishable in the fast-fading evening light, a cornucopia poured forth fruits.

Somewhat heartened by the implied welcome, Alec trod up the steps and faced the choice of a knocker in the form of a pineapple, an old-fashioned bell-pull, or an electric button. He opted for modern convenience.

The youthful lackey who opened the door wore a maroon jacket with brass buttons. A footman, Alec diagnosed.

'May I see Miss Dalrymple?' he requested, and then Daisy Dalrymple,' he amplified. 'The name's Fletcher.'

The youth regarded him with undisguised interest. 'If you care to step in, sir, I'll see if Miss Dalrymple's in,' he said in the sort of voice which indicated he had to check for form's sake though he knew the answer perfectly well. 'Was miss expecting you?'

'Not exactly. That is, tomorrow, not today.'

'Ah,' remarked the footman profoundly. He glanced back as if to see if his superior, the butler, was creeping up on him across the polished marble floor. Reassured, he became confidential. 'You'll likely know what it's all about, then, sir, this funny business?'

'Part of it,' Alec said with caution, taking off his hat.

'That's all I knows meself,' the lad admitted, discouraged. 'Though I *did* think when I obliged Mr. Petrie right at the start that he'd let me in on it Lor, what a sight for sore eyes he were!'

'Oh?'

The monosyllable failed to draw a description. 'Then along come the American gentleman, as hadn't ate his breakfast yet, the which I asked him special. "Ernest," says Mr. Petrie, "you ask him has he ate." So I does, and I tips him the wink on the sly. Have you dined, sir?' he enquired solicitously.

Utterly bewildered, Alec was for a moment under the impression that the question had been addressed at some past time to an unknown American gentleman. Realizing it was meant for him, he confessed that no, he hadn't. 'But I shouldn't dream of presuming on Lady Dalrymple's hospitality,' he added.

'*That's* all right, sit Her ladyship's dining out, and a good job, too. Miss Dalrymple's guests kept putting dinner back, waiting for her to turn up, but . . .'

'Waiting for her ladyship?' Alec asked with a sinking feeling.

Ernest confirmed his suspicion. 'For Miss Dalrymple. Her ladyship's dining out,' he repeated patiently, 'and so's his lordship, of course.'

'And Miss Dalrymple was late for dinner?'

'Hasn't come back yet.'

'Great Scott!' Alec exclaimed, biting back several more forceful imprecations. What the deuce was Daisy up to now, that even her fellow-conspirators were unaware of? What were they all up to? 'I must speak to Petrie,' he said determinedly.

'If you'll please to come this way, sir.'

The footman ushered Alec into a formal dining room. On the white tablecloth six places were set, glasses sparkling, silver gleaming. Five soup-spoons halted between plate and mouth; five faces turned towards the door, premature relief giving way to disappointment, then worry.

And, in Petrie's case, to dismay. He started to rise.

'Mr. Fletcher here'd like a word, Mr. Petrie, sir,' Ernest belatedly announced.

Petrie pushed back his chair, but Lucy Fotheringay intervened. 'I think Mr. Fletcher had better have a word with all of us,' she said with a crispness quite unlike her usual world-weary manner.

'We're all in this together,' agreed a young man unknown to Alec, standing up. 'I'm Pearson, Tom Pearson, and this is my wife.'

The pretty, pixyish blond beside him gave Alec a strained smile. 'You're Daisy's friend, aren't you, Mr. Fletcher? We're awfully worried about her. We expected her back by tea-time.'

'Do sit down, Mr. Fletcher,' Miss Fotheringay invited, her drawl back in place. 'Have you dined? You'd better take Daisy's place.'

Alec did not protest his unwillingness to intrude, nor his lack of evening dress. The footman set a plate of soup before him and reluctantly left the room.

The moment the door closed behind the servant, Petrie said with forced optimism, 'Daisy may have stopped at her mother's for the evening.'

'There's a telephone at the Dower House,' Miss Fotheringay pointed out, scarcely concealing her scorn. 'You said yourself we mustn't ring to see if she's there in case she isn't.'

'If she was, she'd have phoned you,' Alec said. In a voice in which he tried to blend camaraderie with a certain official, no-nonsense tone, he went on, 'All right, you'd better tell me what's going on. Why the urgent messages calling you down here? Where did Daisy go, what for, and why alone?'

He addressed the questions at large. The others deferred to Petrie.

'We're looking for some . . . something.' He sleeked back his already sleek fair hair with a nervous hand. 'It was Daisy's idea for some of us to go out alone, to cover more ground. She was the one who worked out where each of us would go, so none of us is too sure exactly where she was heading after her last telephone call.' He glanced around the table and received confirming nods.

'I stayed here,' Mrs. Pearson explained, 'and the rest reported in now and then.'

'You were expecting trouble, then?' Alec tried not to explode with anger, remembering his own inability to stem the tide of Daisy's determination.

'Lord no!' said Pearson, 'or we'd never have let her go off on her own. We 'phoned in for news, don't y'know. We were just making enquiries.'

'In village shops,' Petrie elucidated.

'Making enquiries in village shops? What the dickens are you looking for?' Alec recalled Petrie's hastily covered pause. 'Or should I say whom?'

Petrie's alarm told him he had struck gold. The young man pressed his lips together, aware too late that he was the last person capable of misleading an experienced detective.

'Miss Fotheringay?'

'We're sworn to silence,' she said with uncharacteristic uncertainty. 'But Phillip, with Daisy missing . . .' Her voice trailed away.

Alec turned a searching gaze on each in turn. Even Petrie's face expressed indecision.

'We can't!' he said, agonized.

'Mr. and Mrs. Pearson, I take it you know I'm a policeman?' They both nodded soberly. 'So do the rest of you,' Alec continued with a sternness he had no need to feign. 'Quite apart from my ... feelings for Daisy, I'm obliged to tell you that I can't simply overlook your determined efforts to keep from the authorities what is clearly a serious matter.'

'I quite appreciate your position,' said Pearson. 'As a matter of fact, I'm a solicitor. I assure you, before I let myself or Madge become involved I ascertained that no crime has been committed by any of us. Nor is our intention to shield any other person who has committed a crime.'

'Thank you, Mr. Pearson, that clarifies matters.'

Taking a spoonful of cooling soup, Alec thought rapidly. He had often noticed that lawyers, though in general the cagiest of men, once they let themselves go frequently gave away far more than they intended.

That a crime had been committed seemed certain. The obvious deduction was that Phillip Petrie had called in Daisy to solve it, knowing her propensity for interfering in police matters. To be fair, Alec was forced to acknowledge that she had two or three times been almost as much a help as a hindrance.

But in this case, Petrie was the instigator of the interference. Why would that generally law-abiding young man choose to try to solve a crime himself, rather than reporting it to the police?

To protect a friend or relative was the most likely answer. Yet Pearson was convinced their purpose was not to shield a criminal, so probably the friend or relative was the victim – and blackmail the crime. If the blackmailer was using a village shop as a convenience address . . .

No, they would know which shop, which they clearly did not since they had been scouring the countryside asking questions.

Only two other possible crimes sprang to mind where, for the victim's sake, the police might not be called in. One was a confidence trick, where the sucker – as the Americans so charmingly put it – was too embarrassed by his gullibility. Alec doubted that would have caused the deadly serious expressions in the five pairs of eyes fixed on his face, as he now observed.

He put down his spoon, having finished the soup without the slightest idea of what kind it had been.

'Am I correct,' he said slowly, 'in supposing your secret is a kidnapping?'

Four faces registered more relief than dismay. Petrie's was horrified, but Alec detected a hint of relief there, too. They both opened their mouths to speak. Alec, with a gesture, deferred to the younger man.

At this inauspicious moment, a butler appeared, his stiff back and impassive face somehow radiating disapproval, and announced, 'Mr. Arbuckle has called.'

Miss Fotheringay glanced around at the others, then, to Alec's surprise, she said in a resigned tone, 'Show him in, please, Lowecroft, and you'd better serve the next course. Set another place for Mr. Arbuckle if he hasn't already dined.'

'As you wish, miss.' Lowecroft departed, stiffer than ever.

'It won't do Daisy any good if we starve,' Miss Fotheringay pointed out, 'and Mr. Arbuckle is going to have to decide what to do about our quick-witted sleuth and his brilliant deductions.

No brilliant deduction was necessary to guess that the unknown Arbuckle was somehow involved. 'Who is ... ?' Alec started to ask. He fell silent as the butler returned with a short, slight, long-faced man in evening dress.

Long-faced in both senses of the phrase, Alec noted. Between the lantern-jaw and the receding hairline was as careworn a countenance as he had ever seen.

While the butler set a seventh place at the table, Petrie introduced Alec – as *Mr.* Fletcher – to Arbuckle. Another surprise: the man was an American. He didn't look at all pleased to meet Alec, even though he was unaware of the police connection.

The footman, Ernest, and a parlour-maid brought in several dishes. During the serving of loin of veal with broad beans and sauteed potatoes, the conversation stuck strictly to the weather. Arbuckle reported lightning over the Malvern Hills. No one mentioned the possibility that Daisy might get caught out in a storm. On the contrary, the prospect of the end of drought and heat was welcome with much false-ringing enthusiasm.

'All very well,' Bincombe said gloomily when the servants had withdrawn, 'but if it really sets in to rain it's not going to make things any easier.'

'Never mind that,' Arbuckle said flatly, with a dismissive gesture. 'There's two things I wanna know: Where's Miss Dalrymple and what the heck is this gennelman doing here?' He glared at Alec, then transferred his glare to Petrie

'Daisy's missing,' said Mrs. Pearson, a catch in her voice. Her husband pressed her hand.

'Missing?' Arbuckle groaned, sinking his head in his hands. 'I knew I shouldn'ta let that little girl ...' Recalling Alec's presence, he raised his head and frowned.

'Mr. Fletcher is a friend of Daisy's' Miss Fotheringay told him. 'He came to see her, and we could hardly conceal her absence.'

'But he don't know ...?'

'He's guessed a good deal,' Pearson said bluntly. He gave Alec an apologetic glance. 'Deduced, I should say. Mr. Fletcher happens to be a Scotland Yard detective, don't y'know.'

Arbuckle looked appalled. 'How much has he figured out?' he demanded.

'That someone has been kidnapped,' Alec said. 'I must assume, someone close to you.' Which meant the man was wealthy enough to make extortion worthwhile. What the connection with Petrie was, Alec could only conjecture.

'No dice, you won't get another thing out of me,' Arbuckle said fiercely. 'Nor my young friends, I hope.'

'Not a word,' vowed Petrie.

'Daisy's missing,' Miss Fotheringay reminded them with equal fierceness.

'Oh lord!' Petrie groaned.

The American shook his head despairingly. 'I know, I know, and I feel real badly about it, you can bet your sweet life. I've taken to that young lady in a big way.'

His patent wretchedness somewhat assuaged Alec's rebuilding fury. 'I'm going to go on guessing,' he said. 'Deducing, if you will. For a start, I believe the victim is your daughter, sir.' A pretty girl was the only possible explanation for Petrie's predicament, the only possible rival for his loyalty to his dead chum's sister. Arbuckle's dropped jaw confirmed it. 'Further, you have been warned not to contact the police if you want her safely returned.'

That was too obvious to surprise Arbuckle, though Petrie was impressed.

'By Jove, Fletcher,' he said, 'I don't know how you fellows do it. Didn't I tell you, sir,' he went on, turning to the American, 'that Scotland Yard knows what's what?'

'You did, son, and I don't doubt it, though I'm doggone sure they don't have much experience at dealing with kidnappers. But anyways, what can they do except join the search? There's no way to keep a posse secret, and the moment word gets out, it's all up with Gloria.'

'Sir,' said Alec, 'I do appreciate your position, believe me. But are you so sure there's nothing else I could do if I knew all the facts? I'm trained and experienced in deciphering the way criminals think and in drawing conclusions from inadequate data.'

'Sure, but . . .'

'In any case, I must insist on being given any information which might conceivably help in finding Daisy – Miss Dalrymple. I take it you all suspect she's in the hands of the kidnappers?' He looked around the table, garnering general agreement. With an effort, he managed to keep his tone calm and reasonable. 'If they are as ruthless as you believe, she's in danger too. You can't imagine I'd do anything to add to the risk?'

Miss Fotheringay cast a half apologetic, half defiant glance at Arbuckle. 'I'll tell you anything you need to know, Mr. Fletcher. Anything *I* know, at least. Daisy's safety comes first, and we haven't the foggiest what to do.'

Her taciturn boyfriend nodded.

'Oh yes,' cried Mrs. Pearson.

'Sorry, old man,' her husband said gruffly to Petrie, 'but she's right, you know. We'll try to give away as little as possible.'

Alec shook his head. 'I can't tell what will be useful until I've heard everything. Nor can I know what will need to be done.' He turned to the American. 'I'm prepared to say I shan't approach the local force unless I consider it absolutely vital, but that's as far as I'm able – and further than I ought – to go.'

Sagging in his chair, Arbuckle yielded, his face becoming an old man's as the tension left it. 'Okay, okay, I guess I know when I'm beat. Tarnation take it, I owe Miss Dalrymple something for the gutsy way she's gone to bat for my girl. If you'll just not spread the word about being a gumshoe, I'll tell you everything. Where shall I start?'

'First things first. Let's see if we can work out where Daisy went today.'

CHAPTER 13

Like the man who had brought their bread and marge, tinned corned beef, and mushy, greyish tinned peas, the kidnapper who fetched their plates wore a scarf across nose, mouth, and chin. In the increasing gloom, his features would have been practically invisible anyway. Daisy wondered whether she would be able to identify the one she had seen in full daylight at the front door.

She rather doubted it. Not only had she seen him very briefly, what attention she could spare from her plight had been concentrated on his black eye and Phillip's probable role in its creation.

He left. The bar thudded into place.

'Will he come back?' she asked Gloria, whose face was no more than a pale smudge beside her.

'I guess not. They never have after . . . dinner.'

'Dinner!' Daisy sighed. Not particularly hungry after Mrs. Barnard's tea, she had eaten the bully beef but had not managed to swallow more than a mouthful of the rest. She suspected she might regret it later. 'Well, it will soon be night outside as well as in here. I'd better get on with it. Help me move the mattress under the hole to deaden the sound if any big bits fall.'

As, blundering in the dark, they hauled the pallet into the other corner, Daisy heard a faint rumble. She could not imagine what their captors were doing. About to ask Gloria whether she had heard a similar noise before, she was forestalled by a second rumbling growl, which she recognized as distant thunder. The weather had broken at last.

She was glad she had not mentioned the sound to her companion. Gloria did not seem to have noticed the far-off drum-roll; if she happened to be afraid of thunderstorms, the longer she remained unaware the better.

'Tell me about the kidnapping,' Daisy invited, feeling for their makeshift plug and giving it a tug. It came loose in a shower of plaster, pieces of lath, and musty, mouldy straw. Coughing, she was pleased to see that the hole, an irregular patch of dark grey in the blackness, had nearly doubled in size.

'I thought Phillip told you. Can I help?'

'There isn't enough room. I'm having to stand with my neck crooked as it is. Phil did tell me, of course, but you might have noticed something he didn't. By the way, I don't suppose you've learned anything more about the kingpin, the man they call the Yank?'

'No,' Gloria said, sounding puzzled. 'They didn't talk in the room below this again. Maybe they realized Phillip overheard them. Does it make any difference who he is?'

'You never know, it could. Phthoo!' Daisy spat out crumbs of plaster, suddenly wondering how many insects made their homes in the thatch, and what sorts. Not that she really cared whether it was spiders or earwigs which landed in her hair, as long as they stayed out of her mouth. 'I can't talk while I'm doing this,' she mumbled through half-closed lips.

Gloria obligingly began to recount the kidnapping and everything that had happened since, which was little enough. Listening, to her disappointment learning nothing significant, Daisy continued to demolish the roof. It was hard work chiefly because she had to reach up to do it. The plaster and straw came down easily, and the lath was not much solider, though she had to pull and twist to break some pieces.

In one way that was most satisfactory. On the other hand, she had no greater desire to fall *through* the roof than *off* it.

A gust of wind blew a flurry of bits of straw in her face. Feeling a sneeze coming, she snorted.

'Shall I take a whack at it?' Gloria asked.

'Would you? It shouldn't take much longer.' Fumbling around each other, they changed places. Daisy heard a closer growl of thunder and began to talk about Phillip and Gervaise's boyhood.

After a few minutes, Gloria interrupted her in a small voice. 'It's beginning to rain, and I think I can hear thunder.'

'So do I,' Daisy admitted. 'Are you afraid of it?'

'N-no. Not exactly, but I don't like it. At least, it's the lightning. We have terrible electric storms at home.'

'They're not so bad here,' Daisy assured her, as though she had a basis for comparison. 'In fact I rather enjoy all the banging and crashing and flashing. Shall I take over again?'

'No, I'm okay. Oh, there's something big and hard here.'

'A proper rafter, or beam, or whatever?'

'I think so.'

'Good, it'll give us purchase. The hole must be about big enough, isn't it?'

'It's hard to tell in the dark. Let me feel.'

A momentary flood of light silhouetted Gloria's head against the hole. She gasped.

'One, two, three, four, five,' Daisy counted, 'six, seven . . .'

Crash, bump, bump, mutter, mutter, mutter.

'G-golly gee!'

'It's still a long way away. Seven miles.' Or was it a count of five to the mile? She couldn't remember and hoped Gloria couldn't either. 'Any noise we make they'll think is thunder,' she said encouragingly, 'and the lightning will help us get our bearings. Let's go.'

'Y-you first.'

'All right We'll roll up the mattress to stand on, and then you'll have to give me a boost, I expect. I'm no gymnast.'

Wobbling on top of the mattress, Daisy stuck her head out into the open. Her shoulders brushed the thatch. Refreshing rain hit her face in dots and dashes, and odd gusts of wind frivolled through her shingled hair. She felt for the beam Gloria had reported.

Luckily, it was on the downward side of the slope. With a bit of a struggle, Daisy managed to raise her arms through the hole and dislodge some of the straw resting on the beam. Then she was able to get her elbows on top of it.

'Give me a shove,' she requested.

A jerk and a heave and a moment later she was on the roof, careful to keep her weight over the beam. The still-dry thatch prickled through her thin linen skirt, but at least it wasn't slippery. She was afraid it soon would be once the rain really got going.

'Come on!'

Hauling Gloria out was more difficult. At last she sat

beside Daisy on the beam. Daisy heard her take a deep breath of fresh air and let it out on a sigh.

'What next?' she asked.

A sheet of lightning let Daisy look up, hopefully, into the sycamore tree above. The nearest branches were within reach, but too thin to support anything larger than a squirrel. A pity – climbing down the tree would be the easiest way to the ground.

The next flash, which followed almost at once, showed Gloria with her hands over her ears and her eyes screwed shut. It also showed Daisy what she had forgotten: the lean-to behind the cottage. Its roof was directly below them, not more than a couple of feet lower than the edge of the eaves, and at its lowest point only four or five feet above the ground.

The heavens crackled and roared. The moment the din ended, in a hush as if the world held its breath waiting for the next onslaught, Daisy reached out unseeing to pull Gloria's invisible hands away from her invisible ears.

'Listen!' she hissed. 'All we have to do is slide straight down. There's a two-foot drop, then another slide, and then a drop of about four feet. Can you manage it?'

'I th-think so.'

'Good. We'll both go at once; we'll be less likely to land on top of each other. Keep still when you reach the ground and I'll find you.'

'Okay.'

'Ready . . . steady . . . go!'

Thatch rasping her skin, Daisy found it quite frightening to let herself slither into the blackness – and she had seen what lay below, however briefly. Gloria could only trust her blindly. Already afraid of the storm, was she spunky enough to obey?

Daisy's feet met thin air. A moment later she *thunked* on her bottom on the lower slope. She had just time enough to wonder if she'd have done better facedown when her feet flew out again. She landed, arms swinging for balance, on something that crunched, a cinder path perhaps.

Gloria landed beside her with another crunch, loud in the unnatural stillness. It didn't sound at all like thunder. It sounded, in fact, like feet on a cinder path.

'Wossat?' The voice came clearly from the cottage. No betraying gleam of light showed, but the men were there and awake.

'Better 'ave a dekko. Coulda bin . . .' The rest was drowned out by a stupendous thunderclap. The lightning was almost simultaneous.

Daisy grabbed Gloria's hand and tugged her away from the building.

Speed was impossible, so there was no advantage to aiming for the comparatively clear ride in front of the cottage, even if they were not starting from the back. They would do better losing themselves quickly in the tangled thickets of the wood, Daisy had decided. Hand-in-hand, lightning-dazzled eyes sightless, they stumbled forward, hands groping ahead for obstacles.

Behind them electric torches sprang to life.

They were spotted immediately, but the long beams spilled past them, illuminating a green wall of leaves. Daisy saw a rabbit path opening to their right.

'Quick!' she cried, and broke into a run.

Footsteps and curses followed. Within a few paces, the twisting path hid the men, but they had the torches to light their way. Once out of range, Daisy and Gloria were blind again.

The skies came to the rescue. Flare after flare banished the dark, amidst continuous blasts and booms and long, rattling rolls. Unable to hear or see their followers, sure they must be gaining, Daisy dived into the nonexistent gap between two bushes, dragging Gloria with her.

They emerged in a space free of undergrowth beneath a larch. Rather, they were more or less in the middle of the larch, for the branches started less than a yard from the ground, continuing up the trunk in what looked to Daisy practically like a ladder.

As the next flash arrived, in a momentary hush, she grabbed Gloria's arm, pointed upwards, and said in her ear, 'Climb!'

In pitch darkness she started up, feeling her way, testing each branch before she put her weight on it, childhood skills taking over just like riding a bike. Thunder rumbled sullenly, but the next flash of lightning was pallid, the storm already moving on.

Glancing down. Daisy realized Gloria had not followed.

The thunder ceased. She heard a crashing in the bushes and swearing voices, then a shout of triumph.

'Got 'er!'

'What abaht the uvver one? Keep looking!'

'Blimey, we'll never find 'er in this, mate.'

The rain was pouring down in earnest now, breaching the leafy canopy in trickles, streams, and torrents. The larch's needles were no protection. Uncomfortably seated on a narrow branch, clinging to the trunk, Daisy was soaked through in no time. She shivered.

They had Gloria again. All Daisy's efforts were for nothing – unless she could get back to Fairacres in time to send the men to the rescue before the kidnappers moved their victim elsewhere.

Yet she dared not descend until she was certain they had given up searching. Fortunately, the thunder was distant now. Through the hiss and plop of falling rain, she listened to the sounds of the hunt dying away.

'Bloody 'orrible!'

Daisy would have jumped a mile if she hadn't been hemmed in by branches.

'Gawd, I can't wait to get back to the Smoke!'

The voices sounded as if they were just below the tree, but through leaves and branches she saw the glimmer of torches and realized the men were on the path. She watched the lights bob away towards the cottage, having kindly helped her find her bearings.

She waited what seemed like an age, then clambered down, though she could not be sure the others were not lying in wait. Pushing through the bushes, she turned away from the cottage and plodded gingerly into the inky night.

Alec scowled at the map spread out on the desk in the viscount's den. 'Here and here and here, Mrs. Pearson?' He pointed to the three villages Daisy had telephoned from.

'Yes.' The pretty young woman consulted her list. 'And she said she had covered these others in between. She didn't ring from each place.'

'So she could have gone on to any of these three, or beyond if she made good time. Has anyone any reason to favour a particular direction?' He glanced around the circle of intent faces.

'She was heading generally back towards Fairacres,' Pearson pointed out hesitantly. 'I shouldn't imagine she'd turn away again.'

'A good point,' Alec approved. 'These two are most likely, then, Astonford and Little Baswell.'

'Astonford's a tiny hamlet,' Petrie put in. 'Doesn't even have a pub, let alone a shop.'

'The shop in Little Baswell will have closed long since,' said Miss Fotheringay, 'but the pub will be open for another half hour.'

'Heck, what does it matter?' Arbuckle asked. 'We might figure out which village she went to but she could be any-wheres now. We can't comb the countryside.'

'And if we could,' Bincombe gloomed, punctuated by a rumble of thunder, 'if we had a hundred men, we might pass within a yard or two of her without seeing or hearing her in this weather.'

Unfortunately he was right. Alec bowed his head in defeat, then squared his shoulders and said reluctantly, 'Yes, we'll have to wait till daylight. Maybe by then I'll have come up with a brilliant plan to find her.'

'Maybe she'll be back,' Mrs. Pearson consoled him wearily. 'You're not waiting up to see, my pet,' her husband informed her. 'Beddy-byes time.'

'You'll all want to be rested for tomorrow,' Alec said. 'You'd better all go to bed, except you, Petrie, if you please. I want to hear everything you can tell me about the kidnapping.

And from you, too, Mr. Arbuckle, if you don't mind staying a while, sir.'

'No sirree. But Lord and Lady Dalrymple may be a mite surprised to find us here when they got home.'

'Great Scott, I'd forgotten all about them! We could go down to the Wedge and Beetle, but I haven't booked for tonight and I don't know wether they can accommodate me.'

'You'd better stay the night here, Mr. Fletcher. I expect we can square it with Daisy's cousins.' Miss Fotheringay eyed him sardonically. 'We'll just tell them she forgot she had invited you. *They* don't know that's inconceivable.'

Acknowledging her mockery with a half-smile, Alec agreed, 'It would be much more convenient to stay. I shan't go to bed anyway, in case Daisy turns up.'

'You need your beauty sleep too,' she told him. 'We'll take it in turns sitting up, won't we?' she appealed to the others.

'Not Madge,' Pearson said firmly, 'but I'll take my turn. I'll make out a schedule.' He sat down at the desk and searched the drawers for paper and pencil.

Alec did not argue. His eyelids felt heavy and gritty after the drive from London following a long day at the Yard, clearing up paperwork so that he could take an extra day off.

'Someone wake me when it's my turn,' Miss Fotheringay drawled, 'or if the missing sheep returns to the fold. I'm for bed. Come on, Madge, darling. If we're gone when the cousins get back they'll assume Daisy's gone up, too, which will spare all sorts of complications – for tonight at least.'

'Good thinking, Miss Fotheringay.'

'I can when I try. I'll tell Lowecroft to have a bed made up for you. Good-night all.'

The ladies departed just in time. Pearson had barely finished writing out his schedule when from the front hall came the sound of voices and a door shutting.

Petrie turned to Alec. 'I'd better introduce you right away, Fletcher.'

'I'll lie low,' Arbuckle said promptly.

Alec followed Petrie out. As they emerged from the passage into the hall, the gentleman handing his dripping umbrella to the footman said irately, 'Dash it, Geraldine, I know a copper when I see one!'

Taken aback, Alec hesitated. Lord Dalrymple could not have caught more than a glimpse of him, was now not even looking their way. Besides, Alec was seldom if ever recognized as a policeman. Not that he himself objected to his profession being known, but he had promised Arbuckle to keep it quiet.

'The small copper is common,' his lordship continued didactically, to Alec's further bewilderment; though not particularly tall, he was above regulation height. Lord Dalrymple, bending to give an absent pat to the spaniel who lolloped to greet him, went on to assert, 'What I saw was a Queen of Spain, a rare visitor. The man was talking through his hat. I should hope I can tell *Issoria lathonia* from *Lycaena phlaeas*!'

'Yes, dear,' soothed Lady Dalrymple, 'but the man *is* a noted authority. That was why he was invited to meet you.'

'Authority!' her husband snorted. 'Ass!'

Petrie turned his head. 'Butterflies,' he murmured, then moved on. 'Lady Dalrymple, will you allow me to present Mr. Fletcher? I'm afraid Daisy forgot to mention to you that she had invited him. He wasn't able to make it until today.'

'How do you do, Mr. Fletcher,' her ladyship said severely,

and at once turned back to Petrie. 'Where is Daisy? She missed tea and had not come in when we left.'

'The ladies have gone up to bed,' Petrie told her misleadingly. 'They had a tiring day.'

'Indeed! This treasure-hunting nonsense of Daisy's has gone on long enough. I shall tell her so in the morning.'

Meanwhile, Lord Dalrymple introduced himself to Alec, and continued eagerly, 'Are you acquainted with the *Lepidoptera*, by any chance?'

'I'm afraid not, sir. I can tell a Peacock from a Cabbage White, but that's about it.

'Large White, my dear sir, Large White. You refer to *Pieris brassicae*, I take it. A pest, to be sure, but not unattractive in its way.'

'Are you coming, Edgar?' said his wife. 'It is late and you *will* insist on going out at dawn.'

'I was going to offer Mr. Fletcher a night-cap, dear.'

'I'm sure you can rely upon Mr. Petrie to do the honours.'

'Please do, my boy. You'll excuse me, Mr. Fletcher. It's true I like to rise early and go out before the heat of the day. Good-night.'

Forbearing to point out that tomorrow was unlikely to be hot, Alec bade him good-night.

At the bottom of the stairs, the viscount turned and said earnestly, 'It *was* a Queen of Spain, I'd take my oath on it. A fritillary, you know.'

Alec rather liked him, but he could see why Daisy didn't choose to make her home with her cousins.

He and Petrie rejoined Arbuckle, Pearson, and Bincombe in the den. The footman came in a moment later with decanters of brandy and whisky.

'*I* knows Miss Daisy's not come in yet,' he said in a hushed, enigmatic voice, with a significant look. 'Mr. Lowecroft's gone to bed. I'm the only one on duty. If there's aught I can do to help, just ring, and you knows, Mr. Petrie, sir, I can keep mum.'

'Good fellow,' said Petrie, turning to Arbuckle. 'Whisky, sir?'

'I could bear to take a drop.'

More appreciative than Petrie of Ernest's offer, Alec soberly told the youth, 'It doesn't look as if there's anything to be done now. Tomorrow's another matter. If Miss Daisy isn't home yet, we may need every man we can get.'

CHAPTER 14

Pearson declined a night-cap. Handing Alec the schedule for the night watch, in an unstated acceptance of his authority, he went upstairs to join his wife. Alec took his seat at the desk and accepted a spot of brandy. Arbuckle sipped his Scotch and muttered something blasphemous about the Prohibition.

Petrie supplied himself and Bincombe with whisky and soda. 'All right, Fletcher,' he said, 'what can we tell you?'

Lord Gerald interrupted in a burst of unwonted loquacity. 'Look here, old man,' he said to Alec, 'Lucy may not show it much but she's deucedly fond of Daisy. Do anything for her. And I'd do abso-bally-lutely anything for Lucy, don't you know. Do a good deal for Daisy, come to that. So you've only to give the word.'

Alec gravely thanked him.

'I mean,' the large young man persevered in his laborious effort to explain himself, 'we all raffled round for Miss Arbuckle, but after all, we don't know her.' He cast an apologetic glance at the kidnapped girl's father. 'Except Petrie, what? But Daisy is . . . well, Daisy, if you know what I mean.'

'I do indeed,' Alec agreed, with a painful clenching of his heart. Where was she? Was she lost, hurt, helpless in the hands of villains?

'That's all right then,' said Bincombe, relieved. 'Wake me when it's time.' Swallowing his whisky in a single gulp, he silently departed.

Turning to Arbuckle, Alec said, 'I'll have your story first, sir. Just a minute while I find some paper to make notes.'

'Nothing in writing! It's too damn dangerous.'

'I find going over notes of a conversation often brings to one's attention points one had not previously noticed.'

'No!' said the American adamantly. 'You want me to play along, you do it my way.'

Alec conceded the point, hoping his memory would prove less fuzzy than his tired eyes. He let the touchy gentleman tell the story without interruption, making mental notes of questions to be asked, points to be clarified.

Arbuckle produced the notes he had received from the kidnappers, which he carried on him at all times. They were printed in pencil in block capitals on ordinary notepaper available anywhere. The wording was uneducated, but in an awkward way which could well be faked. Though Alec had never worked on a kidnapping – they were rare in Britain – he knew such was often the case.

Several instances of American slang, spelling, and phrasing, though possibly also faked, suggested that 'the Yank' Petrie had reported to Arbuckle was in fact American. There was always a chance he was some English criminal whose copied methods had earned him the nickname, but Alec was sure he'd have heard at least a rumour of such a man.

'I guess me telling you about the Yank's just hearsay,' said Arbuckle as Alec pored over the notes, 'but Petrie will confirm it.'

'I'm not concerned about hearsay,' Alec assured him. 'You're not giving a formal statement or evidence. I want to know everything: hearsay, opinion, conjecture, distant possibilities.'

Rather red in the face, Arbuckle said, 'Waal, there's something I told Miss Dalrymple that I've kept from Petrie here. I'm sorry, son, but I didn't want you thinking Gloria's poppa was the kind to go stepping on peoples corns on purpose. The fact is, I've made a few enemies in my time.'

'Which of us hasn't?' said Alec, and Petrie nodded solemnly. His blank look suggested he was trying hard to recall any enemies he had made in his time.

Arbuckle explained how, in the course of his business dealings, he had inevitably offended various people. Asking him to make a list of names, Alec turned to Petrie.

His account, where it covered the same events, coincided closely with Arbuckle's, allowing for different viewpoints.

'Any comments or ideas?' Alec invited.

'Well, there is one thing, Chief Inspector.'

Arbuckle sat up. 'Chief Inspector? That's real high up, isn't it?'

'Pretty high up,' Petrie assented in a modest tone which suggested he accepted the credit for providing a police officer of superior rank.

'Swell! I guess that means you've got some leeway, Mr. Fletcher, when it comes to acting on your own?'

'A certain amount,' Alec said cautiously, trying not to envisage what his Super, let alone the A.C., would think of his present activities. 'What were you going to say, Petrie?'

'Oh, it's just something that's rather puzzled me. If you don't mind my saying so, sir,' he said to Arbuckle, 'I was a bit surprised that the Studebaker had no spare radiator hose in its tool-kit. They're always splitting or getting punctured, or even just falling off. Crawford knowing all about motor engines, I'd have expected him to keep such a basic spare part to hand.'

'Crawford's my technical adviser, not my chauffeur, son. He keeps an eye on the Studebaker but I don't hold him responsible. I left Biggs back home, seeing I mostly drive myself anyhow.'

'Gloria – Miss Arbuckle – drives too,' Petrie told Alec proudly.

'Yet Mr. Crawford was driving you on this occasion,' Alec said to Arbuckle. 'Why was that?'

'Gloria wanted to show me Hereford.' He pronounced it Her-ford. 'When Petrie took her there, she found out Nell Gwynne was born in the city and thought I'd be interested. I'm not real hep when it comes to history – like Henry Ford says, history is bunk – but I took a fancy to that old story of Nell Gwynne, the orange girl, and your King Charles. Now Crawford, he's almost as keen on your history and the countryside as Gloria is. Spends all his weekends exploring. So when he hears we're going to Herford, he says he'd like to come along and he'll drive.'

'It was his idea to go with you, then?' Alec asked.

Arbuckle pondered. 'Gee, I couldn't swear to it. He was interested when we were talking about it, all right, but I've a feeling Gloria asked him along. She was pleased, anyhow, because him driving let her and me admire the scenery. I guess she doesn't pay much attention to the scenery when she's out with Petrie,' he added slyly.

Petrie blushed, confirming Alec's surmise as to the reason for his concern over Gloria Arbuckle.

'So you think Miss Arbuckle invited Crawford to go.' Alec hated to see a promising lead evaporate. 'Tell me, what happens when a radiator hose goes? Am I right in supposing it's quite spectacular?'

'By Jove, yes!' said Petrie. 'The remaining water boils and there's clouds of steam hissing all over the place. You jolly well know it's happening, which is just as well because if you don't stop right away, the engine overheats and can be ruined.'

'Steam?' Arbuckle frowned. 'I'll be darned if I recall clouds of steam.'

'You don't recall whether there was steam,' Alec asked sharply, 'or you do recall that there was not?'

'There was not,' the American said in a flat voice. 'Crawford said over his shoulder something was wrong. He pulled into the gateway and opened the hood. The bonnet, you call it. Then he muttered about the radiator, took some piece out – the hose, I guess. He put it in his pocket and I didn't see it. He said he'd have to find a garage, and off he went.'

'He didn't look in the tool-box?'

Arbuckle shook his head, reluctantly. 'He musta known there wasn't a spare there.'

'You didn't hold him responsible for the Studebaker. He might assume the tool-kit was complete and not check it beforehand, but if so, you'd expect him to look there for a spare hose when it was needed. On the other hand, if he was aware of a deficiency, wouldn't you expect him to replace it?'

'Y-yes. Maybe he just hadn't gotten around to it.'

'I assume in fact there was no spare hose. Petrie, did you look in the Studebaker's tool-box?'

'No. I saw it on the running board, a topping mahogany chest, which would practically hold my whole engine,' Petrie said enviously. 'But Crawford being an engineer, I took it he'd have used the spare if there was one. It's a simple repair. Besides, I was pretty sure I had a piece I could use.'

'So the . . .' Alec started.

Arbuckle interrupted. 'Listen. I know what you're suggesting. But this guy's been with me ten years, my right-hand man. Maybe he did see changes coming, like Miss Dalrymple said, but he knew I'd see him right'

'Changes?' Much as Alec deplored Daisy's penchant for meddling, anything which raised her suspicions was worth investigating.

With a sidelong glance at Petrie, Arbuckle shrugged. 'A business that doesn't change dies,' he said unhelpfully.

Alec appeared to go along with him. 'You drove the Studebaker here tonight?' he asked. 'Petrie, may I ask you to go and take a dekko in the tool-box?'

'Right-oh.' Petrie caught the keys Arbuckle tossed him and departed.

'Changes?' Alec pressed.

'Waal, now, you'll have maybe figured out that that young man is sweet on my girl. Gloria's nuts about him, and I've found no reason to think he wouldn't treat her right, nor that all he cares for is her pocketbook.'

'You've made enquiries?'

'You betcha! I'm not saying he's the smartest cookie in the jar, but he's a decent guy and willing to work, no lounge lizard, and he knows automobiles. That's my business, see, investing in automobile manufacturers, but I'm a real simp when it comes to the technical side.'

'That's Crawford's contribution?'

'As of now. My notion is to train Petrie to take his place. That's if him and Gloria get hitched, if his snooty family doesn't throw a monkey-wrench in the works.'

Mentally translating – if Petrie's blue-blooded family didn't throw a spanner in the works – Alec sympathized. He took a swallow of the superb Cognac Daisy's blue-blooded family had no doubt laid down generations ago.

'Is Miss Dalrymple right about Crawford foreseeing the possibility of losing his job?'

'Could be, but like I told her, he knows I'd see he didn't lose by it.'

'Not financially, perhaps, though I imagine he'd lose opportunities to invest knowledgeably. By the by,' Alec added parenthetically, 'he may resent your having utilised his expertise to make a fortune he can't hope to match. But I was going to suggest he'd lose in status, in closeness to the boss.'

'You may have something there,' Arbuckle said slowly. 'Tarnation, I've wondered . . . Not close to the boss so much as close to Gloria? You see what I'm getting at? I've wondered if Crawford hadn't set his sights on my girl.'

'Or – forgive me – her money. I don't mean to suggest your daughter is not attractive in herself, but your wealth must be an added attraction.'

'Brother, you've said a mouthful. If I had a sawbuck for every fortune-hunter I've seen off . . . ! I can spot 'em at a hundred yards. Petrie isn't one. Crawford . . . waal, I gotta admit Crawford could be.'

'Whether the attraction's money or love, he'd see his chance of winning Miss Arbuckle going down the drain when Petrie came along,' Alec observed. 'What made you think he had hopes?'

'Little things. Lately, this business of suddenly he's so keen on history and the countryside. I had a hunch that was just because of Gloria's interest.' He stopped, looking appalled. 'Aw, jeez!'

Alec had no difficulty following his train of thought. 'You said he'd taken to spending his weekends exploring the countryside. He had every opportunity to find a deserted cottage such as Petrie describes, and to learn the back lanes. And another point: London and Hereford are in opposite directions from Malvern, yet Petrie came across you stranded by the roadside when you were on your way from one and he from the other.'

'He was aiming for his parents' place,' Arbuckle said dubiously, 'not Great Malvern, like us. I gotta say I was a mite puzzled seeing the Malvern Hills first getting closer, then further away. Still and all, you gotta go round, not over, and these lanes of yours twist and turn like a rattler.'

'The kidnapping had to have been arranged in advance for a certain place, though there might have been some leeway as to time.'

Petrie loped in, the ring of keys dangling from his fore-finger clinking like castanets. 'I say, that tool-chest has the whole caboodle, sparking plugs, inner tubes, hand pump, patching kit, fan-belt, even lamp glasses. Just about anything you could need – except hose.'

'That doesn't prove anything,' Arbuckle growled.

'No,' Alec agreed, 'it's just another possibly significant fact to add to the pile. Petrie, can you pinpoint on the map the exact spot where the kidnapping took place? Just there? You're sure? That's quite a way off the direct route from Hereford to Great Malvern, isn't it?'

'Miles. It was a pretty good choice, come to think of it, with all hayfields around, already mowed and stacked so no farmer was likely to come along. It looks as if Crawford's our man, doesn't it? I never did quite cotton to him.'

'Why not?'

Brow furrowed, Petrie thought. 'He was an oily, smug sort of b . . . chap,' he said slowly, 'not exactly pudgy, just sort of too well-fed-looking, like an old maid's cat, but that's hardly . . . No, by Jove, I have it. I never nailed it down before. It was the way he looked at Gloria!'

'Mr. Arbuckle has just told me he suspected Crawford had ambitions in that direction.'

Surging to his feet, Petrie pounded with his fist on the desk. 'By Jove, if the bounder has laid a finger on her . . . !'

Alec laid a calming hand on his arm. 'We must hope he's chiefly motivated by money.'

'I can't believe it.' Arbuckle shook his head. 'Sure, things look real bad for Crawford, but I just don't believe he'd do a low-down, lousy thing like this.'

'As I said, sir, we don't have anything like proof.' Alec had few doubts that he was on the right track, but he would see things clearer after a good night's sleep.

Part of a night's sleep, he corrected himself, glancing at the brass clock on the mantelpiece. 'I want to know more about his movements these past few weeks,' he went on, noting that Arbuckle looked as exhausted as he felt, 'and just what you've said to him about the kidnapping, but that can wait until the morning.'

'I have to go to Lunnon to collect the dough, but I'll come by on my way. I would've anyways, to see if Miss Dalrymple's back. I'll be off, now, and see you in the morning.'

'Will you see Crawford in the meantime?'

'At breakfast, probably, before he goes off to Oxford.'

'Don't say anything to him,' Alec warned. 'Not a word of our suspicions, and try not to alter your manner to him.'

He and Petrie went out to the hall to see the American off. Ernest appeared from nowhere with an umbrella and accompanied the small, somehow crumpled figure down the steps to his motor.

The rain was belting down. Was Daisy out in it somewhere?

Consulting Pearson's list, Alec said, 'You've got the first watch, Petrie.'

'The drawing-room, I should think. There are French windows. If she comes and sees the light, she'll be able to get in easily. I say, Fletcher, I don't want you to think I'm not frightfully cut up about Daisy going missing. It's just that Gloria . . .' Words failed him.

'I know.' Walking with him to the drawing-room, Alec wondered if Petrie could possibly be feeling the same agony of apprehension. 'Look here, I imagine you're known at most of the garages hereabouts? I'd like you to go in the morning and make enquiries at any Crawford might have made his way to that day.'

'Right-ho, old chap.' Petrie opened a door and flicked on a light switch. 'If no one's heard of him, we'll know for sure, won't we?'

'It would be awfully hard for him to argue his way out of it,' Alec agreed grimly, following him into a long room in which the finest furniture of two centuries melded into a harmonious elegance. He waved at floor-length blue brocade drapery on the far wall. 'Is that the French windows? I'll draw the curtains back and make sure they're unlocked.' Opening the curtains, he reached for the handle.

'They're locked, sir.' The footman came in behind them, bearing the tray of decanters and glasses. 'The key's in this here drawer. There you are. Will you be wanting another night-cap, sir?'

'Not for me, thanks, but you might leave it here. Mr. Petrie's staying up. Is the front door bolted and barred?'

'Yes, sir, but it's a Yale lock, the kind you can open without a key, from inside.'

'Good. You can show me the way to my room, then, if you will, and go to bed yourself. Oh, here's the schedule, Petrie. You'll wake Bincombe in an hour or so.'

'Right-ho. Sleep well, old man. I must admit I'm dashed glad you turned up.'

He held out his hand, and Alec was shaking it when from the corner of his eye he saw the handle of the French window move. As he strode towards it, it opened, and over the threshold tottered a tatterdemalion mudlark.

'Alec, thank heaven!' croaked Daisy, and fell into his arms.

He picked her up and sat down on the nearest sofa with her on his lap, holding her tight, disregarding completely the effect on himself, the sofa, and the Aubusson carpet.

Streams of murky water ran from her bedraggled hair and torn clothes. Her face, turned up to his, was scratched and daubed with mud. As he kissed her chilly lips, all he was conscious of was the joyful singing in his heart.

Daisy snuggled against Alec's chest and felt safe for the first time in hours. She could have happily stayed there for just as many hours to compensate, but the reason for her struggling on to Fairacres, resisting the appeal of shelter in barn or haystack, still stood. She was safe. Gloria was not.

Reluctantly she raised her head from Alec's shoulder, and saw Phillip's anxious face.

'Phil, she's all right.' Daisy felt it was most improper to be cuddled on Alec's knee with Phillip, and the footman behind him, looking on, but she wasn't going to move until she absolutely had to. 'They've got her in the witch's cottage in Cooper's Wood.'

'Little Baswell? By Jove, we ought to have thought of it! Right-oh, I'm off.'

'Don't be an ass, Petrie,' Alec said sharply. 'You said there are four bruisers, at least. It'll take all of us.'

'Me too!' said the footman, all agog. 'I knowed there were something up. I knowed it!'

'You too, lad. The two of you go and roust out Bincombe and Pearson, and ask Miss Fotheringay to come and take care of Daisy. Try not to wake her cousins.' As they rushed out, he looked down at her and smiled. 'A hot bath is called for, I'd say. Is there anything else we need to know, sweetheart?'

'Not that I can think of. She's in the upstairs room on the

right. At least she was until we escaped through the roof, and I don't expect they have another room secured. She couldn't get out that way without help. You see, I . . .'

'I see you went rushing into danger when you were supposed to be merely asking questions, without even the elementary precaution of telephoning your whereabouts first!'

'The only public 'phone was out of order,' Daisy said indignantly. 'And I did take precautions. I hid my bike – I hope we can find it – and borrowed a dog for camouflage.'

'A dog!' Alec laughed and hugged her. 'My darling idiot.'

'There speaks a townsman. The wood is far too overgrown for cycling, and the day far too sultry to walk for pleasure, but dogs always have to be walked. They wouldn't have suspected a thing if Tuffet hadn't gone snooping around the side of the house.'

'And you snooped after? Just as I thought. The wood's very overgrown, is it?'

'Even the ride. There's a path of sorts trampled through the thickets, though the beginning of it may be hard to find if they've bothered to conceal it. But Phillip will find it. He knows the wood well, he'll be able to lead you straight to the cottage.'

'Good.'

'You'd never find it otherwise. They have the windows well covered so no light escapes, and they don't let Gloria have a light at all. Poor Gloria! I hope they didn't hurt her when they caught her. She didn't follow me up the tree, you see. I suppose she must have panicked.'

'Maybe she just doesn't know how to climb trees. Not everyone is as resourceful as you, sweetheart.'

'Oh Alec, I do like it when you call me sweetheart!'

He responded in a most satisfactory fashion, but their kiss was interrupted when Lucy swept into the drawing room. She was as elegant as ever in fawn silk pyjamas and matching dressing-gown, even with her hair in a towelling bandeau.

'Daisy darling, what *have* you been up to? Too, too squalid! You'd better come along and have a bath.'

Reluctantly slipping down from Alec's lap, Daisy reeled. He caught her up.

'I'll carry her,' he said to Lucy.

On the landing they met the men. Phillip was still in evening dress but carrying boots, Ernest in his livery, Binkie and Tommy apparently dressed in whatever had come first to hand.

'Well done, Daisy!' said Tommy softly, grinning.

'I'll join you in a minute,' Alec told them. 'Don't forget electric torches, one each if possible. Have we another motor? Five would be a squeeze in mine.'

'I'll get the Lagonda out. It's bigger than Bincombe's Alvis.'

'Ask Bill Truscott to go with you,' Daisy advised, thinking of the four roughs they would be facing. 'Tell him it's by my request.'

'Good idea,' said Phillip. 'He's a good chap. Take care of yourself, old bean. Come on, fellows.'

Alec carried Daisy to the bathroom where Lucy was already running a steaming bath. He deposited her on a chair and stood for a moment gazing down at her, shaking his head.

'Squalid is the word. Straight to bed and I'll see you in morning.'

'Right-oh, Chief,' said Daisy. 'Alec, you will take care, Won't you?'

'You can count on it, love,' he assured her with a grin. 'The last thing I want is to meet your mother for the first time sporting a black eye!'

CHAPTER 15

On Daisy's arrival, now that there was something to be done, all desire to sleep had left Alec. Nonetheless, having picked up the Dalrymples' chauffeur at the lodge, he let the man take the wheel of the Austin. Truscott knew the way to Cooper's Wood – and the rain was still coming down by the bucketful.

Peering through the opened windscreen, the chauffeur followed the red tail-lights of the Lagonda down the lane. Petrie, also familiar with the route, was at the wheel of the car in front. Its owner, Pearson, sat beside Alec in the back of the Austin.

'The others may think I should be in on the planning,' he said self-deprecatingly, 'but I'm quite prepared to leave it to you, sir, don't y'know. This show's a bit different from storming a French village held by the Boches. We couldn't very well go in with machine-guns blazing in the middle of Worcestershire, even if the girl weren't there.'

Alec blenched. 'Ye gods, no! I trust none of you has a service revolver hidden in his pocket?'

'No. Bincombe said something about shotguns but I soon set him straight.'

'You have my eternal gratitude, Mr. Pearson. My superiors are not going to be happy about this caper at best.

If someone got shot, I'd be in the soup over my head and swimming for my life with no land in sight.'

'You'd be back on the beat and I'd be struck off the roll,' said the solicitor wryly. 'No firearms. Right-oh, what's the scheme?'

'Dammit, I wish I'd asked Daisy more about her hole in the roof.'

'Her *what*?'

'She and Miss Arbuckle escaped through a hole in the roof, I gather. Knowing Daisy, she probably made the hole.'

'But how did they get down from the roof?' Pearson queried, sounding stunned.

'I don't know,' Alec said regretfully. 'If there's a ladder, we might use it to climb up and abstract Miss Arbuckle before we tackle her captors.' He raised his voice to be heard above the tattoo of raindrops dancing on the hood. 'Do you know the cottage, Truscott?'

'No, sir, that I don't.' The chauffeur shook his head, silhouetted against the headlamps' light reflected off water sheeting from the sky. 'If you don't mind me asking, sir, what's this about Miss Daisy escaping? From what Mr. Phillip said, I thought we was going to rescue her. I'd do a lot for Miss Daisy, but if she's safe I've the missus and the flippers to think on.'

Letting Pearson explain the situation, Alec tried to devise a plan. Again and again he wished he had asked Daisy more questions. He had been so thankful to see her safe and sound, however filthy, that he hadn't been able to think of anything else.

'So it's Mr. Phillip's young lady's to be rescued?' said Truscott. He gave a philosophical sigh. 'Ah well, I'll do my bit. The missus wouldn't hear of aught else. What was you wishing me to do, sir?'

'We'll all follow Mr. Petrie through the wood to the cottage, with only his torch lit if at all possible. If he directs it at the ground, it shouldn't be visible very far off. Then we'll surround the cottage. I'm assuming it's pretty small, so we shan't be too far apart. If anyone finds a ladder, we'll try to get the girl out first.'

'I take it, sir,' said Pearson, 'your aim is to bag the kidnappers as well as rescue Miss Arbuckle?'

'Ideally,' Alec agreed, unsure whether the 'sir' was addressed to him as a superior officer for the nonce or because of his age. It made him feel ancient, though Pearson could not be more than five or six years younger. 'We'll do our best to take them in,' he continued, 'but the girl's safety must be paramount. Otherwise I'd wait and try to catch the ringleader, as well as his minions.'

'Of course.'

'It means we absolutely must take them by surprise, so that they don't get a chance to use Miss Arbuckle as a shield. They'll have a man on look-out, especially after Daisy's escape. No lights as we get near the cottage. We'll have to work by touch.'

'This rain will cover a certain amount of noise.'

'Yes, we're lucky there.'

'Are you going to invoke the name of the law, sir?'

'I hadn't thought. Given that I'm here strictly in an unofficial capacity, what would you advise?'

'Hmm. In view of the threats against Miss Arbuckle, and the possibility, however remote, that they might get away with her, I'd say not.'

'You're a copper, sir?' Truscott asked. 'A policeman, I mean?'

'Detective Chief Inspector Fletcher,' Pearson introduced him, 'of Scotland Yard. But keep it under your hat. What next, Mr. Fletcher? Say we have the place surrounded but haven't got the girl out. Shall we try to break in or try to draw them out with some sort of sound?'

'The downstairs doors and windows may be barred or reinforced. If we haven't got the girl, we'll try to draw them out. What shall we do? We can hardly just knock on the door.'

'Daisy could, pretending she was lost and cold and preferred shelter at any cost.'

Alec shuddered. 'Thank heaven you didn't come up with that little notion back at the house! She'd have done it.'

'One of us could fake it I've done some amateur theatricals in my time.'

'Let's hear you.'

'Let me in,' Pearson begged in a high voice. 'I'm freezing!'

'Lor, sir, that's Miss Daisy to the life!'

To the discriminating ear of a lover it didn't sound in the least like Daisy, but Alec supposed it would do for a bunch of Cockney criminals. 'Throw in a bit of a stutter,' he suggested. 'Teeth chattering.'

'P-please let me in. I'm f-f-freezing.'

'Not bad. You can perform if we decide to go that way. Any other ideas?'

They discussed other possibilities but came back in the end to the pseudo-Daisy. The men must be eager to recapture her so her voice would bring at least one to the door.

'I'll give you a choice of back-up,' said Alec. 'Petrie, who's the keenest, or Bincombe, who's the best with his fists, I'd guess.'

'Petrie. Deprive him of the chance to get to his girl and he might go off half-cocked and take it anyway.'

'All right. For the rest of us, I'll have to talk to him first about whether there's a back door, and the positions of windows. We shan't be able to see so I hope he remembers.'

'Looks like the rain's lightening up a bit, sir,' Truscott reported. 'Nearly there.'

Before Alec had time to consider the effect on their plan of the end of the downpour, the Austin pulled in behind the Lagonda. Truscott doused the lights. Alec had caught a glimpse of tree-trunks, unobscured by curtains of water. The rain had decreased to the point of no longer penetrating the foliage above.

He stepped out of the cat. A chilly douche promptly hit his hatless head and trickled down his neck. He swore silently.

An electric torch snapped on. By its light, the six men gathered in a huddle, and Alec questioned Petrie about the cottage and its immediate environs.

'There's a back door. We once watched the witch coming out of it to feed her chickens. No windows in the end walls downstairs, only upstairs, I'm pretty sure. Well, almost sure. I haven't been near the place since I was a boy, remember. The other windows are small enough to make it dashed difficult for a man to climb through. I think.'

On that shaky basis, Alec ordered the disposition of his troops.

'All right, Petrie, how do we get there?'

'The beginning of the ride is back here. It's so overgrown I nearly missed it.'

They followed him back along the lane a dozen yards. In the torch's narrow beam, the mass of bushes and small trees seemed to Alec unbroken, impenetrable, but Petrie soon found a path.

He extinguished the torch. 'It's light enough to find the way without,' he said, and plunged between two thickets.

Alec realized the clouds had parted and the first faint light of midsummer's early dawn was painting the world in tones of grey and charcoal. A crow's sleepy caw came from the tall trees edging the ride, and nearby a small bird twittered.

'Wait! That's torn it. I was relying on darkness for surprise,' he explained as Petrie returned, 'as well as heavy rain to cover any sounds.' He held out his hands palms up. The only falling water was dripping from the surrounding leaves.

'We'll just have to storm the place,' Petrie said impatiently, already turning back to the path.

'That's the most risky for Miss Arbuckle. You go ahead, but don't rush in. Pearson and I will study the lay-out and see if we can't come up with a better scheme. All right, fellows, let's go.'

Close behind Petrie, Alec stayed ready to grab him if he seemed about to run amok. He found himself dodging scarce seen branches which whipped back into his face, jerking his trouser turn-ups from the determined grasp of brambles, squidging through ankle-deep mud. His admiration for Daisy, who had traversed this jungle in pitch darkness in a thunderstorm – and in a skirt – grew by leaps and bounds.

Petrie stopped so suddenly Alec nearly ran into his back. 'I think the cottage is under that sycamore,' he whispered, pointing at a tree towering over the brush choking the ride. 'Yes, there's the chimney, see?'

'Good man.' Alec turned his head. 'Pearson, come and have a look.'

They squeezed past Petrie and picked their way forward. The only sound they made was the squelch of the mud beneath their feet, hidden by a rising ground mist, but all around the birds were singing now. Greys paled and hazy colours emerged. The air smelled richly of green, growing things.

The path curved around a gorse bush speckled with yellow blossoms. Alec stopped dead as one end of a thatched roof came in sight.

Motioning Pearson to keep still, he inched ahead. A blotchy wall, a broken window...

He halted, heart in mouth, but nothing stirred.

Another step.

The door stood open, a black hole like a missing tooth in a decaying face. 'Too late,' said Alec with a sigh. 'They've cut and run.'

Warned by the maid who answered her bell that 'her ladyship's in a proper taking,' Daisy toyed with the notion of breakfast in bed.

She dismissed it as cowardly. Geraldine was *her* cousin's wife, and the whole show had been her idea. It was up to her to smooth ruffled feathers.

Besides, she had to find out what had happened last night. Worry had stopped her going back to sleep, though it was still quite early. She had a sinking feeling that if Gloria had been rescued, she would have heard about it by now; but the others might hesitate to disturb her after yesterday's ordeal.

Actually, she felt perfectly well. The stiffness was not much worse than after the first day's bicycling. Some of the scratches smarted a bit, in spite of Lucy's free hand with the boracic. The ones on her face she smothered with a good coating of face-powder before she went down.

In the dining room she found Edgar and Geraldine finishing their breakfasts, and Lucy and Madge in the middle of theirs. The men must still be asleep after the activities of the night.

Lowecroft came in with fresh tea as Lucy shook her head at Daisy, her mouth – already vividly lip-sticked despite the early hour – turned down. No Gloria.

'Lord Dalrymple has caught a lobster,' Madge said brightly. A vision of Edgar in oilskins hauling in lobsterpots crossed Daisy's mind even as she asked, 'Moth or butterfly?'

'A moth, *Stauropus fagi*.' Edgar beamed at her apparent interest.

'A particularly spectacular one?' Daisy queried, crossing to the sideboard and loading a plate with everything in sight.

'The adult form is not spectacular,' her cousin admitted regretfully. 'In fact, it may be mistaken for a bundle of dead leaves. However, I obtained some eggs which I believe it had just laid, and which I hope to hatch. The larva quite ostentatious. It may be said to resemble a lobster in some respects. Its head, for instance, looks somewhat like a lobster claw.'

The diversionary tactic worked only until the butler left the room. Then Geraldine ruthlessly interrupted.

'Yes, dear, I am sure the caterpillar will be a fascinating sight. Daisy, what is this my maid has been telling me? While delighted to welcome your friends, we cannot approve of the sort of high jinks, to use a vulgar phrase, you young people indulged in last night.'

'No, indeed,' Edgar seconded her with a stern frown, changing instantly from the dotty lepidopterist to the censorious schoolmaster. 'Such frolics may suit modern notions, but we choose to preserve the old-fashioned proprieties at Fairacres.'

'Frolics!' Daisy easily suppressed her guilt at having taken advantage of her cousins as she recalled the exhausting, uncomfortable, and at times frightening events of the past twenty-four hours. 'Of course, you couldn't guess, but everything we've done has had an extremely serious purpose.'

'What?' Geraldine asked bluntly, but Edgar looked thoughtful, perhaps remembering the condition in which he had found Phillip.

'I can't tell you the details.'

'Indeed!'

In the face of Geraldine's justifiable scepticism, Daisy decided the moment had come to blow the gaff, at least in part. Sooner or later they would find out that Alec was a police detective, so she might as well make use of him.

She cast a deliberately exaggerated glance at the door, then leaned forward and said in a low, mysterious voice, 'You mustn't tell anyone, but we're helping the police. Mr. Fletcher is from Scotland Yard, a Detective Chief Inspector *incognito*, and we came here to act as camouflage for him when he arrived. Last night he asked the chaps to do something more for him, I don't know quite what. I do know it's absolutely vital to keep his profession secret.'

'Gosh, yes,' said Madge solemnly.

Lucy, the abominable Painted Lady, prudently opened her mouth only to insert a forkful of kedgeree.

'So, please,' Daisy continued, 'if you don't believe me, ask to see his warrant card, but do it discreetly. I'm truly sorry we've upset you. We felt it was our duty to do what we could to uphold law and order.'

Geraldine's face was a study in doubt.

'My dear,' said Edgar, 'perhaps I should have mentioned to you that when I came across young Petrie the other morning, he had clearly not been injured in a motor accident. As a matter of fact, his wrists and ankles were bound.'

'Really, Edgar, you might have told me!'

'I do beg your pardon, dear. I didn't want to alarm you, but I must also confess my mind was distracted by wondering whether it was remiss of me not to have secured the blood vein.'

The four ladies gaped at him. 'Phillip wasn't badly injured,' Daisy said uncertainly.

'Do you mean to say, Edgar, that there was another victim of whatever nefarious business is afoot, and that you let him expire from loss of blood?'

'No, no, good heavens no! The Blood Vein moth, *Calothysanis amata*. Mr. Petrie had an excellent specimen of the larva crawling up his neck when I found him.'

Madge and Daisy burst out laughing, and Lucy smiled.

Geraldine shook her head in despair. 'I should have guessed. Well, I cannot pretend I find it anything but distasteful to be involved in a police matter, however peripherally, but I suppose it is our duty to aid the authorities.'

'I'm sorry,' said Daisy. She was saved from further grovelling as the butler came in.

'Mr. Arbuckle is here, my lady.'

'Good gracious, what ails the man to call at this time in the morning!'

'He asked for Mr. Fletcher, my lady,' Lowecroft informed her with a hint of sympathy.

In response to Geraldine's glance of exasperated enquiry, Daisy nodded.

'Show Mr. Arbuckle in, please, Lowecroft,' said Geraldine, sighing, 'and you had better inform Mr. Fletcher of his arrival. Well, Daisy, we shall take ourselves off. I only hope you know what you are about!'

'So do I,' said Daisy.

CHAPTER 16

'Quick,' said Daisy, as the butler followed her cousins from the room, 'what happened last night? I take it Tommy told you, Madge?'

'The birds had flown. They went upstairs and saw the hole in the roof, which I gather you made? Tommy was frightfully impressed.'

'A fat lot of good it did in the end. We're back where we started, with no idea where Gloria is.'

'Oh no, darling,' said Lucy, 'your disappearance persuaded Mr. Arbuckle to confide in your pet copper, and we have a suspect.'

Madge nodded. 'Phillip told Tommy Mr. Fletcher suspects Mr. Arbuckle's chauffeur.'

'Chauffeur?' Daisy asked eagerly. 'You mean Crawford, his engineer? I thought there was something fishy about him, but I've never met him. I have no sense of his character.'

'Phillip doesn't like him, I gather,' Lucy informed her.

'Phillip's no judge of character. But he takes people at face value, and tends to like them, all things being equal, so if he dislikes Crawford there must be a reason. And if Alec thinks there's good reason to suspect him, we must follow him, in case he contacts ...' She stopped as Lowecroft showed Arbuckle in.

The American's face brightened as he caught sight of Daisy. Only greetings and offers of breakfast could be voiced until the butler left again, but the moment the door shut, Daisy jumped up and demanded, 'Where is Crawford?'

'My dear Miss Dalrymple!' Arbuckle took her hands in his. 'I'm mighty happy to see you safe. I was ...'

'Thanks, but never mind that. Is it true Alec – Mr. Fletcher – suspects your Mr. Crawford? Someone must follow him!'

'Jeez, of course. He's supposed to go to Oxford today, to Morris's factory. Cowley, that is. I guess it's a little town near Oxford.'

'Had he left the hotel when you did?'

'No, he hadn't come down yet. He's nearly finished up over at Morris's, figures a few more hours is all he needs to give me a recommendation.'

'We'll go,' announced Madge, 'Tommy and I. There's not much I can do to help, but I can sit in the car and keep an eye out for Crawford while Tommy drives. I'll go and get him up, poor dear. They didn't get in till after three.'

She dashed out. Lucy poured a cup of coffee for Arbuckle, and Daisy asked him what Alec had concluded about Crawford. He explained, reiterating – though without much conviction, Daisy thought – his belief in his employee's innocence.

Arbuckle was eager to hear why Daisy had gone missing yesterday evening. She did not want to tell him about seeing Gloria until Alec was there to describe the abortive midnight raid on the witch's cottage. He came in sooner than she expected, remarkably alert after so little sleep, if a bit bristly about the chin.

She had never seen him in flannels and a tweed jacket before, since he had always been on duty and thus formally dressed when they met in the country. He looked simply spiffing – or would when he'd had time to shave. Mother would never be able to guess he was a policeman if she wasn't told.

With an apologetic glance at her and Lucy, he stroked his chin. 'Your pardon, ladies. I didn't want to keep Mr. Arbuckle waiting. You've heard about last night, sir?'

'No, sir, I have not,' Arbuckle said anxiously. 'I was just asking.'

Daisy and Alec between them were breaking the news of her capture and escape and Gloria's new disappearance when Madge and Tommy arrived.

'I gather we're off' – Tommy yawned enormously – 'Sorry . . . to Oxford?'

Alec looked at Daisy, his dark, thick eyebrows raised, obviously jumping to the instant conclusion that this was her doing.

'To follow Crawford,' she explained.

'Good thought!'

'Cowley, not Oxford. Mr. Arbuckle, what car does he drive?' Daisy asked, delighted by Alec's approval.

'He has a maroon A.C. Six.'

'Right-oh.' Taking off his glasses, Tommy blinked at the lenses, then took out his handkerchief to polish them. 'We'll try to pick him up in Great Malvern. If the A.C. isn't parked at the hotel, we'll just tootle off towards Oxford, hoping to spot it on the way. And failing that, we'll look around for it in Cowley.'

'The Morris motor-car works,' said Arbuckle, 'that's where he's supposed to be.'

'Do you happen to know which route he generally takes?' Tommy asked. Arbuckle shook his head. 'Never mind. If we miss him, we'll do Cheltenham and the A40. It's fastest.'

'If you're stopped for exceeding the speed limit, I'll pay the fine,' Arbuckle assured him.

'Telephone from Cowley,' Alec put in, 'whether you find him or not.'

'Right-oh. Thanks, darling,' he said to Madge as she presented him with a large roll, hastily buttered and stuffed with bacon. 'We'll buzz off, then. Toodle-oo.'

As they left, Daisy followed her example and went to the sideboard to fill a plate for Alec. On the way, she said to him, 'The men will be bound to contact Crawford after last night, don't you think? And he'll want to see where they've taken Gloria.'

'It seems likely, always assuming he's our man – and we have no better prospects. Mr. Arbuckle, where else has your business taken Crawford?'

'Since we came to Malvern, to Austin's at Longbridge, Sunbeam in Wolverhampton, and a whole bunch of factories in Coventry: Swift, Lea & Francis, Hotchkiss, Humber, Daimler, and Hillman, I think. I guess that's the centre of your auto business, like Detroit.'

Alec groaned. 'So he might have found a place anywhere in the central Midlands, or on the way there, as an alternative hiding place.'

'He wouldn't want them to be too far away,' Daisy argued, setting a heaped plate before Alec, 'or he would have chosen somewhere farther away for the first hidey-hole. He must need to be within reasonably easy reach of both them and Mr. Arbuckle. And he can't move his own base from Malvern without arousing suspicion.'

'Not that it helps how close they are,' Lucy pointed out. 'Wherever it is, we'll never find it unless he leads us to it. So your brain-wave about following him was a work of absolute genius, darling.'

Daisy tried to look modest.

Alec grinned at her, swallowed a mouthful of scrambled egg, then turned to Arbuckle to ask what he had told Crawford about the kidnapping.

'Mighty little, as little as I could get away with, just because I figured the less anyone knew the better. I couldn't keep the kidnapping secret, what with Gloria vanishing without notice and me having the willies, and him getting dumped. Like I told Petrie, he was real mad at being left to walk home. He acted mad enough to fool me, at any rate. He asked was I going to contact the police and I told him no sirree.'

'Do you recall his response?'

'He approved.'

'Did he!' Alec exclaimed.

'No big deal,' Arbuckle insisted. 'He thought I was right for Gloria's sake, and he advised me not to mention it to anyone at all because things have a way of getting out.'

'True enough. Did you follow his advice? You didn't tell him Petrie had turned up again, or about his friends searching for your daughter?'

'Not a word.'

'Good. Anything else?'

'Lessee.' Arbuckle pondered, then said in dismay, 'Rats, yes, I almost forgot. He offered to deliver the ransom for me. If you're right, Mr. Fletcher, that would be handing it to him on a plate!'

'Did you agree?'

'Nah. I said if anyone but me turned up with the dough, it could mess things up but good. I told him to go on same as usual, like nothing had happened, so's not to make anyone nervous.'

'How did he react to that? Did he seem relieved?'

'Not so I noticed. Why?'

'Oh, you might have wanted him to stick close to you, which would have cramped his style. As it is, he's been free to meet his henchmen whenever he wants. He knows you're off to town today to fetch the ransom?'

'I mentioned a coupla days ago I'd have it by today.'

'All right. Just one thing more, unless you have any questions, Daisy? Miss Fotheringay?'

'Yes,' said Daisy. 'Mr. Arbuckle, I realize it goes against the grain to think a trusted employee might have turned on you like this. But it's better than if it was someone out for revenge, isn't it? I mean, at least Gloria's safe? You haven't actually done anything to make Crawford hate you, whatever he may fear for the future.'

'I have not, Miss Dalrymple, not consciously,' Arbuckle said heavily, 'though, like Mr. Fletcher said, it maybe sticks in his craw that I've made more from his know-how than he can ever hope to. But – and believe me, I lay awake half the night thinking about this – if I'm right that he's carrying a torch for my girl, and he knows she prefers young Petrie waal, that opens up a whole new can of worms.'

Even as she wrinkled her nose at the graphic idiom, Daisy acknowledged the validity of his fears. The rejected lover, the mutation of love into hate, had been the basis of uncountable tales of rape, murder, and mayhem throughout the ages.

Lucy had lost her usual blasé expression, and Alec's grave face showed his concurrence.

'I'm afraid you're right,' he said, 'which may make you look more kindly on my last point I most strongly advise calling in the local force and setting up a proper search for Miss Arbuckle.'

Arbuckle stood up, impressive despite his lack of inches as he leaned forward with both fists planted on the table. 'Nope,' he said inflexibly. 'I don't believe they'd find her, and it just might be what sends the guy over the edge. I can't risk it.' He held up one hand as Alec opened his mouth to argue. 'You tell 'em and I'll deny it I'll say Gloria's gone back to the States. No, sir, we have to play it his way, whether it's Crawford or some other bastard I'm going to fetch the ransom.'

His resolute march towards the door turned to a tired trudge before he reached it, but he left, nevertheless.

Alec watched him go, sighed, and turned back to his almost untouched breakfast. Cutting into a sausage, he said, part sour, part admiring, 'Obstinate old so-and-so. I do feel for him, poor chap, but . . . !'

'What are you going to do?' Daisy asked. 'Phillip and I are eyewitnesses to the kidnapping, so his denial won't carry much weight.'

'None, even if Petrie won't cooperate. But I'm caught between the devil and the deep blue sea.' He glanced at Lucy.

'I shan't tell tales out of school, Mr. Fletcher,' she said dryly.

'Thank you.' He gave her a wry smile. 'You see, I have to agree with Arbuckle on several points. For a start, he's correct in saying the British police are not well versed in handling kidnappings. We have very few, whereas I gather there's quite an epidemic in America. In the second place, a search is not likely to succeed when the area to be covered is so enormous.'

Daisy feelingly agreed. 'It was pretty hopeless when we could be fairly sure she was nearby. I only found her by sheer luck.'

'Exactly. And the associated problem is that she may very well not be in Worcestershire any longer. The Met doesn't have the manpower or the local knowledge to mount a detailed search, and I haven't the authority to call out the, forces of half a dozen counties!'

'Who does?' Lucy asked. 'Your superiors?'

'Only the Home Secretary,' Alec told her bluntly. 'Even the Commissioner would have to try persuasion, and before that I'd have to talk the Assistant Commissioner, the head of the C.I.D., into ... Well, suffice it to say it's a long chain of persuasion, and all in the face of Arbuckle's denials. By the time anything was done, the chances are the ransom would be paid and the whole thing over.'

Lucy nodded. 'More than likely. Too, too maddening!'

'There's another thing.' Alec hesitated. 'I hope I'm not letting it influence my decision. The fact is, whenever I report the kidnapping, I'm going to face some awkward questions about why I didn't report it sooner. Especially after last night. The only thing which can save my bacon is a successful outcome.'

'You only found out about it late last night!' cried Daisy, outraged on his behalf. 'I don't see what else you could do when I came in and told you where Gloria was but go and see if she was still there! Any delay would have been madness.'

'So your delinquency only begins this morning, Mr. Fletcher,' Lucy observed. 'Which means the prospect of awkward questions actually weighs on the other side, that is, *for* reporting in now.'

'Confound it, Lucy!' Phillip burst into the room, his usual diffidence towards her in abeyance. 'You're not trying to persuade him to spill the beans!'

'Take a damper, Petrie,' Alec advised him. 'I'd already decided it was more or less pointless to contact my colleagues at this stage, and I wouldn't save my skin at the expense of Miss Arbuckle's, believe me. Not that I'm ungrateful for your *caveat*, Miss Fotheringay.'

'Lucy,' she murmured.

Alec smiled at her. Daisy could have kissed her. If Lucy unbent so far as to invite him to call her by her Christian name, it was a good omen for the Dowager Lady Dalrymple's eventual acceptance.

'Sorry,' said Phillip, abashed. His face was drawn, dark circles beneath his eyes. The hopes raised last night, only to be dashed, must have been harder to bear than his previous state of despondency.

He needed something to do, Daisy decided. 'So it's all up to us now,' she said. 'Tommy and Madge have gone to follow Crawford . . .'

'Tommy! Dash it all, why not me? Why didn't you wake me?'

'We'll all have to take a turn, or he'll get suspicious of the same car always being behind him, don't you think, Alec?'

'Certainly,' Alec said promptly, continuing with his breakfast and leaving present matters to Daisy.

She knew, however, that he would not hesitate to jump in if he disagreed with her proposals. A husband who always knuckled under would be as bad as one who never let her use her own brains, she thought. 'So you can relieve the Pearsons, Phil,' she said.

'I haven't got a car,' Phillip pointed out disconsolately.

'Binkie will lend you the Alvis,' Lucy promised. 'Won't you, darling?' she added as Binkie came in.

'Right-ho. What?'

'Is that an interjection or a question, darling?'

'What will I do?' Binkie asked with a belated touch of trepidation.

'Lend Phil the Alvis.'

'Oh, right-ho! Why?'

'Because the kidnappers pinched the Swift,' Daisy reminded him, glaring the nascent grin off Alec's face. 'Tommy and Madge have followed Crawford to Cowley. When they telephone, Phillip will take over the pursuit.'

'Oh, right-ho. Er, who's Crawford?'

Binkie had somehow been missed out of the general enlightenment. While Phillip, unmoved by doubt, explained that Crawford was the confounded ugly customer who had grabbed his girl, Daisy turned to Lucy.

'I don't think Phillip should go alone,' she said in an

undertone. 'The poor chump's bound to do something silly. Binkie had better go with him.'

'Binkie will never stop him. Besides, a mixed couple will look less suspicious than two men, don't you think? I'll go, unless you want to?'

'No!' Alec swallowed a mouthful. 'Daisy's still rocky from last night. I'd take it as a favour if you'd go, Miss . . . Lucy.'

'I'm perfectly all right,' Daisy insisted. Battling the infuriating blush she felt rising in her cheeks, she went on, 'But actually, if you don't mind going, Lucy, I'd rather like to take Alec to meet Mother later on. Unless there's something else you need to do, Alec?'

'Unfortunately, I can't think of a thing.' It was his turn to flush. 'Unfortunately for Miss Arbuckle's sake,' he said hastily. 'I'm looking forward to meeting Lady Dalrymple.'

Lucy laughed. 'Daisy's mother doesn't actually bite,' she commiserated.

'No, but Geraldine jolly nearly does,' Daisy said guiltily. 'I'm afraid I had to tell her and Edgar that you're a detective – and that we're all here at your request to provide cover for your investigation.'

'Great Scott!' Alec groaned. 'You could at least have confessed that it's I who am embroiled in your affairs, not the reverse! Lord and Lady Dalrymple must think the police . . .'

'What's that?' Phillip demanded. 'The Dalrymples know you're police?'

'I told them, Phil.'

'Hang it all, Daisy, the more people know, the more risk for Gloria!'

'I had to say something. Geraldine was on the verge of

throwing us out after what she described as our "frolics" in the early hours of the morning.'

'They'd know who Alec is sooner or later,' Lucy said, 'and they'd have been fearfully offended to have been kept in the dark earlier.'

'Why the deuce should they ever know?'

'Because Edgar's Daisy's cousin,' Lucy explained patiently, with a sly look at Daisy, 'and when Alec joins the family they can hardly keep his profession secret.'

'Joins ... ? Oh! It's come to that has it?' Phillip looked faintly disapproving. Daisy scowled at him.

'Should have guessed, old man,' said Binkie. 'Invited Fletcher down to meet her mater and all that, what? Have to tell one's people first.'

'Actually,' Daisy fumed, suddenly unexpectedly near tears, 'nothing's settled. Alec hasn't even proposed and after the m-mess we've landed him in, perhaps he never will.'

Alec reached for her hand. 'This isn't quite how I'd envisaged it,' he said wryly, 'but I can't leave you in suspense, my love. This isn't the first mess you've landed me in, and somehow I doubt that it will be the last. Will you marry me?'

'Oh, Alec!' The tears flowed then. He enfolded her in his arms.

The others tactfully disappeared. As the door closed behind them, Daisy was distantly aware of Binkie's plaintive voice: 'But Lucy, I haven't had my breakfast!'

Madge telephoned. She and Tommy had followed Crawford all the way from the Abbey Hotel to the Morris factory.

Tommy was sitting in a perfectly ghastly cafe opposite the works, drinking simply poisonous coffee and keeping an eye on the maroon two-seater, while she reported in. What next?

'I advised her to try the tea,' Alec told Daisy and Lucy, 'to follow if he leaves, and otherwise to hang on until relieved. Bincombe and Petrie should be back soon.'

Phillip and Binkie came in a few minutes later.

'We tried three garages,' Phillip announced. 'The nearest to the kidnap spot's a mile and a half away, and the others four or five miles. They all swore they'd never been asked by an American to go searching the lanes for a Studebaker.'

'Not the sort of thing they'd forget, eh, what?' said Binkie.

'I hardly think so,' Alec agreed. 'I can't see how even Arbuckle will be able to doubt now that Crawford's our man.'

CHAPTER 17

'I've just remembered,' Daisy said in dismay. 'Crawford's met Phillip. What if he recognizes him?'

'Not likely.' Lucy adjusted the cloche to a jaunty angle on her smooth, dark head. 'I won't let Phil get too close, and I'll see he keeps his hat on. With the Alvis's hood up he'll be practically invisible.'

'Having the hood up will look suspicious.'

'Hardly, darling, when it's drizzling.'

'Oh, is it?' Daisy looked out of Lucy's bedroom window. A light but steady rain was falling. Odd, for the past couple of hours she'd have sworn the sun shone. 'That's lucky. Phillip really needs something to keep him busy.'

With quick, expert fingers, Lucy touched up her makeup. A last dab of powder on the nose and they went downstairs. The men were waiting in the front hall, Phillip twitching with impatience.

Alec smiled at Daisy but addressed Lucy. 'I've asked Petrie to ring up at once if Mr. and Mrs. Pearson are gone when you reach Cowley. They'll be following Crawford, so don't waste time trying to find out if he's still there. Bincombe will stay within reach of the 'phone.'

'Hold the fort, darling.' Lucy kissed Binkie's cheek, then turned and kissed Daisy. 'Good luck, darling. Cheerio. All right, Phillip, you can stop fidgeting. Let's go.'

Alec gave Binkie a few last-minute instructions about what to do in various contingencies. 'Don't telephone the Dower House unless you absolutely have to,' he finished.

Binkie grinned and nodded. 'Right-oh. Best of luck, old man.'

'Anyone would think Mother was an ogre,' Daisy said crossly as she and Alec went out under a shared umbrella to the Austin, brought round from the stable-yard by Bill Truscott. Everyone's good wishes had the perverse effect of making her more nervous than she already was. 'She may be a bit difficult at times, but I've seen you cope with much worse.'

'And cope I shall,' he soothed her, opening the passenger door. She was grateful for his forbearance in not pointing out that she had never seen him dealing with a prospective mother-in-law.

He went round, got in beside her, and saying, 'First things first,' he kissed her.

'First things' thoroughly accomplished, Daisy settled back in her seat with a satisfied sigh as Alec pressed the self-starter, engaged the gear, let off the brake, and started down the avenue.

'When we're married,' she said, just for the sake of saying the words, 'will you teach me to drive?'

'I'm not sure its a good idea for husbands to teach wives.'

'Binkie taught Lucy.'

'They're not married. We'd better not wait for the wedding. Daisy, are you quite sure your mother really invited me to lunch?'

Daisy melted at the evidence that he was nervous too. 'Of course,' she assured him. 'When I rang up to see if it was convenient for us to pop in today, she actually offered of her own accord.'

'She wants to vet my table manners,' he said with conviction, adding ruefully, 'Fairacres is rather larger and more impressive than I'd expected.'

'There's nothing wrong with your table manners, dearest. Fairacres is a bit different from the house in Chelsea, isn't it? I dare say that's why it came as a shock.'

'What I don't understand is how you came to be penniless when your father owned so much. The house and land are entailed on the male heir, of course, but still . . .'

'It's because of Gervaise dying in the War. Father had always assumed he'd take care of me, you see, until I married or if I didn't marry. When he was killed, Father was too heartbroken to think about changing his will, and then he died in the 'flu epidemic before he got around to it.'

'I know how it took people by surprise,' Alec said softly. 'Joan left things undone. Dear love, you mustn't mind if I speak of Joan now and then. I love you differently, but just as much.'

'I don't mind. I know Belinda will need to talk about her mother. Alec, I have to tell you about . . .' She stopped as the car turned into the Dower House's short drive. 'Oh, bother, here we are. It will have to wait.'

He put on the brake and turned to her, his grey eyes serious. 'I hope you will always feel able to tell me absolutely anything.'

She squeezed his hand. 'Oh, Alec, I do love you. No, don't kiss me. Mother wouldn't do anything so vulgar as peer through the window, but she might just happen to be standing by it. Alec, when Edgar inherited Fairacres, he offered me a home, and when I refused he offered to settle some money on me. I refused that, too, but I'll tell him I've changed my mind if you want me to.'

'Great Scott, no! I shall expect you to help support the family by writing, not by cadging off your relatives.'

Laughing from sheer lightness of heart, Daisy waved gaily to the gardener, who was pulling the crop of weeds already springing up after the rain.

'You remember Owen Morgan, from Occles Hall?' she asked Alec. 'If we need another man to help rescue Gloria, I'm sure he'd do it.'

'Not another one who finds an appeal from you irresistible?' Alec said indulgently. 'Whatever it is in those guileless blue eyes that persuades people to jump through hoops for you, I hope you'll try it on your mother.'

'Mother's proof against it,' Daisy said with regret.

The Dowager Lady Dalrymple acknowledged her daughter's introduction of the undistinguished stranger with a haughty nod and a cool 'How do you do.' But Daisy saw her eyes widen.

Fearing a penniless intellectual, a wealthy upstart, or even, heaven forbid, a foreigner, her ladyship obviously didn't know what to make of Alec. He was neither scruffy nor over-smartly dressed; his voice, while not Eton-and-Oxford, was accentless; he was, in fine, the very picture of a perfectly respectable gentleman.

Unfortunately, where a prospective son-in-law was concerned, respectability was a damning word. Lady Dalrymple had set her heart on nobility, or, at worst, the upper ranks of the landed gentry.

'Sherry, Mr. Fletcher,' offered her ladyship stiffly, 'or do you prefer one of these modern cocktails? Cook has some gin, I believe.'

'Sherry, please, Lady Dalrymple,' Alec said, and bit his lip. Catching his eye, Daisy was relieved to see he was biting back amusement, not chagrin.

'Alec prefers medium dry, like me, Mother,' she said. 'Shall I pour? Sweet for you?'

'Thank you, dear. You are staying at the Wedge and Beetle, I understand, Mr. Fletcher. I trust you find it comfortable?'

'As a matter of fact, I haven't tried it yet. I spent last night at Fairacres.'

'Indeed! Of course, Edgar and Geraldine have not yet quite found their feet in their new position.' The dowager's tone said clearly that she doubted they ever would, as evidenced by their inviting someone like Alec to stay.

Her mastery of the veiled insult had to be admired, but Daisy wasn't going to let her bully Alec. Not that he was exactly bullyable. He still looked amused, she noted, handing him his glass.

'Edgar and Geraldine seem to have settled in very nicely,' she said brightly.

Her mother sniffed, but she was not to be deflected from her primary target. Sitting down, and inviting Alec to do likewise, she said, 'Who are your people, Mr. Fletcher? I don't believe I'm acquainted with anyone of that name.'

'My earliest ancestors of whom we have any record,' Alec expounded, 'were medieval arrow-makers and bowmen.

By the sixteenth century, the family took a literary turn. I regret to say we cannot claim John Fletcher, of Beaumont and Fletcher fame, but you have heard, perhaps, of Giles Fletcher the Elder? No? He was a poet and author of a book on Russia, and he passed on his gifts to his sons, Giles the Younger and Phineas, both noted poets and churchmen in their time. Giles's sermons were much admired, and Phineas's poems attacking the Jesuits were very well received, though for my part I prefer his delightful descriptions of rural scenery.'

Daisy felt almost as dazed as her mother looked. Continuing, Alec managed to appear to take pity on them.

'I shan't bore you with the next few centuries,' he said with a sweeping gesture which seemed to unjustly exclude swarms of distinguished forebears. 'My father had no literary aspirations. His vocation lay in the world of finance.'

Mr. Fletcher the Elder had been the manager of a North London branch of the Westminster Bank, Daisy knew. Her suspicious glance at Alec was answered with the suspicion of a wink.

Thinking back over what he had said, she realized the record of his early ancestors could well be no more than the name itself. Nor had he actually claimed to be descended from the poetical Fletchers. Oh, the tortuous mind of a detective!

'Finance?' The dowager was at least slightly impressed. 'You have followed in your father's footsteps?'

'No, I decided to dedicate my modest talents to the protection of society.'

'The Army?' Lady Dalrymple asked eagerly. The Army was a perfectly acceptable profession.

'The police,' Alec said blandly.

'Good gracious!' Aghast, Lady Dalrymple stared at him, apparently trying to picture him in a blue helmet, swinging a truncheon. 'I must say, I'd never have guessed,' she admitted in a weak voice, looking daggers at Daisy.

'He's quite presentable for a bobby, isn't he?' Having thrown this provocation into the ring, Daisy decided her mother was ripe for the dénouement. 'As a matter of fact, Alec is a Detective Chief Inspector at Scotland Yard.'

'Oh, *plain*-clothes!' The elimination of the awful prospect of a son-in-law in police uniform mollified her, just as Daisy had hoped. In comparison, a high-ranking detective was endurable. '*Chief* Inspector? Your father was on very good terms with the Chief Constable, Daisy. Colonel Sir Nigel Wookleigh, a charming man. Perhaps you know him, Mr. Fletcher?'

'Not yet, Lady Dalrymple, but I have every expectation of making his acquaintance very shortly.'

Since he didn't mention that he was going to have to explain to the Worcestershire C.C. why he had been operating on his patch without permission, the dowager was pleased. At least her daughter's friend moved in the proper circles. The rest of the visit took place in an atmosphere of astonishing cordiality.

Daisy didn't go so far as to announce that she was engaged to Alec. It was better if Mother believed her approval had been sought in advance. They would break the news before returning to town on Sunday.

If they returned on Sunday! Daisy's mind, otherwise occupied, had lost sight of the kidnapping and Gloria

Arbuckle's plight. Remembering, she was anxious to get back to Fairacres, though Binkie would have telephoned if anything urgent had come up. She extricated Alec from her mother's laments over the parlous state of the world and left her grumbling about the shortness of their visit.

'We could have stayed a little longer,' Alec protested mildly as they drove off. 'It seems a pity to have upset her when we were getting along swimmingly.'

'You did charm her, darling! But in just another few minutes she'd have found cause for complaint in our staying too long. I'd rather she had too little of us than too much. Besides, I'm simply dying to find out whether Phillip and Lucy have picked up Crawford's trail.'

Phillip peered through the rain-smeared windscreen at the dingy building: ERT'S CAFE said the sign painted on the steamed-up windows.

'Surely this can't be the place?' he said uncertainly.

Lucy sighed. 'I'm afraid it must be, old thing. It's right opposite the factory entrance, it only needs a "B" to make it "Bert's," and it looks as if it serves poisonous coffee. And there's the Lagonda, down that alley. Bite the bullet, hold your nose, let's go.'

Jamming his hat down further on his forehead, Phillip stepped out into the drizzle. In the forecourt of the Morris factory, behind the wire fence, he saw a maroon A.C. Six.

He ducked his head back into the Alvis. 'Crawford's still here,' he hissed.

Lucy stopped powdering her nose for long enough to say,

'I should jolly well hope so, or Madge and Tommy really botched it.'

Opening his umbrella, Phillip went round the pointed, 'duck's back' rear of the polished aluminium two-seater and opened the door for her. In her smart, high-heeled strap shoes Lucy perched on the running board, gazing down with dismay at the muddy puddles between her and the café.

'Perhaps I'll just wait here.'

'He may stay for hours yet. Do come along.'

She sighed again, cautiously stepped down, and picked her way to the door. As Phillip opened it, a hot, moist blast of air saturated with stale grease and cigarette smoke hit them.

'Faugh! Hours, you said? I shan't survive five minutes.'

Phillip ignored her moaning. 'There are Tommy and Madge,' he said as every head in the room turned towards them. There were few customers at this time, shortly before the lunch hour. He led the way, squeezing between the close-packed, oil-clothed tables, each with its bottle of HP Sauce, to where the Pearsons sat by the window.

'Thank heaven you've come,' said Tommy, standing up. 'Madge is feeling sick.'

'Poor darling, I'm not in the least surprised,' Lucy commiserated. 'You could cut the atmosphere in here with a knife.'

'How can you make such a fuss,' Phillip burst out angrily, 'when Gloria's in danger?'

'Here, I say, old boy,' Tommy protested. 'Steady! We're all doing everything we can to help.'

'Sorry.' Staring down miserably at the grubby table-cloth, Phillip wished he had never fallen in love. His calm, ordered world, its extremes of emotion the boredom of the office and the pleasure of working on the Swift, had vanished. The joy of knowing Gloria and the hope of winning her had turned into this awful emptiness of dread.

He didn't think he could cope with it much longer.

Madge took his hand in both hers. 'It's all right, Phillip,' she said gently. 'You must feel as I did when Tommy first went to France; you haven't had time to grow numb. Just remember we're with you through thick and thin. You mustn't mind what Lucy says. It's just her way.'

'That's right, darling,' Lucy drawled. 'Tommy, you'd better get Madge out into the fresh air quickly. She's turning green. You might move the Alvis round the corner for us, if you don't mind. It's rather conspicuous and I'd prefer not to be left alone in this frightful place.'

The Pearsons hurried out. Lucy sat down beside the window and, with her handkerchief, retouched the clear circle Madge had wiped in the condensation. Taking the opposite seat, Phillip did likewise.

'The A.C.'s still there,' he said with relief.

'That red car inside the fence? Lucky it's that colour. I'll be able to spot it quite easily when we get going.'

'Yes. Look here, Lucy, I'm sorry I blew up.'

'Not another word on the subject. Are you going to buy me tea? Blast, I forgot to ask Madge if it was any more drinkable than the coffee.'

To a request for a pot of China tea, the slatternly waitress responded that all they had was TyPhoo in the urn, milk and sugar already added. Lucy shuddered. They finally settled on a bottle of ginger-beer apiece.

Before long, mechanics from the works opposite streamed in for their midday meal. Phillip and Lucy garnered many a curious glance, but no one disturbed them. After the first rush, though, the waitress was not too busy to demand that they order something to eat if they insisted on taking up a table.

Lucy decided tinned tomato soup was the safest item on the menu. Phillip ventured upon sausage and mash, which he ate without tasting, his eyes glued to the clear spot on the glass.

The maroon motor-car continued to sit unmoving across the road. The workmen left, streaming back through the gate in the wire fence, past the A.C. Six, into the buildings. Lucy opened the copy of *The Queen* magazine she had brought with her and flipped idly through it. Time passed.

'Suppose he's gone out a back way,' Phillip said, beginning to despair. 'Suppose he's taken a Morris for a spin and he stops off to see his men.'

'Someone from the factory would go with him,' Lucy told him firmly, 'to make sure everything runs smoothly. Anyway, there's nothing we can do about it.'

The waitress reappeared. 'Was you wanting anythin' else? 'Cause I got to sweep the floor afore the next lot comes in,' she said in a disgruntled voice. Phillip saw she had already up-ended the chairs on most of the other tables. 'You been here going on four hours.'

'No wonder I'm stiff.' Lucy stretched. 'I'll have another ginger-beer and some plain biscuits, please, Rich Tea or Marie.'

'Same for me,' said Phillip, massaging the crick in his neck as he turned back to his peephole.

'Let's switch seats so you can bend your head the other way,' Lucy suggested.

'Good idea.' As Phillip sat down on her chair he wiped the window. Applying his eye, he saw two men standing beside the A.C. Six.

He jumped up. 'Come on! He's leaving at last.'

'At last!' Lucy closed the magazine and stood up.

'Hoy!' exclaimed the waitress. 'You going? What about this stuff you ordered?'

'Never mind that,' Phillip cried.

'We'll take it,' Lucy contradicted him. 'Who knows when we'll get another chance to eat?' She stuffed the biscuits into her handbag.

Phillip tossed a form on the table, grabbed the bottles and his umbrella, and ran through the forest of chair-legs to the door. He opened it and held it for Lucy, gentlemanly instinct prevailing, but he beat her to the Alvis although she quickly abandoned her attempt to preserve her shoes from puddles. By the time she wrenched open the door and jumped in, he had the engine started, the hand-brake off, and first gear engaged.

She slammed the door. 'Creep forward till we can see around the corner,' she advised.

Instinct now shrieking at him to move fast, he had to acknowledge the common sense of her suggestion. Slowly letting out the clutch, he inched forward.

'Stop!' said Lucy. 'Damn, if you go any farther the bonnet will stick out and I still can't see the gate. Can you?'

He craned his neck. 'Not quite.'

She groaned. 'All right, I'll get out and stand on the corner. Where's the umbrella?'

'Here. Leave the door open.'

Lucy had barely peeked around the building when she

ducked back. 'He's coming this way,' she said breathlessly, closing the umbrella and hopping in.

'Back into Oxford. Dash it, I hope he's not going to stop in the town.'

'Gosh, yes. We could easily lose him there.'

But Crawford drove steadily through the town centre, turning north at Carfax, then branching left on the Woodstock Road.

'At least he's not heading for the Midlands,' Phillip observed with relief. 'This is the way home via Chipping Norton and Evesham. Oh Lord, do you think he's just going to drive straight back to Malvern?'

'I haven't the foggiest. We'll see, if you don't get too close so you have to overtake or look suspicious.'

Phillip eased up on the accelerator.

Through the village of Woodstock, past the gates of Blenheim Palace; up the long slope into the Cotswolds: then Chipping Norton, Moreton-in-Marsh, Bourton-on-the-Hill – Phillip's spirits sank lower with every mile they followed the maroon motor-car.

'He's not going to stop.'

'We're only half-way. Phillip!' Lucy clutched his arm. 'He's turning off! No, don't slow down, drive on past. He might glance back'.

Reluctantly, Phillip obeyed. Crawford had turned into a narrow, unpaved lane, its entrance half obscured by hedges and overhanging trees on either side. The A.C. Six was already out of sight. Phillip stepped on the brake and put the Alvis into reverse. Lucy closed her eyes, crossing her fingers as he backed along the main road.

A Napier swerved around the Alvis; its chauffeur shook his fist.

Just past the lane, Phillip stopped again and engaged forward gear. They plunged into the green tunnel beneath the trees.

CHAPTER 18

The Alvis squelched, sloshed, and jolted along muddy ruts with grass growing in between. Phillip hoped the suspension was up to it. He wouldn't have chosen to drive his Swift this way.

He remembered sadly that he might never see the Swift again.

They emerged from the tree-tunnel and started uphill. The drainage was better though the potholes were just as bad. The hedges gave way to high banks topped with drystone walls. An occasional gateway showed steep hillsides of short-cropped pasture, where fleeing sheep added to Phillip's impression of the rarity of motor-vehicles.

'No side turnings,' Lucy observed.

'Thank heaven.'

'And I think the rain's stopping.'

The bank on their right ended. Now they could see the sheep-dotted slope rising beyond the low wall. The few trees were scattered, twisted thorns or clumps of oaks in the hollows of the hills.

'There, I saw his hood,' Lucy exclaimed in triumph. 'He's not far ahead, just around a bend or two. Slow down.'

Phillip caught a glimpse of something moving less than a quarter of a mile ahead, before a particularly vicious pot-hole made him clutch the steering wheel. He returned his attention to his driving. If they had a puncture or broke a spring, they would lose Crawford for good.

A moment later Lucy leaned forward and peered round Phillip. 'There's what looks like a farm track up to the right,' she said. 'A pale streak winding back round behind the hill. I don't think it's the lane. Gosh, he's turned up it. Phillip, stop! If I can see him, he can see us. Go back a bit.'

'Are you sure it's not the lane?' Phillip asked in an agony of doubt even as he braked.

'Pretty sure. I can see what I think is the lane curving round to the left between the hills. See, over there. There's a double line of walls. It must be this lane. Go back, he'll see us!'

'No, with no sun shining to reflect off the glass we'll be less likely to catch his eye if we're not moving, and we can watch him, too. Where . . . ? Oh yes.'

The maroon A.C. crept up the track, crossing the slope at an angle. As the car disappeared around the hillside, Phillip started the Alvis forward again.

Around a couple of bends, they came to a gate. As Phillip slowed, Lucy said, 'That's it. Look, you can see the tyre-marks in the mud, and there's the beginning of the track. No!' she exclaimed as he turned the wheel. 'We can't follow him up there. He'd be bound to see us, or even meet us face to face. It looks to me as if the track circles the summit.'

Something tugged at Phillip's memory. Frowning, he got out of the car and went to lean against the gate, staring up at the crest of the hill. An odd shape, as if a handleless frying pan had been set down upside-down on top, it was vaguely familiar.

He turned back to Lucy. 'I have to go and look. Crawford's got to have Gloria hidden up there, somehow. Why else should he go up?'

'There's something fishy up there all right, but you can't drive up and you can't leave the car here for him to find. You're not planning anything asinine, are you, Phillip? Trying to rescue Gloria single-handed will just mean two people for the rest of us to rescue.'

Flushing at the accuracy of her guess, he returned to the driver's seat. 'What shall we do, then?' he asked a bit sulkily.

'Drive on until we find somewhere to hide the car, behind a wall or something. Then you can go off and reconnoitre. At least you had the sense to wear walking boots.' She glanced down ruefully at her muddy footwear. 'I can't go slogging cross-country in these, though they're already ruined.'

'I'm sure Mr. Arbuckle will pay for a new pair,' Phillip consoled her, driving on.

The lane continued to rise for a few hundred yards, curving to the left between a shoulder of the odd-shaped hill and a lower ridge to their left. Then it abruptly swung right and began to descend. Still nowhere to conceal the Alvis. Phillip was starting to fret when Lucy cried, 'Oh, perfect!'

'By Jove, a quarry!'

The flat floor of the abandoned slate-pit was level with the road and thickly overgrown. Phillip pulled over among the trees and bushes.

Lucy took out her vanity-case and powdered her nose.

Between the trees, the ground was stony. Getting out, Phillip saw that the Alvis had left no tracks. He strode back to the lane and turned. The car was invisible.

Returning a few paces, he called to Lucy, 'I'm off. Give me a couple of hours, and if I'm not back you'd better go and tell the others.'

'For pity's sake, don't do anything idiotic,' she responded. 'Don't let them see you.'

Phillip did not deign to retort. For one thing, he knew Lucy could easily squash him in a contest of words. For another, he was in far too much of a hurry. Somewhere on that hill his girl was being held against her will.

His long legs took him at a fast lope up the lane until he had a clear view of the hilltop. Then he clambered over the wall and set off across the short grass.

In spite of his resentment, he was mindful of Lucy's parting injunction. The men probably had a look-out, but he was pretty sure there weren't enough of them to watch in all directions and the chances were they kept an eye on the track Crawford had used. As Londoners, they might well discount the likelihood of anyone approaching cross-country. So Phillip, despite his impatience, headed around the hill.

From every angle, the summit had the same peculiar, truncated appearance. Now Phillip knew where he was. That was Brockberrow Hill, once a favourite place to bicycle for a day's outing.

The excrescence on top was the remains of an Iron Age fort, unless it was Stone Age or Bronze Age or something. The Picts, or Early Britons, or whatever, had chosen a good viewpoint for their fortifications. From the top of the circular mound one could see forever. Inside, one was sheltered from the wind. There was even a ruined shepherd's hut for refuge from showers.

That, of course, was where they had Gloria. How Crawford had ever found the place was a mystery, but Phillip would bet his bottom dollar on it.

He cast his mind back to the old days. The bicyclers – he and Gervaise and various friends and siblings – had always left their cycles at Brock Farm, on the far side of the hill from the track. Buying picnic supplies from the farmer's wife, they used to walk up a footpath to the top.

It had not been much of a footpath, more of a sheep trail. The kidnappers could easily overlook it, or discount its significance, especially as trees hid the farm buildings from the top.

Quite a few stunted hawthorns grew on the upper slopes on that side, Phillip recalled. There were criss-crossing drystone walls, too, dividing pastures and sheep-pens, all good cover for a clandestine approach. And, come to think of it, a clump of thorn trees – more bushes, really – had taken root on the shallower inner side of the fortification mound. If they had survived the years, he could wriggle in amongst them to watch and listen in perfect safety.

Perfect safety, he assured himself, dismissing the faint echo in his mind of Lucy's warning.

Climbing a wall, he saw down to his left the tall beeches around Brock Farm. Ahead was the slope – sheepless at present – scattered with hawthorns, just as he had pictured it. From the shelter of the nearest he scanned the hilltop, wishing he had brought binoculars.

No head protruded above the level brow of the mound; no sign of movement; no sound but the cawing of rooks in the valley behind him, the trill of a lark above, and an occasional far-off *baa*. All the same, Phillip avoided the path itself when he found it, and took full advantage of the cover of trees and walls as he made his way up the gentle slope.

Before tackling the last, bare stretch up to the track encircling the base of the ancient fortification, he paused for another survey. Nothing had changed.

He set off again at a jog-trot.

Pity it had stopped raining. Not only did rain obscure the vision, the discomfort distracted sentries' attention from their business – one of the lessons learnt in Flanders which Phillip had never expected to think of again. He wouldn't be surprised if it was raining again before nightfall, though. Here on the exposed upper slopes, a gusty wind was blowing, warm and damp, from the south-west.

Dashing across the track, he tried to remember the layout inside the fort. The one-time gateway, now just a narrow gap, was round to his left, he thought, a quarter circle from the head of the track, perhaps for some obscure, prehistoric defensive purpose. The thorn bushes, fortunately, were slightly to his right. He hoped.

He scrambled diagonally up the steep bank. Lying prone on the damp grass, his elbow in a patch of scarlet and yellow ladies' slipper, he took off his hat and raised his bare head inch by inch.

No outcry greeted the appearance of his hair on the horizon. He moved up a little farther and found he had perfectly judged his position. The hawthorn thicket hid him from those below. They hid the men from him, too, but he heard their voices.

Listening, he slithered over the top and under the spiky branches.

'. . . don't fink we're gonna let yer pick up the bunce on yer own and scarper back to the States wiv it, do yer? Not bloody likely!'

'Come off it, would I vamoose and leave you guys holding the baby?' Crawford's voice was not so much oily as slimy, Phillip decided with loathing. His chuckle was still more repulsive. 'Still and all, by golly, she's a baby worth holding, which is one reason I won't skedaddle with the dough. I'll be back to . . .'

Phillip missed his next words. Seeing red, he forgot his good resolutions and rose to his knees, prepared to rush down and strangle the bounder whatever the consequences.

A thorn raking down his cheek brought him to his senses. Joining Gloria would not help her. With a silent groan he moved a little further down the slope to where he could see the men and glare his hatred at their oblivious heads.

Crawford and three others stood in a group to the left of the one-room, tumbledown stone shepherd's hut, between it and the gateway.

'Blimey, guv, we don't none of us hold wiv none of that!' one of the men was protesting. Phillip recognized his anxious tone. 'You swore . . .'

Crawford cut him off with an unconvincing laugh. 'That's so. I guess I must have gotten a bit carried away. Oh, well, that's all right. Now, how can I convince you I don't plan to make a get-away without you?'

'Two of us goes wiv yer, or yer can 'and over yer passport, mate, that's what,' the biggest man said menacingly.

In the momentary silence Phillip noticed, beyond them, an Army tent pitched against the bank. At least Gloria did not have to suffer their company all the time, he thought with gladness.

Of course, though it seemed an age since Daisy staggered into the drawing-room at Fairacres, Gloria had only been here since the middle of last night. Phillip vowed that she should never spend an entire night in the hut. He must get back to Lucy and organize the rescue party.

But he didn't dare leave until Crawford had driven off. Besides, he might hear something useful, might even catch a glimpse of Gloria. He checked his wrist-watch: still time enough before Lucy started worrying.

'My passport?' Crawford said uneasily, his hand moving to cover his breast pocket.

''Sright, mate. Long as you're stuck in England, we've gotcha by the short 'airs.'

'Reckon we oughta 'ave one or two of us watching the pickup, too,' said another. ''Case anyfing goes wrong, they can get back 'ere and warn the others.'

'Rats, nothing's going to go wrong.' Crawford sounded distinctly irritable now. 'These plutocrats have nerves of steel when it comes to playing the market, but hit 'em with something like this, and by golly, they crumble faster than a stale cookie. I've jollied Arbuckle along and he's fallen for it, no if, and, or but about it. You should see him. He's in a dandy funk! The old coot hasn't gone within a mile of a cop.'

The men continued to wrangle over collecting the

ransom, then, without a decision, moved on to complaints about their quarters. Crawford told them it was their own fault they had to leave the gamekeeper's cottage. They were lucky he had found them a fall-back, pure curiosity having led him to investigate the significance of the word CAMP on a map.

'It won't be for long, anyhow,' he added. 'Tonight's the night.'

'Then 'and over that there passport!'

Tonight! Phillip glanced at his watch again. If he didn't hurry, Lucy would assume he'd been caught and leave without him. He couldn't wait for Crawford to clear out. He'd have to rely on hearing the A.C. Six start up to give him time to take cover.

Voices raised in a row over the passport allowed him to make a hasty withdrawal from the hawthorns without worrying about rustling leaves. Hat in hand, he crawled back over the crest of the mound and slid down the bank. Bounding down the hillside, he headed directly for the quarry.

Behind him a motor-car engine coughed to life. He raced for the nearest wall, dived over it, and lay flat.

A pair of inquisitive sheep turned their heads to stare, then ambled over to take a closer look. Phillip twitched as one nibbled hopefully at his hair.

'*Pa-aa-ah*!' it said in disgust, and started on the grass two inches from his nose.

Hearing the engine noise grow louder as the A.C. rounded the hilltop, he didn't dare raise a hand to push the beast away.

The sound of the engine retreated. Phillip rose to a crouch and peered over the wall. The maroon car was halfway down the track, heading away from him at an angle, but the driver's side was towards him. He must not move on yet.

He watched the A.C. Six reach the bottom. Crawford climbed out to open the gate, drove through, shut it again, and zipped off back towards the main road.

Phillip rose, sparing a regretful glance for the muddy, grass-stained knees of his flannels. Another pair of bags ruined! He set off at a steady run for the quarry.

The Alvis was gone.

He gazed around, hoping he'd come to the wrong spot, but no, there were the broken, wilting branches he had half noticed before. His watch showed he was five minutes late. Lucy might have given him a few minutes extra! She was on her way back to Fairacres to tell the others he had gone and done something idiotic. Fletcher would think the kidnappers knew they'd been found. What he'd decide to do, goodness only . . .

'Pssst! Phillip, is it all clear?'

'Lucy! Yes. What the deuce . . . ? Where's the Alvis?'

She emerged from the bushes, brushing her skirt vigorously. 'I moved it. There's a van hidden behind those branches and I was afraid someone might come for it.'

'A brown Ford van? With a butcher's name on it?'

'Green, unmarked. It could be a Ford for all I know.'

'Never mind, it must be the one because it's them all right. They'll have painted it, to disguise and camouflage it. I say, suppose I disable it, so they can't get away?'

'No, better not. If they try to go somewhere before we're ready, they'd be forewarned. Come on, we must get back to Fairacres. The Alvis is over here.'

Phillip took two steps after her and stopped. He had been torn from Gloria's side before. He found he simply could not bear to leave her voluntarily, even if she was not aware of his presence.

Across his mind flashed Crawford's description of her: 'a baby worth holding,' and his vow to return for her, ambiguously retracted.

'I'm staying,' Phillip announced. 'If something goes wrong, perhaps I'll be able to help Gloria.'

'Oh bosh!' Lucy turned, exasperated, hands on hips. 'If she's still all right now, nothing frightful's going to happen at least till they have the ransom.'

'That's tonight. What if Fletcher can't get things organized in time?'

'I'm sure he will. I'm coming to have considerable respect for Detective Chief Inspector Alec Fletcher. All the same, he's going to need all the men he can get, and if you go and get yourself caught before the rest arrive . . .'

'I shan't,' he said obstinately, 'unless I absolutely have to try to protect her. Crawford said . . .' His voice got tied in a knot in his throat. He tried again. 'They talked of harming her even after getting the money.'

'I see. But Phil, I'm not at all sure I'll be able to find the way here again. All these hills look alike to me.'

'Daisy knows it. Tell her they're at the ancient fort on Brockberrow Hill, where we used to picnic. Listen, you'd better tell Fletcher they don't trust Crawford so they may have more than one man fetching the ransom.'

'Where from?' she asked, tacitly agreeing to pass on the information, and thus to Phillip's staying.

'I don't know. They'll tell Arbuckle where and when to drop it off, and with luck he'll pass it on to Fletcher.'

'How many men are there?'

'I only saw three, but there was probably one watching the track, and maybe one in the hut with Gloria. Oh, there's a tent, too, besides the shepherd's hut. Don't want anyone falling over the guy-ropes.'

'Draw a diagram,' Lucy suggested.

Her fountain pen ran dry before he had done more than inscribe the broken circle of the mound in the margin of a page of *The Queen*. A search in his pockets produced a handkerchief, two pound notes, small change, a Scout knife, and a propelling pencil with no lead.

'Damn! I mean, dash it.'

'Damn, by all means.' Delving into her handbag again, she sighed. 'Lipstick. It'll be wrecked. Do you think Arbuckle will replace it, as well as my shoes?'

'Give him a list.' With the clumsy implement, Phillip drew the fort on top of an advertisement for a Charity Ball at the Royal Albert Hall. XT showed the position of the tent, XH of the hut, and a dotted line the beginning of the track. He studied his handiwork, dissatisfied. 'Oh well, Daisy knows it. The tent's pitched just round to the left from the gateway.'

'I still think you should come back with me, to tell them yourself.'

Phillip shook his head. 'I'm staying,' he said firmly, and strode off before she could confuse him with useless arguments.

Behind him the Alvis started up. It caught up with him and stopped as he climbed over the wall. Lucy beckoned.

'Here, you'd better take the biscuits and ginger-beer. Toodle-oo, old chap. Do take care!'

He watched the motor-car's duck's back rear disappear up the lane. As soon as it was out of sight, he dashed back towards the quarry. He'd be damned if he was going to let those swine make a clean get-away if he could help it.

His first notion was to remove the van's radiator hose, as an act of poetic justice. But if one of them left for some reason, he would discover the tampering as soon as the radiator boiled, which would be too soon to stop him warning the others. Whatever Phillip did must look like a natural occurrence, he thought as he reached the slate-pit.

No wonder Lucy had found the van. The conspicuous wilting leaves on the broken branches hiding it were another sign of the Londoners' lack of familiarity with the countryside. It was a Ford all right, its green paint spanking new but applied in a decidedly slapdash fashion.

Phillip tried the rear doors, finding them unlocked. There was no tyre pump to be seen, and the tool-box contained no patching kit – in London, of course, such things were readily available.

He let the air out of the spare tyre, then stabbed one front tyre with the corkscrew on his pocket-knife. Considering the state of the lane, a puncture should come as no surprise, and spares often went flat just sitting. They would have no reason to suspect sabotage.

Grinning, Phillip sang softly to himself as he returned to the lane: "'He had to get under, get out and get under, to fix his automobile!'"

A swirl of wind spattered his face with spots of rain as he climbed the wall again, jumped down into the meadow, and set off for his own private thorn-patch.

CHAPTER 19

'Mr. Arbuckle, my lady' The butler's air of long-suffering suggested he was becoming accustomed, if not resigned, to the American's habit of arriving at hours when no real gentleman would call uninvited.

'Show him in, Lowecroft,' said Geraldine, equally long-suffering. 'Edgar, we shall go up and dress for dinner. The rest of you . . .' She paused, and sighed. 'The rest of you and Mr. Petrie and Miss Fotheringay, should they condescend to return, will no doubt forgo that nicety if pressed for time. Daisy, you had better invite Mr. Arbuckle to dine with us.'

'Thank you, Geraldine. You see, he's . . .'

Geraldine held up her hand. 'No, I don't wish to know.'

Edgar looked rather wistful, as if he wouldn't have minded a little elucidation, but he followed his wife from the drawing-room, only pausing to greet Arbuckle as he came in.

'It's sure swell of your folks, Miss Dalrymple, not to shoot off their mouths about all this to-ing and fro-ing,' Arbuckle said. Waving a sheet of blue notepaper, he advanced on Alec. 'Mr. Fletcher, I've gotten the instructions for dropping off the dough. I found this in my suite at the hotel when I got back from Lunnon.'

Alec took it. 'Plain Basildon Bond, like the others, but this one is in ordinary handwriting, rather shaky.'

'Gloria's,' said Arbuckle heavily, dropping into a chair. 'At least she's still alive.'

Daisy, beside Alec on the sofa, craned her neck to read over his shoulder.

'Do tell,' Madge begged.

'It's directions to a quarry in the Cotswold Hills,' said Arbuckle. 'I'm to go alone, at sunset, and leave the dough in the back of a van I'll find parked there.'

'And then they'll let Miss Arbuckle go?' Tommy asked hopefully.

'It's more complicated than that.' Alec frowned. 'Mr. Arbuckle is instructed to go away as soon as he's dropped the money, then return at dawn to pick up directions explaining where to find his daughter. I don't like it.'

'If I do anything different, I'll never see Gloria again.'

'She says they'll be watching him,' Daisy put in.

Restlessly on edge, Arbuckle stood up again. 'So things have got to go their way. I'm doing what I'm told tonight, and I better get back to the hotel so if they're watching they see me leave from there.'

'Won't you stay for dinner? My cousin asked me to invite you.'

He shook his head. 'Please tell her ladyship I'd be tickled to death some other time, Miss Dalrymple, but I'm not fit for company right now, even if I could spare the time. Mr. Fletcher, I sure hope I can trust you not to call out the troopers.'

'Much as I'd like to, it's far too late to organize a police presence.'

'And you won't none of you go near this here quarry.' Arbuckle glanced around. 'Hey, where's young Petrie?'

Bincombe, silent so far, opened his mouth.

Alec gave him a warning look. 'Petrie and Miss Fotheringay went to keep an eye on Crawford. Since they haven't telephoned, we assume they haven't seen anything significant.'

'At this point, it don't matter a hoot if it's Crawford or some hoodlum. There's damn-all to do but follow instructions.'

'All the same,' said Alec, 'you'll telephone if they change your instructions, won't you? Or if you think of anything we can do to help?'

'Surely.' Arbuckle took back the letter and shook Alec's hand. 'Don't think I don't appreciate the support you folks been giving me.'

Daisy jumped up and gave him an impulsive hug. 'Gloria will be all right,' she said. 'This is England, not America.'

He gave her a weary smile. Alec walked with him to the door and closed it behind him.

'I say, Fletcher, what about Lucy?' Binkie burst out at once. 'It's all very well agreeing with Arbuckle, but they've been gone since before lunch. Are we just going to sit on our hands?'

'Steady, old man,' Tommy soothed. 'No sense getting the poor chap upset about Lucy as well as his daughter, don't y'know. And if I'm not mistaken, Fletcher's one step head of us.'

'I wish I were,' Alec said ruefully. 'There really isn't much we can do without more information. I don't imagine you know that bit of country, Daisy. It's rather far from here.'

'I don't know the quarry,' Daisy admitted unhappily. She had brought her friends into this thoroughly nasty business by claiming her knowledge of the countryside would help. A fat lot of use it had been so far. 'We used to cycle that way sometimes, but it's on the outer edge of our range. Oh, blast, I should have copied down the directions. I can't remember them properly.'

Alec promptly recited them.

'Map,' said Binkie, and disappeared.

He returned a few moments later and they were all poring over a map of the north Cotswolds when Lucy sauntered in.

'Don't let me interrupt,' she drawled.

Binkie bounded to her and engulfed her in a hug which made her squeak. 'Where have you been?' he demanded.

'Let me breathe, darling, and I'll tell you.' Released – though Binkie kept her hand in his – she joined the others and gazed down at the map. 'The Cotswolds? You already know?'

'Only where Mr. Arbuckle's to take the money,' said Daisy. 'Lucy, where's Phillip?'

'All in good time, darling. Now let me see. No, it's no good. I never could read a map. Phillip swore you'd remember the place, Daisy: Brockbarrow Hill.'

'Brock*berr*ow.'

'Here,' said Tommy, planting a forefinger on the map. 'It's right next to the slate-pit I'm sure must be the quarry.'

'At least half a mile,' Lucy protested, subsiding with languid grace onto the nearest chair and kicking off bespattered shoes. 'More to the top. Daisy, I'm simply ravenous. You're none of you dressed. Is dinner going to be late?'

'No. Lucy, for pity's sake, what's this about Brockberrow Hill? Did Phillip go there? Without you?'

'Let's hear the story, please, Lucy,' Alec seconded Daisy with a smile. 'If you've brought the information we need, time is of the essence.'

Lucy grinned at him. 'Oh, very well, Chief Inspector, though I was rather enjoying keeping you all in suspense. What it boils down to is that we followed Crawford from Cowley to Brockberrow Hill and Phillip found the kidnappers in some sort of ancient fort at the top.'

'And Miss Arbuckle?' Alec asked sharply.

'He didn't see her, but from the way they talked, he was sure she was there.'

'She'd be in the shepherd's hut,' Daisy said.

'That's right.' Lucy waved the magazine she had brought in with her. Opening it, she said in dismay, 'Oh gosh, it's frightfully smeared. I hope you remember the place well enough to make sense of this, Daisy.'

'Let's see.'

Both pages were a mess of lipstick, but between Daisy's memory and Lucy's and what they could make out, Daisy reconstructed Phillip's diagram.

'This is the fort itself,' she pointed out to the others as they clustered around. 'All that's left is a high bank, of course.'

'How high?' Tommy wanted to know.

'Gosh. I don't know. You couldn't see out from the inside, only sky, but then it's the highest point for quite a way.'

'Could you see the roof of the hut from outside?' Alec asked.

'N-no, I don't think so. No, I'm sure the bank's higher than the hut, so it's much higher than a man. Perhaps ten feet?' she hazarded. 'Twelve? Fourteen?'

'Good enough. How steep?'

'Steep enough to persuade one to go round and through the gateway – here – after bicycling from here and tramping up the hill. But we used to climb it after the picnic, for the view.'

'Phillip must have climbed it,' Lucy said, 'because he saw inside the circle and I hardly imagine he'd have trotted through the gap like a lamb to the slaughter.'

'You didn't go up with him?'

'You're joking, Alec. In those shoes? No, he came down to tell me what he'd found and overheard, then went back to keep an eye on Gloria.'

Alec groaned. 'Understandable, I suppose.'

'I tried to stop him. He did promise not to try any solo attempt to rescue her unless she was in immediate danger.'

'Which means, I take it,' said Madge, 'he expects a mass rescue attempt.'

Tommy nodded. 'If we don't go, goodness only knows what he'll do.'

'He heard them threaten to harm Gloria even if the ransom's delivered as instructed.'

In shocked silence, everyone turned from Lucy to Alec.

'We'll go,' he said crisply. 'I said I don't like this business of Arbuckle having to return to the quarry at dawn to get directions for finding his daughter. I meant it, and now we know Crawford's our man and that threats have been made, I like it still less. Lucy, what else did Petrie overhear?'

'He didn't tell me much. He saw three men besides Crawford, but he thought there were probably at least four. More than one man will go to pick up the ransom, because they don't trust each other. It's to be delivered tonight, but I gather you know that.'

'At the quarry at sunset,' Alec confirmed. 'When does the sun set?'

'Nine thirtyish,' Tommy said, 'with Summer Time.'

They all looked at the clock. Quarter to eight.

'It'll take an hour to get there,' Lucy said uneasily. 'Maybe more if this rain gets any worse. The lane's in a frightful condition, and then there's the hill to climb. Phillip said there's probably a man watching the track, so you'd have to go round. That's assuming you're heading for the hilltop, not the quarry.'

Alec thought for a moment. 'If they have hidden men watching the drop-off, it's too risky to try to grab Crawford there, besides leaving Miss Arbuckle in danger from the others.'

'Start from this side of the hill,' Daisy advised. 'Take the path from Brock Farm. That's the way we always used to go. It could cut off ten or fifteen minutes.'

'All right, Daisy,' said Alec, 'I'll take your word for it. You can explain later. First, does Morgan live in at the Dower House?'

'Yes. I'll go and telephone. Do you want Truscott, too? If he's not up here I can get him on the extension to the lodge.'

'Please. Pearson, find that young footman, Ernest.'

'Was you wanting me, sir?' Ernest advanced eagerly, tray in hand. 'Her ladyship said to bring sherry.'

Daisy hurried out, leaving Alec to recruit the footman and deal with the question of sherry.

In the hall she met Lowecroft, coming from the direction of the family sitting room, where Edgar and Geraldine must have taken refuge.

Will Mr. Arbuckle be dining, miss?' he asked, obviously

put out. 'And do you expect Mr. Petrie to return in time for dinner?'

'No, and no, and I should think Mrs. Pearson and Miss Fotheringay will be the only ones joining my cousins. If you could organize sandwiches for eight in a big hurry – say ten minutes? – it would be much appreciated. Oh, and we'll be taking Ernest with us, I'm afraid.'

She dashed on to the 'phone, leaving the butler with his mouth opening and closing like a goldfish.

Truscott promised to be ready to be picked up at the lodge in fifteen minutes, and Morgan would wait at the Dower House gates. Daisy sped up to her bedroom and flung on a warm tweed skirt and jacket and walking shoes. Alec was bound to try to stop her going along. After all her efforts she was determined to see the thing through, and Gloria would surely be glad to see a female face. Daisy refused to be left behind because they would not wait while she changed.

She had other cards up her sleeve.

Grabbing her mac, she headed for the drawing-room. She entered on the heels of Ernest, whose arms were full of electric torches.

He glanced back at her with a grin. 'Sandwiches coming up, Mr. Lowecroft says, miss. I never seen him in such a pother.' He laid the torches on a table.

'Thanks, Ernest,' said Alec. 'Go put on your oldest clothes and stout boots now. Hurry.'

'Yessir!'

'You two bring the Lagonda and my Austin round to the front, please,' he directed Tom and Binkie, who strode out. They had already changed, as had Alec. 'Daisy, come and show me ...' He stopped as he noticed her costume. His fearsome eyebrows lowered. 'Oh no, you're not coming with us!'

'I can't show you on the map. It's too complicated. I'm not even sure I remember the way to Brock Farm well enough to describe it, but I know I'll recognize it when I see it.'

Alec turned on her the piercing grey eyes which made crooks quiver and subordinates leap to attention. Daisy was glad she was telling the truth. Nonetheless, she brought out another ace.

'Even if you found Brock Farm without me,' she said persuasively, 'the farmyard's the only place to leave the cars and the people there don't know you. They'll remember me. Besides, you'd never find the path without help. It's easy to get lost in the wood before you get to the hillside.'

'Oh no, if you come as far as the farm, you go no further. Someone there will show us the way.'

'How long would it take to explain the situation to them?'

Alec glanced at the clock and grimaced.

Ten minutes later, Daisy sat in the front passenger seat of the Austin as Alec drove down the avenue. The little car shuddered as wild gusts of wind hit it. Though dark, ragged clouds raced overhead against the paler grey overcast, the rain had stopped for the moment.

The Lagonda was close behind, Tom driving, Binkie next to him, Ernest in the back. At the lodge, Truscott stood at the door with another man, older grizzled, but still robust.

'Carlin,' said Daisy. 'Father's gamekeeper.'

The chauffeur stepped up to the Austin. 'Mr. Carlin dropped by for a chat, sir, and wants to know can he go too?'

'The more the merrier. You two join the Lagonda – the extra weight won't slow it. We'll take Morgan.'

They picked up the gardener at the Dower House gates and drove on. Daisy fed sandwiches to Alec as they continued through Pershore and Evesham and up the flank of the Cotswolds to Broadway.

'Turn right at the church,' she said as they entered the village, its amber stone drab dun in the gloom of the early twilight beneath the clouds.

'Off the main road already?'

'There might be a quicker way turning off further on, but I don't know it. We'd only get lost.'

'You're in charge. Morgan, the Lagonda's still there?'

'Chust behind us it iss, sir.'

Alec stuck out his hand and turned. They plunged into a labyrinth of serpentine lanes. For a while Daisy was frightfully afraid she had bitten off more than she could chew, but as crossroads and forks fell behind them, she grew more confident.

'Sharp left at the end of this hamlet,' she said as they came to a huddle of cottages, 'and then the first right. There used to be a finger-post ... Yes, there it is! "Brock Farm Only."'

'Well done! I can see why you couldn't have explained the route.'

The farmhouse and its outbuildings stood close to the edge of the wood where dwelt the badgers which had given the farm its name. The moment the Austin pulled up next to the barn, Daisy jumped out and ran to the house. Barking dogs announced her before she knocked.

A hefty young man came to the door. Daisy didn't recognize him, but he knew her at once in spite of the years and the shingled hair.

'Why, it's Miss Daisy! Mother, Dad,' he called, 'it's Miss Daisy.'

'Good gracious, you can't be little Charlie?'

He grinned. 'That's me, miss, and not so little no more, neither. Step in, do.'

'Not just now, if you don't mind. Good-evening, Mrs. Clay, Mr. Clay,' Daisy said to the couple who came up behind Charlie. 'I've brought my fiancé and some friends to see the old camp. We're running late and it'll be dark soon. May we leave the cars in the yard and cut through your wood?'

'O' course, Miss Daisy,' said the farmer's wife. 'You just hurry along afore the rain come down again, and stop in for a glass o' cider on the way back, if ye've time enough.'

'Spiffing,' said Daisy.

With a wave, she dashed off, but not before she heard Mr. Clay observe sagely, 'They'm all barmy as new beer, the gentry.'

An ominous splatter of rain struck Daisy's face. Shivering, she turned her mind at last to their real errand. If the farmer knew they were out not for a jaunt but to tackle a vicious gang of kidnappers, would he think them less barmy – or more?

CHAPTER 20

'All right,' said Alec, coming to a halt at the edge of the dank, dark wood, 'show us the way through and set us on the right path up the hill, then come back to your friends at the farm.'

Brock Wood was very different from Cooper's Wood. The beeches stood tall and straight, well spaced, with little undergrowth. Instead of narrow, twisting paths which came to dead-ends, the difficulty lay in distinguishing a path from the general openness.

Daisy took Alec's hand and they led the troops under the trees. To hide her uncertainty, Daisy enquired meekly, 'How are you going to find Phillip?'

'That's what I've been wondering,' Tommy said, coming up on Alec's other side. 'If he doesn't know we've arrived, we not only lose a man to help carry out your plan, Fletcher, he'll very likely wreck it.'

'It's a problem,' Alec admitted. 'We can't go hunting for him without the risk of alerting the kidnappers.'

'He'll be hiding in the hawthorns,' said Daisy. 'It's the only place he can watch from without being seen. You'll never find him without me.'

'You're not coming, Daisy,' Alec said firmly and patiently.

'With your facility with words, I'm sure you can describe his position well enough for us to follow.'

'If you manage to stick to the direct path up the hill. There are countless sheep paths to lead you astray so that you come out at a different point on the circle. Ah, here we are,' she said with relief.

Just ahead their path was crossed by a shallow ditch and low bank, perhaps once part of the fortification on the hill above. They climbed over, turned right, and followed the bank, barely visible in the gloom. Alec and Tommy discussed tactics, with Binkie listening in and the four servants following.

They came to a stile in a post and rail fence. Daisy climbed over. Alec followed, then stopped on the top step.

The fence marked the end of the wood. Beyond it rose the bare hillside, its truncated summit standing out against a darkening sky.

'We can find our way without you, love,' said Alec. 'Tell me where to find Petrie and you go on back to the farm.'

Glancing back, past the pale faces of the men to the murk beneath the trees, Daisy remembered her lonely trek from the witch's cottage to Fairacres. She shivered. 'Don't make me go through the woods alone.'

'Make you?' The tender laugh in his voice caused a quite different sort of shiver to run down Daisy's spine. 'When have I ever succeeded in making you do anything? All right, come with us, but *please*, I beg of you, stay close to me until we storm them, and then stay behind. If you insist on going in with us, you'll get in the way and divert our attention to protecting you.'

'I'll keep out of the way,' Daisy promised.

'Good girl.' Alec turned to face his troops. Raising his voice to be heard above the patter of rain on leaves, the sough of tossing branches, he said, 'I take it you all know by now what we're here for. The idea is to rescue Miss Arbuckle while at least one of her captors has gone to fetch the ransom, improving the odds on our side.'

'Already in our favour,' Tommy put in.

'As far as we know. What we don't know is whether someone has already left, and whether they have a look-out watching the track on the far side of the hill. I'm hoping to learn that from Mr. Petrie, who's up there somewhere.'

'If so be there's a guard to be took out, sir,' said Carlin, ''e'll not find a better man nor I at creeping up on poachers.'

Thank you, Carlin, I'll remember that. I'll give you all further instructions when we see what Mr. Petrie has to say. For now, we follow Miss Dalrymple up the hill. If you must speak, keep your voice down. Let's go.'

Outside the shelter of the trees, the blustering wind swooped upon them, flinging random salvoes of rain. Daisy grabbed her hat. As she tugged it down further over her ears, a mighty gust sent her tottering. She clutched Alec's arm.

Hanging on to him, she slogged up the hill at his side. Wetter and wetter, chillier and chillier, she tried to remember why she had insisted on coming.

The path, never more than a stripe of sparser grass across the close-cropped turf, was hard to make out in the dusk. For the most part it led straight up the slope, with here and there a zigzag around a stunted hawthorn. Daisy began to wonder whether her memory of the thorn thicket within the fort was accurate, and whether she was right to assume Phillip would have taken shelter there.

She pictured the interior of the circle as viewed from the gateway, where they had always entered. The hut was somewhat to the right of the centre, she thought, with the hawthorns visible beyond it to its right. According to the lay-out she and Lucy had pieced together, that meant the thicket would be to her right when they reached the track at the top.

'Which way?' said Alec.

'To the right Oh, you mean now?' Rounding a tree, they had come to a fork. The right-hand branch led away around the hillside, the left-hand upward. 'No, left here.'

They trudged between two more hawthorns and faced a bare slope to the top. Alec stopped.

'If they're watching in this direction, they can't miss us.' He looked back. 'Pearson, do you see any alternative approach?'

Tommy came up beside him. Hand sheltering his eyes from the rain, he scanned the surroundings. 'No,' he said baldly, 'but at least it's no Vimy Ridge. I presume they're not waiting with artillery and machine-guns. In any case, I rather doubt they have a sentry out in this foul weather, not being disciplined troops.'

'Let's hope not.' Alec glanced at his wrist-watch. 'We can't wait for it to get any darker. In spite of this gloom, the sun's only just setting and the half-light may linger for another hour. We'll have to risk it.'

There was no way to tell whether they were observed as they moved out into the open. For all they knew, a look-out could be rushing to the hut. By the time they reached the top, perhaps the kidnappers would be hustling Gloria down the track on the far side of the hill.

Might they even mistake the amateur rescue-party for police and kill her?

Daisy forced her weary legs to move faster. She strained her ears: surely Phillip would attempt to save Gloria if they tried to move her, and surely he'd shout as he attacked – before they knocked the poor, gallant chump out again.

The only sounds were the wind and the rain, and the, distant, sleepy bleating of sheep settling for the night.

At last they reached the level track circling the base of the mound. Daisy walked round to the right. 'It must be about here,' she said doubtfully. 'I can't be quite sure.'

She eyed the steep bank without enthusiasm, without the least desire to climb. However, after her insistence on coming, it would be too frightfully shabby to back down now. Moving forward, she reached for a handhold.

Alec instantly pulled her back. '*You're* not going up, Daisy.'

Equally instantly, perversely, she was determined to do it. She racked her brains for reasons why she was the best choice.

'The first thing Phillip sees will be a silhouette. If it's a man, he may think it's one of the villains and raise an outcry.'

'Someone can wear your hat.'

As he spoke, Daisy pulled away from his grasp and started up the bank. After a couple of feet, she promptly slid down again.

'Blast, it's fearfully slippery in the rain. You'll have to give me a boost. And as I'm the lightest, I'm the one to do it.'

The others had gathered round by then. 'I am not hefty, look you,' said Owen. 'It's glad I'd be to go, sir.'

'Phillip might refuse to budge for Owen,' Daisy pointed

out, silently berating herself for persisting in the face of any number of excellent excuses. 'I can talk him into joining the rest of us.'

'Daisy's right,' Tommy said reluctantly. 'Petrie won't be happy to be asked to abandon his vigil at the crucial moment. He'd quite likely disregard a servant.'

Alec conceded. 'All right, but Daisy, if you get up there and see anyone but Petrie, you slide straight back down. Or if you don't see him right away. Don't hunt around for him. Promise?'

'Promise.'

'Bincombe, you're tallest and strongest. See if you can get her to the top.'

It was a fearfully undignified scramble, in the course of which Daisy managed to kick the uncomplaining Binkie in the face. At the last, one of her feet in each of his hands, he gave her a great heave. She shot upwards and only just stopped herself slithering head-first down the reverse slope. The electric torch in her mac pocket thumped her hip painfully.

Gasping for breath, she lay on the ridge, peering down into the bowl. Not a soul in sight, though soft lamplight glowed between the chinks in the stone walls of the shepherd's hut. The wind seemed to have died, and she heard a murmur of voices but failed to make out any words.

The hawthorn-patch was still a bit further to her right. Alec could not have meant she was not to look for Phillip in the thicket just because she had miscalculated its position. She wriggled along the top of the bank, silently cursing the torch, till she was able to peer down among the tangled, spiky branches.

She couldn't see Phillip, but there was only one hole in the thick growth large enough for the passage of a large body, a few feet ahead of her.

Daisy squirmed forward, cupped her hands around her mouth, and hissed, '*Phillip*!'

A rustle and a squeak might have been a frightened rabbit. Daisy hoped it was Phillip – being stabbed by a thorn? A moment later, the soles of a pair of boots came into view. They vanished; there was more rustling; and Phillip's fair head appeared.

'Daisy!' He mouthed the word, or spoke in a whisper too low to be heard over rain pelting on leaves. Her name was followed by what looked like, 'Confound it, what the deuce are you doing here?'

She beckoned. He cast a glance backward, then crawled up to her.

'What the deuce are you doing here?' he repeated in an audible whisper.

'Never mind that. Come on down and explain what's going on.'

Phillip shook his head. 'Something might happen while I'm not watching.'

'Listen, old dear, you can't do anything to help Gloria on your own, and Alec can't plan the most effective help with you playing the loose cannon.'

'Fletcher's here?'

'Of course. A fat lot of use I'd be to you on my own. Alec, Tommy, Binkie, and four servants – eight men with you. Enough to rescue her. Do come on. Time may be important.'

He cast another longing glance in the direction of the hut, then raised himself the last few inches to look down the other side. The others had moved along the track and now stood directly below Daisy and Phillip. Tommy gestured urgently.

'Oh, right-oh,' Phillip sighed.

Daisy was already so sodden she simply sat on the grass and whooshed down the bank. Alec broke her fall, catching her hands and pulling her to him.

'He argued,' she said, breathless but smug, as Phillip landed beside her. 'He wouldn't have come for Owen.'

Alec's smile was maddeningly sceptical. He let her go and said, 'Petrie, have any of the men left yet to pick up the ransom?'

'No. They're all in the hut with Gloria, all four of them. The fellow on watch over the track refused to stick it out in the rain. We can easily bag the lot. Let's go!' He took a step forward.

'Hold on,' said Alec, not budging.

'Steady, old chap.' Tommy put out a restraining hand. 'We need to know a bit more about what we're getting into.'

'Carlin,' Alec addressed the gamekeeper, 'can you sneak around and keep an eye on the gateway without being seen?'

'Aye, sir.'

'Off you go, then.' He eyed the wiry gardener. 'Morgan, you look pretty nippy on your feet. Go with Carlin but keep back, well out of sight. If he sees anyone, you run back to tell us.'

The two went off. Alec turned back to Phillip. 'The hut has only one door, I take it?'

'Yes, doesn't it, Daisy? A narrow opening, round the other side. I couldn't see it from here.'

'So you don't know whether there is an actual door or only a doorway?'

'There never used to be a door, just old, rusty iron hinges sticking out of the wall.'

'They haven't had much time to rig one up,' Daisy said. 'It seems like forever but it was only last night they left the witch's cottage.'

'Could have brought one with them,' Binkie put in. 'Knew they might have to come here, what? Had a tent.'

'True. Damn – sorry, Daisy! – I wish I knew. What about windows?'

'Not even window-holes,' Phillip said promptly, and Daisy nodded agreement. 'No holes in the walls. Actually, though one thinks of it as dilapidated, it's pretty solid except for the chimney. The bit sticking up fell into the inside bit and blocked it up an age ago.'

'No big holes in the walls,' Daisy corrected him, 'but whatever was used to stuff up the gaps between the stones is gone. I saw their light through dozens of little holes.'

'By Jove, you're right! We can peep through and see what they're up to before we burst in. Let's go, Fletcher. We outnumber them two to one.'

'Good odds,' Alec acknowledged, 'but they have Miss Arbuckle. With three, say, to fight us off in a narrow doorway, leaving one to threaten her – no, I don't like it. Pearson?'

'I have to agree. What's more, if we go in through the gateway to spy on them through the chinks in the walls, we risk being seen by whoever comes out to go for the money. All he has to do is run back to warn them and they become virtually impregnable.'

Phillip groaned. 'What do we do then?'

'Wait,' said Alec. 'With one or more gone, we can surround the place unseen and have a much better chance of dealing with the rest. I'd hoped to station men all around on top of the bank, but it looks as if that's out.'

'Impossible,' Daisy confirmed. 'The grass is too short for handholds and much too slippery for footholds. Even Binkie couldn't shove all of you up there.'

'So I'll leave Carlin watching the gateway. Let's see, who's the best runner besides Morgan?'

'Me, sir,' said Ernest eagerly. 'I always win the egg-and-spoon race at the church fête.'

'I'm not so bad myself,' Phillip protested.

'Then both of you go round the other way and keep an eye on the track down to the lane. In case Carlin misses something, see which of you can get back here fastest if anyone goes down.'

Phillip and the footman hurried off around the bend. 'All right,' said Alec, 'with Petrie safe out of the way – Bincombe, do you think you can put Pearson on top of the mound?'

Binkie surveyed Tommy's middling-tall but stocky form. 'Give it a try,' he grunted.

Even with Truscott helping on one side and Alec on the other, Tommy proved too great a weight for Binkie to boost to the crest. After three attempts, Alec turned with a rueful face to Daisy.

'Aren't you glad I came?' she said tartly.

'I could fetch Owen back. He can't weigh much more than you.'

'That would waste time. I'm ready. I just wish I'd thought to bring some chocolate.'

Truscott delved into his pocket. 'Here, Miss Daisy. Never go anywhere without it.'

'Angel!'

This time, tired by his efforts to hoist Tommy, Binkie gave her just enough impetus to reach the top safely. She lay there, nibbling chocolate, her gaze fixed on the hut. Nothing moved.

The murmer of voices came from both the hut and the track below, where Tommy and Alec were no doubt discussing a plan of attack. Every now and then, Alec called up softly, and Daisy responded with a wave to show she was still alert.

She was too damp and chilly to feel the least drowsiness, despite insufficient sleep last night. Though she would have liked sit up and huddle with her arms around her knees, that would make her stand out silhouetted against the skyline. Still, the temptation grew as the risk waned with the daylight.

It was growing dark. Nothing moved.

And then came the growl of a motor engine and a light in the sky, headlamp beams glinting off a thousand raindrops. Footsteps pounded along the track as Phillip and Ernest arrived from one direction, Owen Morgan from the other.

Daisy strained her ears to hear their excited but hushed voices. Not that she couldn't guess what was going on: Crawford had arrived.

A flicker of light crossed the gateway and the engine's rumble was suddenly louder before it cut off. At the same moment Daisy noticed the appearance of a glimmer of light reflected from the rain falling directly beyond the hut. Twisting, she leaned as far down the slope as she could without losing her balance.

'Alec! They have a door!'

'Thanks, love. You have your torch?'

'Yes.'

'Flash once if Crawford goes to the hut, twice if he's carrying a bag, three times if anyone comes out and goes to the car. Got it?'

'Got it.'

She hauled herself back up, just in time to see a torch-beam start to bob along from the gateway towards the hut. While trying to keep an eye on it, she extricated her own torch from her pocket, reached down the bank, and flashed the button on once.

As Crawford came a little closer, the back-scatter of light from his torch revealed a bulging attaché-case in his other hand. Daisy flashed twice.

'Right, miss.' Ernest's low voice, then his footsteps, running.

Daisy glanced down. The rotters had gone and left her!

She looked back at the hut. Crawford's figure stood out momentarily against the dancing raindrops, then vanished. The light from the doorway vanished too, as the makeshift door thudded shut.

The voices within were louder now, but still unintelligible. The only light was the flecks glowing through the chinks between the stones in the wall, a galaxy of irregular stars come to rest on earth.

A shadow eclipsed a patch of stars, a man-shaped shadow. As it moved on, another took its place and then a third.

They were surrounding the hut. Daisy could not decide whether she was sorry or very, very glad she had promised to keep well out of the way. It was agony not to be able to tell what was going on.

For what seemed an age nothing appeared to happen. Then everything happened at once.

Light flooded from the opening door. A man yelled. Alec cried out, 'Police! Come out one by one with your hands raised.' Someone shouted. Gloria squealed.

A few moments of ominous quiet were followed by an urgent voice. Then came a gunshot, and a scream of pain.

Alec? Her heart choking her, Daisy slid down the bank and ran towards the hut.

CHAPTER 21

Alec was pleased with the silently efficient way his men flitted across the grass and took up their posts surrounding the shepherd's hut. The light spilling from the nooks and crannies was just enough for him to make them out.

He had stationed Morgan and Ernest on either side – both were slightly built and too young to have seen combat – and Carlin, strong but slowed by age, at the rear. Their responsibility was to yell for help in the unlikely event of the kidnappers battering their way out through the walls, or to lend their aid if called.

That left the odds even. Surprise was essential.

Petrie, Bincombe, Pearson, and the hefty chauffeur, Truscott, lurked in a semi-circle between the hut and the gateway, beyond the reach of the light when the door opened, by Alec's reckoning. Their eyes were accustomed to the dark. Those emerging from the hut would be framed against the doorway and virtually blinded for a few moments when they moved away from it.

His ear to one of the crevices in the front wall, Alec listened to the hasty counting of rustling banknotes. Turning his head to peep through the hole, he saw the back of a frayed and grimy coat collar, the nape of a still grimier neck, and a chequered cloth cap.

He didn't dare move to another cranny in hopes of a better view for fear of making a noise. In any case, listening was more likely to tell him what was going on, he thought, and once more he pressed his ear to the cold stone.

'You guys satisfied I haven't pulled anything on you, huh?' The American drawl dripped sarcasm.

'Looks orright, mate.'

'Then give me my passport and get out of here!' Crawford snarled.

'Aincha gonna give us a lift down to the van?'

'In a two-seater? Come off it! 'Sides, I plan to spend a while alone with Miss Gloria Arbuckle.' His tone was now smoothly complacent.

Miss Arbuckle's frightened squeak must have drowned out Petrie's gasp of outrage, quickly silenced by Pearson's hand across his mouth.

A different Cockney voice said irresolutely, 'You swore you wasn't going to do nuffing to 'er.'

'Just a little chat, to give her a message for her poppa. Scram, fellas, and don't worry your little heads about us. It's been swell working with you.' The sarcasm was back.

Not for a second did Alec believe the American's disclaimer. As he listened, he wondered briefly whether to let the London roughs pass unmolested, at the risk of losing them, for the sake of concentrating his forces on Crawford. Petrie said he had disabled their van, so it was no great risk.

It was, however, too late to change the plan of campaign. Even as he reached that decision, the door opened and a large man stepped out, turning up his coat collar against the rain.

'Gorblimey, it ain't fit for a dog out 'ere! Can't see a bloody fing.'

'Use yer bloody torch, cock.'

Fumbling in his pocket, the first man walked into the darkness and Bincombe's fist. All Alec heard was a soft *thunk*.

The second man, torch already in hand, moved towards a similar destiny as the third crossed the threshold.

Alec couldn't tell what went wrong. A muffled squawk alerted the third man. With an inarticulate yell he jumped back through the narrow doorway.

Springing forward, Alec cried, 'Police! Come out one by one with your hands raised.'

The door started to close. Alec thrust his torch into the gap. As he leaned his weight against the splintery wood, someone shouted.

The girl screamed.

Petrie and Bincombe arrived neck and neck. Brushing Petrie aside, Bincombe charged the door, an irresistible force Alec only just managed to dodge. He burst into the hut, Alec and Petrie on his heels.

Two scruffy villains faced them, hands reaching for the roof. Behind them, visible between them, a well-dressed, pudgy man with oiled-back hair had his arm around Miss Arbuckle. His other hand held a pistol to her bedraggled blond head.

'Get out or I'll kill her,' he said, quietly vicious. 'Now!'

'Oy!' One of the Cockneys swung round. 'You said she wouldn't come to no 'arm!'

The American was staring at Petrie. 'You!' he exclaimed with loathing, and turned on his henchmen. 'You said you'd disposed of him!'

'We got rid of 'im, but like we told you, we don't 'old wiv murder. Let the girl go.' The man took a step forward. 'We're done for anyways.'

'You dumb yahoos, if we're done for it's your fault!'

'Come on, mate, let 'er go. Least we done nuffing to dangle for.'

Crawford shot him.

His shriek cut through the reverberation of the shot as he fell. Miss Arbuckle wrenched herself away from Crawford, who cringed back, his gun dangling, looking sick.

'Oh God,' he babbled, 'I didn't know it would be . . . I've never seen . . .' He turned away and vomited in a corner as Petrie caught the girl in his arms.

An amateur crook, Alec thought in disgust. Often more dangerous than the pros, because they didn't know what they were doing. He left Crawford and the uninjured Cockney to the others and dropped to his knees beside the wounded man.

Blood welled from his shoulder. His face was deadly pale. ''Ave I 'ad it, guv?' he asked faintly. 'Din't know 'e 'ad a shooter, honest.'

'I believe you. Don't try to talk now.' Alec pressed his handkerchief to the wound. It soaked through alarmingly fast.

He needed help. He looked round to see what the others were doing, just as Daisy burst into the hut.

'Alec . . . Oh, thank God it wasn't you!' She glanced down at the victim and gulped. 'Wait just half a mo and I'll take off my petticoat. Luckily it's a waist one.'

She dashed out again, to return with a wad of white cloth. A glimpse of lace edging brought a twinge of untimely desire as Alec took it and exchanged it for his blood-soaked handkerchief.

'Can you hold it while I take off my shirt to tie it in place? Press hard.'

Pale but game, she took his place. 'Who shot him? Crawford?'

'Yes.' He took off his raincoat and jacket and unbuttoned his shirt, glad he had put on a clean vest this morning. 'You feel all right?'

'I can manage. It's not like in Occleswich, when I'd hit that dreadful man and you were hurt.'

Alec smiled at her. 'I seem to remember you coped very competently then, however frightful you felt. Here, let's tie it round as tight as we can. There's not much else we can do, I'm afraid.'

'He'll be in shock. We must try to keep him warm.'

As he helped Daisy bind the man's shoulder and wrap him in both their coats, Alec spared a fragment of his attention for the goings-on around them. Pearson was competently directing the rounding-up of the prisoners. Petrie still had his arms around Gloria Arbuckle and appeared to be whispering sweet nothings in her ear.

'Petrie!' Alec grinned as the young man started and blushed.

'Oh, er, by Jove, let me introduce . . .'

'Later. I'd like you to take Crawford's motor and send us a doctor. Then notify the police, and Mr. Arbuckle. You'd better take Miss Arbuckle with you.'

'Gosh, thanks. I mean, yes, of course, old man. Police? Local or the Yard?'

'Scylla or Charybdis. It hardly matters,' Alec clarified as Petrie looked blank. 'I'm in hot water either way.'

'The Chief Constable,' said Daisy. 'Sir Nigel – at least, let's assume we're still in Worcestershire, though it could be Gloucestershire. We must be right on the border. A Dalrymple and a Petrie, and throw in *Lord* Gerald Bincombe for good measure, and between us we should be able to talk Sir Nigel Wookleigh round.'

'Right-oh,' said Petrie. Tenderly supporting Miss Arbuckle, he moved towards the door.

Pearson stopped him. 'Just a minute, old fellow. There's no need to tell Wookleigh that Fletcher was in charge of the operation. Say he's here, by all means. That will make the man sit up and take notice. But try to contrive to give the impression that he arrived at the last minute and was dragged along willy-nilly.'

'Right-oh.'

'Hurry, Phillip,' Daisy urged. 'This chap needs proper medical attention. Toodle-oo, Gloria. See you later.'

***

Not for a fortnight did the entire cast of characters – minus villains – meet again. The occasion was a double engagement party thrown by Mr. Arbuckle at Claridge's Hotel.

The millionaire had not only asked Daisy, Alec, and Phillip for guest lists, he invited everyone who had anything to do with rescuing his daughter. Thus, in the true democratic tradition, the Dowager Lady Dalrymple rubbed shoulders with her gardener, Owen Morgan; Colonel Sir Nigel Wookleigh, Chief Constable of Worcestershire, with

Detective Sergeant Tring of Scotland Yard; Lord and Lady Petrie with their neighbours' gamekeeper, Carlin.

Nonetheless, Daisy was not a little startled when her cousin Edgar came up to her and announced, 'I've seen a chimney sweeper, black as the ace of spades.'

'A chimney sweeper?' she enquired cautiously, trying to resist craning her neck and peering around.

'Not uncommon, but they turn brown a day or two after emerging so one rarely sees one sooty black.'

'Butterfly or moth?' said Alec.

'Moth, my dear fellow. *Odezia atrata*. Next time you come down to Fairacres, you must stay longer and see whatever specimens I have on hand at the time.'

Daisy's family had accepted Alec as a future member – her mother and Geraldine with reluctance, Edgar and her sister Violet with equanimity, Vi's eldest boy with sheer joy. His chums at prep school, the nine-year-old confided to his aunt, were bitterly envious of a prospective uncle who was a Scotland Yard detective.

He and Alec's daughter Belinda, the same age and allowed to attend the first hour of the party, were soon thick as thieves. The Dowager Lady Dalrymple and Mrs. Fletcher, though loath to abandon suspicion of each other, at least found common ground in mutual censure of marriage between the classes.

As for the Petries, they were so relieved that Phillip was to be an engineering adviser, not a motor-mechanic, that they welcomed Gloria and endured Arbuckle with gratitude.

Gloria, Daisy decided upon better acquaintance, had not much more sense than Phillip. However, once recovered from her ordeal, she proved a cheerful, good-natured girl, and her father's money would shield them from the world.

Half-way through the evening, Daisy and Alec, Lucy and Binkie, and the Pearsons came together by chance.

'Darling,' Lucy drawled to Alec, 'I've been wondering what's become of the villain Crawford shot.'

'He survived,' Alec assured her, 'thanks to Daisy's first aid. That's all I know.'

'He's recovering,' said Tommy.

'Mr. Arbuckle has retained Tommy to represent him,' Madge explained.

'He'll get off lightly then,' Alec said with a grin. 'Pearson's eloquence is wasted in a solicitor's office. He belongs at the Bar.'

'Tommy persuaded the Assistant Commissioner to forgive Alec,' said Daisy. 'Without ever telling an outright lie, he gave the impression that Alec didn't even know a crime had been committed until he reached Brockberrow Hill. I shall never again believe anything a lawyer says.'

'He did an excellent job of putting the A.C. in the right frame of mind,' Alec confirmed, 'though if anyone can see through legal verbiage, the Assistant Commissioner for Crime is the man. What really saved my bacon, however, and led to complete forgiveness, was his discovery that Daisy was involved. Living in terror of her unorthodox methods of "helping" the police, he relies on me to restrain her.'

'Beast,' said Daisy, but she didn't really mind. Tonight she felt as light as the bubbles in her champagne glass, with only her hand tucked under Alec's arm to anchor her to the earth.

If you enjoyed Damsel in Distress,
Read on for a preview of the next book in the
Daisy Dalrymple series,
DEAD IN THE WATER

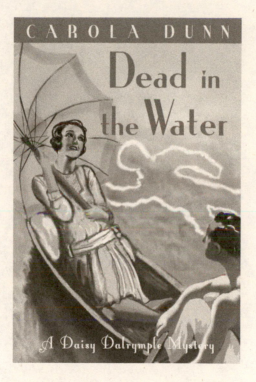

CAROLA DUNN

Dead in
the Water

A Daisy Dalrymple Mystery

CHAPTER 1

Daisy paused at the top of the brick steps leading down from the terrace. The negro butler had said Lady Cheringham was to be found in the back garden, but there was no sign of Daisy's aunt.

On either side of the steps, roses flourished, perfuming the still air. From the bottom step, a gravel path cut across the lawn, which, shaded in part by a huge chestnut, sloped smooth as a bowling green to the river. The grey-green Thames slid past around the bend, unhurried yet relentless on its way to London and the sea.

Upstream, Daisy saw the trees on Temple Island, hiding the little town of Henley-on-Thames. Downstream, the white buildings of Hambleden Mill and the pilings dividing the boat channel from the mill-race marked the position of the lock and weir. Beyond the towpath on the far bank of the river, the Berkshire side, Remenham Hill rose to a wooded crown. On the near side, at the foot of the lawn, was a long, low boathouse half-hidden by shrubs and a rampant lilac-flowered clematis. From it, a plank landing-stage ran along the bank, with two bright-cushioned skiffs moored there side by side. On the landing-stage stood two hatless girls in summer frocks, one yellow, one blue.

Daisy took off her hat with a sigh of relief. The water-cooled breeze riffled through the honey-brown curls of her shingled hair.

The two girls were gazing upstream, hands shading their eyes against the westering sun, still high in a cloudless sky. From her vantage point, Daisy followed their gaze and spotted a racing eight emerging from the narrows to the north of the island. Foreshortened by distance, the slender boat crawled towards them like an odd sort of insect, oars rising and dipping in unison on either side. The cox's voice floated across the water.

'Got you!' The triumphant exclamation came from nearby, in a female voice.

Looking down, Daisy saw a spotted brown-linen rear end backing cautiously out of the rosebed, followed by a broad-brimmed straw hat.

'Hullo, Aunt Cynthia.'

'I keep telling him chopping off their heads won't kill them.' Lady Cheringham, straightening, brandished a muddy-gloved hand clutching a dandelion with a twelve-inch root. Her lean face, weathered by decades of tropic climes, broke into smile. 'Hullo, Daisy. Oh dear, is it past four already?'

Daisy started down. 'Only quarter past. The train was dead on time and your man was waiting at the station.' On the bottom step, she nearly fell over a garden syringe.

'Careful, dear! I was spraying the roses, dealing death to those dratted greenfly, when I noticed the dandelion.'

'Not deadly poison, I hope? It seems to have dripped on your blouse.'

'Only tobacco-water, but perhaps I'd better go and wash

it off. It does stain horribly.' Lady Cheringham dropped the dandelion's corpse by the sprayer. 'Bister simply won't admit that hoes are useless against these brutes, but that's what comes of having a chauffeur-cum-gardener-cum-handyman.'

'I rather like dandelions,' Daisy confessed.

'Never fear, however many we gardeners slaughter, there will always be more.' She stooped to pick up a trug, loaded with pink and yellow cut roses, which lay on the grass at her feet. 'As a matter of fact, I really just came out to deadhead and cut some roses for your room – you're sure you don't mind sharing with your cousin? The house is packed to the rafters.'

'Not at all. In fact it's spiffing. It will give me a chance to get to know her better. Now that Patsy's grown up, that five-year gulf between us won't seem so vast.'

'Tish, dear. Patricia insists on being called Tish these days, Heaven knows why. I dare say I should be thankful they don't address each other by their surnames, she and her friend Dottie.' Lady Cheringham waved at the two girls by the river. 'I gather that is the custom at the ladies' colleges, apeing the men. So unsuitable. I can't help wondering if it was quite wise to entrust Patricia's upbringing to Rupert's brother while we were abroad.' She sighed.

'I suppose being brought up in the household of two Oxford dons must have inclined Pat ... Tish to academic life.'

Daisy hoped she didn't sound envious. Neither family nor school had prepared her for university studies. In fact, the idea had never dawned on her until the newspapers reported Oxford University's admission of women to degrees, just three years ago, in 1920. Already twenty-two and struggling to earn a living, she had recognised that her chance was past.

Her aunt said cheerfully, 'Oh, Patricia has to swot like mad. She isn't really any more intellectual than I am. Luckily – since I suspect she has an understanding with Rollo Frieth. A charming young man but not brainy, though he's an undergrad at Ambrose College.'

'That's the crew you're putting up for the Regatta, isn't it?'

'Yes, Rupert's nephew rows for Ambrose. Christened Erasmus, poor boy, but everyone calls him Cherry.'

'I've met him, I'm sure, more than once but years ago.'

'Very likely. He's practically a brother to Patricia. You'll see him at tea, and meet the rest.'

'I think I saw them rowing this way.'

They both turned and looked at the river. The boat was a couple of hundred yards off, drifting downstream towards them, the rowers in their white shirts and maroon caps resting on their oars. Sounds of altercation reached Daisy's ears, though she could not make out the words.

'I must go and change, and deal with these flowers,' Lady Cheringham said hastily. 'Do go on down and say hullo to Patricia, since she stayed home especially to welcome you. That's Dottie Carrick with her.'

Daisy walked down to the landing-stage. At the sound of her footsteps on the gravel, Patricia – Tish – and her friend looked round.

Tish was a pretty, fair-haired girl, just turned twenty. Slim in pale blue pique, a dark blue sash at the low waist, her figure was admirably suited to the bustless, hipless fashion of the day, Daisy noted enviously.

She didn't know her cousin well. Sir Rupert Cheringham, in the Colonial Service, had left his only child to be brought up by his brother and sister-in-law, both lecturers at Oxford University. Visits between that academic family and Daisy's aristocratic family had been few and fleeting, though Lady Cheringham was Daisy's mother's sister.

To Daisy, Oxford was a railway station, or a place one motored through, between London and her ancestral home in Gloucestershire, now the property of Cousin Edgar. Daisy's brother, Gervaise, might have gone to Oxford had the War not intervened. His death had eliminated that connection. The death of her fiancé had left her uninterested in any men who might otherwise have invited her to May Balls after the War, when demobbed officers flocked to the universities.

Gervaise and Michael were five years gone. The new man in Daisy's life had taken his degree at the plebeian University of Manchester.

'Hullo, Daisy!' Patricia greeted her. 'You haven't brought Mr. Fletcher with you? Alec Fletcher is Daisy's fiancé,' she explained to her friend.

'He can't get away till Friday night. He's booked at the White Hart.'

'Just as well. Mother would have to stuff him into the attics. Half the men are on camp-beds already, sharing rooms, with the cox in the linen-room because he's the only one short enough! Oh, you don't know Dottie, do you? Dorothy Carrick, a college friend – and she's engaged to Cherry. Dottie, my cousin, Daisy Dalrymple.'

Miss Carrick, round-faced, bespectacled, rather sallow, her painfully straight, mousy hair cut in an uncompromising short bob, looked every inch the female undergrad. A frock printed with large, yellow cabbage roses did nothing for her stocky form. Daisy, always at odds with her own unfashionable curves, felt for her.

'How do you do, Miss Carrick,' she said. 'Mr. Cheringham's rowing, isn't he?'

Dottie smiled, a boyish grin revealing even, very white teeth. 'That's right. In both the Thames Cup and the Visitors' – the eight and the coxless four, that is.' Her voice was a beautiful, mellifluous contralto. 'The four won their heat this morning, and we're waiting to hear about the eight. You're here to write about the Regatta, Tish said?'

'Yes, for an American magazine. Harvard and some others often send crews over so the races get reported, especially when an American boat wins, but my editor wants an article on the social side of things.'

'Champagne and strawberries in the Stewards' Enclosure?' said Tish.

'Yes, that sort of stuff. Ascot hats, and watching the fireworks from Phyllis Court. A friend of my father's is a member, and the husband of a friend of mine is a member of the Stewards' Enclosure, and they've both kindly invited me. I'm going to throw in a bit about the fun-fair, too.'

'Hoi polloi's share of the social side,' Dottie observed. 'Jolly good. I'll help you do the research. I've been dying to go on the Ferris wheel.'

Tish shuddered. 'Rather you than me! But I'm a dab hand at a coconut shy. Let's talk Cherry and Rollo into going with us after tea.'

'Rollo?' said Daisy disingenuously.

'Roland Frieth.' Tish's fair skin flushed with delicate colour, as good as confirming her mother's report to Daisy. 'He's Cherry's chum.'

'And the Ambrose captain,' Dottie put in. 'Here they are now.'

'Keep out of their way while they get the boat out,' Tish advised. 'It's serious business.'

Head bobbing, a solitary moorhen scurried for the safety of the middle of the river as the boat nosed gently in alongside the landing-stage, behind the two skiffs tied up there. The cox, short and wiry, with bare, sun-tanned knees knobbly beneath his maroon rowing shorts, jumped out. He held the stern steady while his crew counted off.

'Bow.' Daisy recognised Tish's cousin, Erasmus 'Cherry' Cheringham, a fair, serious-looking young man much larger and more muscular than she remembered him.

'Two.' Another large, muscular young man, dark-haired. He gave a quick, cheerful wave. Daisy assumed they had won the heat.

'Three.'

'Four.'

'Five.'

'Six.'

'Seven.'

'Stroke.' In contrast to the rest, the stroke looked sulky. Otherwise, apart from varying hair colour, they could have been septuplets for all the difference Daisy could see.

On the cox's command, eight large, muscular, perspiring young men stepped out onto the planks, making them bounce beneath Daisy's feet. She hastily moved backwards onto solid ground.

Bow and stroke held the boat while the other six laid the
oars out on the grass. Then all eight oarsmen bent to
the boat.

'Hands on,' ordered the cox. 'Ready. Up!'

With one smooth motion, the boat rose from the water
and swung upside-down over their heads.

'Ready. Split!'

The elongated, many-legged tortoise tramped towards
the boat-house. 'We took the trick,' it called gaily as it
departed. 'Be with you in a minute, ladies.'

Tish and Dottie each picked up one of the maroon, green,
and white banded oars and followed. Eyeing the twelve-foot
length and dripping blades of the remaining sweeps, Daisy
decided against lending her aid.

The cox also stayed behind, staring after the rowers with
a scowl on his face.

'I thought you won?' Daisy said with puzzled sympathy.

'What? Oh, yes, we won all right.' Orotund Oxfordian
contended uneasily with a flat, nasal whine straight from
the Midlands. 'We may be a small college and we wouldn't
stand a chance in the Grand, but we've a good shot at the
Thames Cup.'

'You don't look very happy about it. Oh, I'm Daisy
Dalrymple, by the way, Patricia's cousin.'

'Horace Bott. How do you do, Miss Dalrymple? Of
course I'm glad we took the heat,' he went on gloomily, 'but
even if we win the final, I'll still be an outsider.'

'Because you don't row?'

'Because I haven't got the right family, or accent, or clothes,
or instincts. When I won the scholarship to Ambrose,
I thought all I had to do was prove I'd earned it, but I could

take a hundred Firsts with Honours and my father would still be a small shopkeeper.'

'There's nothing wrong with being a shopkeeper,' Daisy encouraged him. 'Napoleon said the English were a nation of shopkeepers, but we beat him all the same.'

'Nothing wrong as long as we know our place,' Bott groused, 'which isn't at Oxford competing with our betters. 'Betters,' my foot! Half the stuck-up snobs who treat me like dirt only got into Ambrose through their family connections, and with all the private tutoring in the world they'll be lucky to scrape by with Pass Thirds.'

Daisy didn't care for his peevish tone, but she suspected he had reason for his disgruntlement. If Gervaise had gone up to Oxford, it certainly would not have been on the basis of academic brilliance, nor with the intention of excelling academically. She rather thought he would have scorned those who did, and he had certainly not shared her willingness to hobnob with the lower classes.

'Do you join in the other stuff?' she asked, adding vaguely, 'Acting, and debating, and rags, and sports, and so on ... Oh, sports, of course.'

'I thought sports'd do it, coxing, and I play racquets – got my Blue in that last year, actually.'

'You play racquets for the university, not just the college? Congratulations.'

'All very well, but the toffs still don't choose to hoist a pint with me after a match,' Bott said resentfully.

His lack of popularity might have less to do with his birth than with the way he wallowed in his grievances, Daisy guessed. She nearly said so, then thought better of it. He would be sure to take advice amiss, however well-meant, and though she felt sorry for him, she did not like him.

He took a packet of Woodbines from his shirt pocket. 'Smoke?' he offered.

'No, thanks.'

He lit up the cheap cigarette, flicking the match into the river. 'I suppose you never touch anything but Turkish.'

'As a matter of fact, I don't smoke at all. I don't care for the smell of cigarettes.' Pipe smoke was another matter, especially Alec's pipe.

Bott moved a step away, wafting the smoke from her with his hand. 'Sorry. My girl doesn't like it, either. She's coming down this evening – booked a room in the town – so once I've finished this packet, I won't buy another for a few days.' His momentary cheerfulness at the prospect of his girl's arrival faded and gloom returned. 'Can't really afford them, anyway.'

Tempted to start listing the things she couldn't afford, Daisy was saved by the return of the others from the direction of the boat-house. Beside it, the racing shell, too long to fit inside, now rested upside-down on supports.

Three of the men started up the lawn towards the house, a Georgian manor built of age-mellowed red brick with white sash windows. A shout followed them: 'Don't hog all the hot water!'

Tish, Dottie, Cherry, and four others came towards Daisy and Bott.

'Daisy, you remember Cherry?' said Tish.

'Yes, of course.'

'How do you do, Miss Dalrymple?' the fair-haired bow-oarsman greeted her.

'Daisy, please. We're practically cousins, after all.'

A grin lit his, face. 'Daisy it shall be, if you promise never to call me Erasmus.'

'I promise!'

During this exchange of social amenities, two of the men picked up a pair of oars each and returned towards the boat-house, while Daisy heard the dark number two rower say to the cox, 'Jolly good show, Bott.'

'Thanks to St. Theresa's hitting the booms,' the fifth oarsman said sarcastically. He was dark-haired, like Number Two, but his hair was sleeked back with pomade. Daisy thought he was the sulky stroke.

'Lots of boats are hitting, with this experimental course being so deucedly narrow. Bott's steered us dead straight. We'll beat the tar out of Richmond tomorrow.'

'Not if we're all poisoned by those filthy things he smokes.'

Bott gave the stroke a malevolent look, then turned and headed for the house.

'Oh, come on, DeLancey, pack it in,' said Number Two. 'Not everyone's so frightfully keen on those foul cigars of yours.'

'It sticks in my gullet taking orders from that beastly little pipsqueak twerp,' DeLancey fumed.

'All coxes are small . . .'

'Bott's no twerp!' Dottie interrupted, flaring up. 'He's brainier than the rest of you put together.'

'Oh, I say,' Cherry protested.

'Well, nearly,' his fiancée affirmed, unrepentant. 'You've got a good mind, my dear old soul, but his is tip-top.'

Cherry looked chagrined.

'Better watch it, Miss Carrick,' DeLancey said nastily, 'or you'll be an old maid after all.'

'Here, I say!' Cherry stepped forward. 'You mind your tongue, DeLancey!'

Tish put a hand on his arm. 'Don't come unbuttoned, old thing. The best way to make him eat his words is to stay engaged to Dottie.'

'I shall!' her cousin snapped, 'but I'd like to stuff his rotten words down *his* gullet, all the same.'

'This isn't the time for a dust-up. You've got a race to row tomorrow,' Tish reminded him.

'Common sense and pretty, too,' DeLancey applauded mockingly. 'A girl with your looks is wasted on books and lectures. I'd be glad to show you how to have a good time.'

Tish turned her back on him.

Number Two, his face red with suppressed fury, said through his teeth, 'Didn't I tell you it's your turn to help with the oars, DeLancey?'

'So you did, Captain, so you did.' With insolent slowness, DeLancey strolled towards the remaining two oars.

Captain – so Number Two was Tish's Rollo, as Daisy had already surmised. Fists clenched, he stared after DeLancey, then shrugged and turned back to the others.

'I'm so sorry, Daisy,' Tish apologised unhappily. 'What a welcome!'

Daisy murmured something soothing.

'Oh, didn't introduce Rollo, did I?' The ready blood tinted her cheeks. 'Roland Frieth, the crew captain.'

'And a pretty sorry specimen of a captain you must think me, Miss Dalrymple,' Rollo said ruefully. 'Unable to squash dissension in the ranks.'

'I thought you squashed it very neatly,' Daisy said with

a smile. 'The oars are on their way to the boathouse, aren't they?'

They all glanced at DeLancey's, retreating back.

'I ought to have introduced him, too,' Tish worried.

Dottie snorted. 'He hardly gave you much opportunity.'

'One of these days,' said Cherry darkly, 'he'll go too far and get his teeth shoved down his precious gullet.'

Rollo shook his head. 'I doubt it. He's a boxing Blue, remember. What I'm afraid of is that one of these days he'll biff Bott.'

'Oh, Bott! He can scramble Bott's brains with my good-will, as long as he waits till after the Regatta.'

'But, Cherry, he's twice Bott's size!' Dottie protested.

'I can't see that stopping him,' said Rollo. 'For all his pater's an earl, the way he goes around insulting ladies proves he's no gentleman, and he's really got his knife into Bott.'

'Bott's no gentleman either,' Cherry muttered, 'even if he is a bloody genius.'

'Oh darling!' Standing on tiptoe, Dottie kissed his cheek. 'Bott's brains are absolutely the only thing about him I admire. I wouldn't marry him for a million in cash. I mean to say, how could I bear to be called Dottie Bott?'

Laughing, they all moved towards the house.

July, 1923. Daisy has been invited by an American magazine to cover the Henley Regatta. But unknown to her, she steps right into a class war between two members of the Oxford rowing team. Cox Horace Bott – a shopkeeper's son and scholar student – has always hated rower Basil DeLancy – younger son of an earl and all-round cad and bully. And after a particularly brutal public humiliation by DeLancy, Bott swears revenge – so when DeLancy keels over and dies mid-race, it would seem he's made good on his promise.

Yet Daisy isn't convinced, and with the help of her fiancé Detective Inspector Alec Fletcher of Scotland Yard, she dives into a tangled web of jealousies and secrets, where appearances are everything and good breeding may just be a cover for a killer intent on keeping Daisy mum ...

978-1-84901-332-1

It is 1925: Daisy and her dashing Scotland Yard detective husband, Alec, have moved house to an idyllic, suburban setting. But the discovery of a man's body in the adjoining gardens disrupts their peace with talk of bootleggers, American gangsters and black ship rum-runners. While Alec is assigned to the case, Daisy must mingle with her new neighbours to establish the dead man's identity and uncover his murderer.

978-1-84529-866-1

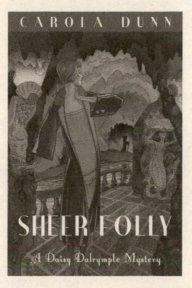

CAROLA DUNN

SHEER FOLLY

A Daisy Dalrymple Mystery

Daisy Dalrymple, at work on her book of architectural follies, heads for Appsworth Hall, reputed to have the best grotto in the country. But Daisy's plans are thrown off course when the grotto explodes and kills one of the houseguests, Lord Rydal. Faced with an array of suspects, all with good reason to want the abominable, tactless, and womanising Lord Rydal dead, it's sheer folly for Daisy even to attempt to find the killer.

978-1-84901-121-1

Thea Harrison is the pen name for author Teddy Harrison.
Thea has travelled extensively, having lived in England and
explored Europe for several years. Now she resides in northern
California. She wrote her first book, a romance, when she was
nineteen and had sixteen romances published under the name
Amanda Carpenter.

Visit her online:
www.theaharrison.com
www.facebook.com/TheaHarrison
www.twitter.com/theaharrison

Also by Thea Harrison

Elder Races series:

Dragon Bound
Storm's Heart
Serpent's Kiss
Oracle's Moon

Lord's Fall

THEA HARRISON

piatkus

PIATKUS

First published in the US in 2012 by The Berkley Publishing Group
A division of Penguin Group (USA) Inc., New York
First published in Great Britain as a paperback original in 2012 by Piatkus

A CIP catalogue record for this book
is available from the British Library.

ISBN 978-0-7499-5831-2

Printed and bound in Great Britain by Clays Ltd, St Ives plc

Papers used by Piatkus are from well-managed forests
and other responsible sources.

MIX
Paper from
responsible sources
FSC
www.fsc.org   FSC® C104740

Piatkus
An imprint of
Little, Brown Book Group
100 Victoria Embankment
London EC4Y 0DY

An Hachette UK Company
www.hachette.co.uk

www.piatkus.co.uk

≈ ONE ≈

Even though feeling like a drama queen sucked donkey's balls, it was still true—leaving Dragos and New York behind was one of the hardest things Pia had ever done.

What sucked worse than that? Leaving was her idea. She had even argued for it, loud, long and vociferously.

And what sucked the absolute worst of all? She couldn't even pretend she was leaving all her troubles behind, because she wasn't. All her troubles came along with her in a nicely matched portable set, because of course she had to travel with a bunch of psychos.

She had just gotten used to one set of psychos, the Wyr sentinels. Not all of them liked her, but most of them had, more or less, accepted her. She even fancied that a few of them loved her, and she loved them, even though she thought they were all certifiably crazy, and to be fair, she was pretty sure they thought she was crazy too.

And now here she had to break in a whole new set. This crew was fresh and energetic, while she was just goddamn tired and feeling bitchy enough to start tearing off heads for no reason.

That'd win her some brownie points.

Three of the group traveled with her in one black Cadillac Escalade. Three more traveled in another Escalade behind them, also black. In fact, both SUVs quite illegally had the same license plate numbers and were identical in virtually every way, in case the group had to split up and one SUV had to act as a decoy for the other—which would end up being whichever one Pia was traveling in at the time.

In the Escalade following them were Miguel, Hugh and Andrea. Miguel was nut-brown and dark-haired, with a tight body coiled with lean muscles and dark, sharp eyes that never stopped roaming. Hugh was rawboned and rather plain. He had big hands, a slight Scottish burr, and a sleepy demeanor that Pia didn't believe for a moment, because if he was really that sleepy and slow moving, he wouldn't be traveling with her.

Andrea looked just like Pia from a distance, which had been intentional. She had the same leggy five-foot-ten body type and the same thick blonde hair that fell past her shoulders and could be pulled back in a ponytail. Andrea's hair had been carefully lightened so that it matched Pia's blonde shades.

They couldn't pass for each other close up. Andrea looked to be possibly five years older than Pia's twenty-five, although with Wyr, guessing someone's age could sometimes be difficult, and Andrea could be as much as thirty years older. Pia's face was more triangular. Andrea's eyes were green, not midnight blue. Still, Pia got an eerie feeling whenever she caught sight of Andrea moving around in the distance. It was like looking at a doppelganger of herself.

The three traveling in Pia's Cadillac were James, Johnny and Eva. James was the tallest of the crew and actually handsome, with dark hair that fell into blue eyes and a strong nose and jaw that looked great in profile. With his fine features and light brown hair, Johnny appeared so boyish that he looked downright innocent—which was another impression that Pia knew had to be false.

Then there was Eva, who was the alpha and captain of this particular pack of lethal whack-jobs. Eva had the whole

Venus Williams Amazonian splendor thing nailed, with her honed, six-foot-tall body, rich ebony skin that rippled over strong muscles and a black, bitter gaze that had dissected Pia so thoroughly the first time they met, Pia was not exactly sure she'd found all the pieces and got herself put back together quite right afterward.

Most of her six attendants were canines of some sort, wolves, mongrels or mastiffs, although they had one winged Wyr who would provide aerial support if it ever became needed. Hugh was one of the demesne's rare, prized gargoyles.

They all came from the Wyr's version of Special Forces, the unit that was the most gifted and volatile in the army. They were the first into any conflict and acted as advance scouts, the rangers sent in to places too dangerous for the regular troops. They were the ones that patrolled the shadowed corners and slipped past enemy lines to take down their opponents from behind. The only Wyr more dangerous were Dragos's sentinels and, of course, Dragos himself.

They were not good at conforming. They never wore a uniform, they didn't salute and they didn't bother to hide their opinions about things. And it was clear they didn't think much either of Pia or the babysitting job they had been shackled with, which meant they were all in for a shitty trip if things didn't change.

Pia slouched in the back behind the driver's seat, arms crossed as she watched the dirty white, winter scenery scroll past. She could sense Dragos flying overhead, although they didn't talk telepathically. Everything had already been said, shouted and argued out a while ago. After following the two-car cavalcade for about forty minutes, she could feel him wheeling and beginning the return flight back to the city.

She shifted restlessly in her seat. Her head pounded. On the sound system, 2Pac rapped "Ballad of a Dead Soulja." Beside her, Johnny slouched in fatigues and a T-shirt, his light brown hair pulled into an untidy ponytail. He was totally absorbed in playing a handheld game.

Eva drove while James rode shotgun, literally, with the butt of a late-model SCAR (which, Pia had been told, stood for Special Operations Forces—SOF—combat assault rifle) resting on the floor between his boots. Eva's kinky black hair was cropped short, emphasizing the graceful shape of her skull. As Pia looked at the rearview mirror, her gaze collided with the reflection of Eva's contemptuous glance. Pia's already strained temper gave up trying to control her behavior. It slunk away and took her better half with it.

She said, "I want to listen to Kenny G now. Or maybe Michael Bolton."

Johnny's head came up. James twisted to look at her.

"You've got to be fucking kidding me," Eva said. She turned to James. "Tell me she's fucking kidding me."

Pia felt childish, petty and vindictive. The drama queen had turned into a two-year-old, and the toddler was having a tantrum. She said to James, "Change it."

"Woman wants it changed," James said, expressionlessly. He punched buttons. Easy listening music filled the Cadillac.

"That's just fucking great," Eva muttered. "We're going to be stuck in a goddamn elevator for the rest of the goddamn day."

Pia hated elevator music too. She smiled and settled back into her seat. Now everybody else was almost as miserable as she was.

Time dragged along with the miles that scrolled behind them, and the urban scenery remained the same, dull brick factories, black railroad lines ribboning through dirty snow, rows of houses and the occasional shopping center. Nobody spoke, at least not out loud. The two Cadillacs wove smoothly through the sporadic Sunday morning traffic on the interstate, not always staying together to avoid drawing too much attention, but always keeping within sight of each other.

As Pia watched the passing landscape, she couldn't help but think of the last time she had made this trip, seven months ago. The two trips were almost perfect opposites of each other.

4

Last May she had been on the run, frightened, exhausted and alone, while everything around her had been bursting into bloom. This time she was mated, pregnant—her hand curled protectively over her stomach's slight bump—and surrounded by the most effective, if surly, soldiers in the Wyr demesne, and it was flipping cold outside, as winter held New York by the scruff of the neck with sharp, white teeth.

January in Charleston would feel positively balmy in contrast, with daytime highs up to sixty degrees and night-time lows around thirty-eight to forty degrees. Mostly what Pia was looking forward to, though, was the lack of snow on the South Carolina coast. In late December, New York had been hit with one of the worst blizzards on record, and it would take months for all the mountains of snow to melt.

Ninety minutes into the trip, she stirred. "I have to stop."

Eva glanced at her again in the mirror. "Does her?" said Eva in a baby-talk kind of voice. "Where would herself like to stop?"

James stirred and said, "Evie."

"What?" Eva snapped. "We barely got on the road, and princess already wants to take a break. And while I'm on the subject, why are we driving and not flying? We could be there in a couple of hours, instead of the trip taking the whole goddamn day."

"It's none of your fucking business why we're driving instead of flying," Pia said icily. "And princess here doesn't give a shit where we stop, just as long as we do in the next ten minutes. Got it?"

"Sure, doll-face," Eva said. "Any little thing herself wants, herself gets."

As Eva signaled and cut right from the fast lane to the exit lane, Pia watched the other woman in the mirror and thought, Imma have to kick your ass before the day's out, aren't I?

Yeah, it was shaping up to be a great trip so far.

And they were on a mission of diplomacy.

The other Cadillac cut across traffic to join their SUV,

and the two vehicles took the next exit ramp. Their choices for stopping included two gas stations, a McDonald's, a Denny's and a Quik Mart. Eva pulled into the McDonald's lot and parked. Pia stepped out and headed for the restaurant. The other six surrounded her so casually it seemed to happen by accident. The psychos had smooth moves, she would give them that much.

Feeling an increasingly urgent need, she found her way to the restroom, accompanied by Eva and Andrea. So far the seven-month pregnancy didn't show much—a fact that pretty much freaked her out if she thought too much about it—and she could keep it completely hidden if she dressed strategically. But the peanut, bless him, was beginning to exert some influence on her bladder. That was going to get much worse before it got better.

The women's restroom was more or less clean, and empty. She pushed past the other two women, slammed the stall door shut and enjoyed a few minutes of what was likely to be the only alone time she would get that day.

Resentment and antagonism were two of the troubles that had followed her. Pia hadn't really gained acceptance from the Wyr over the past seven months.

Oh, she had from some of the sentinels. All the gryphons had embraced her, and Graydon had become one of her best friends. They also knew what kind of Wyr she was, and why she and Dragos kept it secret.

The gryphons were the only ones who knew. Not even the other two sentinels did, although that didn't seem to cause gargoyle sentinel Grym any problems, but then it was hard to tell what he was thinking since he didn't talk much. And she had achieved a kind of uneasy truce with the harpy sentinel Aryal—at least enough to spar with the harpy on the training mat several times a week, although they didn't share confidences or socialize.

As far as all the other Wyr went, in the early days of her mating with Dragos, expectation had turned to puzzlement, and then suspicion as the whispering began.

She didn't reveal to anyone what kind of Wyr she was because she was stuck-up.

No, she was a fugitive from some other demesne, because Dragos wasn't the only one she had stolen from.

Or, she didn't bother to reveal what kind of Wyr she was, because she was one of the antisocial ones, and she didn't care if she made friends or fit into any of the packs, herds or prides.

She was stuck in a box, her options limited. She couldn't just pretend she was a horse or a deer and dismiss the subject. Nobody would believe her if she tried, because her scent was too strange.

For the Wyr, it was hard to warm up to someone who kept something so fundamental to their nature hidden from everybody else. Knowing that and understanding the reasons why it was there weren't much help. The low-level resentment and subtle ostracization still felt sucky.

Over half a year later, Pia still felt like an uneasy guest in what was supposed to be her own home. The only real friends she felt like she had were Graydon, who knew everything; the new Dark Fae Queen, Niniane, with whom she steadily corresponded; and a few people from her old job working as a bartender at Elfie's.

Quentin, the bar owner, didn't need to know all of her secrets, and she didn't need to know all of his. And of course there was Preston, the half-troll barfly, who liked to describe himself as an eight-foot hunka burnin' love, and who really was a sweetie through and through. Preston didn't care if anyone had any stinking secrets. If you were willing to share a dozen orders of baked potato skins, lathered with cheese, bacon, sour cream and chives, and drink beer while watching the NBA playoffs, you were all right by him.

But Graydon was increasingly busy, and letters from Niniane, while fascinating and wonderful to receive, weren't enough to satisfy her social needs. Quentin was absent more and more from Elfie's these days, and anyway Pia couldn't

hide out at the bar twenty-four/seven. She could only visit a couple of times a week.

As far as she was concerned, there were only two things that made living in Cuelebre Tower worth it. One of them was the peanut—and she really had to stop calling him that, because the little fetus was already so smart, she could tell he thought his name actually was Peanut.

The other was Dragos, who was primitive, powerful, domineering, calculating, manipulative, infernally clever and tactless, and who she adored with all of her heart. Dragos, who created as many problems as he solved, and who loved her too, fiercely, so much so he had mated with her. Their lives had become inextricably entwined, and they had to work together for things now.

Which meant they needed to figure out how to be partners in more places than just the bedroom. (Because Pia was pretty damn sure they had nailed that part the first time they had made love.) And which also meant coming to an agreement about what they worked toward, even if reaching that agreement took months and sometimes felt like pulling giant, dragon-sized teeth.

The Wyr demesne and Dragos himself were facing too many challenges at once to deal with any one of them effectively. Dragos had broken several treaties with the Elves in his pursuit of Pia last May, and those treaties had not been repaired. Border strife continued with the Elven demesne, along with an ongoing trade embargo that had put several New York businesses under and was seriously hurting several more. Dragos's multinational corporation, Cuelebre Enterprises, had bailed out several floundering companies and provided low-interest, long-term business loans to help out others, but they were all stopgap measures that didn't really resolve the core issue.

In the meantime, Dragos's corporation, along with the rest of the world, had taken its own hits in an ongoing global recession. Diversification, along with aggressive streamlining and retrenching, had kept the corporation leaner but run-

ning strong, but that had taken harder work and more top-heavy manpower at a time when Dragos could ill afford to expend the energy.

Then there was the problem of being critically short staffed. Dragos had lost two of his seven sentinels in quick succession last summer. The first one to go was his warlord sentinel, Tiago Black Eagle, who had mated with the new Dark Fae Queen, Niniane Lorelle. Then Dragos lost his First sentinel, Rune Ainissesthai, who had mated with the Vampyre sorceress Carling Severan. Dragos and Rune had parted badly, and Dragos still refused to talk about it. He had moved two people into sentinel positions as a temporary stopgap, but now he had to go through the process of setting new sentinels into place.

To top it all off, there was the amorphous Freaky Deaky Something that hung on the horizon, the strange voice that Dragos had heard through an impromptu prophesy given by the Oracle of Louisville, Grace Andreas. The Oracle and her family had since relocated to Miami, where Pia and Dragos had traveled to meet with her in a follow-up consultation last autumn. Unfortunately, Grace couldn't add much to the original vision since, as she said, specific prophecies did not repeat themselves.

Grace did offer them a piece of advice, while they sat at her kitchen table and two young children played outside with, of all things, a very large, indulgent and good-looking Djinn. "The person or Power behind the voice from the vision is either already in your lives, or it will be," Grace told Pia and Dragos. "Don't let that knowledge weaken you. There's no point in trying to avoid it, because the actions you take might actually cause you to come into contact with it sooner than you would otherwise. Act from your strengths, and live your lives in a state of readiness. You were lucky. You were given a warning. Most people don't get that."

The memory of that conversation played through Pia's mind as she exited the bathroom stall and washed her hands. She also thought of all the other issues, along with

the added stressor of having just left her mate. Eva's antagonism shouldn't even be on the list of challenges she had to face.

The psychos were a well-trained unit. They would have a strongly defined internal order she didn't yet have a handle on, and that would be reinforced by the five canines' pack instinct. Each one would be highly opinionated and would make up his or her own mind about Pia, but none of them would go against their alpha, and no doubt several of them would take their cue from how Eva and Pia's relationship developed. Right now Pia was just an annoying, disliked outsider they had to bodyguard. She had to turn that around and establish a different working relationship with them now before Eva's lack of respect became too entrenched.

The other two women had taken advantage of using the facilities too, first Andrea, then Eva, while one remained on guard at the door.

Pia dried her hands deliberately, then turned. Andrea guarded the door. Pia met the other woman's gaze. She said, "Get out."

Andrea's blonde eyebrows rose. She glanced at the closed bathroom stall, which opened. Eva stalked out, her whole magnificent body flowing like gleaming black oil.

Pia said to Andrea, "Wrong response."

Eva jerked her chin. "Go on."

Andrea opened the door and backed out without a word.

Pia went to the door and flipped the lock. The *snick* sounded over-loud in the silent restroom. It wouldn't keep anybody out who was determined to get in, of course, but it was a strongly symbolic barrier—and the sound would tell any sharp, listening Wyr ears to stay out of what happened next.

She turned, leaned back against the door and met Eva's sardonic gaze. Pia said, "I thought briefly about just kicking your ass, but we would have to take that outside and I don't feel like getting wet and muddy. Besides, you're not worth it."

Amusement sliced across Eva's bold features, and her black eyes sparkled. "You're sadly deluded if you think you could take me, princess."

Pia didn't smile, and her gaze remained level. "I can take the gryphons," she said. Eva's face froze. "For the past seven months, I've been sparring with Aryal almost daily. With the harpy, it's more like fifty-fifty, since she doesn't pull her punches. She doesn't give a shit if I'm a female and Dragos's mate. If anything it makes her hit harder, because she doesn't like me much. So, you tell me, Eva. Can I take you?"

Okay, so some of that was bluffing. The other woman was a trained soldier and versed in battle, combat tactics and weaponry in a way Pia never would be. If they were in the wild and engaged in guerilla warfare, Pia was pretty sure that if she didn't succeed in running away from a confrontation, Eva could wipe the forest floor with her. But they weren't in the wild. On a training mat or in a McDonald's parking lot, Pia didn't have a doubt she could take the other woman. That was the certainty she let sit in her gaze.

"You have two choices," Pia said. "You can either change your attitude completely right now, no second chances, or you can give me the car keys and make your own way back to New York, because I'm not going to put up with your shit. It's pulling my mind off what I need to be thinking about, and not only that, it's unprofessional—from the both of us. We don't have to be girlfriends. We don't have to like each other. Believe me, I'm pretty used to that by now. But if you choose to stay, you've got to come to terms with the fact that, for anything that doesn't involve a combat situation, you're not the alpha in this group. I am. If we're ever facing a fight where you're the clear expert, that's a different story, but until then, you do as I say."

She watched as fury and instinct warred in Eva's face. The other woman was dominant, and she lived a violent life. Her Wyr side would be much closer to the surface than it was for others. It would be difficult to give up her alpha status without a fight, especially to someone who was an

herbivore, not pack. If they were both purely animals, Eva would try to hunt Pia down for lunch.

Of course Wyr were much more than just their animal natures, but even still, some things bled through in subtle and not-so-subtle ways. Predator Wyr often had a condescending attitude toward more peaceful herbivores. Usually that dynamic was nothing more than a social irritation, but in this situation, it added more tension.

But she would not want to be in Eva's shoes if Eva chose to head back to New York. No doubt that was the deciding factor in Eva's response, along with the fact that the other woman would never abandon her unit. Eva said expressionlessly, "Got it. For this trip, you're alpha. We done?"

Pia sourly poked at her lower lip as she noted Eva's specific wording. "No," she said. "I'm not finished." She raised her voice slightly for the benefit of whoever was listening on the other side of the door—which by that point, she reckoned, was all the others. "No doubt you all wanted to stay and watch the Games this week, and find out who wins the sentinel positions. And I get that you're irritated, but you people need to change your attitude about this assignment. I don't think you realize how important this trip is, or what an honor you've been given."

"We get that you're special, being Dragos's mate and all," Eva said.

"No, knucklehead," she snapped. She might have to take Eva out into the parking lot and kick her ass after all—whatever the other woman said, Pia wasn't sure Eva could really give up her alpha status without it, even if Eva honestly tried. "We're not on some kind of pleasure jaunt or shopping trip, and I'm not just going to have tea and cookies and go shopping with Beluviel. We're going to try to fix one of the biggest problems the Wyr demesne has right now, repair treaties and better our relationship with the Elven demesne. It's something Dragos can't do, since he's the one who broke the treaties to begin with—the Elves have threatened war if he enters their demesne without permission again, and besides, he has to settle the sentinel

issue, which means he has to stay in New York to preside over the Games."

She could tell when Eva stopped sneering long enough to actually begin to think, and then the shift happened. Suddenly their trip south was no longer an unwelcome babysitting job for an unpopular mate but had become much more.

She continued, more quietly, "The outcome of our trip matters to a lot of people, Eva. I'm not going to risk failure because you and your idiots don't know how to rein in your snark, or take orders from someone who is not pack and is nonmilitary. I get that your more usual assignment involves solving problems that are more the point-and-shoot kind. If you can't handle this, say so. We'll turn around right now and go home, and I'll start over with another crew that can."

"Okay," Eva said after a moment, relaxing from her rigid stance. "I was told you were meeting with Beluviel and possibly the High Lord, but I wasn't given details beyond our mission objective—to travel with you and keep you safe."

"Well, I am special and all, being Dragos's mate," Pia said dryly. Eva snorted, a near-silent exhalation that sounded almost amused. "And by the way, we're not taking a flight because Dragos thought we would have more survival capability on the ground. Incidences involving planes tend to have high fatality rates." Plus only one in their group had a Wyr form with wings, which seemed to bother Dragos quite a bit. He couldn't imagine flying high in the sky without having the capability to jump out of a plane and take flight if he had to. "Not," she added, "that I plan on explaining every little decision to you in the future."

"Fine," Eva said with a scowl, evidently not liking the sound of that. Then her expression changed. "I would like to ask you just one thing, though."

Pia studied the other woman. She would make more of an ally with Eva through cooperation than not. Maybe this could be a bloodless coup after all. They might never grow to like each other, but achieving a partnership before they reached South Carolina would be good enough for her. So she said, "Shoot."

Eva ran her black gaze down Pia's body as she sucked a tooth. Finally she looked up and met Pia's stare. "You even pregnant?"

Pia's eyebrows rose. She hadn't realized people were beginning to gossip about that as well. "You can't tell from my scent?"

"You have a strange scent," Eva said. "None of us have smelled anything like you before, and we don't know what to make of it."

Her face twisted into a wry grimace. Fair enough. She beckoned with her fingers and said, "Come here."

Eyes sparkling with curiosity, Eva stepped forward. Pia reached for her hand, and Eva allowed her to take it. Pia settled Eva's flattened palm over the small bump of her stomach and waited. She watched Eva's face transform into wonder.

The dampening spell that Pia used to camouflage the natural luminescence of her skin also seemed to mask the peanut's presence from others, at least from a distance. The pregnancy didn't remain hidden when someone actually came in contact with Pia's body. Even though the peanut was still very small for twenty-eight weeks, the muted roar of Power at her midsection was unmistakable even for someone who was not medical personnel.

Wonder rounded Eva's eyes. "Holy shit," she whispered.

Pia rubbed her eyes with thumb and forefinger. Yeah. Holy, as it were, shit.

"I'm confused," Eva said, frowning. "It doesn't seem very big but it's carrying a helluva wallop."

"I'm about twenty-eight weeks along," Pia told her. She could see Eva doing the math.

Eva's frown deepened. "Shouldn't it be bigger?"

"Nobody knows," Pia said with a tired sigh. "The doctor says he's quite healthy, and that's all that matters. Based on his current development, she's estimating a gestation period between seven hundred thirty and seven hundred fifty days." She watched the other woman do the math again.

Eva blanched. "You're going to be pregnant for two years."

"Seems likely," Pia said between her teeth. "Did you know elephants have a gestation period of twenty-two months? Apparently dragon babies might be more complicated. And before you think to ask, no, I'm not laying an egg so he can gestate the rest of the way outside my body. No, no such luck. This baby's going to be a live birth."

Somehow.

Eva looked at her in poorly concealed horror. "Won't he have . . . claws? And not cute tiny, puppy ones?"

"We're a little concerned about that," Pia said grimly. "And he hasn't yet shown any sign of his human form." Some Wyr babies were born in their animal form, and others were born in human form. Still others, if they were not already in the same form as their mother, shapeshifted while in utero, although that was more rare. "The doctor wants to plan a C-section."

"I see." Eva pulled her hand away and stepped back.

They had roused the baby. Pia felt an invisible presence settle around her neck and shoulders, a bright, fierce loving innocence. It was a waking version of what she dreamed so often these days, the peanut draping his graceful, delicate white body around her, his long, transparent wings tucked close to his body. Nobody else but her could sense when he did that, not even Dragos. She put a hand to the base of her neck with a small, private smile.

"Guess we better get you to Charleston," Eva said. "You got a job to do."

"I guess we'd better," said Pia.

"I just want to know one more thing," said Eva.

Pia turned to unlock the restroom door. "What's that?"

Eva put her hand on the door and held it shut while she met Pia's gaze pointedly. "Tell me we can change radio stations now."

Pia bit back a chuckle. "Yes, please. Let's get off the elevator."

15

Eva took hold of the handle and pulled the door open. The other five in their group were hanging in the hallway, looking thoughtful, their arms piled high with food bags and drink carriers. Johnny was already eating a sandwich.

Reaching a détente with Eva was one hurdle down. Now all Pia wanted to do was reach their rented estate and settle in for the evening. She wouldn't be meeting with any Elves until the next day.

She couldn't wait for nightfall. She only hoped she wasn't so excited that she couldn't fall asleep, because that would seriously screw up everything.

≈ TWO ≈

After seeing off Pia's mini-cavalcade, Dragos flew back to the city.

He missed her ferociously already, the ache so bad it hurt his chest. Each wing stroke that took him further away from her felt wrong as hell. They had not separated since they had come together and mated last May.

Wyr could survive separations from their mates, sometimes for years if necessary, but it always felt like privation. He almost called her back to him a half-dozen times. Only the thought of their shared mission kept him silent, although his massive jaws ached from how hard he clenched them.

When he reached Manhattan, he spiraled down through the frigid air to land in a large, cordoned-off area in a parking lot by Four Pennsylvania Plaza. After he shimmered into a shapeshift, he let go of the cloaking spell and strode toward the main entrance of the massive, round Madison Square Garden building.

He glanced up as he approached. The banner had gone up weeks before. It was several stories tall and very simple. It read SENTINEL GAMES, with the dates for this week down

below, along with the simple graphic of a gigantic, crimson dragon rampant.

That'd do.

The twenty-thousand by ten-thousand-foot arena seated 19,500 and it had all the latest multimedia technology, with giant television screens to show spectators in close-up the details of what occurred down below. The arena had undergone extensive renovations over the last several months, heavily subsidized by Cuelebre Enterprises, down to and including the Cuelebre Enterprises Executive Suite, which perched above the rest of the arena like an aerie.

All the tickets for the week of the Games were long gone. The tickets were for four-hour slots and had been free on a first-come/first-serve basis to any Wyr or resident of New York State who applied. The first ones to go were on the last day, when the final round of contests would take place and he would name his next seven sentinels. A limited amount of seating and suites had also been made available, for an exorbitant price, to any of the other races who were willing to pay.

And they were all willing to pay. Dignitaries from all the other Elder Races, along with many human nationalities, would be attending.

People would watch the Games for a variety of reasons. Some would be evaluating the strength of the Wyr demesne and making notes of the personalities involved. The week would showcase a lot of talent, so no doubt some, including Cuelebre Enterprises, would be headhunting for a selection of opportunities that lay outside the sentinel positions.

Also, many Wyr would gain a sense of security from knowing their demesne remained strong and capable of handling any threat. Still others would watch for the blood sport, which was barbaric, of course, but Dragos had never made any bones about the fact that the Games themselves were barbaric. They were supposed to be. PETA members were completely outraged and utterly confused.

The weeklong event would also be televised on pay-per-view cable worldwide, which would help to defray some

of the massive cost, but the bottom line was the Games still remained the single most expensive project he had personally sponsored in generations.

In this case, profit was not the point. This was governance, a calculated, lavish display of wealth and an exercise of raw, brutal strength.

Just as humans had many different countries splattered across the globe, all the other Elder Races had different demesnes—in the continental United States, in Europe, Asia, Africa and other places.

All except for the Wyr. The Wyr had different communities, such as the gargoyles in northern Scotland, the wolves of the Great Steppe in southwestern Russia, the gazelles of the African plains and the mysterious, ancient kraken of the North Atlantic who rarely interacted with others or came to land.

But there was only one Wyr demesne, one Wyr ruler.

Cuelebre, the Great Beast.

And there had been only one event like this in the last thousand years. That had been the first Sentinel Games, when his original seven had fought their way to their current positions. Then, he had recruited the most Powerful of the Wyr throughout the world. They had come together to establish who was the strongest amongst them, and they had fought for the chance to rule by his side.

He had been working toward this point since Tiago and Rune had left their positions last summer. This time the worldwide recruiting and screening effort had been conducted electronically. Notices had gone out, job application forms had been posted, and an entire team of recruiters and HR personnel had spent the last several months screening and checking references for all the applicants.

They had arrived at a short list of 448 contestants, and most of those were predator Wyr. There were any number of lions, of course, and several gargoyles. Dragos liked the gargoyles. They were community minded, and when they changed into their Wyr form, their stone-like surface was almost impossible to penetrate in hand-to-hand combat.

There was one of the two other known thunderbirds in existence aside from Tiago, a clash of harpies, and a very interesting, rare individual who was mixed race but whose Wyr side was strong enough that he could shapeshift. Most interesting of all to Dragos, there was a rare pegasus. While Powerful immortals, as herbivores pegasi were peaceful creatures, and it was unusual for one to seek out such a public, potentially violent position.

All-predator sentinels made for a hawkish group, a fact that was brought home to him when Pia, with her more peaceful outlook, began to sit in on conferences and voice her opinions. It might not be a bad thing to have a pegasus as a sentinel—as long as he could establish his prowess in physical combat. If he couldn't fight worth shit, there was no point. The pegasus could go push some pencils in a bureaucratic position somewhere. Right here? It was call of the wild, baby.

The shortlist of contestants also included all five of his current sentinels, who had to participate in the Games to prove they were still the strongest and the best, because while the Wyr demesne adopted modern technology, legal concepts and principles, at its heart it was still a feudal system. It had to be; his sentinels needed to be the strongest and most capable of taking down any other Wyr who might go rogue, and they also had to be capable of leading a world-class defense against any potential attackers.

Might did not always equate with right, but it did provide damn strong security in an uncertain, often brutal world.

Still, the participation of the five sentinels was probably just a formality. Probably. The only stipulation Dragos had made was that they fight other contestants, because the point of their inclusion wasn't to find out which of them was the strongest against each other. The real question was, were they stronger than anybody else?

Everyone was on edge, and more tempers than just his had flared frequently over the last few weeks. Crews had been laboring overnight to put the last touches on the com-

bat arena. It was a simple area, a huge cordoned-off space with a sand-covered floor. The sand could be raked in between bouts to get rid of the blood.

Because there would be blood.

With all the paperwork and formalities out of the way, the Sentinel Games had just one objective: beat your opponent by any means possible. One fight, Wyr to Wyr. No weapons, no second chances, no holds barred.

There was just one rule: don't kill anybody.

At least not on purpose.

Nobody wanted to talk to Dragos these days. No doubt it had something to do with him being so snarly. He was liable to bite off somebody's head if they so much as looked at him funny. That wasn't winning him any friends.

Which was all right with Dragos. He didn't need friends, and he didn't want to talk to anybody else, anyway. He could probably stand to not talk to anybody for the entire length of Pia's trip away.

Yeah, that could potentially save lives and maintain inter-demesne alliances. Unfortunately, that strategy wasn't on his agenda for the foreseeable future.

Approximately twenty thousand spectators were on site, along with countless staff and security, a team of medical personnel on standby for the week, the four hundred and forty-eight contestants, a gaggle of assorted dignitaries, some protest groups and a shitload of press.

Whenever his five current sentinels were not competing, they would be working with Wyr divisions in NYPD to maintain an extra-sharp vigilance throughout the city. This week would be particularly challenging for them, for they would have virtually no downtime between rounds in the arena, other than what they might need to physically heal from any injuries. They were all taking the rigors of the week as their own personal challenge to excel.

Lines went down the street. It was taking a while to usher

in all of the people. While Dragos liked putting on a show, he really hated crowds, even when he was the one who instigated the gathering. He clenched his fists and kept a stern hold on his temper, turning his face away when someone pointed a camera at him.

Cuelebre Enterprises' new head of PR, Talia Aguilar, was already on site and talking with several camera crews in the main lobby area. Talia was a selkie, a seal Wyr, with a sinuous rounded body, golden skin, brown hair and large, soulful eyes that the camera loved. She had been part of Tricks's staff when Tricks had been Head of PR.

Last summer Pia herself had recommended Talia for the position, after she had briefly considered whether or not she wanted or even could do the job.

"Why her?" Dragos had asked.

"Because not only is Talia qualified, she's freaking adorable," Pia told him. "Have you noticed her? People fall over themselves to do things for her. They open doors for her and shit—and she never says shit. And Dragos, as much as I love you I have to say, you need someone who is really adorable in that position."

"You're adorable," he said.

"Really? Aw." Pleasure sleeked her down. She gave him a creamy smile. "I'm not, you know. But, aw."

"Why shouldn't you take the position?" he asked, curious as to her reasoning.

"For one thing, I'm not qualified," she said.

"So?" He didn't care if Pia wasn't qualified. In this instance, he was fully prepared to act in unabashed nepotism. She would learn the job in time if she wanted it, and in the meantime she wouldn't screw up too badly.

Pia sprawled across his body, her head on his chest. She liked to draw light circles around his nipples with her soft, gentle fingers while they talked. It drove him absolutely crazy. Plus they had just finished making love. At that point he was inclined to give her anything she wanted. He was most amused to note she didn't seem to be aware of that fact.

"For another thing, you've got people on staff who actu-

ally *are* qualified and deserve the promotion, like Talia," she told him.

He kissed her forehead, almost closing his eyes as he inhaled her beautiful scent. When they were intimate, he always insisted she take off the cloaking spell that hid her full nature from anyone else. Her pearly luminescence filtered through his dark lashes and lit all the dark corners inside of him.

He said, "I'm still at the 'so?' part of this conversation."

She yawned and told him, "Third, I believe it's a big mistake to take any position that would make me your employee. You'll just think it gives you that much more right to run roughshod over me."

He whispered huskily, "Is that what I do when I'm over you?"

Her throaty chuckle was barely audible. It brought to the forefront of his mind fevered images of what they had just done together. What he had done to her. What he would do to her, with her, again soon. "Seriously," she said. "I may be your lover and your mate . . ."

"That's not all you are." He gathered up her left hand and kissed her fingers where the diamond in the ring he had given her gathered all the light in the room and threw it out in a spray of rainbow sparkles. "You're going to be my wife too, as soon as we have time to do it right."

She paused, then said, "Okay, I'm a little intimidated by what you mean when you say 'do it right,' and I'll be your wife at some point, but the real point I'm trying to make is that I have no idea how to be your partner. I think that job is the wrong way for us to go."

"Fair enough," he said. And that had been that.

Now he strode through the crowded space of the arena, and Talia registered his presence with a quick, smiling glance, but she never stopped speaking to the reporters in front of her, and he maintained his distance. The selkie was all right, he supposed, as he maneuvered through the crowd to the elevators. There was just one big problem with her: she was scared to death of him.

While that might be a reasonable reaction to him, her fear saturated her scent whenever they were within proximity of each other. He didn't know a single Wyr who would believe anything she had to say when she was in that state, so at the moment they were limited to televised appearances together—and Dragos almost never did televised appearances.

Plus there was another unfortunate consequence. Her fear drove him crazy. Not a tolerant male at the best of times, he felt the urge to smack her upside the head whenever they got in the same room. It made for a poor working dynamic.

When he reached the Cuelebre Enterprises Executive Suite, he surveyed it with satisfaction. It had been customized perfectly to his specific requirements.

The interior would have surprised anybody outside his inner circle. Most suites at the arena were designed for high-end entertaining, either personally or for business clients. Cuelebre Enterprises had taken over the arena's new "supersuite" that had the capability of entertaining up to three hundred people, with comfortable lounge-style furniture, stylish decor, kitchens, full bars and fireplaces.

For the duration of Dragos's use, however, the supersuite was currently furnished as a mobile working office, with secure laptop systems that had been personally couriered over by his assistants, office desks and chairs and a lounge area by the windows. It was fully plugged in, with high-speed internet, phones, and fax, print and scan capability. After several months of hard work and negotiations, they were finally at the end stages of some critical business deals. The office would allow Dragos to maintain a presence at the Games without losing a full week of work he could ill afford to lose.

One of his assistants, Kristoff, was already present and hard at work, talking on his phone while he typed on his keyboard. No matter how well dressed Kristoff was, he always appeared to be slightly shaggy and shambling. Kristoff was an ursine Wyr whose untidy, self-effacing demeanor

disguised a sharp, quick wit and the kind of sturdy disposition needed to work around Dragos on a daily basis. Not only that, Kris was a Harvard-educated MBA who thrived on aggressive corporate maneuvering. Dragos paid him well for those traits.

Nodding to Kris as he strode in, he went immediately to the window look out over the arena. The sand on the combat floor was pristine, all footsteps raked smooth.

The door slammed open. Dragos looked over his shoulder, one eyebrow raised. One of his sentinels exploded into the suite. The harpy Aryal's furious gray gaze fixed on him and she stormed toward him. In her human form, she was a six-foot-tall, powerfully built woman with dark hair that was tangled more often than not, and she had a strange, gaunt beauty that had nothing to do with dieting. In the harpy's Wyr form, both strangeness and beauty were accentuated.

Naturally it would be Aryal who dared to storm and seethe around him that day. Chick was crazy, but no doubt that was axiomatic. All harpies were.

Dragos turned back to the arena, which was mostly full and still filling. Fifteen minutes to showtime. He said, "What is it?"

"I just saw the final list, and I cannot fucking believe my eyes." Aryal stopped at his side and glared at him. "Quentin Caeravorn is *PART WYR*?"

"Yes."

"How can he be Wyr without any of us knowing it?"

"His dampening spell was just that good, Aryal. And recruiters saw him change. If his Wyr side is strong enough for him to change, he's eligible to enter the Games."

"He's a goddamn criminal!" she snapped. "You *know* he is!'

"I gave you six months to close down an investigation on him," Dragos said, "and you've not been able to pin anything on him. His qualifications and references are impeccable. The law says he can compete." Besides, he was extremely interested in what Caeravorn's possible motives could be

25

for competing. Those motives would surface eventually, if Caeravorn was given enough time. And rope.

"Screw the law!" she shouted. *"You're* the law. You can disqualify him, for crying out loud—or won't you do that because he's Pia's former boss and special *friend*?"

He pivoted to stare at her with a molten gaze and cold face. He growled, "I created that law, and I will abide by it. So will every other Wyr in my demesne. And so will you, or I will take you down myself right now, so hard you will need much more than a week to heal."

They stared at each other. Aryal's fists were clenched, the muscles in her jaw leaping with furious tension. If Dragos put her out of commission, she wouldn't be able to fight, which would disqualify her from the Games—and that meant she would not be considered as one of the final seven.

Dragos waited a pulse beat. He said softly, "Now if you're quite done, get the fuck out of my face."

Aryal hovered on the edge a moment longer than any other living creature would have dared to. Her particular brand of insanity included an insane kind of courage, he would give her that.

Dragos tilted his head. He flexed a hand.

Her gaze dropped. She looked like she was about to explode, but she held her silence as she whirled and stormed out of the suite.

It wasn't a bad thing to force her to confront her own reckless temper without Grym around to pull her back from the brink. The two sentinels had developed an odd kind of relationship, a nonsexual friendship where Grym took it upon himself to haul Aryal back from whatever trouble her tempestuous nature got her into. But Grym wouldn't be there for her in the Games.

In the end, the arena was like facing the dragon—it was every one for herself.

"Sir, it's time," Kristoff said quietly from behind him.

He stirred. "Tell them I'm on my way."

He went down the elevator and through security, to the tunnel entrance onto the main floor of the arena. The Games

manager was a Wyr gray wolf named Sebastian Ortiz, army retired. Like most gray wolves, Ortiz's hair had turned salt and pepper as he had aged. He had a lined face, sharp yellow eyes, and a lean, tough body that said the old wolf could still be dangerous. Ortiz and Talia were waiting for him just inside the tunnel entrance, along with a few security Wyr.

All of the contestants were already lined up along the arena floor. Talia handed Dragos a field microphone. He nodded to her, gestured to Ortiz and strode into the arena while the Games manager followed.

As he cut across the floor, making the first tracks in the pristine raked sand, the crowd shouted. The sound grew until it rang in his ears. Somewhere a rhythm began. It swept through the arena, turning into a chant: *"Dragos—Dragos—Dragos."* And: *"Wyr—Wyr—Wyr."*

Then Dragos caught a whiff of a long-familiar scent, one single thread of identity in a mélange of over twenty thousand other scents, and it was so unexpected, his stride hitched. Almost immediately he controlled himself to move forward until he stood in the center of the arena. He pivoted, inhaling deeply as he looked over at the crowd. The hot, white blaze of lights was no deterrent for his sharp, raptor's gaze that could detect small prey from over two miles away.

He took his time as he searched. The thunderous roar of the crowd continued for several minutes then began to die away. A heavy anticipation pressed against his senses.

There.

His vision narrowed. He clenched his jaw to bite back a snarl.

High in the stands, his former First sentinel Rune sat quietly with his mate. Rune leaned forward, elbows braced on his knees and chin resting on his laced hands, his expression quiet and serious. His mate Carling sat back in her seat, also watching with a serious expression, one hand resting on Rune's back.

Rune and Dragos had not talked privately since an ill-fated cell phone conversation six months ago when they had

27

parted badly. They had not seen each other since an early morning confrontation in a meadow soon after.

Dragos heard updates, of course. He knew that Carling's quarantine had ended successfully, and that Rune and Carling had settled in Miami. He also knew that a trickle of bright minds and talents had begun to gather in Florida—the Oracle who had once lived in Louisville, a brilliant medusa who was a medical researcher, a sharp legal mind from one of the premier law firms in San Francisco, along with others—enough talent so that disconcertment was beginning to ripple through the seven demesnes. Dragos also knew that the other sentinels kept in touch with Rune, and he did not forbid it.

He had not forbidden Rune or Carling from entering the Wyr demesne either, so he should not have been surprised that they would attend the Sentinel Games.

A strange, tangled knot of emotion gripped him. He felt the urge to shapeshift and attack, along with something heavier, something like sadness or regret.

Or maybe it was the weight of all the years they had worked together in partnership, years that had flown by to become centuries. They had accomplished so much together. For a very long time their different natures and talents had showcased each other's so well that Dragos had once told Rune he was his best friend.

Or perhaps it was the burden of words they had left unsaid. Words like "I'm sorry," and "how are you." And, "you should have fucking said something sooner."

And especially, *"you left the demesne—OUR WORK—for a woman."*

And not just any woman. The former Queen of the Nightkind, one-time Elder tribunal Councillor, fellow Machiavellian thinker and occasional ally. The one woman in the entire world Dragos would not completely trust as mate to his First.

Which meant that even if Rune wanted to, Dragos would never let him work as one of his sentinels again.

All of those words and more strangled unsaid in his tight-

ened throat, because if it had been him and Pia, he would have done the same thing. Unquestionably. He would have left anyone and anything for her, and he still might over the long unknown years of their future. For Pia he would walk away from what had turned out to be his life's work, the Wyr demesne, if he ever had to, and he would do it without a second's hesitation or a second look back.

Gods damn it.

Rune was looking back at him, lion's eyes steady.

He realized he had crushed the field microphone as he clenched his hands into fists, and twenty thousand people had fallen into silence.

He gave his former First a curt, slight nod, and despite the distance, he knew that Rune's own sharp gaze would have caught it. Rune returned the nod.

Then the Lord of the Wyr turned his attention to his waiting people.

He projected his voice so that it filled the arena.

No speechwriter had written what he said. It was unpolished, blunt, straight to the point and televised.

"A long time ago, I made you a promise. I said there would be law in this demesne, and I said it would be a fair one. I told you there would be protection for those of you who could not protect yourselves. As a result, the Wyr demesne remains one of the strongest Elder Races demesnes in the world, and the sentinels are a key part of that promise.

"Six months ago I put out the call, and Wyr from all over the world answered. Every candidate who will fight in this arena has chosen to be here, including each of my current five sentinels who have already served both you and me for a very long time. They could have taken the opportunity these Games presented to retire with honor. None of them chose to do that.

"Of the others, we have screened each applicant carefully until only the most qualified Wyr will enter this arena. They're smart, experienced and capable, and I would be proud to have any of them stand at my side. But not all of them will. The only thing we have left to discover is which

of these contestants are the seven strongest. Those will be the Wyr who stand by my side on Friday. They will keep the peace, uphold the law, protect our borders and *both they and I will hunt down anyone foolish enough to try to harm the Wyr in any way.*

"That continues to be my promise to you and to the rest of the world. Today we start with four hundred and forty-eight contestants—the best and the brightest of the Wyr. Each will fight, and if they lose, they're out, including my current five. Tomorrow we start with two hundred and twenty-four. Friday morning, there will be fourteen left. By Friday evening, the Wyr demesne will have its seven. That way everyone will know beyond a shadow of a doubt that the strongest and the best Wyr hold this demesne safe."

Then he took a deep breath, filling his lungs. He brought his Wyr form close to the surface and let it glow like lava in his eyes.

With enough Power to shake the entire building, the dragon let out a deep roar.

"LET THE GAMES BEGIN!"

Both the crowd and the contestants surged to their feet and roared with him. He walked off the floor while the Games manager took over. It was a strong beginning to the week, a show of Wyr solidarity to the watching world and no doubt it made damn fine TV.

And, bloody hell, he was glad it was over.

Because he couldn't wait for nightfall.

Pia had better be able to get to sleep. If she couldn't, their plans were fucked.

═ THREE ═

The rest of the road trip down to Charleston held more challenges for Pia, after she and the others piled back into the SUVs. Despite the antinausea charm she wore almost constantly, the concentrated smell of so much greasy meat from the many breakfast sandwiches the others had ordered from McDonald's, combined with traveling in the passenger seat, caused her a miserable spell of nausea.

She never actually vomited, but they had to roll down the windows and let frigid air blow through the vehicle until the others had consumed their food. Then they had to stop again to throw away the bags so the smell would really dissipate from the SUV. She couldn't even stand to keep the hash browns they had bought for her. McDonald's used "natural beef flavor" in their hash browns, and she couldn't tolerate how they smelled.

Eventually the group could roll up the windows again. In sharp contrast to the barbed tension and outright antagonism from earlier, the others were really very good about it all—patient and concerned, and without a hint of irritation.

So at least she had made some progress.

The temperature warmed as they traveled south, but the day never brightened. They drove into a steady drizzle, again in almost perfect contrast to her previous trip. This time too there was no need to stop at a superstore for supplies—a pair of mated Wyr had traveled down a couple of days earlier to prepare the estate Dragos had rented. The couple would keep house and provide any cooking that the group would need, which included high-end catering for any guests Pia might invite. They were especially versed in vegan cuisine and coached to provide meals for Pia that were high in protein.

Charleston was a gray smear of rain-dulled cobblestone streets, the windows of gracious homes shining with warm, golden light.

The estate had a large historic home that was beautifully built and attractively positioned on an acre of land, and surrounded by a decorative black wrought-iron fence. She knew the details, at least on paper, and she had seen several digital photos. There were six bedrooms, four full baths, a large dine-in kitchen, a full formal dining room, a formal living room/parlor, a family room with a fireplace, a back terrace and an "in-law" apartment over a detached garage where their housekeeping Wyr would stay.

As the group pulled up the driveway, Johnny pointed out that the house was also positioned well for defense, with a minimum of landscaped foliage around the bottom of the building. She pretended to listen, but mostly she was busy soaking in the sight of their own golden lights shining in welcome in the windows.

Miguel, Hugh and Andrea went into the house first while the rest of them waited, their SUV idling halfway down the drive in case they needed to pull out quickly. As soon as Miguel appeared again in the front doorway and waved an all clear, they headed in.

The interior was a blur, and so were the two Wyr who waited with expectant smiles to greet her. She was sure the whole place was perfectly, outrageously splendid, because

gods forbid that the Lord of the Wyr's mate stay anywhere else. Dragos had probably bought an entire house full of linens, housewares, antiques and crazily expensive artwork just for the duration of her stay. In fact she would bet money on it. He wouldn't allow any Elven guests—or potential spies—to witness anything differently.

At the moment she didn't care, and she didn't want to know. She could scent a whole array of cooked food, including *meat*, which smelled good while at the same time it made her nauseated all over again.

"I appreciate everything you've done to get ready for our arrival," she told the man and woman. She would ask one of the others for their names again later. "And I would enjoy a tour some other time. Right now I need to go to my room. Would you please bring a supper tray up for me?"

"Of course!" said the woman. "Please come with me."

Pia followed her up the stairs along with Eva, while the others brought in their luggage. As soon as the woman had shown her the way, she left with a smile and the promise to return in a few minutes.

Naturally Pia had been given the master suite, and it was—as she'd known it would be—perfectly splendid, decorated with an array of her favorite colors, a large four-poster bed, two beautifully preserved antique wardrobes, a cozy sitting area around a fireplace with a hearth inlaid with hand-painted tiles and a luxuriously appointed bathroom.

Pia walked to the bathroom doorway and contemplated the toilet. Eva took one thoughtful look at her then went around the suite opening windows.

"Thanks," she said without looking around.

"It always this bad?" The other woman sounded leery.

"No." She stirred, inhaling the cold waft of air deeply. "Usually it's nowhere near this bad. The trigger was smelling the meat again on an empty stomach, on top of traveling in the car all day. Now that we're not traveling anymore, it'll probably go away if I can manage to eat something."

Hugh sidled into the room with her luggage and set the

two suitcases in front of one of the wardrobes. She thanked both him and Eva, sent them off to their own suppers, and relished the privacy as they closed the door behind them. As soon as they were gone, she pulled out her iPhone and typed out a text.

We're here.

Within moments, her iPhone pinged with a reply.

How are you doing?

She smiled to herself. Dragos never used abbreviated words in his texts.

Fine. Tired. That's GOOD.

She had a brief impulse but backed away from it. He also wasn't somebody you LOL'd at.

I'm going to eat, clean up and go to bed. You?

The same. See you soon.

All she had to do was *text* with him and read those simple words, and her stupid pulse started racing. Stop. Stop. Adrenaline would wake her up.

A knock sounded at the door. She said, "Yes?"

"I have your supper," said the woman whose name she had forgotten. "Would you like me to leave it here in the hall?"

"No, that's all right." She walked to the door to open it. "I appreciate you bringing it up. Thank you."

"You're welcome." The woman carried the tray in and set it on the small table by one of the two armchairs in front of the fireplace. "Did you find the TV?"

"No," Pia said. The smells emanating from the covered dishes on the tray were good in all the right ways, and her stomach rumbled as she sniffed appreciatively. She confessed, "I'm so tired I forgot your name."

The woman smiled at her. "It's Fran. Shall I help you unpack, or would you rather wait until tomorrow morning?"

"Tomorrow would be great, thanks."

Fran showed Pia the cleverly designed panel over the fireplace that hid a flat screen in a recessed area. "If you would like to set your tray outside your door when you're through, I can pick it up later without disturbing you again."

"Perfect."

She waited until the other woman had closed the door, then she uncovered the dishes. Supper was a southern-style red beans and rice dish, with slices of spicy tofu sausage, a spinach and tangerine salad and a peach cobbler. Pia's nausea vaporized. She fell on the feast and didn't stop until it was all gone.

A full stomach and a hot shower later, she opened up one of her suitcases. She had stolen one of Dragos's T-shirts out of the hamper and wrapped it in a plastic bag. Shaking out the voluminous black material, she slipped it on. It gapped at the neck and fell nearly to her knees, but she didn't care what she looked like. The T-shirt carried his masculine scent, and almost immediately after she put it on, the knot of anxious tension eased at the base of her skull.

It would be all right. He had promised.

She closed most of the windows but left one cracked open, slid in between clean sheets and . . .

She lay there in the strange bed, listening to the quiet, distant sounds of strange people moving about in the strange house. A crazed, frustrated despair lurked around the edges of her mind, looking for an opening to sink its hooks into her and really wake her up.

That was the absolute worst thing, when she needed to go to sleep, she really needed it so badly that it interfered with her actually going to sleep. Then thoughts rabbited around in her mind like rabid bunnies on crack, and oh my gods, this trip was going to be one long-drawn-out hell if she didn't sleep, except she had to sleep some time, didn't she?

Even if it took days. . . .

A warm breeze caressed her skin as she relaxed on her lounge chair on the terrace. She wore one of Dragos's T-shirts and was wrapped in her favorite silk throw as she looked out at the magnificent spray of lights that was the New York City skyline at night. The French doors to their room were propped open and gauze curtains rippled. Despite all the issues and her continued discomfort at living in

Cuelebre Tower, the good things were crazy, out-of-this-world fantastic.

Wait, was she supposed to be in New York? She strained to remember the last events of her day. Man, it had been a long one. A car ride.

"You're thinking too hard," Dragos said from within their room.

It never changed and never lessened, that fierce leap of joy she felt whenever she heard his voice in greeting or whenever she saw him again. She sprang to her feet and ran into their room.

Their bedside lamps were turned on low, and a fire had been lit in the freestanding fireplace, making soft light and shadows dance along the walls. Pia had made a few changes to warm up the austere room. The white carpet was gone, replaced with honey-colored oak floors and woven rugs, and she had added deep gold and jewel-toned pillows to their bed and to the couches. She could tell whenever Dragos's gaze lingered on the rich textiles that he enjoyed the changes.

Magic and Power filled the room, rich like champagne and so imbued with his presence she basked in the feeling.

Dragos stretched out on the top of their bed, hands laced behind his head. He was dressed in one of his casual outfits, simple jeans, boots and a T-shirt. One long leg draped over the side of the bed, his foot planted on the floor as if he had just lain down. His bronze skin looked dark against the white bedspread, and his gold eyes glowed, brilliant and witchy.

She smiled at him, and he smiled back, his hard-edged face softening. He said, "It took you long enough."

"I'm in Charleston," she said. "I couldn't get to sleep."

"You managed it in the end." He held a massive, long-fingered hand out to her.

She went to the bed, and he pulled her down to him. As he wrapped his arms around her, she settled into place. Her body knew him so intimately. It recognized the longer, much stronger shape of his body, every muscle and bone,

36

bulge and hollow. Her cheek knew to rest just there, in the dip on his shoulder, and her arm understood the most comfortable way to lie crooked across his wide chest. She nestled the curve of her pelvis against the jut of his hip with his heavy, muscled thigh slightly between her legs, and they both sighed and relaxed.

It was one of her best-loved places, a necessary place, like when she curled on her side and he spooned her from behind, wrapping her tightly in his arms. He kissed her forehead, and she was home.

"I missed you," she said.

He whispered against her forehead, "I missed you."

Unlike the beguilement he had sent after her when she had run from him last May, this was a simple dream sending. Then, he had set a trap for a thief only to trap himself as well, and the desire they had discovered together had ratcheted into a desperately miserable fever pitch. This time the magic was gentler, as Dragos had explained it would be, and their dream would be whatever they chose to make of it.

"What I want to know," Pia said, "is why you didn't put us in some silk-draped tent in a desert, so we could act out a sheikh fantasy."

His wide chest moved in a low chuckle. He told her, "I'll keep that under advisement. You maintained control of your dampening spell this time."

She stirred, murmuring, "I'll take—"

He clenched her tight and said sharply, "No, don't!"

She froze, looking at him with eyebrows raised.

"Two reasons," he said to her unspoken question. "The shift of your magic might break the dream. And even if it didn't, if you take the dampening spell off here, you might actually remove it from your physical body too. You never know if one of the guards might have to wake you up for any reason. Remember—you told me when you woke up in the motel room the first time, the spell had slipped and you had to recast it."

She scowled, intensely disliking the idea of anyone

37

walking into her bedroom when she was asleep, or possibly breaking the dream without warning. "Okay. Makes sense."

Now that he mentioned it, the whole thing did feel a little dreamy. His arms were around her, and yes, they felt strong and sure, but somehow they did not seem quite as solid as they should. Deep down her bones knew the difference because she had experienced the real thing. She buried her face in him and held on tightly.

He tapped her forehead with a finger. "You're thinking too hard again."

"What, are you afraid I might wake myself up?" she said, muffled against his T-shirt.

"You might. Mostly I don't want you to get so tangled up in details that you mull and stew the night away. The time we have is limited. We need to make the most of it."

"Whose genius idea was this again?" Her mutter was truculent. "Oh yeah, it was mine."

He laughed quietly, took hold of her hand and played with her fingers. "Tell me, how was your day?"

Freaking miserable. "We drove a lot. Then we got here."

She debated whether she would tell him about her sort-of confrontation with Eva then decided against it for now. She had no idea if he would be calmly pragmatic, or if he would go all evil alpha and threaten to ruin Eva's army career, or something else equally over the top and disastrous.

And there would be no point to any of that, especially when she suspected the issue had been resolved enough as it was. Eva was no Aryal—thank God. Pia and Aryal might have reached a balance so that they could spar together, but Pia knew Aryal had never forgiven her for the mistakes she had made last spring, and it was likely Aryal never would.

Argh, harpies. Look them up under the definition of *trouble*.

She glanced at Dragos. He had tilted his head and was watching her closely. "What are you glossing over?"

She sighed. "Anything else I might have to say would be a complaint."

"Tell me," he said.

She could tell by his expression that he meant it. "I got carsick and couldn't eat all day. It was awful. The house is magnificent, but you're not here. That's awful too. I'm trying to spare you a long, boring litany of whine."

He frowned. "Were you able to eat supper?"

"Yes, I stuffed myself." She paused. "Actually there's nothing to whine about that supper. It was just damn good." She peeked at him. "Except you weren't here to eat with me."

"And there it is," he said. "I knew you could get there if you really wanted to."

She pulled her hand from his and touched his lips. He had such a severe mouth. Like the rest of his hard, rough-edged features, it was stamped with temper and the force of his personality.

Only she knew how tender and gentle that hard-looking mouth could be. It wasn't fair, to love someone this much and to have it returned in such a fierce, undying tidal wave of passion and devotion. It was completely unfair, that fortune should lavish upon her such an extravagant, rare gift.

"How was your day?" she whispered.

"It went as expected," he said. "Mostly. No one died. All of the sentinels went through to the next round, but then nobody believed anything different would occur. Graydon—" His gold eyes danced suddenly. "You know what a big motherfucker Graydon is. He turned into a gryphon, and then he just sat down and looked at his opponent, who forfeited. It was the fastest bout of the day."

She giggled. Mostly she was relieved to be away from the Games, and they had deliberately arranged for her trip to occur on the same week. She knew it would tie her into wretched knots to watch people she cared about going through the bouts of combat, even though they chose to go through it, and the fighting was in a good cause.

But she didn't think she could resist watching and fretting if she was in town. At least this way she occupied herself with something that really mattered, and Dragos would stay busy while she was gone.

She said, "I would have liked to have seen that."

"I'm sure many, many people in the Tower are DVRing the Games. I'll get somebody to edit that segment out for you."

"Thank you." She tilted her head. "And how did Quentin do?"

Dragos said simply, "He's an elegant fighter. He put his opponent down quickly, and neither one got hurt. But it may not always go so neatly for him. The bouts will get messier and harder as the week progresses."

She asked, "Was that the unexpected bit of the day?"

The laughter in his eyes died, and his face grew edged and dangerous. For a moment he looked like what he was, a natural-born killer, and she could see the dragon moving at the back of his gaze. Before she could say something the dragon eased back, and then there were other things in his expression, a frown of pain or regret, his mouth tightening in frustration or anger.

He said, "Rune and Carling were in the stands."

She had wondered how Rune would feel about the week, and if he would watch the Games. She had never really bonded with Rune, other than to reach a place where they exchanged friendly banter and agreeable pleasantries. There hadn't been time before he and Aryal left for Chicago to help investigate the assassination attempts against Niniane. Then they had traveled to Adriyel to witness Niniane's coronation. After returning and only spending a week at home, Rune had left again to pay his debt to the Vampyre sorceress.

He had never come back to New York until now.

She asked gently, "Did you talk with him?"

Dragos shook his head, his face hard.

Such a stubborn, proud male. She stroked his inky, silken hair, the short strands flowing through her fingers like water. Even more gently, she asked, "Did you want to?"

His jaw set. "No."

That was too complex an answer to be either a truth or a lie. It felt like neither, and both. She didn't know how to help Dragos with this, other than to listen. She was just glad they were finally talking about it, at least a little. She had tried

40

to broach the subject before a couple of times, only to run into a rare stone wall. "Were you angry when you saw them?"

His eyes flashed again. "Yes."

She rubbed his chest soothingly. "Maybe somewhat hurt too, or regretful?"

"Those are useless emotions," he growled between his teeth.

She nodded. Definitely hurt and regretful. "And I'm guessing jealous too." She met those angry, dangerous gold eyes. "Carling took something of yours that you valued highly, and you're never going to get it back, at least not in the same way."

His expression went blank. For a long moment she waited as he stared into space, and she did not know where he went in the complex, serpentine pathways in his head. Then his gaze snapped to hers, and he was back with her again. He lifted a shoulder. "And I also understand," he said, his voice deepening. "Because if I had to, I would leave everything for you too."

They looked into each other's eyes. Then they moved at the same time to hug each other tightly.

Dragos rolled her across him gently so that she lay on her back. He spread his hand over the slight rounded swell of her stomach, brought his head down and kissed her. She murmured, fingering his hair as a heavy, languid pleasure drenched her body.

Their mating frenzy had eased after a month or so, which had almost been a relief. The frenzy was still there if they reached for it, but now desire had grown deeper, richer. Dragos slid his hand under the hem of the bulky T-shirt, and she lifted her torso so that he could pull the shirt over her head.

He palmed her breast and kissed her again, his hand and mouth gentle, lingering. Without clothing the changes from her pregnancy were visible. Her abdomen swelled where before it had been flat, and her breasts were growing fuller, the full pink, jutting nipples more sensitive.

"I love watching your body change," he murmured as he kissed down her throat.

"What, you didn't like how I looked before?" she said.

His head reared back. He glared at her in sharp incredulity.

She lowered one eyelid in a slow wink at him.

Laughter creased his features. She smiled as she stroked his face, glad she could lighten his mood for a little while. He was such a hard male, and sometimes that hardness bruised others, but sometimes it bruised him most of all.

He cupped her breast and took her nipple in his mouth, running his tongue around the soft, swollen peak and then flicking it with the tip of his tongue, so gentle and sensuous she melted for him, molding her body to his and crooking one leg to rub along the side of his with her naked thigh.

He knew how much she loved it when one of them was nude but the other remained fully clothed.

Once he caught her by surprise. He had dressed for a business function in a black suit that had been hand stitched by some foreign designer. She had chosen to have a lazy day and spent the afternoon reading, stretched out on one of the couches in the penthouse's great room.

When he returned to the Tower, he was still wearing his sunglasses. The dark lens turned his brutal face into that of an impenetrable stranger's. She smiled at him as he strode out of the elevator, her heart kicking at the sheer fluidity of power in his massive body as he moved across the floor.

As he neared she lifted her face, expecting him to kiss her before he went to their bedroom to change.

Instead he knelt on one knee, put his hand over her mouth and pushed her down on the pillows.

She froze and stared at him, her heart rate jettisoning into the stratosphere. Her book fell from nerveless fingers. The thud as it landed on the floor sounded a sharp report in the silent penthouse. He took his time looking at her sprawled body, her crumpled T-shirt and cotton shorts, and the light summer blanket tangled around her slender legs. He yanked the blanket off of her.

An insane arousal stabbed her. She fisted one hand in the lapel of his suit and grabbed hold of his thick wrist with the other. The tiniest of veins at his temple beat a hectic tempo, and oh my God, she had to be one twisted pervert, because when he took hold of her T-shirt by the neck and ripped it down the front, she groaned against his palm and almost came.

He tore her shorts away too with an almost leisurely ease, while his half-hidden expression grew darkly flushed with sexual intent. She lay sprawled on the couch, naked except for the simple white wisp of panties. His head turned. She knew he was looking down the length of her. He hooked his fingers into her panties.

Maybe he meant to slow down and tease her. But she let go of his lapel and gripped his penis as it strained against the expensive trousers. Then the muscles in his arm flexed, and her panties were nothing more than ruined shreds of silk.

He yanked open his trousers as she scooted around to face him, and he gripped her by the hips to lift her up to him. It arched her spine, a strange position, so that her shoulder blades pressed against the back of the couch. She hooked her heels on the edge of the cushions, but she was completely off balance, half suspended in air as he held her entire body weight in his grip. With an exhalation that was more like a whimper, she guided the thick head of his cock into place. She was so wet, so wet.

He thrust in and in, an immense, slick invasion that didn't stop until he was buried all the way inside. His shoulders were bowed, his white teeth clenched. His breathing sounded like bellows. He looked entirely urban and utterly barbaric at once.

Then he fucked her. Hard, slow, rhythmically, steady as a piston. No foreplay, no kissing. She watched his danger-ous, half-hidden face, moving her hips to match his rhythm until she sobbed and climaxed, and then he fucked her some more, until he bowed over her and shook all over with his own spurting release. He never once said a word to her.

43

And she loved all of it.

It was good to love and trust someone so much you could just have sex sometimes, just mate for the sheer rutting pleasure of your bodies moving together in primitive sync.

Now in the dream, she thought back to that earlier time with a small, bittersweet smile. Now wasn't one of those times.

She knew he was right there with her. They could talk on the phone afterward and both would remember the same things—how he suckled at her so gently, how she wound her arms around his neck and cradled his head— but there was still that dreamy, unreal edge to their lovemaking. It made her even hungrier for him in a way that had nothing to do with enchantments or beguilement, and it also made her a little sad.

She tugged at his shirt, and he obeyed her unspoken request, lifting away from her breast so that he could shrug out of it. She ran her hands over his wide, heavily muscled bronze chest as he unfastened his jeans. He rolled to his back to kick off his boots, then he shoved off the jeans, and my gods, there was so damn much of him, and he was all nude, all hers.

As he turned back to her, she put her arms around his neck to hug him tightly. She whispered, "If we climax, will it wake us up?"

"I don't know," he said. He flattened his big hands on her back and pressed her to him. "It could. Do you want to try?"

She twitched a shoulder. "We might as well find out. Otherwise we'll just wonder until we try it."

She felt him exhale in a silent laugh. "There's a rousing endorsement for making love, if ever I heard one."

She tapped her fingers against his bicep, the merest, gentle hint of one of her smacks. "You know what I meant," she muttered.

"I know what you meant."

He eased her onto her back again and came over her.

The laughter died, and his expression turned serious. She parted her legs and guided his cock as he kissed her, and there was another one of her very best-loved places, as he covered and penetrated her while she raised her legs and cradled him. Their bodies were perfectly aligned in a way that said this was home.

She adored it, adored him. He leaned his weight on elbows planted on either side of her head, and he lowered his head until they were nose to nose, staring deeply into each other's eyes as their bodies flexed together gently.

But it was all just a little too dreamy.

Her eyes filled. She said, "I still miss you."

He stroked her temple with the back of his fingers as he kissed her. His gold gaze filled with quiet pain. "I still miss you too," he said.

⇒ FOUR ⇐

Rain pattered outside and left silver streaks against windowpanes when Pia woke early the next morning. She lay twisted in her bedsheets, staring around her lovely bedroom. She remembered the play of his long, clever fingers down the most sensitive places on her body and the sound of his hitched breathing as she tasted his skin, and her overheated body thrummed with frustration.

While the dream with Dragos had been wonderful for comfort's sake, neither one of them had been able to climax as they made love. Not only had the dream experience felt too unreal, but she, for one, had not been able to relax enough while knowing that anyone could walk into her bedroom and wake her at any time. Whatever the reason, meeting in dreams might not be quite the solution they had hoped for.

After another quick shower, she dressed in jeans and a sweatshirt. Her iPhone buzzed. She snatched it off the bedside table and checked the screen. It was another text message from Dragos.

One week.

He had been confident he could create a dream spell for

them to meet in, but they had agreed she would shorten her stay in Charleston if they ran into any issues. They might have managed to make a connection, but hell.

She rubbed the back of her neck, blew out a breath and texted back.

Yes.

Now it was time to see what they could accomplish in seven days. She could repair all the broken treaties while Dragos fixed the internal problems in his demesne. Then they could get back together before the Freaky Deaky came along to screw with them.

But no pressure, right?

Her muscles tightened with nerves. As Dragos's mate, she had traveled with him and attended various functions, such as the world-famous winter solstice Masque at Cuelebre Tower, but this trip to South Carolina was her first time actually flying solo. She had worked hard and learned a lot over the last several months, but she still felt woefully inadequate for the task she had set herself.

Hell, she *was* woefully inadequate. There wasn't a single thing that qualified her to act as the Lord of the Wyr's mate, except that she was actually his mate.

When she confessed how nervous she was about the trip, Dragos hadn't exactly been unsympathetic. But he had certainly been less than helpful. Once he finally conceded to her arguments and she accepted the Elves' invitation to visit, the whole subject occupied the area of *settled* in his mind.

"You're going to be great," he said. "Don't sweat it. Just be yourself."

"You're no help at all," she mumbled into her pillow.

She sounded drugged. She felt drugged. She was lying on her stomach on the bed while he massaged her neck and shoulders, his powerful hands digging into her muscles with slow, sensuous care. Whenever he touched her, he moved his hands as if he savored every sensation, every curve and hollow of her body, and that was possibly even more intoxicating than the actual massage itself.

47

"Of course I'm not any help," Dragos said. "I don't actually want you to go." He paused, then scratched the edge of his fingernails lightly along the bare skin of her back as he asked slyly, "So does that mean you're going to cancel the trip?"

She shivered all over and sighed. "No."

"Then shut up and go," he told her. His gentle tone was in direct contrast with the brusque words.

She lifted her head and stuck out her tongue at him. It was a stupid, childish thing to do, especially when she had been enjoying that back rub so very much.

He retaliated by rolling her onto her back, taking hold of her jaw gently and leaning over her with a machete smile. Just before he brought his mouth down to hers, he muttered, "I've got better uses for that, you know."

Boy howdy, did he have better uses for that.

While the Offices of the Elven High Lord, Calondir, were located in downtown Charleston, his consort Beluviel had invited Pia to Lirithriel House at three o'clock for tea. The house, along with its famous gardens, was the public face of the Elves. It was located an easy half an hour's commute from Charleston and it bordered the actual heart of the Elven demesne, Lirithriel Wood.

The rain had stopped late in the morning. They traveled through a green countryside that sparkled in the pale yellow light of a winter afternoon sun. As they drove north, the sense of land magic grew more powerful. They passed through a small town with several shops and restaurants along the stretch of road that approached Lirithriel House. Pedestrians packed the quaint, Colonial-style cobblestone side streets. The Elven-run businesses enjoyed a robust tourist trade, no matter what the season.

Eva drove Pia's SUV again. Everyone maintained the same positions they had traveled in the day before. All the psychos wore black. Pia couldn't decide if that actually dressed them up or made them look like drug dealers.

Maybe both. It did make them look scarier, at least as far as she was concerned.

She tugged at the edge of her lavender Dior wool Grisaille Bar jacket and checked her patent leather, peep-toed pumps for scuff marks. Beluviel was famous for her beauty and style, and Pia had looked hard for the right kind of outfit to wear for their first meeting. With the help of Stanford, the personal shopper Dragos had retained for her, she had settled on a suit that conveyed a sense of Jackie Kennedy's suits—or at least she hoped it did. The jacket, matching dress and shoes cost as much as a quality used car.

Just months ago she would have been really happy to own that car. She and her mother had lived frugally throughout her childhood, while her mother had put their diminishing resources into hiding escape packs with cash and new identities in various places throughout New York.

Her mother's version of setting aside nest eggs for a rainy day had been more like preparing for immediate evacuation in case of catastrophe. After her mother's death, Pia had honored those choices by leaving the escape packs untouched while she had lived on the modest income she made tending bar.

She thought it might boost her self-confidence if she wore something high-end and classic when she met Beluviel, but instead that morning the expensive suit just added to her nervousness. She was going to spill something down the front of that gorgeous wool suit or break a heel, she just knew it.

You can take a girl out of a Target store, she thought, but you can't take the Target store out of the girl.

"Stop fussing," Johnny muttered under his breath. "You look fine."

Pia took a deep breath and looked sideways. Johnny had his nose buried in his video game again. Compared to the others, his narrow bone structure was almost delicate. "How can you tell? I don't think you've looked up once since you turned that thing on."

An angelic-looking smile touched his lips, an expression

that was there and gone again so fast, she would have missed it if she hadn't been watching him. "Scoped you out when you came down the stairs earlier. I'd commit murder to borrow that suit. Those shoes would be too small for me though."

She turned to look at him again. In the front seat both Eva and James had gone still and watchful, and while she applauded their protective instincts, it wasn't necessary.

She said, "Are you any good with makeup?"

Johnny's gaze lit up, and he looked from his game.

Eva snorted. "He's better than anyone I know."

"Wish somebody had told me that sooner," Pia grumbled. "I could have used some help when I got ready earlier. I had to redo my eyes three times before I got them right."

Eva and James relaxed. Johnny's grin returned, wider this time. "Next time give me a holler. I'll see what I can do."

The two SUVs made the correct turn and traveled at a sedate pace up an immaculate avenue lined with massive old-growth southern live oaks. The iconic trees towered around fifty feet tall, their gigantic thick limbs rippling outward in twisted sprays.

A three-story mansion sprawled at the end of the avenue. Lirithriel House was a perfect example of Greek Revival architecture. The building was balanced and spare with a front gable design, Ionic grand columns, tall elegant windows and a spacious front portico. Built with a light yellow sandstone facade, the house was famed for its golden glow in the early morning hours.

Behind the house lay extensive flower and herb gardens, complete with a labyrinth maze. Beyond that towered Lirithriel Wood, a dark massive presence that was so intense everyone in the car drew a collective breath. Land magic saturated the air, witchy and intoxicating. The lure of the Wood was so strong Pia could hardly look away. The wild creature that lived inside of her yearned to plunge into the tangled green mystery.

The size of Lirithriel Wood was estimated at around

eighty square miles, including a secluded stretch of beach between the barrier islands that dotted the coastline.

The Wood was roughly a fifth of the size of its neighbor, the Francis Marion National Forest. In 1989 Hurricane Hugo had devastated the national forest until virtually none of its old growth survived, but Lirithriel Wood had somehow remained unscathed, dense and wild with ancient trees and a profuse tangle of undergrowth.

Aerial photographs invariably showed an impenetrable canopy of green, the Wood so dense that little of the underlying landscape was visible. A river meandered to a coastal outlet, but it never seemed to run the same path from one photograph to the next.

A river didn't just change its course arbitrarily. Since the Wood contained the crossover passageway to the Elven Other land, speculation had it that the magic of the passageway warped both digital and chemical photos alike.

Pia met Eva's wide gaze in the rearview mirror. She was vaguely surprised that she managed to think of something coherent to say, as she asked, "Have you ever been here before?"

The captain shook her head. "Never sensed anything like that in my life. Can see why people think the Wood is an actual entity."

James stirred in the front passenger seat. "I've heard it called the Bermuda Triangle of South Carolina. A company of Union soldiers disappeared around this area and they were never found again. That's almost a hundred people who vanished into thin air."

"Didn't the Elves adopt a laissez-faire attitude during the Civil War like all the other Elder Races?" asked Johnny. "I thought they claimed that the war was a purely human conflict."

James said, "I don't think official politics would have had anything to do with those soldiers getting lost in that Wood, and if the Elves knew anything about what happened, they never said."

"Weird," said Johnny. He turned off his video game and tucked it into a pack between his feet.

Pia had also heard more modern stories of hikers who had gone missing in the Wood, to emerge confused and disoriented days later. Legend had it the Wood itself did not like uninvited guests.

She glanced one more time at the avenue of enormous oaks. They weren't quite the size of Angel Oak, which was located a short distance southwest from Charleston. Angel Oak was reputed to be the oldest living oak in America, perhaps the world. But these oaks had to be at least several hundred years old.

Was it just her imagination, or did their branches stretch more toward the Wood than anything else? What would it be like for them to live so close to the Wood and yet unable to become a part of it? Or maybe they were close enough that they were a part of the Wood. Maybe they passed ancient secrets through the air with the rustling of their leaves, and she just didn't have the ability to sense it.

As the SUVs pulled around the wide circle in front of the mansion, the double doors opened. A tall, slim Elven woman dressed in a raw silk pantsuit stepped out of the house. Pia recognized her from countless magazine articles and TV news segments, and from the teleconference last summer. She was Beluviel, consort to the High Lord.

Other people exited the house, all Elves, but Pia's attention remained fixed on Beluviel, who was breathtaking. Dark, sleek, shining hair fell down to her long, slim waist, and her face was beautiful, with high cheekbones and wide, gracious dark eyes. Her hair was tucked behind the tip of one long, elegantly pointed ear.

But Beluviel's physical beauty wasn't what made her so striking. America's media was saturated with the physically beautiful to the point of boredom. What made Beluviel unique was her rich, full radiance of presence.

All the immortal Wyr had a certain forcefulness in their aura, especially those who had been born at the beginning of the world for they carried a spark of creation's

first fire. Energy and Power radiated from Dragos. It seethed in the air around him. Pia's own Power lent a natural pearl luminescence to her skin that was unique to her Wyr form.

What Beluviel carried was entirely different, the sunlit green of an eternal springtime. All Elves carried something of that brightness along with the sense that they walked lightly on the earth, but, Pia realized, it was stronger in Beluviel because the Elven woman was older than any other Elf she had met before. Instead of age weighing more heavily on her, it seemed to have the opposite effect. The High Lord Calondir was also one of the ancient Elves. He would carry that same shining, ageless light, tempered with a stern, elegant Power.

The other Elves had stopped just outside the house. Beluviel walked forward alone, her step as light and eager as a girl's, a smile of joy on her bright face.

Suddenly it didn't matter what Pia wore, or the nature of her troubles and insecurities. The political tensions that had brought her to South Carolina, along with the two SUVs filled with bodyguards, all seemed somehow inconsequential.

Stay back, she said telepathically to Eva as she climbed out of the car.

Oh fuck, said Eva with disgust. *You gonna kill me, princess.*

Just do it. As Pia walked toward Beluviel, she saw the Elven woman's eyes fill with tears.

Beluviel said, "I see your mother in you even more strongly in person."

The love and sadness in Beluviel's voice were unmistakable. Everything blurred as Pia's eyes flooded with moisture too. She put out her hands blindly. They were taken in a slender, strong, infinitely gentle grasp.

"I met your mother a very long time ago," Beluviel said. "So long ago, it was a different age entirely, and humans had not yet begun to walk the Earth. She was always wary but predators had not yet forced her into reclusiveness." A

53

smile of reminiscence softened her lovely features. "The world was once a much larger place."

"I never knew," Pia said.

They sat outside at a wrought-iron table on a flagstone terrace overlooking the extensive gardens that held heirloom azaleas and camellias, gardenias, lilies and roses of all kinds. The gardens were dotted with magnolia and crepe myrtle trees, and the entire garden was profusely, brilliantly in bloom. Even though Pia had been raised a city girl and had never tended anything other than potted plants, she was fairly certain that the other gardens in the area would not be quite so colorful in January.

The day had warmed and the sunlight had grown more intense, or at least it was where they sat. The sun burned away the morning's rain, and the evaporating moisture shrouded the nearby Wood in a ghostly, shining mist.

She told the consort, "My mom rarely talked of anything that was not in the present. I loved it when she did, but I think remembering made things harder for her. Also she didn't want to emphasize how different we were from each other. I only just came into my full Wyr form last year, and she had died several years earlier, so she never knew."

"I know she adopted a variety of different names throughout the years, but to us she embodied something sacred, and we called her Silme." Beluviel pronounced the name *seel-may*, and her musical voice made it beautiful. "It means moonlight."

"I didn't know that," Pia whispered. It hurt to think there was so much about her mother that she didn't know, but that was an old ache that was so familiar it was almost comforting. She sipped her tea. The clear golden liquid was a strange, complex floral brew, and the taste and fragrance filled her with a sense of wellbeing and refreshment. "This tea is wonderful."

"It is a flowering herb from our Other land," Beluviel said. "Among its many restorative properties, the tea is quite effective for bouts of nausea. It would be my pleasure to give you some when you leave."

54

She looked up quickly. Beluviel's gaze had dropped to Pia's waist, and a wistful shadow darkened her brightness for the merest moment. While children were rare for all the Elder Races, they were rarest of all for the Elves. She wondered if Beluviel had borne any children. Of course it wasn't the kind of thing one asked.

Instead, she said, "That's very kind of you. Thank you."

"Your father must have been a special man," Beluviel said.

"I think he was, although I never knew him," she said. "He died when I was little." She smiled at the other woman's quick, questioning look. When Wyr mated they did so for life, and when mated Wyr lost their mates they invariably died. "My mother lived long enough to see me grown."

Sadness passed over Beluviel's face. "She was very strong."

"I think so."

"Did you grow up in New York?"

She nodded, and time winged away as Beluviel asked her questions about her childhood and they reminisced about her mother. "I was very drawn to her," Beluviel said. "I adored her wildness. We are so often drawn to that in the Wyr."

Insight and opportunity dangled in front of Pia. She tried to decide how to take advantage of it without seeming to push too far, too fast. She liked Beluviel so much, and up until that moment she had been happy just to build a rapport in their first real conversation. And the last thing she wanted to do was to come across as being too manipulative or driven solely by an agenda.

As she hesitated, a young Elf boy brought a tray of berry cakes to the table. While he served them, she sat back in her seat and looked around.

Eva stood still and expressionless several feet away, her hands clasped behind her back. The others had remained at the front of the house. Probably they were being served berry cakes too, since apparently the Elves didn't have any problem with Wyr. They just had a problem with Dragos.

Pia had not been able to convince Eva to stay with them even though she was convinced the Elves meant her no harm. After a brief, intense telepathic argument when they had first arrived, Pia had given in rather than create an awkward moment in front of Beluviel.

Pia glanced at Eva now, uneasy with how much the other woman was hearing of their conversation. The subject of her mother, along with her Wyr form, was like watching a long, slow train wreck.

All she did was tell one secret to her ex-boyfriend Keith. That's all. Just one.

Now not only did Dragos know what her Wyr form was (and she was completely and totally okay with that), but all the gryphons did too, along with Beluviel—and that Elf Ferion, wherever he was—and God knew how many other Elves, and what was Eva piecing together in that quick mind of hers?

Pia had known this trip was going to be a challenge, and she figured she was going to have to do some pretty fancy tap dancing, but now the reality of that was beginning to sink home. Now she was no longer sure if she was tap dancing, or if she was hopping about like a cat on a hot tin roof.

"Calondir was looking forward to meeting you too," Beluviel said. "Unfortunately it looks like he might not be able to do so."

Pia's attention snapped back to the consort, and she struggled to hide her dismay. "Is he away?"

"In a manner of speaking," Beluviel said. "We have received word that an emissary from Numenlaur will be arriving soon."

"Numenlaurian Elves?" Pia's gaze widened. Numenlaur was the Other land connected to Europe and the seat of the oldest Elven demesne in the world. They had withdrawn from the outside world so long ago that the details of their existence were shrouded in myth. "I've heard it's rare for them to make contact with the world outside of their borders."

"It is," Beluviel said. "We once lived in Numenlaur but have not spoken with our brethren for a very long time.

Whatever has compelled them to make this trip must be of overriding importance to them. They would not be comfortable staying in Charleston, and Calondir has gone into the Wood to prepare for their visit. After your stay, I will be joining him."

Pia savored the last of her delicious berry cake, using it as an excuse to take a moment to think. How much of a roadblock did this represent? While she didn't exactly have Dragos's enthusiasm behind this trip, she knew that she had finally gained his approval for trying to repair their relationship with the Elves.

As the High Lord's consort, did Beluviel have any independent authority to remove the trade embargos levied against the Wyr demesne? If she didn't, Pia might very well just be having tea and cookies with her. As enjoyable as getting to know Beluviel was, Pia did not plan on enduring a separation from Dragos just for that.

She said slowly, "I was hoping to talk with Calondir while I was down here."

Beluviel looked down as she adjusted the position of her fork on the table. She asked, "Might you possibly consider traveling into the Wood for a few days as our guest? I'm sure we would both be honored to have you visit our home."

The wild creature that lived inside of Pia yelled *hell yeah* and strained to gallop headlong into the underbrush right then and there. She whacked at it mentally and fought to get in control. "I would be delighted to visit with you in Lirithriel Wood," she said. "If you think Calondir would be able to take time from his preparations to meet with me."

Beluviel's smile was positively conspiratorial. "I believe that he might value greatly the effort you would make to speak with him."

"If we did this, we would need to do it right away," Pia said. "I promised Dragos I would stay in the Charleston area for just the week."

Beluviel's smile widened. "The Wood does not like machinery, so we must travel in on horseback. Would you be comfortable with that?"

"Certainly," said Pia, her mind racing. Of all the contingencies she had packed for, she didn't think to pack for anything like this. Damn. She really would have to go shopping.

"Then we can leave in the morning. Would seven o'clock be too early?"

"That would be fine," she told Beluviel. Eep, that meant shopping tonight.

Pia could tell Eva didn't like the direction things had taken, but she ignored the other woman's wooden expression and stiff posture as Beluviel walked with her through the exquisitely decorated showcase mansion.

When she turned to Beluviel just outside the front doors, the Elven woman hugged her. Touched and warmed by one of the few physical gestures of outright affection she had received from anyone outside of Dragos in months, Pia hugged Beluviel in return.

"I am so glad that you came," Beluviel said.

"I am too," she told the other woman. "Not only is it wonderful to meet you, but it's been especially wonderful to talk with someone who knew and loved my mom. I can't tell you how much I've missed her."

As she turned to walk to the SUVs where the others were waiting, Eva fell into step beside her.

Pia managed to bite back saying anything until they were almost to the vehicles. Then she said telepathically, *If you say anything to anyone about what you overheard, I will break every bone in your body.*

Eva's jaw angled out. *Princess getting cranky again?*

I mean it. She glared at the other woman. *That was a private conversation.*

Shew, don't get your fancy knickers in a twist. Captain Psycho opened her dark eyes wide. *I know who I work for, and it ain't you but he be bad. I figure he would want me to keep my mouth shut about your momma. I also figure he won't like your plans to go on an impromptu camping trip.*

They climbed into their SUV. As soon as the doors were shut, Pia said aloud, "What Dragos does or doesn't like is none of your business either, Eva."

"It's my business when it comes to me doing my job," Eva said, her expression grim.

"What's going on?" James said.

"Princess going to party in the Wood with the Elves tomorrow morning," Eva said, her voice turning crisp. "So we get to party with the Elves too."

"Sa-weet," said Johnny.

Eva glanced at Johnny sourly as she continued, "Beluviel say that Wood don't like machinery, and to me that sounds an awful lot like an Other land. That means we pack the guns and pull out the swords tonight. Starting tomorrow, we go on rotation and stay with princess twenty-four/seven, no matter where she go, who she see or what she do. It's the only way she going to get to talk to the High Lord and since that's why we came, that's what we're going to help her do."

Angry, Pia had opened her mouth to verbally smack down on Eva, but she held back as she listened.

"She bitch-goddess sexy when she throw down orders like that," Johnny said to James.

"You can call me bitch for short," Eva said.

$=$ FIVE $=$

Blood sprayed crimson over the sand of the arena.
    It was the pegasus's blood. What was his name
again? "Alexander somebody," murmured Dragos.

"Alexander Elysias," said Kristoff from behind him.

Dragos stood at the window of the supersuite, arms
crossed, as he watched the latest contest. He could see his
assistant's reflection in the glass. Kris had never looked
away from his computer screen. Kris probably knew by
heart the names of all the four hundred and forty-eight
original contestants.

Dragos glanced over the VIP boxes. Virtually every
demesne in the United States had some representative in
attendance. He noted that Jaggar, the kraken who repre-
sented the Wyr on the Elder tribunal, sat with the human
witch Councillor, Archer Harrow. Jaggar was a dominant
personality. One of the reasons why he and Dragos got
along was that the kraken attended to his tribunal duties for
the Wyr but otherwise spent most of his time offshore.

The Elven Councillor, Sidhiel, was also present, her pale
blonde hair pulled into a classic chignon. Sidhiel was one of
the ancient Elves, at least as old as Beluviel and Calondir

and perhaps older. She watched the arena, her expression perfectly controlled and composed. She and Dragos loathed each other with the passion of those who remembered old grudges well. No doubt Sidhiel was staying at the Plaza, where the Elven demesne kept a suite. He wondered what she thought of Pia's trip to Charleston.

He switched his attention back to the combatants. Elysias was limping badly as he turned to face his opponent of the day, one of the harpies. The pegasus was one of the most popular of the contestants, especially with the females. He had a kind of imperious beauty that somehow missed being feminine, and a ready, gleaming smile. His human form was lean and graceful, and his mahogany skin gleamed with sweat under the strong lights.

The gash in his thigh was long and deep, and it bled freely. His footing had slipped in the sand, which was an unfortunate mishap. The harpy had been all too quick to take advantage, and she struck at him hard and fast. The wound heralded the end to their battle. The harpy wouldn't allow him any time to bind it, nor should she. Either Elysias would have to put the harpy down fast, or the bleeding would do him in.

The harpy wore a sharp, predatory grin. Since the contestants went into the arena without weapons, all they had to use in battle was what nature had given them, and nature had favored the predator Wyr prodigiously. She had shifted into her Wyr form, and her long sharp talons dripped with the pegasus's blood. Her hair, wings and the short feathers on her powerful legs were a fiery red.

A harpy with a redhead's temper. Dragos exhaled in a silent snort. Talk about overkill.

Legend said the skies tore when the harpies screamed into existence. He remembered that day well. The legends were correct.

The heavy, rich scent of blood tinged the air. Elysias wasn't the first to have bled in the arena today. Many had sustained wounds of some sort, although thus far his five sentinels and Pia's friend Quentin had remained unscathed.

Dragos breathed evenly. The dragon was close to the surface, angered that Pia was gone and constantly roused by the spectators from other demesnes or countries who were neither allies nor friends. It liked the blood and the violence, and it wanted to enter the arena, but it had no true opponent in this place. There would be no satisfactory battle for him to find here; he could only turn the arena into a slaughterhouse.

Once, the dragon would have enjoyed such a slaughter. Ancient memories moved deep in his thoughts like a subterranean tide. He was a more primitive creature without Pia. She had a clean decency that brought out the finer things in him. With her, he almost understood what it meant to be kind, and he had just barely begun to understand tenderness. As he had told her once, she was his best teacher.

In the arena, the harpy moved to make another strike, hands splayed wide with all ten talons extended like knives. They would be sharp enough to slice through metal. They could definitely cut through the pegasus's bones if she struck him hard enough.

Elysias feinted, and when the harpy fell for the maneuver he surged forward on a burst of speed and power. With an immense leap he twisted and kicked out with his good leg. He threw the full weight of his body behind it, and as his heel connected, the crack of the harpy's spine was sharply audible over the sound system. She shrieked in rage and pain. They both dropped to the ground.

Silence washed over the audience. When Elysias rolled to his knees and pushed to his feet, his struggle to get upright was evident. He must have torn his wound open even further with his last leap, for he couldn't put any of his weight on that leg.

The harpy didn't rise. Her back was broken, and she wouldn't be able to stand upright for weeks. The fight was over. Elysias had pulled it out at the end and won.

The crowd roared, and medics ran out.

The door to the suite opened. Dragos turned away from

the window as Graydon poked his head into the room. "You wanted to see me, Chief?"

"Yes, come in." He said to Kris, "Take a break."

"You got it," said Kris, who shut his laptop, tucked it under his arm and left, no doubt to ignore what Dragos said and work elsewhere. His obsession for work was another reason Dragos paid him so well.

Graydon strolled in. He was the brawniest of the four gryphons, a good thirty pounds heavier than the others. In his human form he stood nearly six foot five, and all of it was hard, packed muscle. He took the ugly road to handsome, with a strong face that most often wore a good-natured expression, and rugged, slightly irregular features, sun-darkened skin and gray eyes. He kept his tawny hair no-nonsense short and his clothes plain, and somehow whenever drama plagued the occupants of Cuelebre Tower, he was nowhere to be found. That was a useful talent to have.

A couple of months ago, curious, Dragos had asked Pia, "Why do you have such a soft spot for Gray?"

She smiled, and the part of him that would always be selfish and acquisitive took jealous note of how her face softened whenever Graydon's name was mentioned. "Because he's got this bluff, gruff exterior, but underneath that he's true, right down to the bottom of his soul."

True, faithful. Loyal.

Unlike many other predator Wyr, including several of the other sentinels, Graydon often pulled his punches when he struck at someone else. He was well aware of his outsized strength. So far, Dragos had noticed, the gryphon was pulling his punches in the arena as well. With the intimacy of long acquaintance, he knew that Graydon would only hammer down when the occasion called for it.

Dragos frowned and turned toward the window again. Graydon joined him and looked out the window too. "I have every expectation that you will be one of the final seven again," Dragos said. Graydon nodded without speaking, plain even in this. Dragos told him, "When Friday comes, I want to announce you as my First."

63

Out of the corner of his eye, he saw Graydon give him a quick look. After a few moments, Graydon said, "I suppose you know that Rune has been in the audience."

He nodded.

"So you've talked?"

"No," he said.

Graydon said, "I wish you both would get over this shit."

That one sentence was the most any of the sentinels had said to him on the subject. He said, "Will you consider the position and let me know?"

The other male sighed. "When do you want me to get back to you?"

"Thursday evening would be fine." Then, driven by an impulse he chose not to dissect, he said, "You keep in touch with Rune, don't you? You all do."

"Yep," Graydon said. "Some of us are mad at him. Some are mad at you. Some of us are mad at both of you."

Dragos rubbed his face. "Has he ever talked about what happened?"

"Nope. Far as I know, he hasn't told anybody about it. Well, maybe he's talked to his mate, Carling, but he hasn't talked to any of us."

There were different ways to manifest loyalty, Dragos thought. Maintaining silence was one of them.

As he considered the events of last summer, he thought he could see the cracks in Rune's own behavior that had indicated the volatility of a Wyr in the early stages of mating. While Rune was known for his even temper, he had snarled at everyone when he had returned from Adriyel, even Dragos. Dragos remembered his own volatility when he was mating with Pia, and how he had nearly choked Rune to death over something that had been entirely innocuous.

How readily Rune had seen what was happening and forgiven him then. Fuck.

He gritted his teeth. Talking to Pia was so much easier.

He growled, "If you are inclined to take the position, you should consider. I was not easy on Rune. He bore the brunt of my temper often, and when he started to show

strain, I did not take notice or change any part of what I did. When he asked for me to pause and listen to him, I did not. I issued orders."

He had specifically ordered Rune to return to New York and abandon Carling, who had at that time been an ally to the Wyr. The Elder tribunal had put Carling under a kill order. While normally Dragos might have involved himself in the issue, last summer the Wyr demesne had been facing border tensions with the Elves, and had been too deeply entrenched in the Dark Fae problems for too long. Overextended, understaffed and short on political tolerance, he had decided, to use a fisherman's term, to cut bait.

It had been the right decision, goddammit, and one Rune might have agreed with, if he hadn't become so deeply invested in Carling. Hell, probably even Carling would have agreed with it. She knew the necessity of doing what was politically expedient in order to survive.

If Dragos had it to do all over with the same information he'd had at the time, he would make the same decision again. But it had been the right decision delivered badly, and he had not given Rune a chance to weigh in on the subject and change his mind. Then it had been Rune who had cut bait in favor of his mate.

Graydon's thoughts must have followed in a similar vein, because he said, "You all went crazy when you mated. I may want a mate, but I don't want to go crazy."

Dragos smiled wryly. "I may remind you of that someday."

"Yeah well." Then the other male said, wistfully, "Don't suppose you could tell Rune all this and apologize."

"Things cannot return to what they were, Gray," he said. "Even if I were to apologize—even if Rune apologized for his part in creating what happened—we cannot go back. Maybe we can find a new definition, but he will not ever be my First again. That time is done."

"Well," said Graydon. "Suppose I had to ask." He sounded disappointed but not surprised. "Do you mind saying— why me?"

Dragos considered. "Because not only do I trust you but Pia does too. It matters to me that she loves you, and that you're close to her. I want you to talk to her if you ever feel the need. I know she's young, and she may not have experience with administrative shit, but she has more understanding and compassion for people than I will ever have. I think that may lend us a stability that Rune and I didn't achieve in the end." He smiled. "She won't let me be too hard on you."

His rugged face sober, Graydon said, "Thank you for telling me."

Dragos nodded to him. "Let me know when you've decided."

"I've decided," Graydon told him. "I'll do it."

They talked for a few more moments, then the gryphon took his leave, and with that Dragos reached his limit on meaningful talks for the day. He needed out. Out of the crowded complex that was filled with so many vulnerable creatures and such a strong scent of blood. Out of the crowded city.

He left the building and launched into flight, and let the burn of the icy winter air take him until solitude gave him a measure of balance. He would stay in the air until darkness covered the land. Then he could hope to find peace with Pia, in a dream.

He supposed this was love. The thing of it was, he had seen examples of love that were twisted, small-minded and unhappy, so he wasn't quite sure. The immensity of experience he had with Pia was so much more than that.

When they came together, he felt a deep knowledge in massive bones that were as old as the Earth. The knowing was a vibration that altered the fabric of his existence. It became the sound that mystics claimed was the absolute reality in the universe. Having never, ever embraced mysticism, he thought he must have gone more than a little mad.

She was *his*, his only true treasure and one possession, and part of what created that trueness was that she chose it too, and she claimed him, and he was *hers*. What existed

between them was active and passionate and elemental, a hinge upon which everything else pivoted.

A Prime, indivisible. That pure, that strong, that essential.

Without this, he had nothing. Everything else might cease and pass away, but this one thing would never fail. And the rest of his life became as if seen through a glass, darkly.

Since he knew Pia's true Name, bringing her into a dream was easy. Still, he took time with this one and worked to get the details right, brushing them into place with his mind like an artist putting the finishing touches on a painting. Then he cast it out, an invisible net woven with Power, and he went to sleep himself and waited.

Part of him marked the passing of time even as he drifted quietly. Then he felt her presence slide into the dream, and he came alert.

The setting was cool and quiet, and a light, delicate wind blew. He had recreated the subtle hues of night.

She was outside. The light, musical tinkle of bells danced through the air. "What the . . ." she said, sounding disoriented and puzzled. Then she laughed, and the sound was more beautiful than the bells.

He smiled, rose from the couch where he had been reclining and lifted the flap of the tent to look out.

Sand dunes rippled underneath the silvery cascade of moonlight. Several feet away from the tent a small oasis of water, little more than the size of a comfortably large hot tub, was surrounded by a collection of ferns and palm trees, which didn't make any ecological sense, but still, the scene was pretty.

Pia stood on the path between the tent and the oasis, looking down at herself. Pleasure washed through Dragos. She was a symphony of the precious colors he loved the most, silver, ivory and gold, and those gorgeous sapphire eyes. Her loose hair rippled down her back, and the harem outfit he had devised for her to wear was skimpy in all the

right places. Bracelets and anklets of tiny bells adorned her graceful wrists and ankles, and her slender, arched feet were bare.

She looked up, still laughing. "You made me look like a belly dancer . . . oh my. Oh, very much my."

"What?" he said, strolling toward her with a slight smile. He was barefoot as well. He wore a simple linen robe that wrapped and belted at the waist, with thin cotton pants underneath. "The belly dancer outfit was my favorite part."

"How very sheikh-ish you look." Her face tilted up as he neared, and her midnight-colored eyes were wide.

He played with her jewelry, letting the dangling earrings slide over his fingers. The heavy, gold linked necklace at her neck was shamefully erotic. It highlighted the delicacy of her throat and collarbones, and evoked the concept of bondage. He said deeply, "You should wear jewelry more often."

The bells at her wrist tinkled as she raised a hand and laid it at his chest where the robe parted. Her fingertips were cool on his bare skin, her hand unsteady, resting against him as light as a trembling butterfly. "It's at times like this that I want to say something incredibly foolish," she said. She sounded breathless.

He captured her fingers and brought them up to his lips. "Like what?"

She murmured, "Like I'll wear anything you want me to, whenever you want."

"I see nothing at all wrong with that statement." He mouthed the words against her fingers.

She snickered. "Of course you don't. And I'm *not* saying it. I'm only confessing to the impulse."

He told her, "You should always tell me your foolish impulses so that I may take advantage of them."

"That is not going to happen, your majesty," she informed him. "The ones I do tell you are bad enough." She looked down at herself and her voice grew mournful. "This outfit makes me look fat, doesn't it?"

"You've got to be kidding me," he growled. He had started

to bend down to her for a kiss, and he reared his head back to glare at her. Without a clever layering of clothing to hide it, her slender waist flowed gracefully out to a lightly rounded belly, and her breasts were lush and ripe, the creamy skin soft as a white peach. Everything inside him tightened at the sight. "You look utterly incredible."

She swayed forward. He put an arm around her as she leaned against him, and his head came down over hers. He rested his cheek in her thick, soft hair, and for the first time that day the dragon's constant, rogue urge to violence subsided. What it left behind was a deep, hungering ache. He wanted to drag her to the ground and ease his cock inside of her while she gripped him with her inner muscles and rocked him with her strong, supple body until he spilled everything he had into her. He was the hardiest of all creatures, but good *gods*, these dreams were going to kill him.

He slid a greedy, possessive hand down the front of her body to cup her rounded belly. A pang of disappointment lanced him as he realized the familiar, young bright spirit was absent. "I didn't notice before," he murmured. "The baby isn't here."

She tilted her head back, gaze darkening in ready sympathy. "I can sense him, but I guess he isn't dreaming?"

He shook his head and shoved the disappointment away. "No."

She rubbed his back. After a moment she asked, "How did . . . everything go today?"

He answered her real question. "Everybody is fine. All the sentinels and, yes, your friend have won through to the next round."

"That's good." She searched his gaze. "Right?"

"Yes." Suddenly the playful, pretty scene was no match for his darkening mood. Setting his teeth, he let go of her and turned away.

Silence fell between them. He gazed over the endless-seeming, empty desert with a scowl. When he heard tinkling and a splash, he looked over his shoulder. Pia sat by

the edge of the oasis with her feet in the water, harem trousers rolled over her knees. She had taken off the anklets. She straightened one leg and lifted her pretty foot out, looked at it then let it fall with a splash back into the water.

Somehow she knew when not to push him. Yes, she was wiser sometimes than he would ever be. He walked over to ease down behind her until she sat between his legs, and when he put his arms around her again she leaned back with a sigh. The feel of her body in his arms felt maddeningly familiar and yet somehow incomplete. Damn these dreams, yet he would not go the week without them.

He said, "I asked Gray to be my First, and he said yes."

She turned her head slightly. "That's great news."

He sighed. "We also talked a little about Rune and what happened last summer."

She said gently, "That must have felt complicated."

"It did."

"I'm glad you finally talked to someone about it. Did it help?" She rubbed slender fingers soothingly along his forearms.

"Yes, actually, it did." He pressed his mouth to the place where her neck met her shoulder. "How was your day?"

"Complicated too in its own way." She reached behind her and cupped the back of his head, stroking his hair in a brief caress. "I like Beluviel, and she told me some things I didn't know about my mom. That hurt, but it was kind of a good hurt, if that makes any sense. I think we really connected. She told me something interesting that may throw a monkey wrench into my visit. They've received word that an emissary from Numenlaur is coming to meet with them."

Dragos raised his head. "Did they?"

She twisted to look over her shoulder, searching his expression. "Calondir has gone into Lirithriel Wood to get ready for their arrival. Have you ever heard of Numenlaurians visiting the U.S. before?"

"No." He regarded her thoughtfully. "Are you sure that Beluviel said Calondir went into the Wood? She didn't

70

say that he crossed over to prepare for the emissary in their Other land?"

She frowned and scooted around until she could face him fully. "Yes, I'm sure. Why?"

"Do you remember how I once described Other lands like bodies of water, from small lakes to large oceans, with streams or rivers that sometimes linked them together?" She nodded, and he continued, "I know their Elven Other land is quite large, and I've suspected for some time that it has several connections, or crossovers, to Earth and to Other lands. I think they've had the ability to travel to and from places in Europe."

"What makes you think that?"

"Stories of arrivals and departures," he told her. "People disappearing and then reappearing in other places."

She cocked her head. "Sometimes sudden appearances and disappearances can be explained when the Djinn are involved."

"Yes, they can, but these accounts are different," he told her. "Beluviel and Calondir were involved in rescuing Jews during World War Two. A few of the survivors described journeys that sounded like they traveled in an Other land until they suddenly arrived in America."

Her eyebrows rose. "I'd like to learn more about that sometime, but what is the connection here?"

"I wonder how the emissary is traveling. I find it hard to imagine that members from an enclave community would travel from Europe on this side if they had any choice to travel in an Other land. If they are making the journey from the Other land, why would Calondir choose to host them in the Wood, here on this side? Why not host them on the other side of the crossover, where they would be more comfortable? The pieces don't quite fit together in my mind."

"Maybe I'll get a chance to find out how they fit together," Pia said. "Beluviel said that she and Calondir were originally from Numenlaur. I wonder why they left."

"Do you remember, you also once asked me why Elves

might not keep their word?" he asked. "You had said you'd never heard anything bad about their integrity."

"Yes, we were just leaving Charleston after you got shot. You called my car a POS." She frowned, thinking back. "You also said that every race has had its moments now and then, so I suppose that means the Elves had a moment."

He played with her bracelet of bells. "They had more than their fair share of moments. They were responsible for one of the greatest wars in prehuman history."

"Who did they fight?"

"Themselves. They fought until Elven blood ran over the land, and they finally drove themselves into a diaspora. Did you know that the Light Fae and the Dark Fae are children of the Elves?"

"I had no idea." Pia watched him with a fascinated gaze. "I guess it makes sense since the similarities between the three races are pretty obvious. They're all long lived, and magical in some way, and of course they all have the pointed ears. But there are some pretty obvious differences too."

He said, "The Fae races came out of that original Elven diaspora. I believe their differences evolved because of their differences in environment. The Dark Fae are most often found in northern lands, with their pale skin, dark hair and affinity for metal. The Light Fae, with their brown skin, lighter hair, aversion to certain metals and a strong affinity to water, are most often found in more southern climates."

"Then there are the Elves," she said. "And they feel like no other creatures in the world. At least no other creatures that I've met."

It was his turn to raise his eyebrows. For someone of her relative youth and inexperience, she had a remarkably refined sensitivity to creatures of Power. "Interesting. You sense a difference in how they feel?" She nodded. He told her, "You are correct. Their Power is different from any others. It's elemental, literally."

"What do you mean?"

"Their Power comes from the five elements—air, fire, water, wood and earth. Like the Wyr and many of the other

Elder Races, the Elves grow in Power as they age. The ancient Elves can control weather, shift tides, cause landscapes to shift. In many ways the Earth was a different place before they warred with themselves."

"That sounds terrifying," she muttered.

"It was," he said. "And I still have not forgiven them for it."

A shudder ran through her, and she looked up at him. "Lirithriel Wood. Is it something they created?"

"I believe it is at least something they started," he said. "It was born out of their Power and is combined with the magic of one of the strongest crossovers passageways in America. The Wood appears to have achieved a certain intelligence that is entirely wild and not necessarily safe."

"I think it's beautiful."

"And I suppose it is that too." He laced his fingers with hers.

She made a sudden moue. "That's probably my segue into telling you that Beluviel invited me to their home in the Wood so that I can speak with Calondir."

In an instant, his uneasy sense of peace and balance vaporized, and the dragon roared to the surface. He snapped, "Absolutely not."

She froze, her mouth open, and stared at him. "Excuse me?"

"I said no," he growled. "You do not go deeper into the Elves' territory. I have allowed you to go this far, but I will not allow that."

She blinked several times. She said slowly, "So when Beluviel invited me, and since it is the only way I can speak to Calondir on this trip, I said yes. We leave first thing in the morning."

"Pia, I said no, dammit!"

Her expression grew cold. "I heard what you dictated the first time," she told him, shaping each word deliberately. "I chose not to respond right away so that you could have a moment to think about what you just said, and how you said it to me."

He went nose to nose with her and hissed, "You will not disobey me on this. I forbid it. *They are my enemy.*"

She flinched but did not back away. "Yes, Dragos," she said. "They are *your* enemy. They are not mine."

He said between his teeth, "That is a foolish attitude. My enemies are yours. You are my mate—if you die, I die."

"Just because our lives are linked together, I do not believe that makes the Elves my enemy too. When Beluviel made the invitation, she was clearly trying to help." She pushed to her feet, and he rose too. She lifted her gaze, and the hurt, anger and disappointment in her eyes speared him. She said with quiet bite, "Now I am going to figure out how to wake myself up, and I'm going to turn off my phone. That should give you more time to think, because we have also had this conversation before. I am *NOT* your employee, *NOR* am I your servant, and I never promised to obey you. And what's more, Dragos, you should not speak to your employees or your servants like that anyway. If what happened with Rune taught you anything, it should have taught you that."

He sucked in a breath. Maybe to roar, or maybe to apologize. Not even he knew what he intended. Perhaps both. Whichever it was he was too late, for she turned away from him.

His mate *turned away from him*. As she did so, she faded from the dream.

The dragon woke up with a growl. He lunged to his feet, then glared at the bed.

It was so appallingly empty he took hold of one end and threw it against the wall.

≡ SIX ≡

"You look like something a cat coughed up," Eva said in a helpful tone of voice.

Pia gave Captain Psycho a dirty look as she tied the laces of her new boots. "Have I told you yet how much your witty repartee means to me?" she said between her teeth. "No, wait. I believe I haven't."

Beluviel had told her that the Elves would provide for her group's needs, but she had still needed to get a few things suitable for horseback riding and a stay in the Wood. She had brought only one pair of jeans, the ones she had worn on the trip down.

The group had stopped at a superstore directly after leaving Lirithriel House so that she could buy a couple extra pairs of jeans and the boots. She had brought enough sweaters, and although they seemed a bit dressy, they would do. She packed one nice slacks outfit to meet Calondir in, left her fine wool dress coat in the wardrobe and threw the more serviceable anorak she had worn on yesterday's car trip on top of her pack.

Eva crossed her arms and lounged against the doorway, watching Pia's final preparations. "You sick?"

"Nope."

"Deranged?"

She gritted her teeth. "Just didn't sleep well." She had, in fact, lain in a furious, hurting clench for hours after she had woken up. After a brief, horrible struggle with herself, she did exactly what she told Dragos she would do, and she turned off her iPhone. Then she glared at the damn thing for the rest of the night.

She wanted to turn it on. So. Badly.

But it would be truly awful to turn the phone on only to find out he never called or texted. And it might actually be just as awful to turn it on and find out that he left a terrible message of some sort, something cold or hateful about *disobeying* him.

And it would be especially awful if she turned on the phone to find out that Dragos was remorseful and apologetic. In pain. If he did something horrendously unusual like beg her not to go. Because then she was afraid she would totally cave in, and what's more, she might gallop back to New York, and that wouldn't do anybody a lick of good, not the Elves, not the Wyr demesne, not Dragos and especially not her, because this was a line she had to draw that she could not back down from.

He simply had to acknowledge and treat her like his partner, and work with her to figure out what that meant. He could not give lip service to the subject only to revert whenever he lost his temper or he didn't like how things were going, and sure, he was a dragon and a man, and that meant he had all kinds of communication issues, but *this one time*, he had to be the one who gave in.

"So," Eva said. "There's no reason to call off this trip."

Pia froze as an especially, super-duper terrible idea added itself to the litany of terrible possibilities. "Why?" she bit out. "Did somebody ask you to try to stop it?"

Eva stared at her like she might have lost her mind. The other woman might have a point. "Just thought I'd double-check."

"There are lots of reasons to call off this trip," she said. She stood and walked over to Eva, and looked into the other woman's eyes. "I just happen to think all the good reasons to go outweigh the others. Got a problem with that?"

Eva cocked her head. "You got a touch of bitch-goddess sexy too, don't you, princess?"

She twitched a shoulder. "I guess I do."

One corner of Eva's mouth lifted an insolent notch. "Your goddess ain't as sexy as mine though."

"Who cares?" said Pia. "Because you're my bitch now."

Surprise flared in Eva's gaze, then she burst out laughing. With that, they both went down the stairs to load the SUVs, and the group drove out of Charleston.

The early morning was cool, damp and gray. Low-hanging clouds blanketed the sky, dark and lowering. They might be in for a wet, uncomfortable day's ride. Pia flipped her cell phone over and over in her hands, scowling at it for the duration of the trip. She only looked up when they drove the final approach to Lirithriel House. As they pulled up to the front doors, an Elven male stepped outside to direct them to follow the drive around to the back of the property where they could leave their SUVs by the stables.

The drive took them around the edge of the garden, which was lush from every angle. Between the magnolia trees, Pia caught a glimpse of a gap in a high green hedge, bordered by two elegantly carved marble pillars. That looked like the opening to the labyrinth.

The stables were already a hive of activity. A couple of the Elves smiled at the newcomers. Several of them walked horses that were already saddled. Their horses were gorgeous, thoroughbred-sleek with gleaming coats, long, slender legs and intelligent eyes. Pia saw one horse mouthing affectionately at the hair of the Elf attending it, who bore the attention with a tolerant smile. They clearly loved their horses, and their horses loved them.

The animals were also quite large up close. While the rest of her group double-checked their packs, Pia took a

deep breath and turned to Hugh, who carried her pack slung over one shoulder along with his. "I suppose now's the time to mention that I don't have a lot of horse-riding experience."

"Not to worry," Hugh said. His smile transformed his rather plain, bony features. "I'll make sure they give you a suitable mount."

"Thank you."

Pia fingered her phone again as Hugh left to talk with one of the attendants. Her stomach was a tight knot of nerves. She ran her thumb over the power button, looking down at the black screen. She would take just one quick peek. She never said she would leave it off forever. And she ought to check on things anyway, since the phone probably wouldn't work when they went into the Wood.

She couldn't go all day without some sort of contact, she just couldn't, not with how they . . . *she* had left things. She thumbed the power button on at the same moment that Beluviel walked out of the stables, caught sight of their group and walked toward her.

Beluviel looked even more exotic than she had yesterday, her long, dark hair braided for travel. She wore leggings and a tunic of a rich, soft green cloth, with a bronze jacket so intricately embroidered, it could have been a museum piece.

She was also more luminous and vibrant than ever, and a sense of refreshment wafted over the scene at her arrival, bringing with it optimism and hope. At first Pia thought she had imagined it, but then she noticed how the other Elves looked to Beluviel as well, smiling. Even the other Wyr did, although they didn't lose their sharp-eyed alertness.

A useful attribute, that. It had to be much better than looking and feeling like something a cat coughed up.

Her phone pinged. The small sound sent a hot prickle over her skin, and her stomach clenched. She glanced down at the screen. She had several text messages.

"Good morning," Beluviel said. "I'm so glad you were able to start early. We can make the journey in one day, but

there is quite a lovely resting area where we can stay the night if you find yourself getting too tired. Please don't hesitate to say something if you feel the need to stop."

"Thank you, that sounds terrific," said Pia. She tried to smile too, but the muscles in her face felt rigid. She hoped her expression didn't look as ghastly as it felt. "I'm sorry, I don't mean to be rude, but these messages won't wait. I hope you don't mind if I take a few minutes to check them."

"Not at all," Beluviel said. "Your phone won't work in the Wood, so take the time you need now. We can leave whenever you're ready."

"I appreciate that," Pia told her. "I'll be as quick as I can." She turned away, her heart knocking like a crazy thing.

Suddenly Eva was right beside her, asking telepathically, *You all right, princess?*

Pia's stiff smile died a miserable death, and good riddance to it. *I'll be ready to go in a few minutes, Eva.* Even to her own mind, she sounded tired.

Like the lady said, take your time, Eva said quietly. The captain stopped at the rear bumper of their nearest SUV and took a casual position, relaxed yet unmistakably standing guard.

Pia nodded in Eva's general direction as she stepped between the two vehicles for a modicum of privacy. She was an idiot. She shouldn't have waited so long. She should have checked for messages in real privacy when she had the chance.

As soon as she was a few feet away from the other woman, she looked at the screen of her phone again. She had nine text messages from various people. Most of them were from Stanford, who tended to be high maintenance.

Only one text message was from Dragos. It had been sent a few minutes after she had woken up and turned off her phone.

She clicked the message open and read it.

Talk tonight. Be safe.

Her vision blurred. The message was terse and to the point, as were all of Dragos's messages, but was it enough?

She had to admit, she had boxed him into a corner in her mind where almost nothing he could have said would have been right, and silence would have been the worst thing of all.

But those four words said a lot. They said he had backed down and accepted her decision, even though he had to have still been angry when he sent the message. They weren't enough, but they set a platform and were a promise of more.

Then she was able to take a deep breath for the first time since she had awakened. She texted him back.

Yes.

Almost instantly her phone pinged again.

Six days.

He had been waiting all that time for her reply. The starch left her spine, and she rubbed her face. Probably it was good to make him wait now and then, but hell's bells, that was a hard road to take. *You're impossible, impossible*, she mouthed at the phone as she gripped it in both hands and shook it. *You make me crazy.*

She started and deleted a couple of replies, all too aware that her six guards, as many Elves, the High Lord's consort and all their horses were waiting on her.

Her phone pinged again.

Pia.

Of course, she sent back.

Ping. Dammit! She opened that message too.

Until tonight.

Her fingers moved rapidly over the small keyboard.

Until tonight. Cell phones won't work in the Wood. I must shut down now.

She hit send and, gritting her teeth, forced herself to turn off the phone. Then she squared her shoulders and turned to join Eva, who said nothing but walked with her back to the waiting group.

Afterward she never remembered what she said. She knew that she smiled, exchanged pleasantries and admired the tall, sweet-natured chestnut horse that was to be hers

for the trip. When everybody mounted, she did too, while Hugh held on to her horse's bridle for her.

Beluviel rode a gorgeous, gleaming black mare, with a proud arched neck and startling blue eyes. After a quick glance to make sure everyone was ready, the High Lord's consort rode first toward the Wood, and the rest of the group fell into place behind her.

As Pia nudged her mount, the two female Wyr, Eva and Andrea, came up on either side of her. Hugh and James took point, and Miguel and Johnny fell in behind, surrounding Pia completely. She gritted her teeth, feeling trapped and boxed in, but she held her peace for the moment. None of them knew what to expect when they passed underneath those trees for the first time.

Behind her, Miguel muttered, "There better not be any Tom Bombadil skipping and singing this early in the morning, or any hobbit-eating trees. That's all I got to say."

A light Elven voice said, "Tom Bombadil is a completely fictional character, of course, but we make no promises about any flesh-eating trees."

Pia glanced over her shoulder, as did Andrea and Eva. An Elven girl had ridden up beside Miguel, a longbow and quiver strapped to her back. The girl had an immaculate seat on her horse, her slender body held straight and relaxed. Her short hair, skin and twinkling eyes were a lustrous dark brown, the pointed tips of her ears showing pixie-like through the fluffy strands. She had dyed the end of her hair blue.

Miguel appeared frozen in his saddle.

"Class it up, jackass," said Captain Psycho irritably.

The Elven girl laughed, a bright, sharp sound that rang out like knife play. Then she chucked her horse into a gallop that sent her to the front of the party where she fell into step beside Beluviel.

Miguel looked after the young Elf hungrily. "Somebody please tell me that chick ain't underage."

Pia closed her eyes briefly. If she could only start over

from eight o'clock yesterday morning. No, make that two days ago. Then she could have packed differently too.

Up ahead, Beluviel rode toward a wide path that led to a break in the trees. Pia could have sworn that neither the path nor the break in the trees had been there a moment ago. The Wyr fell silent at the same time the Elves did, and by some trick of acoustics the sound of the hoofbeats seemed muffled as the group entered the Wood in twos and threes.

Intensely conflicting emotions ricocheted through her when it came her turn to pass the border, a deep elation along with a sense of panic. She was both an urban-raised girl and a forest animal, and the dense foliage called to her deepest instincts. She wanted to back out, turn on her cell phone and call Dragos, or worse, race to one of the SUVs and break the speed limit all the way back to New York. She also wanted to throw herself out of the saddle, change into her Wyr form and plunge crazily into the deepest, most Powerful heart of the Wood.

Of course she did none of those things. Instead an ancient, wild presence enveloped her as her horse stepped underneath the green, green trees.

They traveled at an easy pace through the morning. Once they had all entered the Wood, Beluviel fell back through the group to travel with Pia and talk of a variety of things. In contrast to their open heart-to-heart from the previous afternoon, they both kept the conversation light and suitable for multiple listeners.

The Elven girl with the blue-tipped hair traveled back with Beluviel to tease Miguel unmercifully. Miguel did not appear to mind in the slightest. In fact, by the end of the morning his dark, observant gaze had glazed over slightly, and he was looking both smitten and disturbed, much to the amusement of the other Wyr and the Elves.

The party stopped for lunch in a beautiful spot where a huge tree had fallen and the wood had been carved into a massive table. The table had been surrounded by stone benches that had also been carved, their thick legs covered

with moss and lichens. Diffuse light filtered through the green leaves overhead. Pia could hear the faint trickle of running water nearby. The scene felt peaceful and very old.

Pia's double, Andrea, came up to take the reins of Pia's horse as she eased out of the saddle, her thigh muscles quivering from the unaccustomed strain of riding all morning. Come evening she was going to be in a world of hurt.

Clearly Beluviel had no such trouble, as she sprang lightly from the back of her mare. When the Elven woman joined her, Pia said, "This place is gorgeous. The tree must have been immense."

Beluviel regarded the scene, her expression inscrutable. "Yes. I was very saddened when she fell."

Pia looked from Beluviel's youthful face to the table again. This time she also took in the hollows on the stone benches along with the wear underneath on the forest floor.

Dragos, Beluviel. Her mother. It was easy, she thought, to speak of ancient beings without really taking in just what that meant until the reality hit home at moments like this.

Someday, someone might look at her and realize the same thing. But nobody would look at her that way for a long, long time. She was just in her twenties, which was young by human standards, and she had mated with one of the oldest known creatures in the world. How could she expect to become his partner in anything? Even worse, how could she expect him to accept it? It was beyond crazy. Discouragement turned her limbs leaden.

While she tumbled into her private funk, Elves brushed off the top of the table and laid out flasks of wine and water, along with fruit, nuts and stacks of their indescribably delicious wayfarer bread. At the end farthest from Pia and Beluviel, they set out a variety of meats and cheeses.

Pia's mouth watered at the sight of the loaves. She had eaten Elven wayfarer bread just once in her life, when she and Dragos had been kidnapped by Goblins and imprisoned in an Other land, and she had never forgotten the taste.

She glanced upward, but the sky was too obscured by

83

thick tree branches and clouds to see the sun. It wouldn't sound good to ask how soon she might be able to go to bed. "How long is the journey from here?"

"We'll arrive before dark," Beluviel said. "Sunset is around five thirty, which is something around forty-five minutes later than New York at this time of year. That is, if you're up for the rest of the trip? There are a few quite comfortable cabins just an hour away if you would rather stop."

"Not at all," Pia told her. "I think we should travel the whole distance today." After all the sooner she got there, the sooner she could talk with Calondir, accomplish what she came to do and go home.

She was not well adjusted at all. Most people would be thrilled at the rare privilege to see inside the Wood and travel into the heart of the Elven demesne. All she did was think about leaving as soon as she could.

Because she might have put too positive a spin on Dragos's texts. The tricky thing about terseness was that it left so much open to interpretation, and he had only sent her nine words in total.

And it was probably pathetic that she had counted them.

Her stomach tried to clench up on her again. She shoved away the impulse and focused on eating. The other Wyr cycled behind her, always keeping two on duty while the others ate. No one remarked or looked askance at that, although she noted Beluviel's attendants did not keep the same kind of vigilance.

She tried to think of ways to ask Beluviel about the Numenlaurians' impending visit but she couldn't figure out how to broach the subject without sounding like she was prying, mainly because she *would* be prying. In the end she said nothing, opting to wait, watch and listen. She could always ask questions later.

The group finished lunch quickly while their horses were watered, and soon they were on their way again. After traveling with her for another half an hour or so, Beluviel excused herself and moved forward to take the lead again.

An invisible hot poker settled at the base of Pia's spine.

The backache grew worse as the afternoon wore on, and her new boots rubbed blisters on her heels. The unsettled euphoria at having entered the Wood had worn off. Now its presence made her feel claustrophobic as it seemed to press on her from all sides. She could sense the crossover passage somewhere ahead as the group grew closer to it.

Eva never left her, although the other five Wyr took turns riding on her other side. Johnny and Andrea carried crossbows, and all the Wyr had swords strapped to their backs. Eva's powerful body moved in lithe rhythm with her roan mare, her lean dark fingers handling the reins with confident ease as her black, alert gaze never stopped roaming over the scene.

Pia sank into a miserable haze, only jerking straighter as Eva said telepathically, *You looking like something a cat coughed up again, princess. Need a break?*

No, she said. She needed for the day to be over, and a break would only prolong her misery.

Eva turned to look her in the eyes. *Are you sure, Pia?*

She took a deep breath, and the muscles in her sore back throbbed while the peanut slept oblivious to it all, his energy strong and steady. *Thank you, I'm sure.*

You know, I don't remember hearing Beluviel make any promises, Eva told her. *In fact, I thought she sounded a little cagey.*

What nonsense are you talking about now? She sighed and shifted in her saddle, but there wasn't any position she could get into that would alleviate her discomfort.

The consort said "might" and "possibly" yesterday, Eva said. *She hung with Calondir all these years, seems she could be more definite about whether or not the man would like it if you showed up on his doorstep. It's possible he might not be as pleased as he could be. If the Numenlaurians arrive while you try to get his attention, you might be knocking yourself out like this for nothing.*

She scowled. She hadn't considered any of that. It had sounded to her like Beluviel was just being polite. Great. She grumbled, *Just once I'd like you to say something I*

85

really want to hear. Besides, that's all the more reason to push hard to get there. I need to try to talk with Calondir while I've got the chance.

Point, Eva admitted.

They rode for a while in silence. Just ahead, Miguel and the young Elven girl were sniping at each other again. Pia watched them as she thought. She asked Eva, *Do you know anything about the prehuman war among the Elves?*

You mean a civil war? Eva said, lifting her eyebrows.

Yes.

The captain shook her head. *Before my time, princess.*

Pia snorted, and a grin played at the corners of Eva's mouth. *Apparently there was one, and it was big and nasty. Dragos said it changed the landscape of the Earth, caused the Elves to scatter and eventually gave birth to the Light and the Dark Fae.*

Shew, what a lot of drama, said Eva. The captain paused. *If Numenlaur is the "old country," then that's where the war began?*

Sounds likely, Pia replied.

Eva remarked, *Makes me curious why they coming to visit Calondir and Beluviel.*

Pia said, *Me too. Keep your eyes and ears sharp in case you get the chance to overhear something, will you?*

You bet. I'll pass the word to the others to do the same.

Silence fell again between them, and that was the last they spoke for a while. Wowzer, thought Pia, after her and Eva's rocky beginning, it seemed almost peaceful.

The light was beginning to wane when one of the Elves broke away from the group and ran ahead. Pia hoped that meant the Elf was taking word of their arrival to Calondir, and their destination was close at hand. She had long since stopped trying to talk with anyone and rode in a cloud of increasing tiredness.

She must have fallen into a doze, because the next thing she knew a shout of greeting sounded up ahead. She jerked into alertness.

Those at the front of the party passed around a huge age-darkened granite boulder. She looked up at the massive stone. As she neared, what had appeared at first to be random bulges and hollows aligned into an Elven face with noble features and an inscrutable expression. It was impossible to tell if the face was male or female. The sculpture held her mesmerized until she came too close to discern it, and then the stone became just a stone again.

"Will you look at that," Eva whispered.

"What?" She glanced at the captain who was staring forward, and she looked in that direction too. At first she didn't notice anything that might cause Eva's wonder. The travelers from the front of the group had stopped in a clearing at the foot of a rocky waterfall, the fast-flowing, turbulent river ribboning into the trees. Elves dismounted with smiles of pleasure. They called out to others who came to greet them.

Then her perspective shifted as it had with the massive stone face, and she saw the building. It spanned the top of the waterfall, by some trick of architectural genius seeming as if suspended in the air. The building had several levels, its lines modern and ultra-plain. The outside walls were covered in plain sheets of reflective glass so that it all but disappeared from sight.

Once she saw it she couldn't look away, and she only dismounted when Eva nudged her knee. Beluviel approached, looking as fresh and bright as she had that morning. The consort said simply, "Welcome to our home."

Pia blinked and forced herself to concentrate on the other woman. "Thank you. It's stunning."

Beluviel regarded the building with the same inscrutable expression from earlier when they had talked about the tree table. "We loved the Frank Lloyd Wright house in Pennsylvania, Fallingwater, so much we chose to emulate something of that style. We finished rebuilding in the 1970s."

She and Eva walked with Beluviel to the wide, winding staircase that had been carved into the stone by the fall, while

the other Wyr gathered their packs from the horses and followed close behind. Pia forced her strained, quivering thigh muscles to work and matched the consort step for step.

As they climbed, two tall, Powerful Elves, both male, appeared on the landing at the top of the stairs and watched their approach. One of the males was Calondir. The other was Ferion, whom Pia had met last May in Folly Beach.

Both Elven males wore serious expressions. The High Lord's hair was long and sable dark, and bound back tightly, his eyes a bright, startling blue. In the May teleconference, Pia hadn't noticed the resemblance between Ferion and Calondir, but in person, the similarity between the two males was unmistakable. They both had the same strong, elegant bone structure.

Beluviel paused on the top step, and instinctively Pia paused with her. The High Lord and his consort faced each other with cool, perfect courtesy.

Calondir said, "Lady."

"My lord," Beluviel murmured.

Pia's eyebrows slid up before she could get in control of her expression. Maybe she and Dragos would greet each other so coolly too, after they had been together for a bajillion years, but somehow she didn't think so.

Then Calondir turned to her and inclined his head. "Greetings, Lady of the Wyr."

Greetings, not welcome. Even though Calondir didn't show any hint of his emotions, she was suddenly convinced that the High Lord was blazingly furious.

Clearly he was not falling over himself with excitement at her arrival.

Oy vey.

≈ SEVEN ≈

The undercurrents that swirled around Ferion, Beluviel and Calondir were stifling. Pia received the distinct impression that the three of them exchanged an intense storm of telepathic words while she faced the High Lord's ageless, closed expression. Meeting his cool, Powerful gaze was one of the more challenging things she'd done since, well, since she'd argued with Dragos in the middle of the night.

Suddenly the pressure from the last two days, hell, the last seven months, welled up, and it had to go somewhere outside of her body or she would combust. She cast about mentally . . . where, where . . . but in the end, there was really only one place for it to go.

She said in Eva's head, *I'm in so far over my head in so many ways, I don't even know where shore is anymore.*

Steady on, Tinker Bell, Eva said calmly. *Man shits like anybody else do.*

She did not just hear that. Her poise, having already grown precarious, splintered. She bent sharply at the waist and leaned her hands on her knees. Vaguely she was aware of a ripple of reaction passing through the others.

A strong, brown hand curled around her bicep and

gripped her hard. "There's no need to be alarmed," Eva said crisply. "She just isn't much of a rider. She has been suffering from a leg cramp, that's all."

Captain Psycho's speech was polished, educated, and her grammar beautifully correct. And damn that woman, she could lie. Pia's truthsense insisted on Eva's sincerity.

"Yes, I'm all right," Pia said hoarsely. She kept it simple, not even attempting to match Eva's duplicity. "My apologies." She told Eva, *You're pure fucking evil, and I hate you passionately.*

I know, my bitch goddess too hot for some to handle, Eva said. Even in her telepathic voice, she sounded complacent.

SHUT UP.

Opposite Eva, Beluviel took Pia's other arm for support as she straightened. The consort's wide gaze was warm with concern. Beluviel asked, "Are you able to walk?"

"Yes, thank you," Pia said.

"Other issues need my attention," Calondir said. "I'll take my leave now."

Pia saw everything she had worked for slipping through her fingers as the High Lord turned away.

Anger sparked. Sure, an upcoming visit from Numenlaurians must be hugely important, but the Elves had invited her first, dammit.

She said, "Sir."

Calondir paused to look back at her, one eyebrow raised in imperious inquiry.

In the end, she spoke as plainly as she had several months ago when she had first addressed him. "I know you are very busy, and you have a great deal on your mind. That is why I was so honored at your invitation. I've made it my priority to visit despite the distance and the important developments occurring in my own demesne." She knew the original invitation had come from Beluviel, but just as Dragos had to agree to the visit, Calondir had to have put his stamp of approval on it, and she couldn't afford to let him wriggle out of granting her an audience. People in the Wyr demesne

needed for her to succeed at reestablishing trade agreements. She finished, "I hope you might find time for a short talk."

He regarded her unsmilingly, then inclined his head. "Thank you for your effort in making the journey. I appreciate your dedication and hope you have a restful evening. Good night."

Argh, that was it? No promise to talk later? Just a dismissal? What the fuck? Pia's lips tightened as Calondir turned his back to her again and walked away.

She looked at Beluviel. The consort stared after Calondir, her posture stiff. "Ferion and Linwe," said the consort, "would you kindly show Pia and her people to their rooms?"

"Of course," Ferion said immediately.

Pia looked around to discover who Linwe was. She found the blue-haired Elven girl standing just behind the consort. The girl bounced a little on the balls of her toes. After Calondir's Powerful, mature presence and tension-filled greeting, Linwe's blue-tipped hair seemed cheerfully barbaric. The sight lifted Pia's spirits quite unreasonably.

Beluviel said to Pia, "Please don't hesitate to tell either Ferion or Linwe if there is anything that you or your group requires. Perhaps if you are interested, one of them can show you around tomorrow. In the meantime I will say good evening as well."

After the warmth and support Beluviel had shown over the last two days, her abrupt departure on top of Calondir's rebuff felt like a slap in the face. Pia didn't know if she was angry or just confused. She did know she didn't trust herself to speak. She gave the consort a curt nod.

Beluviel hesitated, dark gaze searching Pia's expression. Then the consort said telepathically, *Forgive me for bringing you all this way only to abandon you this evening. The emissary from Numenlaur arrived this afternoon, several days earlier than expected, and their mission is one of some urgency. Calondir and I are needed elsewhere at the moment.*

The emissary was already here? No wonder Calondir looked less than thrilled at her arrival. This trip was rapidly going from bad to worse.

I understand, Pia said, because in the end there was nothing else she could say.

I will be in touch. Rest well. Beluviel brushed her cheek with cool lips and followed in Calondir's footsteps, her long stride rapid.

Pia bit back her impatience. It had been another long, frustrating day. Her back ached like a bastard, and no matter how much she wanted it, she couldn't expect an instant resolution to any of the issues that had brought her here. At the rate things were going, she might not even get a chance to talk with Calondir at all.

At least this meant she could go to bed soon, right?

That thought did not exactly put her in a more cheerful mood. She and Dragos had too much unresolved between them. But the interminable day was nearly over, which meant she could hope to get on a better footing with him. Missing him had turned into a deep ache, only now she didn't just miss his physical presence. She also desperately, fiercely missed their lack of rapport.

She turned to Ferion, who regarded her with a faint smile. "Lady, please forgive our preoccupation with other matters," he said. "Your visit deserves better than this. It is good to see you again."

Somewhat mollified, she said, "Hello, Ferion. How are you?"

"I am well, thank you," he said. "Although I will always regret that you did not come to stay with us last summer."

Her returning smile was wry. Ferion had led the party that had responded to her distress call when Dragos had crossed the Elven border without permission and had broken his treaties with them. The Elves had shot Dragos with a poisoned arrow, and then someone had told Urien, the Dark Fae King, what had happened.

A lot of bad things had come out of that. She and Dra-

gos had been kidnapped, beaten and nearly killed. But a lot of good had come out of it too, like the first time she and Dragos had made love. They would probably never know which Elf had been Urien's informant, and so much had happened since then that the information had become irrelevant. Urien was dead, and whatever alliances or loyalties any Elf might have had to him were dead also.

"All of that is water under the bridge now," she told Ferion.

If he heard the double message in that statement, he didn't show it. With a polite gesture, he invited her to walk with him, and Linwe and the rest followed.

It had been impossible for Pia to get a sense of how large the house really was when she had been looking at it from below. The reflective outside walls had messed with her sense of depth perception, as her mind kept insisting that she looked at sky and trees.

Inside, Ferion led the group down halls of flagstone, carved granite and wood, and they made several turns, which indicated that the house was very large indeed. Finally he stopped and opened a door that led to a spacious, gorgeously appointed apartment that had a central common room with a large fireplace and several couches, a couple of bathrooms and three bedrooms.

Since two of the psychos would be awake at any given time, the others could double up in two of the bedrooms. The rooms had rich, dark hardwood furniture and gleaming floors, handwoven rugs and intricately sewn tapestries with ocean and woodland scenes populated with fantastical creatures. The largest tapestry hung on the inside wall and depicted several Elves on one of their historic, sleek ocean-faring ships. One of the figures was a male with a long braid of dark hair, apparently Calondir, who held a gold cup. While the cup was relatively small in comparison to the rest of the scene, the gold thread gleamed brightly against the deep, rich colors used throughout the rest of the tapestry, drawing the eye immediately to it.

The outside wall of the apartment had large windows that overlooked the moonlit river and the Wood above the waterfall. She went to look out.

Ferion followed her. The Elf stood quietly, hands clasped behind his back, as they gazed at the beautiful scene. She glanced at him, and the resemblance to Calondir struck her all over again. The two males had to be related to each other in some way. They could be father and son. If they were, she wondered if Beluviel was Ferion's mother. Given the coolness she had seen between Beluviel and Calondir, anything was possible.

The Power that Ferion carried indicated that he might even be old enough to remember the Elven war in the far-distant past. She wondered what he made of the Numen-laurian's visit, but she could not quite bring herself to ask.

She said to him telepathically, *I would count it as a great favor if we did not discuss my mother in front of others. I don't know if you have heard, but I've not publicly revealed my Wyr form.*

He looked at her quickly and bowed. *Lady, I would be honored to keep that in confidence.*

Thank you.

Aloud, he said, "I will see to it that supper is brought up shortly. Is there anything else that you require?"

"Everything is beautiful," she told him.

He bowed again with that touch of Old World charm, excused himself and left. Linwe left with him, and the Wyr were alone for the first time that day.

Eva set the others to inspecting the apartment then she joined Pia by the window. She said, "The man had a point. I've seen better welcomes."

Pia grimaced. "Beluviel told me telepathically that the emissary arrived this afternoon. Apparently they're several days earlier than expected."

Eva pursed her lips. "Well, that complicates things."

"Yes, it does," Pia said grimly.

Calondir and Beluviel might have invited her first, but the gods only knew how long it had been since they had

seen Elves from Numenlaur. In contrast, they had only seen seven months of border tensions with the Wyr demesne. To people of their immense age, seven months must seem like nothing more than a passing moment.

But the trade embargo had to have hurt the Elven demesne as much as it did the Wyr. They had held out and made their statement successfully. Wouldn't they be just as relieved to let it go as the Wyr would?

She felt like her mind was spinning from one thing to the next. It seemed like she did nothing but move from one pitfall to another. She couldn't wait to see Dragos tonight and to put things right between them. Then maybe she could turn things around tomorrow and make something good come out of this damn trip.

The others made short work of thoroughly inspecting the apartment. Pia claimed the first bedroom they cleared, shut the door, stripped off her dirty clothes and staggered into the bathroom to take a long, warm bath.

Her Wyr healing abilities, along with the soothing soaps and water, soon eased the aches and pains of the day away but left her exhausted. As she climbed out of the bath, Eva knocked and brought in a tray laden with strange, delicious foods. Pia stuffed herself, shoved the tray outside the bedroom door afterward, climbed into the soft comfortable bed and was out before her head hit the pillow.

Despite her quick plummet into sleep she tossed and turned. Several times she came partly awake, frustrated and searching. She couldn't find the right connection. Every time she reached for Dragos, all she could see was a male with green eyes. He held out his hand and beckoned to her, but it was much too dark where he stood. Every time she saw him, she shuddered and turned away.

Then she came awake in a rush.

Disoriented, she thrust out of bed and went to the window. The sky was growing lighter. It was early in the morning, and she hadn't dreamed of Dragos.

They hadn't dreamed.

Panic throbbed like a migraine at her temples. She strode

to the door and snatched it open. James and Andrea were talking quietly, keeping watch in the common room. Both came to their feet at her appearance.

James put a hand on his sword. He asked, "Everything all right?"

"No," she said. "Get Eva."

"I'm here," Eva said from one of the other doorways. She was barefoot but otherwise dressed in black cargo pants and an army green T-shirt that fit snugly against her lean torso. She strode across the room quickly, black eyes sharp. "What up, princess?"

She said to Eva in a low voice, "Dragos has been casting spells so that he and I can dream together, and I didn't dream last night. Something's wrong."

And she couldn't make a simple, goddamn phone call to see if he was all right.

Eva's gaze had widened as she talked. "Okay," the captain said. "Let's talk it through. Has he ever had problems dream casting before?"

"We've only done it together a couple of times," Pia said. She rubbed her mouth and tried to get in control of her panic, to force herself to think logically. "The Power in the Wood interferes with phone calls. Maybe it can disrupt Dragos's spell."

"He's Powerful as shit and older than dirt," Eva said, her voice steady and not unkind. "Rather than something happening to him, it's much more likely that the Wood interfered with his spell, don't you think?"

Suddenly Pia grew calm. "That makes sense, but he doesn't know that, and last night was important. We had things to discuss."

What would Dragos do now?

He would be doing the same thing that she was doing, working his way through the possible reasons for their missed connection. She had the advantage. She knew he went to bed safe in his home territory, whereas to him, she was deep in the heart of enemy territory.

Would he watch and wait for word? If he didn't—if the

Elves discovered that he had crossed the Elven border again without permission, she didn't think there was anything she could say then that would repair the treaties, and they might not be able to avoid war. The Elves had been quite clear: they would treat any further trespass from him as an act of invasion.

She said, "We need to send someone out and hope they get out of the Wood in time to make a phone call before Dragos decides to come in after us."

Eva's eyebrows rose. "Sounds like we better get someone out fast."

Throwing their bed against the wall hadn't done anything to improve Dragos's mood. He knew Pia felt stressed about the trip, and he had no intention of arguing via text messages, but he was utterly *furious* with her.

How dared she rebuke him, leave their dream and turn off her cell phone? How dared she bring up that old issue of servants and employees, and throw Rune in his face?

Did he not allow her to do as she wished in most things? *How dare she disobey him?*

Yeah, he heard that.

He tossed the king-sized bed back into place, showered, dressed in black fatigues and a thin, black silk sweater, and left the Tower.

Another heavy day of fighting was scheduled for that day, so the bouts started at five A.M. Despite the early beginning, all the seats were filled. Tension had ratcheted up. One hundred and twelve contestants would start the day. By tonight there would be fifty-six.

When Dragos arrived at the mobile office, he told Kris and his other assistants, "Find somewhere else to work today."

None of them asked questions. They took one look at his expression and scattered, leaving him to prowl the super-suite and fume in isolation.

All the sentinels were scheduled for early combat. By

some trick of chance, none of them had yet drawn Quentin Caeravorn as an opponent. Aryal, Grym and Bayne had cycled through their fights already, and now Constantine was on the floor.

Con was brawny and blond, as were all the gryphons. He was also what his fellow gryphon Bayne liked to call a "man slut." It was a testament to Constantine's actual skill set that he was so effective at his job while remaining so aggressively promiscuous, because from what Dragos heard, Con never got a full night's sleep.

His current opponent in the arena was one of the gargoyles, and both contestants had shifted into their Wyr form for the fight. The gargoyle had morphed from a mild-looking man into a seven-foot winged monster, with a demonic face, huge batlike wings and a tough, stony gray body.

Their fight caught even the raging dragon's attention. Dragos paused at the window to watch.

A human would have had a difficult time following the fight without the benefit of instant replay and slowing the action down, but Dragos had no trouble at all making out every detail.

Con was not Graydon. He had broken one of the gargoyle's legs and a wing, and now, catlike, he played with the guy, letting him get close and then batting at him with a giant paw. Constantine was just plain nasty in a fight, whether he was in gryphon or human form. The gargoyle was done for, but apparently he was too stupid or stubborn to quit.

Dragos shook his head and turned away.

He had been an autocrat for so very long, and he was utterly used to absolute rule. Then Pia came along. She coaxed his arrogance into laughing and charmed him into easing up, giving in. He had convinced himself he was growing more tolerant in indulging her wishes, but the brutal truth was *tolerance* and *indulgence* were simply other forms of the autocrat.

Pia had said, *The real point I'm trying to make is that I have no idea how to be your partner.*

More brutal truth: he had no idea how to be her partner either, or anybody's partner, for that matter.

She was always going to be a softer personality than he, immensely younger and less experienced. More peaceful. And yet here she was his best teacher again, for she had already shown him how she could bend to his will when he needed it. That, he realized, involved a profound kind of trust in him.

Now he had to learn how to bend to her will when she needed it.

Not tolerate, allow or indulge. Really bend, despite his mood, the circumstances or his temper. As old, strong willed and entrenched in the habit of power as he was, this was a lesson he might have to relearn over and over again.

But Pia also had to learn, there would only be so far he could bend. He was simply too dominant. They were in uncharted territory, and he did not know how far he could go. Plus he had been on edge for months, ever since the economy had taken such a serious downturn, Tiago and Rune had followed their mates and left him and the other sentinels running at full throttle, and the Oracle had made her uninvited, impromptu prophecy last summer that hung in front of Dragos like a mushroom cloud.

He would never forget the strange, dry voice that had come through the Oracle's Power, or the quiet way it had spoken and what it had said.

It had spoken of stars dying in agony, and the nature of evil, of Light and Dark as creatures, and Lord Death himself having forgotten he was a fraction of the whole.

"I am not form but Form," the voice had claimed, "a prime indivisible. All these things were set in motion at the beginning, along with the laws of the universe and of Time itself. The gods formed at the moment of creation, as did the Great Beast, as did Hunger, as did Birth along with Finality, and I am the Bringer of the End of Days. . . ."

Which, when it came right down to it, was insane gibberish. It made no fucking sense, and his atavistic reaction

99

to it was just as nonsensical. But every time he thought of that voice he remembered the Power in it, and the hair at the back of his neck raised and the dragon clawed its way to the surface and looked for war.

But it had not targeted Dragos specifically. It had only mentioned him. In a way the real significance was not what had been said but that the prophecy had come to him, and when he and Pia had consulted with the Oracle a second time, the Oracle had said the events might not surface for months or even years.

They could not live their lives in fear. He would not. When Pia brought up the possibility of visiting with the Elves, he listened, eventually. Just as the Elves had intended, the trade embargo had caused damage, and it was time to explore ways to end it.

Not only that, but Pia and Dragos were natural lightning rods. There was always going to be some kind of shit happening, because some kind of spotlight was always going to be trained on them, and they lived eventful lives. If any shit happened while they were separated, they would deal with it.

And so he tolerated, allowed and indulged.

Gods damn it. The hardest thing to break was a habit, and the attitude crept in when he wasn't looking. When all was said and done his behavior had been boorish and typical. He . . . owed her an apology.

And how strange it was, to recognize how he had grown to need someone after being autonomous for so very long.

He counted the time until he could go to bed and cast the dream spell. Then he counted the time as he waited, and she didn't come, and she didn't come.

Dawn bled a pale, colorless light over the eastern sky, cold and bleak as death. When he rose he did so silently, full of cunning, for the world he inhabited was filled with prophecy and predators. The dragon was not a safe creature at the best of times, and that was true especially now that he was without his mate.

He had questions and he needed answers, and while

those answers could be found within the forbidden Elven Wood, there was a quicker and more efficient way he could get them, another place he could go that was much closer to home.

He called Bayne and made some arrangements.

Then he went on the hunt.

He found his prey easily within the hour. She wore a classic black two-piece suit, four-inch heels and another sleek chignon, but Dragos remembered another image of her from an age long past, wearing armor, covered in blood and screaming at the sky as he soared overhead, her face twisted with rage and hate.

The early morning was still dark gray and bitingly cold, and huge mounds of dirty snow were piled everywhere, but like Dragos, the Elven tribunal Councillor did not bother with an overcoat. She stepped out of the front doors of the Plaza Hotel on Fifth Avenue followed by two attendants.

If the Elf had seen him coming, she would have tried to find some way to avoid him, so he had not given her the opportunity.

Dragos could cloak himself so completely while he was in dragon form that a mouse could run over his talons and never know it. Usually he did not bother with casting such a strong spell, but he did this time. He cloaked himself while standing on the street curb and added a small, subtle aversion spell so that pedestrians somehow avoided the spot where he stood, until the Elven Councillor reached a spot just a few feet away.

Dragos said, "Sidhiel."

She screamed and spun, her sophisticated poise shattered, and there was his old adversary again. Despite their designer clothing and their urban setting, and the laws and traditions they had surrounded themselves with, civilization remained the thinnest of veneers after all.

≈ EIGHT ≈

The Elven Councillor's attendants had whipped around also, drawing weapons. Dragos regarded them contemptuously. Pulling guns on him was a stupid move. Firing on him would be even more stupid.

It had been a very, very long time since he had killed an Elf. He raised an eyebrow and almost smiled.

"Put away your weapons, fools!" Sidhiel snapped. Looking shaken and wild-eyed, the two attendants holstered their guns. The Elven woman regarded Dragos with abhorrence. "This is outrageous, Wyrm. You have no business approaching me for anything."

"Quite the contrary," said Dragos. "Talking to you has become the most important priority of my day."

"I have nothing to say to you," she gritted. "But I will have a great deal to say to the Elder tribunal if you do not leave me alone immediately."

"The tribunal is not here," Dragos said in an exceedingly gentle tone of voice. "Would you like a cup of coffee, Councillor? Perhaps a ride to the Garden."

She hissed and yanked a BlackBerry out of her suit pocket.

Moving faster than sight, Dragos grabbed her wrist. He held her effortlessly as she struggled to free herself.

Sidhiel's attendants stood frozen. Dragos told them, "You are out of your league. There is no shame in acknowledging that. Do nothing." They watched him unblinkingly and didn't move.

Sidhiel's eyes widened as her BlackBerry grew hot. "Stop. Stop it!"

He said nothing. With a gasp the Elf's fingers sprang open, and her BlackBerry tumbled to the ground. As both he and Sidhiel watched, the phone glowed red and melted into a dangerous, acrid smelling puddle that steamed on the frozen sidewalk.

Sidhiel's gaze raised, her features sliced with impotent fury. "You are a blight upon this Earth."

"I'm always amused at how the Elves insist upon vilifying me," he remarked. "Your pot is much blacker than my kettle. Yes, I hunted some of you long ago before I grew and evolved. But you killed so very many more of yourselves than I ever did, and you tore up the Earth while you did so."

"My gods, I loathe you."

"About that cup of coffee," said Dragos. As she turned woodenly toward the hotel entrance, he told her, "Not in a public restaurant. Your suite or my limo. Or even my suite at the Garden, if you prefer."

After a brief struggle with the choices he offered, she turned to her attendants. "Go. Wait for me at the main entrance to Madison Square Garden. If I am not there shortly, call the head of the tribunal and tell him what has happened."

"Councillor," said the taller of her attendants.

"You can do nothing here," she said through white lips. "But you can bear witness to my absence." She threw a scathing glance at Dragos. "You will be held accountable for anything you do."

"You should be careful when you talk of accountability, Sidhiel," he growled. "I am not a patient man at the best of

times. Now my mate is visiting your demesne, and I cannot get in contact with her."

She stood rigid, her startled gaze searching his face. Then she gestured to her attendants, gave him a curt nod and strode with him to the sleek black Mercedes limousine that idled at the curb.

In the back of the limo, Dragos settled back in his seat with his arms crossed. He watched indifferently as the Elf positioned herself so that she avoided any accidental contact with his long legs. Without any further preamble, he said, "You may not have heard, but Beluviel invited Pia into Lirithriel Wood so that she could talk with Calondir. They traveled in yesterday morning."

Sidhiel's gaze flickered. "No, I had not heard." She added slowly, "Someone should have warned you that cell phones do not work in the Wood."

"I already know that," he said impatiently. "What I want to know is if the Wood can block spells."

"What kind of spells?" Sidhiel asked suspiciously.

He studied the Elf, his mouth tight. He was secretive by nature, and he hated to give up any kind of information to her, but there was no other way for him to find out what he needed to know. He said, "I have been dream casting, but last night either it didn't reach Pia or she didn't sleep. I chose to talk with you before I went down to South Carolina to discover for myself if she is all right."

The Elf sucked in a breath, but she replied calmly enough. "There is no reason for alarm or for acting hastily. I believe in this case the Wood might have caused interference. Spell casting from within its borders is quite a different experience from casting a spell from the outside. It is important to keep in mind, Cuelebre—the Elves do not regard Pia in the same light as we do you. No one wishes her any harm."

"So everyone has said," he replied, eyeing her coldly. "Which is why I finally agreed to her visit in the first place. It does, however, occur to me that not everyone may have the same definition of *harm*. For instance, someone might think that taking my mate hostage would be a good way to

try to control me. Then of course once you start talking about taking hostages, a whole new chessboard emerges."

He watched realization dawn, and the Elf's face went ashen. Her gaze darted to the scenery passing by outside the limousine's windows. Madison Square Garden was several blocks southwest of the Plaza Hotel, and they were nowhere near the vicinity. The Councillor whispered hoarsely, "You do not want to do this."

"Do I not?" He settled himself more comfortably. "Since we are talking, perhaps you can tell me why Numenlaurians have decided to visit Calondir."

Sidhiel made a sharp gesture. "No one knows the answer to that except the Numenlaurians."

"Speculate," Dragos said.

"That would be pointless and irresponsible," she bit out.

"Very well, if you won't, I will," he said softly. "I can think of one reason why Numenlaur would contact Calondir after silence for all these years. It's the same reason that drove you to war in the first place when you fools discovered the Deus Machinae, and you thought you could control them."

The Deus Machinae. The God Machines, items of Power that the seven Elder Races gods had cast to Earth at the time of creation in order to enact their will. The Elder Races had many myths of the Deus Machinae. At times the items appeared to be weapons or pieces of armor, and at other times jewelry or a tool. Their forms did not remain fixed. Their real nature was something infinitely more Powerful.

The Elf shifted in a sudden movement, her body oddly graceless, and a haunted expression entered her large, blue eyes. "We didn't know then what we know now," she said. "We thought the Deus Machinae had been given to us to use. We didn't realize the Machinae would use us."

"You thought they were yours to use as you saw fit, just as you thought you had the right to reshape the Earth," he said, his quiet tone scathing. "You were ever arrogant that way."

He had long held a fascination with the underlying patterns in the world—magic systems, science, the ever-shifting

reality of economics and politics—and in the back of his mind, he was constantly piecing and repiecing together bits of information, like working on a gigantic puzzle of the universe.

Several pieces of information snicked into place, and another potential pattern came together in his head.

These things were set in motion at the beginning, along with the laws of the universe and of Time itself.

That voice from the Oracle's prophecy. Numenlaur. The Deus Machinae, the seven items from the seven gods of the Elder Races, thrown to Earth at the beginning and working the will of the gods as they tumbled through history. Pure and primal, not form but Form, indivisible.

The world was not just filled with prophecy and predators, but it was filled with Power too. So much of the drama that played out on the modern-day stage came from the first things and the first creatures. First among those creatures were the gods themselves.

It was clear he would get no more out of the Elf. Once her usefulness to him ended, he lost interest in her.

The limousine pulled smoothly up to the curb at Cuelebre Tower. As the vehicle rolled to a stop, a young Wyr male ran out of the Starbucks on the ground floor, wearing a green apron and carrying a covered cup. As the Starbucks employee reached the limo, Dragos opened the door and climbed out.

He took the cup and bent in the open door to hand it to Sidhiel, who took it cautiously as though she expected it to explode in her face. "Here is your coffee, Councillor," said Dragos. He met her gaze. "Don't try to leave New York until I know for sure my mate is free and safe. I don't think the journey would go well for you. Enjoy the games today."

Color washed her pale features, and her pale gaze glittered with equal parts fear and fury. He stood back and watched the limo pull away from the curb. Then he pulled out his iPhone and hit speed dial.

Bayne answered on the first ring. "Yup, got two people following the limo now."

106

Dragos said, "She can do anything she wants as long as she doesn't leave town. If she does try to leave, call and let me know."

"You got it."

He clicked his phone off. Sidhiel would make sure that there were repercussions for him frightening her and issuing threats, but that was an issue to face on another day.

A slicing winter wind whistled down the tall corridors created by the skyscrapers, stinging his skin. He ignored it and turned to face south while logic and instinct clashed inside, building pressure. These days there was always more pressure.

Logic said that Pia was all right, that the Wood's influence was just as Sidhiel said it was, and that it interfered with spells cast from the outside. While he had sensed a great deal of hate in Sidhiel, at that point in the conversation she had spoken plainly and he had not sensed any insincerity in what she had told him.

Logic also reminded him that Pia had five days left of the week they had agreed upon. Five days was a very short amount of time, despite the Powers that were active and moving through the world. In the meantime, he knew Pia was also awake and thinking about their missed dream date. He should give her time to send him a message, at least a day and perhaps two.

But instinct was a much more simple and overriding imperative. It drove him unmercifully and roared that she was gone, gone.

And the fact of the matter was, he was not actually needed at the games today. The contestants would fight each other, and half of them would lose, and tonight there would be twenty-eight left. And Kris could shoulder for the short term whatever business crisis hit, just as he always did when Dragos had to travel. Bayne and the other sentinels would call if they needed to get in touch with him. Dragos's presence wasn't essential until the final round of combat, the day after tomorrow.

He should not cross the Elven border.

And he never did well with things he should not do.

The intolerable pressure that had built up inside him eased as he took to the air. It was an unutterable relief to fly south.

He would go as far as the city limit. That was all.

Once he reached that point, he would decide what he would do next.

The fastest messenger in the group was Hugh, the gargoyle who could fly out in a few hours the distance that had taken them an entire day to travel by horseback.

Theoretically.

Pia thought of the stories of the lost hikers, and her stomach tightened at the possibility that the Wood might somehow interfere with Hugh's flight. What if it screwed with his sense of direction so that he flew in circles? If that happened, who knew when he might emerge?

Eva didn't like the idea of sending out their only avian capability, but then Pia was pretty sure that Eva didn't like anything that she thought of. "Stop wasting time," Pia said. "You know it's got to be Hugh if we're going to have any chance of getting in touch with Dragos quickly."

"Fuck," said Eva. "Fine." She turned to Hugh. "Get ready to go."

"You got it," said Hugh.

By then everybody in the apartment was awake and alert. While Hugh prepared for the journey, Pia sent Johnny out to look for an attendant. Johnny returned almost immediately, followed by a pleasant-faced attendant who wore the High Lord's plain green-and-brown house uniform.

"Good morning, Lady," the Elf said, smiling. "Would you and your group like breakfast brought up to your rooms?"

Nobody outside the group needed to know the reason for Hugh's journey. Pia told the Elf, "I must send a messenger to Charleston right away. I need to know how safe he will be traveling through the Wood."

The Elf blinked rapidly. "You are the High Lord's welcome guests," he said. "The Wood will not harm either you or your messenger, but if you are concerned in any way and can wait for a short while, I'm sure the Lord or Lady would be most happy to send an escort."

Pia looked at Hugh, who had returned to the room. The gargoyle balanced on the balls of his feet, his long rawboned body coiled with readiness. His sword and crossbow were strapped to his back, and he carried a belt filled with crossbow bolts angled across his chest along with a long knife in a sheath tied to one thigh. He no longer looked sleepy. He looked interested and capable, and very deadly.

Hugh shook his head at Pia's unspoken inquiry. "I'm good."

Once again, Pia thought back to the events in May. It had taken Dragos and her several hours to make the journey back to New York, but part of that time had been spent traveling out of an Other land.

If Dragos chose to travel south this morning, there was no guarantee how he would make the journey. If he took the corporate jet, he could hit the Charleston International Airport as soon as two hours from the point of departure. And who knows when he might decide to take off? The only thing she felt confident about was that he would wait as long as possible in case she had simply been very late to bed. Now that morning was officially here, it was possible he was already airborne.

"Go as fast as you can," Pia said to Hugh. Telepathically, she added, *If you don't get through to Dragos right away, call Graydon or Bayne.* She paused. Dammit, there was no way for them to know which sentinel might be fighting when, or if they might be recovering from an injury. *Actually, try all the sentinels until you talk to a live person, but don't just rely on them to pass on a message. Keep trying yourself to get through to Dragos and call to him telepathically as well. He has a much larger telepathic range than anyone else.*

All right, Hugh said, frowning. *But since I've never talked*

with him telepathically before, I don't know if I'll be able to connect.

Exasperated, Pia said, *Look, Dragos might already be in South Carolina by the time you get out of the Wood, so just try everything you can to get in touch with him, and don't stop until you get through and actually talk to him yourself. If you tell him I'm okay, maybe we don't have to have anything turn into a disaster, all right?*

Right, Hugh said.

Eva walked out with Hugh and the Elf. Several minutes later Eva returned alone, and she asked, "Now what?"

Pia had gone to the window to stare out. The early morning was shrouded in a thick veil of fog. She could barely see the water down below. The only details that she could see when she looked toward the horizon were black tree branches that appeared in the dull white fog like dismembered limbs. She shuddered at the thought.

"Now we figure out how to get some breakfast, and I'll send a request to speak with Calondir," Pia said. "Maybe either Ferion or Linwe will show us around like Beluviel suggested. And we wait."

And as for herself, she would be crossing her fingers that the day did not end badly.

Breakfast turned out to be a simple and social affair. The same Elf from earlier returned to ask if Pia would like food to be brought up to her apartment, or if she would prefer to come down to the main hall. After washing and dressing in a clean pair of jeans and sweater, Pia was more than ready to leave their rooms.

The main hall was quite large with several tables, a high ceiling, more flagstone floors, two fireplaces at either end that were so massive a grown man could walk into the ash pits, and walls that were mostly windows and that provided more views of the river and the forest. The trees and rocky forest floor were dark with moisture and occasional patches

of startling green moss, and tendrils of fog drifted along the foaming water at the foot of the falls.

One of the hallways must lead to the kitchens, for a couple of servers moved back and forth from that direction, carrying full trays of breads, fruits and meat to sideboards that were set against one wall. People ate and talked in clusters, sometimes in English but quite often in their lyrical tongue. Most of those in the hall were Elves, but a smattering of other races were also present: a couple of dwarves, three humans with sparks of Power that identified them as witches, and an elderly male medusa whose head snakes trailed a few inches along the floor.

The atmosphere was relaxed and cordial. Pia and her group served themselves and sat at one end of a long table to eat, nodding and smiling at folks as they returned morning greetings. Calondir, Beluviel and Ferion were all absent, and Pia didn't think any of the Elves in the hall were from Numenlaur.

For one thing, it looked like people knew each other with the ease of long acquaintance. Also, most of them were dressed in a mix of Elvish and modern American clothing, an unlikely combination for someone from an enclave society. Leggings and sneakers seemed to be a popular combination. A few wore leggings, tall boots, tunics and jeans jackets.

Folks looking street chic, Eva remarked in her head. *Lookee there. That homeboy got a hoodie.*

I have not forgiven you for yesterday, Pia said. *Just so we're clear.*

That okay, princess. I surviving juuust fine.

Pia's gaze slid sideways to Eva, whose wide black gaze remained innocent. She compressed her lips. Clearly Eva needed no encouragement, but she might actually get worse if Pia smiled or laughed.

On the captain's other side, James, Hugh and Miguel discussed the Sentinel Games. Pia realized they were making bets on who would win through to the final seven positions.

Johnny ate silently with quick economy while he drummed the table with the fingers of one hand. No doubt he missed his *Angry Birds*.

Then she noticed the top of a blue-tipped head weaving its way through a knot of talking people at the other side of the room. Linwe shouldered between two people and walked toward them.

"Oh look, here she come," crooned Miguel. "I love that girl. I love her." As Linwe stopped beside their table, smiling, Miguel said to her, "Please tell me you starred in a spring break video called *Elf Babes Gone Wild*."

At that both Pia and Eva swiveled to stare at him. Miguel glanced from one unsmiling face to the other. "Come on, I asked her if she was legal," he said. "She's thirty."

Linwe grimaced. "I lied. I'm only sixteen."

Miguel looked stricken. Eva pointed at him and said, "You gonna get your ass arrested someday. That's if you lucky, and I don't beat you to a pulp first."

Linwe's bright peal of laughter rang out. Dancing brown eyes met Pia's. *I am actually thirty, but please don't tell him,* Linwe said.

I won't, Pia promised grimly. *He deserves to sweat a little. I apologize for his behavior.*

Please don't feel that's necessary, Linwe said. *I'm at least partway to blame, since I goaded him all day yesterday.* Aloud, the Elf said, "I heard you would enjoy a tour."

"Yes, please, as long as the High Lord can contact me if he becomes available for an audience," Pia replied.

"If that happens, a runner will find us."

"Very well." Pia stood, and all the others stood too. She said to Miguel, "No." As his face fell, Pia told Eva, "Two on. You pick."

"Me and Johnny," Eva said immediately.

"Fine." She smiled at Linwe. "Thank you for showing us around."

"That is entirely my pleasure," Linwe said.

For the next hour Linwe took Pia on a tour of the heart of Lirithriel Wood, while Eva and Johnny followed silently.

The High Lord's house had four levels, two of them deeply carved into bedrock.

By the time they stepped outdoors the fog had dissipated, leaving behind a gray, overcast day. Underneath the heavy blanket of old-growth trees, the landscape itself was full of curves and ridges like the whorls of a fingerprint or a gnarled tree trunk.

Many other small buildings dotted the area, cleverly hidden in nooks between the trees, and Pia was fascinated to find, there were more of the subtle there/not there Elven faces carved into large boulders. She started to look for them in rocks of any size, but several times they still surprised her, one moment hidden and the next moment coming visible.

Throughout the entire tour Pia could feel the crossover passageway, but either the underlying curl of the land itself or the Wood's presence kept her from pinpointing where it was until suddenly they came upon it.

Pia jerked to a halt, staring. Behind her, Eva and Johnny had to pull up hard to avoid running into her back.

Just ahead the trees opened up to a small clearing where stairs had been carved into the stony ground, leading downward and reshaping the floor of what must have once been a natural ravine. On the other side of the stairs, the walls had also been shaped and carved with a graceful, interlocking pattern. Even though she was standing several yards away, the Power of the passageway tugged at her.

She said, "I'm amazed the sculptors were able to keep their equilibrium long enough in the passageway to carve anything, let alone something so intricate and beautiful."

Linwe said cheerfully, "They were old." She grinned as all three Wyr laughed. "I meant that. Our ancients are very strong in their affinity to the elements."

"Do you have an affinity to an element?" Pia asked.

"Yes, as a matter of fact, I do. Mine is air." Pia blinked as a sudden breeze tickled her cheek. Linwe said, "I'm quite young, though, and that's the extent of what I can do. One of our most Powerful ancients could take that same affinity to

113

air and create a storm the size of Hurricane Rita." The Elf held up a slim hand. "Not that I'm saying that creating a storm of that size would be a good thing. And one or two of our ancients, the ones who are especially gifted, have an affinity to more than one element. Those tend to be compatible with each other. Fire and air. Water and earth. That sort of thing."

That was the best conversational opening Pia had seen yet, and she took it. "Speaking of ancients, I hear that Elves from Numenlaur are visiting."

A shadow darkened Linwe's animated expression. "Yes, although very few people have seen them. They have been closeted away ever since they arrived. I heard one of them might be ill."

Whatever Pia might have expected to hear, that wasn't it. She wasn't aware Elves could suffer from illness. "I'm sorry."

Linwe shrugged a slender shoulder. "It's gossip. I don't know anything for sure."

"Do your ancients ever talk about why they warred with each other?" Pia asked.

Johnny and Eva's silence grew more intense. When she looked over her shoulder, the other two Wyr stood several feet away and appeared to be studying the carved patterns in the passageway.

She could also tell by Linwe's wide-eyed glance that she had surprised the other woman. "You know of that?"

It was her turn to shrug. How much should she admit to knowing? Keep it simple, stupid. She said, "Dragos is my mate."

That seemed to have more impact than she had expected. Linwe's eyes rounded, and she took a deep breath and blew it out so that her blue-tipped bangs bounced in the air. "Yes, of course," Linwe said. "Then you must know of the Deus Machinae."

The whosie whatsit?

Pia smiled. She said, "I don't know the details of the story the way you learned it."

Either Linwe didn't notice that Pia was pumping her for information or she didn't care. The Elf said, "I was taught that there are things on this Earth, Powerful things that were put here by the gods to enact their will. They have had many forms and have been called many names over time, but ever since the time of the classic Greek poets—Horace, Euripides, Aeschylus and such—they have been called the Deus Machinae, or the God Machines."

Pia shook her head and murmured, "I haven't had much of a classical education, but wasn't the deus ex machina a plot device in Greek plays?"

Linwe's gaze touched hers briefly. "Yes, it literally means the 'god from the machine.' Anyway at one point, or so I've heard the story go, the Elves had possession of all seven of the Deus Machinae at once, and they agreed this was a significant event. Then they began to argue about which of them was meant to rule and how."

"I take it that didn't go so well," Pia said dryly.

"No, not so well. Some said the one who possessed Taliesin's Machine was destined to rule, for Taliesin is the god over all the other gods. Others said, no, Inanna, the goddess of Love, should reign supreme. Or perhaps Azrael, the god of Death. Or the bearer of Hyperion's item, since Law is the cornerstone of any civilization. Whether it was their ambition or the Power of the Machinae themselves, the ancients couldn't agree. Instead they—we—came to blows. Apparently we nearly destroyed ourselves."

"Dragos said it caused a diaspora," she said softly.

Linwe glanced at her. "Yes, those who survived finally came together and made a covenant. They split into seven groups, and each group took an item. Numenlaur was one of them. The other six groups promised to travel far away from each other, so that they would dissipate the Power of the Machinae, and end the war and all the chaos that had come with it. All seven groups were supposed to cast their items into the world, letting the gods' will work where it would."

Pia became aware suddenly of a cold, steady wind that blew along the crossover passageway. The wind must have

come from the Other land for it smelled strange, and it felt wet and heavy with a sense of snow that the Wood didn't have on this side of the passage. She shivered, pulled her anorak close and asked, "Did they do it?"

Linwe shook her head. "Nobody knows for sure. Maybe they did. Maybe some of the groups lied and said they did, but instead they kept their items. Or maybe they tried to keep them only to have the Machinae slip out of their grasps, because no one can control the will of the gods. Some of the original groups disappeared, and Numenlaur closed itself off from the rest of the world. All I know is that our High Lord and Lady kept their word."

Maybe those groups that had disappeared were the precursors to the Light and Dark Fae. Linwe's faith in her demesne rulers was touching, but Pia couldn't help but wonder if it was naive. She ducked her head, trying to keep her expression neutral. She asked, "Whose item did Calondir and Beluviel carry away with them?"

"Inanna's, the goddess of Love," the Elf said, smiling. "At the time, Inanna's Machine appeared as a golden chalice that fit into two cupped hands." She held her hands together to demonstrate the size. "The goddess was depicted as riding a chariot around the bowl, and seven gold lions circled the base."

"It sounds like it must have been striking."

"I've heard that it was so beautiful, apparently everyone who saw it wanted to drink from it. The High Lord's group sailed west across the ocean. When they sighted land, everyone in the group drank from the chalice one last time so that they all felt the goddess's Power, and then he threw it overboard."

"Dramatic but effective," Pia murmured, recalling the tapestry with Calondir and a gold cup in their apartment. She wondered which group ended up with Taliesin's item.

Not only did the convoluted Wood mess with her sense of direction, but with the sky so overcast, she couldn't guess how much time had passed. She glanced skyward, then at

Eva, who said, *Been a couple hours. Hugh should have made it out by now.*

Which told Pia exactly nothing. She took a deep breath and tried to ease the tension that had knotted the muscles at the base of her neck. Either shit would hit the fan or it wouldn't. Apparently that was the story of her day.

Story of her life, come to that.

After thanking Linwe for the tour, Pia chose to go back to their rooms. The others played chess, did sit-ups and push-ups and napped. Johnny coaxed Pia into playing a game of chess too, but she knew little beyond the basic moves and she was too preoccupied to focus well, and he trounced her thoroughly. Afterward she went to her bedroom to pace.

Calondir did not grant her an audience. Neither Beluviel nor Ferion appeared. Pia did not hear anything from Dragos or about him. Beluviel did send a note of apology and promised to see Pia the next day, but other than that nothing at all happened for the rest of the day.

Nothing, nothing, nothing.

⇒ NINE ⇐

The group had lunch brought up to them and by evening Pia couldn't stand the sight of the apartment any longer. They went to the main hall for supper, which was filled with quite a few more people than had been present at breakfast. Supper was robust winter fare, hot and filling: roasted deer, rabbit and pheasant, white and sweet potatoes, roasted chestnuts, loaves of chewy honey nut bread, pumpkin and cranberry tarts, baked apples and plenty of wine, beer and water.

Linwe joined them, along with a few of the other Elves that had traveled with them on the previous day, and the meal passed with plenty of lively conversation. Most of the people in the hall didn't leave when they had finished dining. Instead a few fetched musical instruments, and soon the sound of flutes, fiddles and drums filled the hall.

After several people called out in encouragement, a slender male with a sensitive-looking face stood to sing a ballad in Elvish. Even though Pia didn't understand a word of the song, the music and the flow of the lyrical words were haunting.

Pia watched and listened in silence. Everyone was friendly, the music was excellent and she had not heard anything *bad*, not from Dragos, Hugh or Calondir.

So that meant everything was fine, right? The evening should have been pleasant.

Table lamps and the firelight from both massive hearths gave the hall a warm, golden illumination. Sparks of Power from individuals glowed in her mind's eye like fireflies lighting a warm summer night, and the wild, secretive Wood's presence blanketed them all. She could sense so much Power, and it was all undiluted by distractions from technology like television, cell phones and street traffic.

A few especially strong glows seemed to shine in the distance. Perhaps those were Linwe's "ancients." Two of the glows might even be Calondir and Beluviel.

But underscoring everything was a sense of dread and anxiety she could not overcome. She had to force herself to unclench her fists. Then only a few minutes later she discovered that she had clenched them again. She ate because she was starving and eating was compulsory these days, but the food sat in her stomach like a rock. An unseen pincer gripped her by the back of the neck, causing a dull, throbbing ache.

Her tension roused the peanut whose awareness draped around her neck, his bright, loving energy unsettled. She put a hand over her abdomen, whispering silently, *I'm sorry, baby.* She tried to soothe him, but she didn't really know what she was doing, and she was still tense and filled with dread herself. His presence sharpened until it felt spiked with invisible claws. For the first time since she had become aware of his existence, he felt dangerous.

Oh great, go ahead and scare the dragon baby, why don't you? Knucklehead. She breathed deeply and evenly. Calm down.

She could just see how the future was going to go. If the peanut really turned out to be dangerous after he was born, Dragos might have to be the one to take care of him

whenever he had a toddler tantrum. Yeah, it was going to be fun to get the answer to that question. For the first time that whole, rotten day she felt an evil, sneaking sense of cheer.

Gradually the baby calmed down again. As she turned her attention away from him she felt again the sense of something lying stealthy and quiet underneath all the other sparks of Power, and her fists clenched.

Realization struck. Yes, she was worried and anxious, and she missed Dragos horribly, but whatever the hell she was sensing, it wasn't her own fear. It definitely existed outside of herself.

Had it always been there, only she had been too preoccupied to notice? Or had it crept in since they had arrived? The words *dark* and *light* didn't seem quite accurate when describing nonphysical qualities, but that stealthy, quiet thing felt like the antithesis of those sparks of Power that glowed so brightly against her mind's eye.

She turned to Eva, who sat beside her and murmured, "Do you feel anything odd?"

Across the table James's gaze flickered to them even as he laughed at something one of the others said. Beside him, Miguel shifted his seat back and settled into a lounging position that, Pia noticed, also happened to free his legs so that he could leap easily to his feet. Even though the others appeared relaxed and were clearly enjoying themselves, they had not sacrificed an iota of their alertness.

Like Pia, the captain had also been silent as she listened to the conversation. Eva sat in her chair at an angle, legs crossed at the ankles. She rested one elbow on the table, chin in her hand as she watched not only their group but also everyone else in the hall. Her black, alert gaze considered Pia thoughtfully.

Eva asked telepathically, *Like what?*

Following Eva's lead, Pia switched to telepathy. *How strong is your magic sense?*

This time Eva didn't bother with any taunting street talk. *Pretty good. Miguel is the real magic user in the group, though, so his is the best out of all of us.*

Pia rubbed the back of her aching neck as she tried to come up with the right words. *I just picked up on something. It's very quiet.*

Hold on.

As Pia waited, she ran her gaze over the main hall again. Whatever it was, she didn't think it was in the hall, but pinning a physical geography to the feeling was as difficult and slippery as trying to explain it with physical descriptors.

Then Eva said, *None of us are sensing anything. Can you get any more specific?*

She thought of how she had sensed the Goblins who had kidnapped her and Dragos in May. Dragos hadn't sensed the Goblins either. Frustration gripped her. The feeling was growing all too familiar on this trip.

I can feel different Powers in the area, she said. *Some of them are definitely people, although I can also sense the Wood. This other thing is lying underneath all the rest. It's like a patch of black ice on the road. You might not be able to see the ice very well even though you know it's there.*

How dangerous do you think it is?

Dragos had thought her sensitivity to the Goblins might be connected to her Wyr form. Should she open that can of worms with Eva?

She shook her head. I don't know. I've never felt it before. It's making my stomach knot. I don't know if I just became aware of it, or if it's something new to the area since we arrived. She looked into the other woman's sharp gaze. *The last time I felt something strange, I was beaten and nearly killed. But this is a different situation. I don't think this . . . thing is physically here in the hall. I'm not even sure that what I'm sensing is active.*

Yet, Eva said. *It might not be active yet. Bombs are inert until they go off.*

Pia grimaced. *Point.*

Think we should take a walk, see what you pick up from different areas. I'd like to get an idea of how localized it is, if we can. Maybe Miguel can get bead on it somewhere else, or we can get a direction on it.

121

Pia said aloud, "After such a big meal I could stand to stretch my legs a bit." She stood, and the rest of the people at the table, Elves and Wyr alike, politely stood with her.

"Miguel, come with us," Eva said to their group, smiling. "The rest of you, relax and enjoy the music."

Miguel winked at Linwe, stood and fell into step behind Pia and Eva as they turned away.

Pia kept her stride casual and her expression calm, while her heart rate sped up. Stupid, but there it was. She returned nods and smiles to people while she, Eva and Miguel worked their way through the crowd to the doors that led outside.

The night air was chilly and damp, and patches of fog had begun to appear again, drifting over the area like aimless ghosts. The other two kept silent as Pia chose to descend the main staircase beside the falls. Two lit braziers illuminated the bottom of the stone steps and other braziers dotted the open area, marking the entrance to paths into the forest.

Other people were outside, walking and talking quietly, with the occasional outburst of laughter ringing out over the clearing. A few were couples, arm in arm. She felt jarred and disoriented as she glanced around again and realized that the scene was actually quite pretty, and people were out to simply enjoy the night.

Choosing a direction at random, she walked across the shadowed clearing and stopped by the boulder with the subtle face. The Wood's presence felt stronger at night. It pressed against her skin, unsettling and intoxicating at once. She resisted another urge to change and disappear into the dark foliage. Some Wyr went wild and never returned to their human form. For the first time she began to understand the lure.

Then she turned in a slow circle. At first she couldn't sense anything beyond the Wood, but she cast out further with her mind.

There. She felt certain that the nearby quiet, intense glow of Power was Miguel, and that the weaker one was Eva. Then other, different glows came clear.

And there it was again, that slick, subtle patch of black ice. Certainty settled inside, and she knotted her fists. "It's in the building," she said.

"Damn." Eva sighed. "Okay."

Miguel said, "I still got nothing. I can't pick up on whatever you're sensing."

"That means we have to rely on you," Eva told Pia. "And if we aren't going to leave, you need to speak up immediately if you feel it change."

She nodded, frowning. Beluviel had been very kind to her, and it wasn't the consort's fault that events had given her a surfeit of houseguests and issues to attend to. While Pia was wary of putting herself in the shoes of someone who was so different in race, age and outlook, she couldn't help but do so this time. Pia would want someone to tell her if something like that black . . . thing was lurking anywhere around her home.

She said, "I need to talk to Beluviel."

Even in the shadows, she could see Eva and Miguel exchange a look. "For all we know, she might be responsible for it," Miguel said, his voice pitched very low. "Needs to be considered."

Pia shook her head and spoke just as softly. "I don't believe that. It feels entirely alien from Beluviel's energy, and even though there are some Powerful Elves here, it's possible none of them can sense this anymore than you can." She looked at Eva. "You know that experience I mentioned earlier? Dragos didn't sense what I picked up then either."

Eva sucked a tooth and looked sour, but she said, "All right. Let's go find her."

They walked across the clearing and up the stairs, and Pia stopped the first Elf in a house uniform that they came to, a woman with hair so blonde it was almost white.

"Please take me to the consort," Pia said.

The woman regarded her with wide eyes. "Perhaps I can take a message and she can get back to you."

"I know it is late," Pia said gently. "And I know the consort

has been very busy. But I need to talk to her right now, and you need to take me to her."

The Elf's posture grew rigid, but she said, "Yes, ma'am."

What, you ain't gonna tear her up none? I feel betrayed, Eva said telepathically. *You lied to me. You ain't got no bitch in you.*

Keep pushing, Pia told her. *And you'll get to find out how much bitch I've got.*

Sound like a good time to me.

Pia, Eva and Miguel followed the Elf through corridors and up a flight of stairs. They reached the end of a hallway where two attendants stood in front of double doors. Their escort spoke rapidly in Elvish, and one of the other attendants replied.

Pia asked in Eva's head, *Any clue what they're saying?*

Eva turned to Pia with her most limpid innocent look. *They arguing.*

Apparently Eva couldn't straighten up and fly right for long. Pia angled out her jaw. She told Eva, *I still hate you passionately.*

Yeah, I still surviving, princess.

The Elves' conversation had grown forceful. Finally the door attendant slipped inside the apartment while their escort studied the floor with her mouth folded tight. Clearly the woman felt like Pia had put her in a bad position, and Pia supposed she had.

A pungent herbal scent had wafted out when the attendant had opened the doors, along with a faint, unsettling whiff of blood. On either side of her, Eva and Miguel shifted into a tighter position until their shoulders brushed hers, and the invisible pincers at the back of Pia's neck tightened as they waited.

She had lost her internal vision when they had traveled back inside, and she fumbled to retrieve it. Her concept of where the various sparks of Power had shifted with the change in her position, and that flat, black patch was so quiet and subtle anyway. . . .

The door opened again, and Beluviel herself stood in the doorway. For the first time since Pia had become acquainted with the other woman, the consort looked disheveled and tired. Beluviel wore a simple loose tunic and cotton trousers, and her long dark hair was bound haphazardly back from her face.

Pia's internal vision settled into utter clarity. Whatever the dark thing was, it was in the apartment behind Beluviel. Could it be the emissary's illness that Linwe had mentioned?

The strong, medicinal herbal scent, mingled with the scent of blood, wafted through the air again. Even though Beluviel held the door partially closed, Pia could see several individuals in the apartment behind the consort and hear quiet-voiced conversation. She glimpsed a few familiar faces of people she had seen in the main hall earlier that day. They stood in a tight cluster around a tall male she had never seen before.

All the Elves were striking in some way, and this man was no different. He had his own particular charisma, with gleaming chestnut hair pulled back from precise features, and eyes that were as green as the Wood and just as compelling.

The man turned and looked at her. Such green eyes, like a sunlit, beckoning glade that called so seductively to her.

A glade for her forest creature to get lost in, reveling in mystery and silence.

No, she was wrong. She *had* seen this man before. Of course she had. Somewhere. He was more familiar to her than any of the other Elves that were present. She had talked with him at length at some point, perhaps at one of the functions she had attended over the last seven months. Perhaps over dinner. . . .

With an effort she yanked her attention back to Beluviel. She said, "I'm sorry to interrupt you so late in the evening—"

Beluviel interrupted her gently. "This is not a good time, Pia. I am attending to something that cannot wait."

She said to Beluviel in a low voice, "I understand this isn't a good time, but I wanted to warn you about something I sensed. . . ." As she spoke she glanced at the man again. He smiled at her conspiratorially as though they were the very best of friends. And they were, weren't they? The very best of friends. It seemed as though they had known each other for forever. She heard herself saying, ". . . But it appears you are already aware of it. Again, my apologies for interrupting you."

The man nodded in approval and winked. It was wonderful to see her friend again, so wonderful she wanted to shoulder her way into the apartment and ask the man what his name was.

"Thank you for coming to find me," Beluviel said. Pia yanked her attention back to the consort, who looked puzzled. "Let's talk in the morning."

Pia couldn't help herself and looked at the man again. Yes, the man's bright gaze promised her. We'll talk. Soon.

"Certainly," Pia said. Who was she answering again? She couldn't remember. "Good night."

Beluviel closed the door, and Pia turned to Eva and Miguel, who were frowning at her. Eva said telepathically, *Did you tell Beluviel everything you needed to tell her?*

Of course, Pia said.

She sent the Elf who had escorted them to the main hall with a message for the others, and soon Andrea, James and Johnny joined them in their apartment. Eva and Miguel updated the others while Pia stayed silent, lost in thought.

She felt like she was forgetting something. What was it? If only she could chase it down. The feeling was driving her crazy.

Eva asked her, "What did Beluviel say when you told her about what you sensed?"

"Hm?" Pia said.

Was it something she had forgotten? Or was it someone? Eva studied her with a frown. "You did say that you told

Beluviel about what you were sensing, so you must have had a quick exchange telepathically. What did she say?"

Pia frowned back at the captain. She did know that she had told Beluviel everything, while someone had watched her. Who was it again? He had such green, green eyes.

She had a feeling of something slipping past her, like a train of thought almost but not quite recovered. She told the other woman, "You heard as much as I did. She said we would talk in the morning."

Eva's lips tightened. "Fine," said the captain. "Extra vigilance on watches tonight. I'll take a double, since Hugh's gone. Miguel, I want you on the second shift. Maybe you can get a better reading when things quiet down and at least most people are asleep." She looked at Pia. "Anything else you want to add?"

It was a relief to turn her mind to other things instead of trying to chase down that maddeningly elusive memory. Pia said, "Maybe I should check on things during the second shift as well, to see if I can sense any changes."

"Smart," Miguel said.

"Other than that, we can see if Beluviel can give us more news or clarification." She straightened her back, which had started to ache again. "Depending on how that talk goes, we may be leaving tomorrow. This whole trip may just be a case of poor timing all the way around, but there's no reason to stay if we can't accomplish what we set out to do." And then because she had been a good, good girl that whole damn day, she looked at Eva and let herself ask, "I don't suppose Hugh might still show up this evening with any news?"

Eva shook her head. "Not unless it's urgent. He won't try to fly into this Wood at night."

Fuck. Unsurprised but still disappointed, she nodded.

Even though Eva's gaze remained fixed on her, it was clear the captain was lost in thought. After a moment Eva said, "Everybody pack. There might be a simple explanation for what's going on, but right now we don't understand what we know, and I want to be able to move at a moment's notice if we need to."

"I'm never going to hear the end of this," Pia muttered. "Somehow this will all end up being my fault."

Eva slapped her on the shoulder. "'Course it will, princess. That's 'cause it is."

For the barest moment Pia resisted her impulse. She should not stoop to Evil Eva's level. But then there it was. Her hand came up without her permission, and she flipped the other woman her middle finger.

Eva and the others laughed. As Pia went to bed, she consoled herself with the thought that at least the psychos' laughter was friendlier than when they had first started out on the trip. Anyway, that was her story and she was sticking to it.

When she went to bed, she expected to toss and turn, and to chew on all her worries, but instead she fell asleep almost immediately.

Someone stood over her, swathed in shadows, looking at her with green eyes. He bent over to touch her.

No. That wasn't right.

There wasn't a man in her room. Someone was growling.

The peanut lay stretched out on her torso, long wings sleek against his supple back, his head on her shoulder. He was such a beautiful white dragon baby, every delicate feature etched in perfect miniature. She stroked a hand down his body and whispered, "Ssh, sweetheart, it's all right."

He lifted his head to look at her, and his dark violet eyes glowed with ferocity. Wow, he really was unsettled. He was going to be quite a force to be reckoned with when he grew up. She looked out the window where he had been staring. While the night sky was clear, there were no stars.

The sky looked so wrong that dread jolted through her. She gathered the peanut up in her arms and rolled to her feet to go to the window. Oh, thank God, there were some stars sprinkled across at least part of the sky.

As she watched, a few of the bright lights went dark. A man stood at her shoulder and whispered, "Nothing shines forever. Their deaths will pave a way to a new age."

She glanced back at him. Green eyes smiled at her.

"No," she said. Was she agreeing with him, or refuting him?

The peanut's growling grew louder. She hugged him tightly. Either the stars were dying, or they were being smothered or eaten. Despite what the man said, it was horribly wrong, the most horrible thing she'd ever seen. A harsh, discordant clash sounded like a dirge, or perhaps it was an inhuman scream, and dread soaked the landscape like blood.

The dread was everywhere. It beat a dark, oily sludge in her veins and tried to black her out, swallow her whole. The man reached out to put his hand on her shoulder, and suddenly the peanut's little head whipped around and he actually *bit* her—

She plunged awake, her skin damp with sweat. Dammit all to hell, that wasn't the kind of dream she had been hoping she would have. A vague nausea roiled and she curled on her side, breathing deeply.

The baby was roused again, his presence draped over her, an invisible protective cloak spiked with aggression. She put a hand on her rounded stomach. What the hell?

The dark sense of dread had intensified. It saturated the air so thickly, she felt as though she were actually breathing it in like wood smoke.

Smoke.

She came fully awake, stabbed to alertness by a knife of adrenaline.

The acrid scent of smoke hung in the air. A sharp clash of metal sounded in the distance, along with shouting, and a red-tinged fog drifted across the window outside.

Or maybe that wasn't fog. Her head ached fiercely and her ears rang as if she heard a high, thin scream.

There was no sound of movement in the apartment. Lunging to her feet, she ran out of her bedroom.

The embers of a fire pulsed brightly in the fireplace in the common room. James sat on the floor, slumped against the hallway door. Andrea sat in an awkward heap in front of the window.

129

They couldn't be dead. They couldn't be. Pia leaped to James and slapped him. He came upright with a growl and pressed the tip of his sword against her throat before she could jerk back.

The sharp tip nicked her skin. They stared at each other, wild-eyed. Then James jerked his sword away and said, "*FUCK*, don't ever do that again. I could have sliced your throat wide open."

She hissed, "You were asleep."

Affront flashed across his handsome features. "I never fall asleep on watch."

"Keep telling that to yourself as you go wake Andrea up!"

The sharp clashes of metal in the distance—those were swords. James leaped toward Andrea's slumped figure as Pia raced for the nearest bedroom. Eva would never sleep through this kind of commotion, not unless she'd been drugged.

Eva and Miguel lay in a large bed. Miguel had the bed-covers pulled up to his chin while on the other side of the bed Eva lay stretched on top, wrapped in a blanket.

Having learned her lesson the hard way with James, Pia slapped Eva's ankle hard and jumped back out of the way as the other woman lunged to her feet with a growl.

"You know that bomb you mentioned earlier?" Pia said. "It went off."

She didn't bother to stay and chat about things. Eva would figure it out. Instead she ran to her bedroom to get dressed, yanking her clothes and boots on with unsteady hands. She unwrapped her light crossbow—the only weapon she was comfortable enough with carrying—and slung a belt of bolts around her neck. If only she could get her head to stop ringing. That sense of a high, thin scream just on the edge of her hearing felt like someone was shoving a needle into her brain.

Eva strode into the bedroom as Pia shouldered her pack. By the growing light in the window, she could see that the other woman was dressed and armed. Red tinged Eva's bold dark features and sparked in her furious black eyes.

"Every last fucking one of us was goddamn *fucking* asleep," Eva said. "Every last one. I'm gonna kill us."

Pia told her tersely, "It wasn't your fault. Something wanted us asleep." Even as she said it, she knew that wasn't quite right. She remembered the shadowed figure of a man, and the oily black sludge trying to take her over before the peanut bit her and shocked her awake. "Not something. It was someone, and I think he wanted more than just our sleep."

Eva's gaze narrowed. "Got a description of this guy?"

"Call me crazy," she said, scowling, "but I'm pretty sure he's got green eyes. I keep . . ." Her voice trailed off as something slipped into place. "I just remembered. I'm pretty sure I dreamed about him the first night we were here."

"Did you, now?" Eva moved to the window to look out, hands on her hips. "Dreams, spells and fire. That ain't good, princess, but whoever this fucker is, he ain't our problem. I sent Johnny and Miguel to scout out our best exit strategy."

Pia didn't argue. Eva was right. There was a time for sticking things out, and this wasn't it. When they got safely back to Charleston, or better yet, New York, she could send a sympathy card to Beluviel and Calondir for whatever this disaster turned out to be.

She went to stand beside Eva. There wasn't much to see outside, other than the smoke or the fog, except for a patch of dark water below that glittered with a tint of red. Man, her head ached like a son of a bitch. She said, "I wish we could see what was burning."

"The walls, floor and ceiling are cool and our air quality is good," Eva said. "Same out in the hall. If this building's on fire, it hasn't gotten close yet. We're going to have to rappel out the window if the exits are blocked."

Pia took a breath. Their windows looked over the river at the top of the falls, and the water rushed underneath the building to plunge over a deadly number of rocks before hitting the bottom. "I assume you have a plan to avoid going over the falls?"

Eva said, "One of the building's main support pillars is

underneath the common room window. We can use the pillar as an anchor and cast left with ropes. River's edge is three pillars to the left. It's awkward, and we'll get wet and cold, but we can do it."

Of course Eva would have thought of that. She had probably scoped that out as an emergency exit option when they had first arrived. Pia rubbed the back of her aching neck. If only she could think past this needle in her brain.

Eva said in an ultracasual tone of voice, "Guess this is when I point out how much help Hugh would be if he were still here."

Pia just looked at her. They had made the only decision they could, given the information they had at the time, and the other woman knew it. "So why'd you let him go so easily, captain?"

The other woman laughed softly. "Touché."

Light, running footsteps sounded just outside in the hall, and someone pounded on their door. Eva and Pia strode quickly into the common room as James checked outside. He stood back almost immediately. Miguel and Johnny had returned, and they brought Linwe with them. The Elf's face was tear-streaked, her dark brown eyes stricken.

Pia said, "What's happening?"

"People are fighting each other," Miguel said.

"We knew that," Eva snapped. "Be specific."

"You don't understand. People aren't just fighting each other," Linwe said. Her voice sounded hoarse and scraped raw. "*Friends* are fighting each other. It doesn't make any sense. I just saw—I-I just saw Elyric cut down his best— his best—"

Johnny put an arm around her as she stuttered into choked silence.

Eva's face had turned grimmer than ever. She said, "What's burning?"

Miguel's expression held an echo of the same horror that Linwe's did. He said, "The Wood. The blaze is all around us. Someone set the whole damn place on fire."

Pia's stomach gave a sickening lurch as she realized

what was causing the needle in her brain. The strange, beautiful Wood was screaming as it died.

If she thought Dragos was mad at her before, this was going to send him ballistic.

She muttered, "I'm *never* going to hear the end of this."

≡ TEN ≡

D ragos didn't stop at the New York City limit.
Instead he continued to fly south until he reached
the Wyr/Elven border. The seven Elder Races demesnes in
the United States did not follow any human geography, and
state lines were not demesne border lines. The Wyr/Elven
border cut through Lumberton, North Carolina, south of
Fayetteville.

Once he reached Lumberton, he decided to pause and
think. He landed on the shoulder beside I-95 South. Lumberton was a small town, with around twenty thousand
humans and three thousand more of a smattering of the Elder
Races. Even though Lumberton was several hours' drive
away from New York, it was just as gray, cold and dreary
as the city had been.

Still keeping his presence cloaked, he changed into his
human form to check voice mail and text messages, scroll-
ing through them quickly while trucks and cars roared past
on the interstate.

There. His vision narrowed. He'd gotten three phone
calls from Pia's iPhone. The first had come in almost two

hours ago, and the others had come at intervals of every half hour afterward.

He didn't bother to listen to any of the messages. Instead he punched speed dial. When a male answered his mate's phone, his talons sprang out and the growl that came out of him shook the ground.

The male spoke rapidly, ". . . Is quite well. This is Hugh Monroe. Again, your mate is quite well. Pia sent me out of Lirithriel Wood to tell you that she is fine, and that she thinks the Wood is interfering with your communication with each other. She gave me her cell phone because she wanted to be sure I reached you, sir, and I promise you, that's the only reason why I'm using her phone right now."

Monroe. It took Dragos a second to place the name. He was the gargoyle from Pia's bodyguard team. Dragos took a deep breath and relaxed fractionally. Although he hated the gargoyle's voice coming from Pia's phone, he said, "Tell me everything."

Hugh obliged by telling him about their trip into the Wood, along with every detail of the High Lord's home, how Pia's evening had gone last night and how she had sent Hugh with the message within minutes of waking up.

As Dragos listened in silence, he strode south down the shoulder of the interstate while traffic whizzed past, oblivious to his presence. Snow began to fall in fluffy, fat flakes that swirled over the dark gray land. The snowflakes that fell around him hissed as they boiled to nothing before they reached the ground, until a cloak of mist trailed behind him as he walked.

Fifteen more yards. He knew it like he knew the back of his own hand, just as he had known to a penny what had been in his original hoard before he downsized it. He knew to a precise inch the many miles of border that surrounded his demesne.

Monroe fell silent after he described flying away from the High Lord's home. Dragos asked, "Where are you now?"

135

"I'm on the north side of the Wood, in the Francis Marion National Forest," Monroe told him.

"You've done what you were told to do," Dragos said. "Now go back in."

Ten yards.

"I will certainly give it my best shot," Monroe said. "But I'm not sure I can. I could feel the Wood close behind me as I left."

Five.

"Try," Dragos said. He hung up.

He checked through the rest of his messages, but there was nothing that couldn't wait. Bayne had texted that Sidhiel had not made an effort to leave town. He sent out a blast message to his sentinels in a brief update and then he turned off his phone.

The thing about laws was, at their essence they were a decision. Before he had met Pia, Dragos had counted law as his finest achievement. Law was the necessary bridge he had needed to build between him and other creatures when the world had become so goddamn crowded.

But at his essence, he was a lawless creature. Other imperatives ran much deeper.

He would not tolerate being separated from Pia, nor would he let this Elven Wood keep his mate from him. If Pia herself was angry or upset with his decision, why then, so be it. They would just have to figure out a way to get past it.

And he would not let any other race dictate his actions.

Not when Numenlaur was involved, and prophecy might be at hand.

As he stepped across the Wyr/Elven border, he changed back into his Wyr form, launched into the air and continued south.

Choosing to copy the gargoyle's actions, he landed in the Elven Wood's much larger neighbor, the national forest. Coming to ground about a quarter mile out from his goal, he changed and walked the rest of the way through the new, slender young trees.

He had left the snow behind, but the chill, damp, cloudy day was little better. Even though he did not expect it, he kept his senses sharp in case the Elves chose to send periodic patrols around the Wood's border.

Despite his wariness he did not encounter any Elves or any hikers either, for that matter. He sensed the Wood well before he came upon it. Then the visible landscape changed as he saw the dark, tangled edge of the old growth forest up ahead, and for the first time he came toe-to-root with Lirithriel Wood.

The Wood was aware of him. He could feel it watching and waiting. He pushed at it gently with Power, and it pushed back. It was wild and wary, and it did not want any part of him inside its borders.

He respected that. He just didn't accept it.

He walked along the edge of the Wood and studied it. A couple of times he thought he had figured out how slip past its barriers, but when he rose into the air to try to fly inside he felt the Wood turn in on itself, and he lost his sense of direction. When that happened he wheeled immediately to fly away again until he broke clear again of its influence.

Eventually he settled on a wide, flat bluff, his head between his paws as he regarded the dense forest with the patience of a very old predator. It had been successful in keeping him out thus far, but he knew one thing it didn't. He knew that he would find a way to get inside. He was far older than the Wood, and smarter, and much, much more convoluted. It was only a matter of time.

Sometime midafternoon, a male voice said in his head, *Sir, did you still come south after we talked?*

He said, *Monroe?*

Yes, sir. I can't get back inside.

Various facts moved through Dragos's thoughts like chess pieces journeying across a black-and-white checked board. Across the chessboard in his head the face of his opponent might vary, but there was always an opponent.

He said, *Go to Lirithriel House. Explain to them that*

you were sent out to deliver a message and ask to stay there while you wait for Pia and the others. It is a reasonable request. I would like to know more about what happens inside that house, especially now.

Yes, sir, Monroe said.

Update me when you have a chance.

He could think of no possible good reason for those at the house to deny hospitality to the gargoyle. That might prove useful. And if they did turn Monroe away, Dragos would be most interested in learning why.

Once he had settled that matter, his attention drifted back to the Wood. He was not surprised at its stubborn rejection of his presence. It was, after all, a creation of the Elves. And it was impossible to reason with something that had no language.

Night slipped slyly across the sky, a stealthy assassin that murdered the bleak, lonesome day. The more the Wood resisted, the angrier Dragos became until his rage burned as a feral fire deep in the pit of his chest.

He could break it. He could splinter it to pieces and tear his way in. He was not only older, smarter and more convoluted. He was much stronger as well.

But Pia thought this tangled, obstinate piece of real estate was beautiful, and he supposed that counted for something, so he would hold on to his temper for a little while longer.

Then Monroe said, *Sir, I'm at the house, and they've agreed to give me a room.*

Very good, he said, for the first time pleased with how something had gone that day. *Contact me if you notice anything out of the ordinary.*

With that he launched into the air and flew east toward the coast, following the Wood's border.

By now there were twenty-eight contestants and only two more days of the Games. He expected that all five of his sentinels would have made it through to the semifinal round, and he suspected that the elegantly fighting, disin-

genuous Quentin Caeravorn would have too. He was also very interested in finding out if Elysias had won through.

That was when a part of him noticed a small but entirely logical curiosity.

When he stopped pushing against the Wood, it stopped resisting him. That was all, and it was a remarkably simple fact, yet instinct had him changing his course minutely while he kept the main focus of his attention on the events in New York.

Then he slid into the Elven Wood obliquely, as if by accident, and he allowed himself a slight, predatory smile.

In the next instant, he lost his smile. Now that he was past the border, he could scent on a billow of wind the acrid bite of wood smoke and the dark taste of a chaotic Power that was so familiar to him even though the last time he had sensed it had been so long ago.

The Power came from one of the Deus Machinae. Someone was wielding one of the God Machines.

The damned fools were doing it again.

Pia.

He flung himself forward, hurtling through the sullen, deadly night.

"Are you saying we can't break through the fire?" Eva demanded as she stared at Miguel.

"That's what it looks like," he said. "Leaving the building shouldn't be an issue. All the exits are useable. The problem is leaving the area. That blaze is going like gangbusters and it doesn't seem to matter that the forest is damp. If I didn't know any better, I'd say it's been burning a while, couple days at least. That blaze looks mature."

"So we hit the river below the falls," Eva said. "And swim past the line of fire."

"Not a good option," Miguel said. "Some fuckers on the other side of the river are shooting at the swimmers, and we don't have time to send someone to take them out."

Linwe sobbed softly and covered her face with both hands, and James started swearing, a low vicious litany.

Pia said, "That leaves only one way to go, unless it's blocked off too. The crossover passageway."

She knew just exactly how Dragos would spell ballistic. It began with a capital *I'm going to kill somebody so fucking dead for this*, and well, after that point, it didn't matter if you spelled the rest of the word right.

Eva snapped out several swear words as she drew her sword. "This smells like a setup, but it doesn't sound like we have any choice and the fire can't last forever. We make for the passageway, and we keep Pia surrounded. Johnny, take point, and James and Andrea, take either side. Miguel and I will bring up the rear."

Pia took Linwe by the arm. The Elf looked at her blankly. She had gone into shock. Pia told her firmly, "You're coming with us."

"I should do something to help," Linwe said.

"Right now, staying alive is what helps," Pia told her.

"Enough," Eva snapped. "Move, everybody. And don't engage with anyone if you don't have to."

The smell of smoke grew more intense as soon as Johnny opened the door. They slipped out of the apartment and worked their way through the building. Pia kept her grip on Linwe's arm, carrying her crossbow one handed.

Elves ran down the halls, shouting to each other. James pressed against Pia's shoulder, forcing her and Linwe against the wall, but nobody paid any attention to their group. They worked their way down a flight of stairs and the sound of fighting grew louder. When they pushed outside, it was like stepping into a scene from hell.

Towering golden red flames crackled and roared in the Wood, throwing great swirling spires of glowing sparks into the sky, and acrid smoke blanketed the scene in swathes of hazy white that blurred details and gave the scene a nightmarish quality. Heat throbbed against Pia's skin. The fire would reach the building soon.

She could see a patch of the river, which looked blacker than ever, its surface covered with dancing red light. The heads of a couple of swimmers speared the surface until crossbow bolts took them. More Elves ran past them, and clusters of people dotted the clearing, fighting savagely.

Just as Linwe and Johnny said, they were fighting each other. Pia couldn't make sense of it, and she saw the same incomprehension on the faces of the others.

With a sharp gesture, Johnny led them to the path that would take them to the crossover passageway. Pia's grip on Linwe's arm slipped away as they jogged, but she saw that the Elf had come out of her shock somewhat and stayed with the group.

The path twisted and suddenly they came upon a large group of Elves engaged in an intense battle. A clash of Power swirled dizzyingly in her mind like fierce lights and glistening black. Pia glimpsed Calondir in the thickest part of the fight, wielding a bright silver sword, his expression stern and deadly. Blood streamed down one side of his face.

Johnny spun and pushed at her. "Turn around," he said. "Go!"

"There's nowhere else to go," Pia told him, even as Eva and Miguel pressed up behind her, urging her forward.

The fire advanced behind them all, driving them to the clearing. The forest on either side of the path was dense with shadow and hellish light, and for a moment the group was all in a tangle. Somebody struck her ribs with an elbow, knocking her crossbow out of her hand. She had no idea where Linwe had gone.

Because Johnny was facing her, Pia saw the battle spill toward them before he could. She called out a sharp warning, and Johnny pivoted, and then he engaged in a sudden sharp flurry of movement. James lunged forward too, and the world turned into a grunting, churning mess of a melee that she couldn't track . . . goddammit, she was no good at any of this war shit. . . .

Eva grabbed her from behind and bodily yanked her back from the fighting. Beside them, Miguel flung out a hand, fingers splayed, and he said, *"Lux."*

Power flew out with the word, and the area filled with brilliant light. For a few moments everything was clearly illuminated. They were much closer to the passageway than Pia had thought. Not only did she see Calondir, but she saw Ferion too. And Beluviel stood in the group that faced them, her eyes great hollows of darkness in her perfect face, her hair bound back and a sword in one hand.

Wait. Was Beluviel fighting with Calondir and Ferion, or *against* them?

With the flare of light, the battle paused. It resumed with redoubled fury, and chaos spun around them like a hurricane.

Johnny said, "Shit."

Through some trick of timing Pia heard him distinctly over the sounds of battle, even though he didn't shout or even speak loudly. He went to his knees, and James roared and fought even harder, and Andrea and Miguel lunged forward too.

Eva shoved Pia roughly behind her and said, "Stay *back*, goddammit."

Pia stared at the other woman incredulously; like she was so crazy that she would leap into that battle. Then the captain did just that as she leaped forward, and the Wyr clicked into a seamless fighting unit. They were a hell of a sight to see, she supposed, as they formed a protective barrier around her and Johnny, but she didn't bother to pause and admire their prowess. Instead she fell on her knees beside Johnny who had sagged forward.

"Hey," she said stupidly to him.

His head turned slightly toward her. She blocked out all the chaos and noise and put an arm around him, and he fell against her. Trusting the others to do their job, she eased Johnny to the ground, and in the fading light of the spell Miguel cast, she saw the profuse cascade of blood down his front. Oh shit.

She tore his clothing open, and it was bad, very bad. As a Wyr, Johnny had a strong aptitude for self-healing, but this, oh *shit*, he wasn't going to get over this.

And there wasn't time for any fucking thing, let alone time to stew over a decision when she couldn't think straight anyway, not with that horrible, unending scream in her head, so she took her knife, slit her palm and let a trickle of her blood flow over poor Johnny's torn-up chest. Power flowed out along with her blood, but probably no one would notice because the entire world had gone insane, and everybody else was busy making too much noise to pay any attention to anything she did anyway.

Right?

Eva knelt on the other side of Johnny and grabbed her wrist. *What the fuck are you doing?* she hissed in Pia's head.

Pia yanked her wrist out of the other woman's grasp. *I will HURT YOU SO BAD before I kill you if you say anything about this.*

Eva didn't bother to answer, but instead tore off some of Johnny's shirt to put pressure on wounds that Pia knew were already closing under all that blood. *I have healing potions in my pack. Dig in the left pocket—*

Johnny coughed, sat up and said, "Oh man, that sucked."

Eva's eyes rounded. She yanked Johnny's shirt open wider and ran a hand down his lean torso, searching for a wound that was no longer there. "Princess, you got some kind of bitch-goddess mojo I ain't never seen before."

"It wasn't that bad," Pia said desperately to Johnny. "Quit whining and get up." She stuck a finger under Eva's nose. "And you shut the fuck up."

The rest of the world snapped back into focus. She jumped up and Eva helped Johnny to his feet just as the last of Miguel's spell faded, leaving the clearing washed in a hot hellish red again.

At the same time the screaming in her head reached a crescendo. For a moment it was so loud she couldn't see straight. Then with a *snap* it broke off into silence.

What did that mean? Had the spirit of the Wood died?

Something had happened when she wasn't looking. The chaotic Power had vanished, and the fighting had come to an end, although all of the psychos stood braced and ready. Suddenly Elves surrounded them.

"Lady," Ferion said as he shouldered between two Elves and came to an abrupt halt in front of the business end of James and Miguel's swords. Ferion wore leggings and a loose tunic, and he was blood streaked too. "You need to join us."

Pia coughed, looking beyond Ferion for Beluviel, but she was no longer in sight. Pia could still see Calondir. He stood partially turned away as he shouted and gestured to someone. Her voice hoarse from smoke inhalation, she said, "This is where you tell me what the fuck, and you do it quickly, Ferion."

"There's too much to explain quickly," he said. Linwe slammed into Ferion's side, and he put an arm around her, hugging the young Elf tight against his side. "One of the Numenlaurians used a very old Power against us. Telling the rest of the story would take time we do not have."

Calondir approached, and the Elves that surrounded them backed away. The High Lord glanced over the other Wyr to Pia and gave her a curt nod. "The fire's very close," Calondir said. "We're going to have to cross over, and if they're waiting on the other side, we'll have to try to fight our way through."

Fight their way through what? Or whom?

"Where's Beluviel?" Pia asked.

"She has been taken, along with many others," Calondir said. "They've already crossed over."

"Taken how?" Eva demanded sharply.

The High Lord did not appear to take offense at her tone. Calondir said, "Many of us were taken over while sleeping, and they rose to attack the rest of us." His gaze moved over them. "I see all of your party is intact."

Then the entire conversation became *blah blah blah* as the only thing that mattered in the world happened.

Dragos growled in her head, *Pia.*

Wild joy transformed her, blazing brighter than the fire. *It's not my fault,* she groaned. *Oh my God, I missed you.*
I'm coming in fast, he said. *Where are you?*

We're with Calondir in a clearing by the Elves' cross-over passageway. He said that Beluviel and others have been taken over. I think he means they've been controlled, because the Elves have been fighting each other. We—we're going to have to cross over, Dragos. The Wood is on fire all around us, and it's getting close.

No! Do not cross, he said sharply. *Not unless you have no other choice. Please, Pia. Wait for just a little while longer and trust me.*

Please. There it was, and not when he was cajoling, and not when it was comfortable. Her hair was practically on fire, and she was surrounded by Elves. She was even with Calondir, whom she was pretty sure occupied the bull's-eye in the dartboard of hated people in Dragos's head, and yet Dragos still said please. It was better than any apology he could have crafted.

She told him, *I'll wait.*

Then she said aloud, "We're not crossing over."

Everyone turned to look at her as if she was crazy. Yeah, she got that a lot. Pretty much ever since she had mated with Dragos, in fact. She focused on Calondir and said, "You said 'they' may be waiting on the other side of the passageway, and Ferion mentioned one of the Numenlaurians. Is he by any chance a male with green eyes?"

"Yes," Calondir said, his expression bitter. "If he is not waiting for us on the other side, then some of his people will be. The fire is driving us like cattle toward them."

"Dragos is coming," she told the High Lord. "He said to wait and not cross over, not unless we absolutely had to." Well, he hadn't actually included Calondir in any of that, but she had to think on her feet here with some pretty tight time restrictions, so she figured she was entitled to some broad interpretation.

The High Lord stiffened. "The risks you and your mate decide to take have nothing to do with me or my people."

She strangled the sudden urge to slap him. She said, "Calondir, I know you hate Dragos, and to be perfectly frank, he hates you too." Heh, this next bit was actually kind of funny, although she was glad Dragos wasn't around to hear her say it. "But he *allowed* me to travel down to talk with you and to try to make peace with your demesne. In the meantime you say someone is on the other side of that passageway, waiting to cut you down as you try to cross. I wouldn't like those choices if I was in your shoes, but I really think you ought to wait. Dragos is not going to let me get hurt."

Calondir studied her, his face cold. Then he looked around at the waiting Wyr, and at his own people, many of whom were wounded. As Pia looked around too, she realized that most of them weren't dressed for fighting. They wore a hodgepodge of casual clothes, and some of them appeared to be in pajamas. They were in no shape to face another battle.

"Who has water?" the High Lord asked. Several people raised a hand, although none of them were the psychos, even though Pia knew fully well that they each had a canteen in their packs. "Tear strips of cloth and wet them. Be prepared to tie them over your nose and mouth, and move over to the passageway. We'll wait." His gaze came back to Pia. "For as long as we can."

Fair enough. She nodded to him.

Eva said to the other Wyr, "It's good advice. Do as he says." They each tore strips of cloth and wet them. *Getting toasty, princess. Hope the Old Man gets here quick.*

He said he's coming in fast. Pia gave into temptation and used her wet strip to mop her hot forehead and cheeks.

Eva scanned the nearby blazing tree line. *It won't do any harm to hang with the High Lord by the passageway, just in case.*

Whatever, Pia said irritably. The cloth came away streaked black with soot. She grimaced, hoping she wouldn't have to tie it over her face. *He'll be here.*

Eva gestured to the others, and they moved over to where the Elves stood in a tense huddle around Calondir. Eva told Pia, *You and me, when we get out of this mess we talking about what happened with Johnny.*

Pia said, *You go on telling yourself whatever story you want to hear.*

The flames were clearly visible between the trees, and smoke covered the sky. It was growing harder to take a real breath, and several people had covered their noses and mouths already. Pia looked from the small group of pale, silent Elves down to the number of bodies littering the clearing. Those bodies were the Elves' friends, families and lovers. Her heart went out to the survivors.

Pia. Eva gripped her shoulder. She looked up. Eva's gaze glittered brilliantly in the uncertain light. *However you did it, I know you saved his life. I wanted to say thank you.*

Pia looked away. *I have no idea what you're talking about.* But she couldn't keep the pretense going in the face of Eva's emotion, and she reached up to squeeze Eva's calloused hand briefly before pushing it gently away.

A sharp, cold wind blew over the clearing. It dissipated the smoke and brought some much-needed fresh air. A patch of night sky appeared overhead, revealing sharp, bright stars, and a wave of elation washed over her. He was almost here, almost here. She felt as giddy as if they were about to go on their first date.

Not that they had actually dated. Seemed like she should have at least gotten a dinner and a movie for all her trouble. She cocked her head and frowned. Unless she counted that one awful dinner when they fought, and he stormed out for hours, and he made Graydon give her that necklace as a present.

She loved the necklace, but nah, she wasn't going to count that as a date.

An immense bronze-and-black dragon flew over the trees and plummeted down, his wingspan spread out to the fullest and blocking out the night sky. A couple of the Elves cried

out sharply. The dragon landed, not in the small clearing, but directly in the fire, snapping burning trees underneath him like they were matchsticks.

Pia's pulse thudded as she stared. She knew he could touch coals without getting burned and he could breathe fire, but she had no idea he could immerse himself so completely in a blaze and not be injured.

His gigantic, horned head lifted along a long neck. Great witchy, Powerful eyes fixed on her. Wings still outspread, the dragon drew in a breath. He began to glow brighter and brighter until he shone like molten gold. The brighter he glowed, the duller the forest fire became around him, and the dangerous heat cooled. He was pulling the fire into himself.

Wow, that was a crazy kind of . . . um, hot.

She danced from foot to foot, barely able to contain herself until it was safe enough to approach him. She just loved him so goddamn *much*.

Then the fire in the forest died completely away, and the only illumination in the clearing was from the shining dragon himself. Gradually he began to dim.

As soon as her skin didn't throb from the heat, she ran forward. She barely felt her feet touch the ground. As she approached him, Dragos shifted into his human form and raced toward her, his bronzed, machete hewn features thrown into dark shadow by the intense glow in his eyes.

When she was still a few yards away, she leaped. He snatched her out of the air and clenched her to him as she wrapped arms and legs around him. He went to his knees, holding her so tightly she couldn't breathe, and his Power enveloped her. One tremendous hand cupped the back of her head. She closed her eyes and laid her head on his shoulder as he put his face in her neck.

Neither one said anything. Their bruising hold on each other said it all.

That lasted all of thirty seconds or so, until Dragos lifted his head. It took Pia a few moments to realize the vibration

she felt in his chest was the source of the deep, rough sound she heard. He was growling.

She straightened to look at him sharply. Still gripping her tight, his brutally handsome features were savage with anger and hatred as he stared over her shoulder.

She raised her eyebrows and looked over her shoulder. A few of the Elves had lit torches, and reflected firelight danced across the clearing again, while in the background the ravaged forest looked black and stark, the burned trees still smoking.

The High Lord stared at them, his face bitter with animosity. Several Elves stood with six-foot longbows, arrows aimed at Pia and Dragos. Well, she was pretty sure they were meant for Dragos, but that meant she was definitely in their sights as well.

As for her psychos, they had stationed themselves in a line on either side of Dragos and Pia. Their crossbows were loaded and aimed at the Elves, and their bodies drawn dangerously tight.

Somebody better think of something fast.

Until that happened, she patted Dragos soothingly on the chest.

"Now, honey," she said. "You've got to stop getting so worked up, or you'll have a heart attack when you hit middle age."

═ ELEVEN ═

Dragos's fierce gaze came back down to her, and everything he had ever promised her was there in his eyes.

I never stop thinking about you. You're with me everywhere I go, but I miss you when we're apart.

I've already shown that I will kill for you. I would also die for you.

You make me laugh. You make me happy. You're my miracle and my home. If you as much as twitch, I get a hard-on.

I will always come for you, always want you and always need you.

As she remembered every word, she saw past those promises in his gaze to what lay underneath them. He had been so afraid for her it had driven him away from the Games and into possible war.

"Dragos," she said, very low. "They're just scared of you. I don't fully understand what happened, but I believe Calondir didn't do this. And when I told him you were coming and asked him to stay, he did."

The feral vibration underneath her palm stilled. That had to be good, right?

Still holding her, he stood upright. Her legs loosened from around his waist, and as she landed on her feet, he swept her gently behind him and held her there.

Oh no. That had to be bad.

"Lower your weapons now," Dragos said to Calondir. "My mate is present."

Pia fisted a hand in the thin silk sweater that stretched across Dragos's wide back and held on to the material tightly. The tension between the two demesne rulers reverberated with the memories of ancient confrontations and unresolved grudges, but she couldn't keep intervening every time they were rude to each other. At some point Calondir and Dragos had to be the ones to take the next steps.

"And my consort has been taken, along with many loved ones," Calondir said, his voice ragged from smoke but still filled with Power.

Along with many loved ones? Pia's fist tightened as any sympathy she felt for Calondir evaporated. They were all under a lot of strain, and now was probably not the best time to parse his words, but damn, that was cold. She didn't need to hear details, explanations or an apology for misspeaking. He said that in public, and nothing else mattered. She was on Beluviel's side and ready for divorce court.

Calondir had continued. "I do not have time to fight with you, Cuelebre. Ferion, have your men put up their weapons and go look for survivors. We must gather the largest force we can and prepare to cross over quickly if we are to have any hope of recovering them."

As Pia peered around Dragos's arm, Ferion gestured and the Elves lowered their bows. Dragos's hold relaxed, and she stepped around to his side. She said, "You too, Eva."

To Captain Psycho's credit, she didn't try to argue, nor did she look at Dragos. Instead she said, "Ease up, kids." The other Wyr relaxed and unloaded their crossbows.

"Spread out," gritted Ferion. "Comb the area for survivors."

"Go help them," Pia told Eva. At that the other woman

did hesitate, turning to face her. Pia said telepathically, *You're not needed here at the moment.*

Eva's gaze flickered to Dragos. She said to the group, "You heard her. Let's go." The unit joined those who were gathering at one end of the clearing and after a quick consultation, the whole search party dispersed into the Wood.

Ferion stayed with Calondir, along with another tall, Powerful Elf. They bristled as Dragos strode forward. Pia followed more slowly, concerned about further confrontation and taken by the differences between Dragos and the other males.

Dragos's Power was a roaring inferno that eclipsed the others. Calondir and his two companions were some of the most muscularly built males she had seen among the Elves, but they looked willowy against Dragos's broad bone structure and raw solid strength. They would need an army to even think about trying to take Dragos down, and at the moment they didn't have one. Also, as Calondir said, they didn't have time. She let herself relax slightly.

Dragos stopped several feet away from the other three males, his hands planted on his hips. Ignoring Ferion and the other Elf, he said to Calondir, "Who was it this time?"

For the first time since Pia had seen him, the High Lord looked vulnerable as he took a deep breath and straightened, visibly bracing himself. "Amras Gaeleval, one of the Guardians that closed the Numenlaur passageway after the war. He came with two others."

His voice heavy with sarcasm, Dragos said, "And you just thought they wanted to catch up on old times so you invited them in."

Ferion snapped, "They came to us asking for help. One of them was suffering from an old wound that would not heal. Our best seers scanned them, but no one sensed that Amras possessed one of the Machines until he wielded it tonight."

Pia chewed her lip as she listened, and something else slipped into place.

"I might have sensed it," she muttered. Dragos swiveled to face her, his expression growing intent. "I picked up on

something odd at supper, and I went to tell Beluviel about it earlier this evening, but something stopped me. There were several people present along with this one man who caught my attention. I'm pretty sure he messed with my head. I remember thinking he was one of my best friends when I know I've never met him before. He was in my dreams too." Scorching gold eyes turned murderous. Dragos put a hand on her shoulder, gripping her tightly as she finished, near to tears. "I didn't say anything to Beluviel that I had originally intended. I just remembered that."

Calondir, Ferion and the other Elf were watching her closely as well. Calondir said, "Amras is one of our ancients and adept at persuasion, along with other arts. Do not take the burden of this onto your shoulders. It does not belong there."

The muscles in Dragos's body had coiled dangerously tight, but his hand was very gentle as he touched her cheek. She felt the brush of his Power along hers, sliding hot and possessive along her cooler energy. Coming up next to the reality of him was an intense shock to the system after the slightly unreal dreams they had shared. It felt like a feast after she had starved for days.

"I do not sense any lasting influence," he murmured. "But I would like to check more deeply later."

She could see out of the corner of her eye that all three of the Elves were staring at Dragos as though he had sprouted two spare heads. She had grown used to seeing that expression on other people, and she chose to ignore it. Instead she focused only on Dragos just as he focused on her, and for one fleeting, enchanted moment they shut out the entire world.

She told him, "I dreamed that I went to look out the window and saw that stars were dying. He was there and he said 'nothing shines forever,' along with something about paving a way to some kind of new age. This is what the Oracle prophesied, isn't it?"

Dragos smoothed a strand of her hair back. "It sounds like it."

It was possible that the search parties would find many

more survivors than she believed they would. But even if they did, the Elves had suffered a devastating blow. More people had been asleep than had been awake. The number that might be able to cross over with Calondir and do battle to recover those who were taken would be pitifully small. They prepared for a suicide mission, and she could tell by the High Lord's expression that he already knew it. Then those that remained would be lost, along with Beluviel and so many others.

And while the concept of the Deus Machinae was new and strange to her, barely more than a passing story, she was pretty sure that it wasn't a good idea to let one stay in the hands of someone who could willingly cause so many deaths.

She took Dragos's much larger, harder hand in both of hers. "You know we have to help them, don't you?"

He turned his hand and curled his long fingers around hers, squeezing lightly.

He said, "I have already summoned the Wyr."

He had summoned the Wyr as he raced toward a magical fire that destroyed the Elven Wood and lit the night sky for miles.

The Deus Machinae were only dangerous in proportion to the Power of those who wielded them. When they fell into the hands of those with little Power or no real understanding of what they possessed, the Machinae influenced the world in subtle ways.

The last time Dragos had seen a Machine was almost two hundred and forty years ago. Although he had not touched it, he was fairly certain it had been Hyperion's, the god of Law. At the time it had appeared in the shape of a quill pen, and one of the most famous human lawmakers in American history had used it to sign the Declaration of Independence.

Now an Elf wielded one of the Machinae again. Only an ancient Elf with an affinity to the elements had the Power

to use a Machine to such devastating effect on the environment, and he was *NOT GOING TO LET THEM* tear the Earth apart again.

The fire had killed the spirit of the Wood. He spared a thought for how that would sadden Pia, as he reached out to Monroe telepathically.

You will call Graydon, he said to the startled gargoyle. *Tell him to halt the Games. The High Lord has been attacked, and the Elven Wood is broken. Graydon is to bring a hundred of our strongest, as fast as he can. As soon as you deliver that message, get your ass back to your unit.*

Yes, sir, Monroe said. The gargoyle sounded much calmer than he had when he'd answered Pia's cell phone. *I'll be right there.*

Then Dragos raced toward the fiery horizon, willing Pia to be safe with every ounce of his energy. Even though he spoke to her telepathically, his world only settled into rightness when he laid eyes on her. She was bedraggled, sweaty and smeared with ash from the fire, but she was calm, and despite the streaks of blood on her clothing that caused his heart to pound in heavy slugs, she was unharmed.

Now as she looked up at him with such earnestness, he knew what was going on in her mind. She counted the cost of the Elves' struggle in the lives they lost, and she responded to that loss out of compassion.

He did not share her compassion. As far as he was concerned, the Elves could keep killing each other until they wiped themselves off the face of the Earth. But she would always be finer than he was, and more generous.

His gaze shifted to Calondir. "My people will be here in just under two hours," he said. "Accept our help or not as you choose. But you and I both know that you do not have the strength to confront another one of your ancients if he is wielding a Machine."

He watched with interest as Calondir struggled. It was not his job to ease the High Lord's path or make him feel better. He did not bother to point out to the Elf Lord that he had already summoned the Wyr because he was going

after Amras Gaeleval whether Calondir accepted his help or not.

Like Constantine, he never pulled his punches.

"I accept," Calondir said. Ferion and the other Elf stood beside the High Lord, their postures and expressions eloquent with bitterness and resentment, but they also clearly recognized the necessity for a Wyr alliance for they said nothing. Calondir told his two lords, "We will cross over when the Wyr have arrived."

Just then two runners, a Wyr and an Elf, came back from the search party with a preliminary report. The loss of life was devastating but not a surprise. The big news was that much of the main building was still intact, as a group of Elves had banded together and used their combined Powers to slow the progression of the blaze.

"There are a lot of survivors," said the Elven runner, who was a slender girl. She had a tear-streaked face and short, fluffy brown hair that was dyed blue at the tips. "There are many more alive than we had feared. Healers have set up a station in the main hall to tend to the wounded."

The three Elven males' expressions lightened. Calondir said, "Survivors, shelter and supplies. It is the first good news I have heard this whole gods-cursed night."

The Wyr runner was one of the males, the magic user of Pia's guards. He had tightly coiled muscles, strong, high cheekbones and restless dark eyes, and his spark of Power glowed steady and strong. Dragos was interested to note that the male did not look at him but at Pia when he spoke. "They also captured several of the attacking Elves and are holding them in a secured area, but they won't let any of us near enough to examine them."

Pia turned to Dragos quickly, who said, "I no longer sense the Machine in the area, so I assume Gaeleval crossed over to your Other land."

"Yes," Calondir said. "He took Beluviel and the others."

"Now that he's no longer present, I want to know how much of his beguilement has lingered on the captives," said

156

Dragos. That was just one of many questions to which he intended to find answers. He also still wanted to know how Gaeleval had traveled to reach the Elven demesne in the United States, and he was very interested in finding out what happened in Numenlaur before Gaeleval left. Dragos looked down at Pia. She was as filthy as all the others, and she was the most beautiful, most precious thing in the world to him. He told her, "But first, I want to make sure that you are clear of any influence. I do not like how he was able to enter your dreams."

Her lips tightened and she nodded.

Calondir said nothing, either in acknowledgment of what Dragos had said or in negation. Instead the High Lord led the way through the decimated Wood to a building at the top of a waterfall. One side of the building was charred and shattered glass lay all around. Braziers lit the open area and bodies lined one end of the clearing, covered in blood-spotted sheets.

Dragos noticed that a few limp and unmoving head snakes from a medusa trailed out from under the corner of one of the sheets. Elves weren't the only ones who had died here tonight.

Pia averted her gaze from the sight, blinking rapidly, her eyes reddened. Dragos put an arm around her shoulders and drew her close against his side.

The unit captain from Pia's guards came out to meet them. Eva, that was her name. Dragos had met with her personally before Pia's trip. Just as her unit mate had done, she nodded to him but spoke to Pia. "Whole place is a mess, inside and out. Our rooms smell like smoke, but then everything does right now. Other than the smell, the apartment is fine if you need it."

Pia said, "Get the others, and have something to eat and rest while you can. We've allied with Calondir. Troops will be here in less than two hours, and then we're crossing with the Elves to go after those who were taken."

The captain's face sharpened. "You got it."

The captain jogged away to round up her unit. Dragos asked Pia, "Where are those rooms?"

She looked up at him thoughtfully. "Not far."

He frowned. Her earlier fierce outburst of joy had become tempered with other things, and he could no longer tell what she was thinking. He told her, "I want to go there."

Pia hesitated as her gaze traveled to two Elves who half carried an injured third person into the building. For a moment he thought she would insist on helping them, but instead she said, "All right."

She led him through the building to the apartment. Other than a dim red flicker of coals that were still glowing in the fireplace, the rooms were almost totally in shadow.

The other Wyr would be arriving soon. Dragos asked, "Which room is yours?"

"This one." Now she kept her gaze averted as she took him to the bedroom, and his mouth settled into a grim line. As they stepped inside, she pulled away and went to look out the window where torch lights from the working Elves dotted the shoreline and were reflected on the black surface of the river.

He shut the door. This room also had a fireplace. Wood for a fire had been laid but it had not been lit. With a flick of his fingers, he set it alight.

He said, "Look at me."

She did, sidelong, as he walked over her. He took hold of her shoulders and turned her fully around. "No, really *look* at me."

His tone must have conveyed the seriousness of his intent, because she complied, gazing up at him with wide, dark violet eyes. He cupped her face, stroking his thumbs along the rose petal softness of her skin and slipped quietly into her mind.

Last May he had removed an intricate citadel of spells that Pia's mother had woven around her mind. Her mother had intended to protect her, but ultimately the spells had prevented her from fully accessing her Wyr form once she had matured into adulthood. Now her mental strength was

wholly her own—and she *was* strong, with a slender, wholly feminine thread of steel that ran right through her core.

Obsessively, carefully, he examined every part of her, and she allowed it, resting her hands on his wrists, open and trusting to his mental touch. Finally he pulled back and released a deep breath. "You are clear. There isn't any lingering influence."

Relief lightened her lovely features. "Oh, thank God. I was really shaken when I realized how much he had messed with my thinking."

"What did you dream about?" he demanded. "What did he do to you?"

"Nothing," she said. Then her eyes widened as she caught the full implications behind his fury. "There weren't many more details other than what I already told you. He kept trying to put a hand on me, but it wasn't sexual. I think he was trying to control me, and he was probably trying to control the others as well. They had all fallen asleep, including the two that were on watch. Not even the smoke or the sounds of fighting woke them." She frowned. "But I also dreamed about the baby, who was lying on me and growling. He bit me, which woke me up and then I woke the others."

"The baby *bit* you?" Dragos laid a hand on her abdomen, where his son's strong, bright spark nestled.

Her expression turned wry. "Yeah, that was my reaction. I really believe he wasn't trying to hurt me, just startle me. It worked."

"Way to go, little man," Dragos told the spark.

He knew that Pia thought the baby believed his name was Peanut. Dragos thought it was more likely that the baby responded to the love he felt when his mother talked about him, and in reality he comprehended little more than love and danger. Still, he had acted twice now to save his mother.

A fierce wave of emotion caught Dragos off guard. He clenched his jaw, blinking.

He had a son. The concept was still new and shocking after several months. He had a son, a delicate and small very Powerful creature, and already he was so proud of him.

"All right," he said, his voice deeper and rougher than usual. "You're safe. The baby's safe. Next item of business."

Pia raised her eyebrows, her expression turning cautious. "We have items of business?"

"Yes," he said. "I'm sorry."

She sighed. "Dragos, we have enough to think about. We don't have to talk about that right now."

"I do," he told her. "I'm a bad-tempered bastard at the best of times, and I was on a hair trigger. The border problems with the Elves, the sentinel issue, all the business problems, and to top it all off, you were gone. None of that is an excuse, and I'm not trying to make one out of it. I'm just telling you, and I want you to know that I heard every word that you said. And I'm sorry."

Her expression softened, and his world became brighter. "You're right, it's no excuse. But I know you have been under a lot of strain."

"I can't promise we won't run into this issue again," he said. "I've been used to solitary rule for a very long time."

"We're both feeling our way," she murmured.

"And it's too easy for me to slip into old habits and difficult for me to change on something so fundamental, but I am asking you for patience. I promise that I am trying, that I will continue to try."

A small grin tugged at the corners of her lips. He raised an eyebrow, not at all sure that his carefully crafted and quite rare apology should elicit such a reaction. "I knew you were sorry," she told him, "when I was standing in the middle of a forest fire with Calondir of all people, and I was about to cross over to the Elven Other land, and you still said 'please.'"

He narrowed his eyes. "What part gave it away?"

She laughed out loud, a silvery sound of pure pleasure that danced in his old, wicked soul, and he felt the magic again, how she lifted him to a better place.

She put her hand to his cheek. "Well, I'm probably going to regret this, but I've got to say it's a good thing you don't

listen to me all the time," she told him. "Wait, did Hugh ever get in touch with you?"

"You mean Monroe? Yes. He called me and then I sent him to Lirithriel House. That's how I summoned the Wyr. I told him to call New York and then get his ass back here. He was coming in from the opposite direction I was, and he should be arriving soon." He gave in and did what he had been wanting to do for a while now. He pulled her close and held her tightly. She put her face against his chest, slipped her arms around his waist and heaved a big sigh.

She told him, "If you had listened to me, you wouldn't have flown south, and you wouldn't have been close enough to respond to the fire. Shows what I know."

He pressed his lips to her forehead. "If I hadn't listened to you," he said, "you wouldn't have come south in the first place."

"I wasn't going to mention that one," she muttered.

"I didn't mean that the way you think." He slid his fingers underneath her chin and tilted her face up. "It was a good thing you came south. Not only were your original reasons valid, but believe me when I say this—it is much better to find out about Gaeleval now so that we can act before he has the chance to acquire more Power. He will only become harder to stop as time goes on."

"I just don't understand why someone would do this," she whispered. "Kill so many people, cause so much damage and take so many others."

"He took too many people," he said, thinking. "If he wanted hostages, he would have taken a smaller selection of the most influential Elves. They would have been more mobile and easier to control. If he is the voice I heard in the Oracle's prophecy, he has an ambitious agenda."

She shuddered. "I remember you said that the voice talked about all kinds of grandiose shit, birth and death, and gods, and time."

"It also claimed to be the bringer of the End of Days," he said dryly. "But if all Gaeleval wanted was pure destruction,

161

he would have stayed here with the Elves he controlled and he would have fought until everybody was dead. You said he mentioned something about paving a way to a new age."

She nodded. "Yes."

"Then I think he must be building an army," he said. "And not only did he conscript a substantial addition to his troops, but he crushed any effective resistance from Calondir. Those are the moves I might make if I were building an empire."

She looked even more troubled. "Persuasion and beguilement are all very well and good, but how can he control them all at the same time?"

"For that, I'm positive he's using the Machine. As I flew in I could feel the Machine being used before its Power cut out. That must have been when Gaeleval crossed over. It's amplifying the Power and skills he already has. I've seen it happen before. And the more he uses it, the more it will work on him and affect his mind." He shook his head. "We will confront him soon enough. Right now our meeting time is limited and we need to move on to our next item of business."

She cocked her head. "I didn't know we had an agenda."

"I did," he told her.

He bent his head and kissed her, and there it was, the real thing, not some made up, distant dream. Her gorgeous lips softened and molded to his mouth, just as her slender body molded to his.

He had been *afraid*. What a horrendous emotion. He had been scared for her, and the room smelled like ash and the whole area looked devastated. Aggression and tenderness fought for supremacy, and tenderness won.

He ran his hands down her body, rock hard and aching for her. He knew this hunger for her would never ease, never die away. "You are never going to get trapped in a magical forest fire again," he growled against her lips. "Do you hear me, Pia? That flight took millennia off my life."

"I'm sorry," she whispered. "It won't happen again."

"Goddamn right it won't," he said between his teeth.

Gaeleval was a dead man walking; he just didn't know it yet. Dragos would find and stop him because he wouldn't allow the kind of destruction that had come before. But he was going to rip Gaeleval limb to limb because the Elf had put Pia in danger and because he had dared to try to take her.

She threaded slender fingers through his hair as she kissed him, and he bent to pick her up and carry her to the bed. Then he laid her on top of the covers and came down on her, and he covered her body with his. In a move that was as natural as breathing, she wrapped her long, fabulous legs around his waist and her arms around his neck. She held him with her whole body, and he was home.

Home. It was a concept to which he had never given much thought. Self-contained and solitary by nature, his home had always been within himself, but not any longer.

"I love you," she whispered against his mouth.

He lifted his head to look at her. She smiled at him, golden-skinned in the firelight, her eyes as rich as sapphires. He laid his fingertips along the exquisite, delicate curve of her cheekbone.

The dragon came to a realization and was amazed. In the unending years of his acquisitive existence, despite all his hoarding of the treasures of kingdoms and emperors, he had never been rich before this. She had come into his life to steal from him, and in the process she had given him everything she had.

"I love you," he said.

═ TWELVE ═

As he spoke the words her gaze flared, and her lips trembled. For one split second he stared at her, utterly mystified. She had never seemed to mind before that he hadn't said the words.

She couldn't be upset that he had said them now, could she? Fucking hell, he was no good at this romance shit.

In the next moment he realized that mirth filled her eyes, not sadness.

He growled, "What."

She told him, her voice trembling with laughter, "You just sounded so surprised when you said it."

He took a slow, deep breath and let it out gently. "I am," he said.

He kissed her again, savoring the light play of her lips before deepening it to explore the lavish intimacy of her mouth. She groaned and rotated her hips so that his cock pressed against her pelvis. They rocked together, fully clothed, both remembering how it was to be together and promising each other more. His hunger spiked higher, and he palmed one of her breasts.

She pulled back slightly to mutter something, her warm

breath against his cheek. He had no idea what she said but it sounded urgent and sexy. Then she kissed him hard, and her eager, feminine aggression caused everything within him to glow hotter than the forest fire and brighter than a newly minted coin.

"Take it off," he whispered.

She knew what he meant and removed the dampening spell that cloaked her body's natural luminescence.

She was simply dazzling. She was his beacon to what others called decency, not because she told him how to act but because she made him want to try.

They shouldn't be doing this. They didn't have time. But he slipped one hand under her sweater anyway to tease at her nipple, rolling the soft, delicate jutting flesh between his thumb and forefinger. Her eyes glazed with passion, she thrust up with her hips and he hissed as the friction drove him out of his mind crazy. . . .

A sharp rap sounded at the door, and he snarled as he lifted his head.

Pia grabbed him by the ears. It startled him enough to make him pause.

Their eyes met.

She said, "Count to ten."

Hm, he had heard of that technique before. One, two, three . . .

She called out, "Yes, what is it?"

Eva's voice sounded through the door panel. "The High Lord requests that Dragos attend him downstairs. I guess those Elves that were spelled aren't doing so well."

He expelled a breath between his teeth. It sounded like steam hissing in a kettle. "I got to ten," he told her. "It didn't help. Stay here and follow your own advice. Eat something and rest." He raised his voice. "I'm coming."

He rolled away from her, careful to avoid putting any real weight on her abdomen, then stood and strode out of the bedroom.

Eva stood just on the other side of the door. She gestured to the unit's magic user, who waited across the room by the

hall entrance. "Miguel knows where to go. He'll show you where they are being held."

"Fine," he bit out. "Let's go."

Just before he turned away, he saw Eva glance into the open doorway of the bedroom, and her eyes grew very wide. Realization flashed. *Fuck*. He spun back, even though he knew he was already too late.

Eva asked in a hushed voice, "Uh, princess? Are you aware that you're illuminated?"

It was an idiotic mistake.

Pia had lifted her head off the pillows to watch Dragos stride away, her body thrumming with frustrated hunger again. She felt like they hadn't made love in months, not days. He should always dress in black, because he sure did give Satan a run for his money on being wicked hot. He moved so fast and light on his feet, it would be disturbing to see in such a large, muscular man if it wasn't so damned sexy.

He was already preoccupied with what lay ahead of him, and she was distracted with lust and just plain stupid. She realized it as soon as Eva looked in the bedroom and her black gaze went wide. Even though Pia threw the dampening spell back on that very instant, it was too little too late.

Remember that slow-moving train wreck? The one you were just bitching about the other day? And who was driving that train again, dumb ass?

You, that's who.

She launched off the bed and moved faster than she ever remembered moving in her life. As she leaped toward Eva, she called out sharply, "I'll take care of it, Dragos."

She reached the doorway, registering every shift in Eva's expression, the simple astonishment shifting to shock at her urgent speed. In the next instant, Pia had her hand fisted in the front of Eva's shirt. Eva grabbed her wrist reflexively, glanced at Dragos and froze.

Pia looked at Dragos too, at his calm, expressionless

166

face and the death in his gold eyes. I am mated to the biggest psycho of them all, she thought. She said strongly, "I said I'll take care of this."

His attention shifted from Eva to her. There was no way to tell what he was thinking. She shifted her body so that she came between Dragos and Eva, and she pointed toward the hallway door and Miguel, who also stood frozen. *"Go."*

Dragos tilted his head at her in wordless acknowledgment, turned and left, taking Miguel with him.

She took a deep breath and only then realized that she was shaking. So much to do, so much to do. Build a relationship, stop Armageddon, save a Wyr here and there. It really did never rain but it poured.

James, Andrea and Johnny had been in the other rooms, but they weren't any longer. Something that had been said, or perhaps some instinct for danger had roused them. They stood tensely in the doorways of the other bedrooms, Andrea and Johnny in one, James in the other. Quickly she calculated the angles of the doorways in relation to each other. None of them could have seen into her bedroom, and Miguel had been standing by the hall door, so he hadn't seen anything either.

Pia told the others, "Go back to bed. Now."

Slowly, they backed into their separate rooms, even though she could tell all their fight-or-flight instincts had kicked into high gear.

Only when they shut their doors did she turn her attention to Eva, who hadn't moved or spoken. It was the first time she had ever seen Captain Psycho truly subdued.

Pia loosened her hold on Eva's shirt and pointed silently into her own bedroom. As the other woman stepped inside, she followed and closed the door behind her.

She asked quietly, "You haven't by any chance been talking telepathically with any of the others in the last few minutes, have you?"

"No," Eva said, very low. She turned around, her sober black gaze fixing on Pia's face.

Even though she was pretty sure that Eva got the full

implication of what had happened, she still said, "You realize you saw something you weren't supposed to see. Your life is on the line here."

Eva said, "I got that."

The tension in Pia's body wouldn't let her stand still, and she started to pace. "This isn't your fault," she said, still keeping her voice very soft. "This is all my fault. I was careless and preoccupied. This should never have happened, and I'm so sorry, Eva."

"This is about your Wyr form, isn't it?" Eva whispered. "Why you don't talk about it, or identify what you are."

She moved to the window and looked out, rapping out a hectic, uneven rhythm on the pane with her fingers. The shadowed river was beautiful, but one end of the pile of covered bodies was visible, and she couldn't keep her gaze from drifting to them. So much unnecessary death, so much pain.

She looked at the silhouette of the ravaged tree line as she tried to formulate how she should answer. Eva was quick and clever. Even now some part of the other woman had to be whispering, *What is she? What?* And running through all the possibilities in her mind.

"The problem is that people talk," she murmured. "One person might swear that they'll keep a secret, but then they tell their best friend just one thing. 'I trust you not to tell anyone,' they say. 'Oh, I promise, I won't,' their best friend says. And everybody is quite sincere at the time. Then the best friend tells someone else. Someone they trust. Someone who says, 'I promise, I won't say a word.'" She laughed, the sound abrupt and humorless. "You know I wouldn't be standing here if I hadn't done that very thing myself and had it backfire on me. Now I'm mated to one of the most visible figures in the world. The gryphons know what I am, along with several of the Elves. Fuck, don't even get me started on the Elves. I have no idea how many of them know."

A hand settled on her back. "You keep getting your fancy knickers in a twist, don't you?" Eva said. Her voice was gentle, even after everything that had happened.

168

Pia turned her head. The shock had eased somewhat from the other woman's face. "He will kill you if you breathe a word of what you saw. He will kill you if you even think of breathing a word." He probably would have killed Eva already if Pia hadn't stopped him. All because he had been preoccupied, and she had gotten careless. She said, "And I don't want your life on my conscience."

Eva gave her a crooked smile. "I'm not going to say anything, Pia, and not because the Old Man scared me shitless, even though he did. I'm not going to say anything because you're ours to defend. Besides, I owe you for Johnny's life."

She shrugged irritably and grimaced. "Nobody owes me anything."

The other woman chuckled. It sounded indulgent. Then Eva sobered. "You realize, don't you, that the others know you did something important, even if they don't quite know what it is. And I think Johnny's been too busy to really think about what happened, but sooner or later he'll remember and get to wondering."

"He was passed out by the time I did anything," Pia said.

"He'll remember being wounded."

She blew out a heavy sigh and looked at the tragedy outside again. "Yeah, I guess we all remember when that happens."

"I guess we do."

Pia thought of the Elves that Dragos had gone to examine. She wondered how bad off they were, and what Dragos would find out. If he could do anything for them. He was not a healer, but he was probably the world's foremost expert on beguilement.

Her eyebrows rose. Maybe he could beguile Eva into forgetting what she saw. He had tried to beguile Pia more than once, but it hadn't stuck. What if, for whatever reason, it didn't stick on Eva either? Then Eva might feel betrayed and resentful, and that was never a good combination in someone when you needed them to keep a secret.

Maybe it was smartest to just trust her, but damn, that was another uncertain road to travel. She tapped the glass

a few more times. Maybe she had better think about it some more and talk to Dragos later.

In the meantime, he had given her good advice.

She said, "I'm so hungry I could eat my boots."

Eva stirred. "We better get some food to that baby before he chews a hole in you."

"There's a concept I could have lived without," Pia muttered.

A vision of the baby monster breaking out of John Hurt's chest in *Alien* came to mind. Yeah, she needed that image to stick with her for the rest of this long, weird pregnancy like she needed another hole in her head.

Eva went into the common room. Pia dug through her pack for the handful of soy protein bars she always carried with her, then she joined the other woman. She settled at one end of the couch while Eva brought her a bowl of nuts and fresh fruit from table by the window. After plowing through several protein bars, most of the nuts and half the fruit, she was finally able to make herself stop.

Eva ate a couple of MRE meals she carried in her own pack. Even though they had taken pains to keep their conversation low, somehow the others sensed that it was okay to reappear. They did so quietly, bringing their own supplies of food to eat.

Then the door to the apartment opened, and Hugh walked in.

He said, "Hey, kids."

"Yes!" Andrea leaped across the room to smack both his upheld hands and throw her arms around him. Johnny leaped on the pair, and all three staggered, laughing.

James grinned, and Eva said, "Good job, bucko."

The gargoyle shrugged loose of Andrea and Johnny, walked over to Pia and dropped her cell phone into her hands. His plain, bony face crinkled in a smile. "I don't mind telling you, answering that phone when the Old Man called was one of the braver things I've done. He did not like the sound of my voice coming over on your frequency."

It was just a phone. See, like she said. Biggest psycho of them all.

"Thank you, Hugh," Pia said.

"No problem." He threw himself on the couch, dug through his own pack for food and ate with all the others.

Pia drifted, listening to the psychos talking smack with each other. They had a rough-and-tumble camaraderie that reminded her of the sentinels, and in spite of all the issues that waited back in New York, listening to them made her homesick. Like the sentinels, this group was used to facing death and danger, and they had a kind of emotional ballast for dealing with violence that she might never achieve.

You're gonna have to toughen up fast, chickadee, she told herself. There's more violence on the road in front of you.

Because she had no intention of letting Dragos cross over to the Elven Other land without her, and while he had backed away from Eva when she had told him to, he had still carried death in his eyes when he left.

And call her crazy, but she was pretty sure he wasn't planning on having tea and cookies with Gaeleval when he caught up with him.

Dragos strode with Miguel through the halls, his sharp gaze taking in the damage to the building along with the nervous reactions of the Elves that they passed. The scent of fear and stress littered the air along with the stink of ash and blood, and the fires in wall sconces flickered in a macabre echo to the forest fire.

Once he might have enjoyed seeing his old enemies when they were so devastated. Now he thought of Pia's distress when she had looked at the pile of bodies. He frowned, and an Elf who was coming toward them from the other direction shrank back against the wall until they had passed.

Miguel led him down a flight of stairs. There was a minute change in air pressure and scent, along with the lack of

windows. He was unsurprised. Underground was the best place to have holding cells. As pretty as this place had once been, it was still the seat of the Elven demesne and they had to house prisoners somewhere.

They reached a spelled and bolted door where a pair of armed Elves stood guard. The guards regarded Miguel and Dragos with stony faces but unbolted and opened the door right away. The sound of screaming boiled out as soon as the door was cracked, along with the quieter undertone of people engaged in intense conversation.

Just as Dragos had expected, beyond the door was a block of cells. This cell block was probably where people were held until judgment had been passed. There would be another, more permanent place where the Elves would hold criminals sentenced to prison terms, but this was a solid temporary holding area.

At the moment the cells were packed with bedraggled, bloody people, all in some state of half dress. Calondir stood with a cluster of armed guards and a few other Elves. Their focus was turned inward to an area that they circled. That area was also the source of the screaming.

A few of the guards turned to face them as they entered the block, but their attention was fractured and they looked distressed. One of the guards tapped Calondir politely on the shoulder, and the High Lord turned to face them as they approached.

Dragos studied the occupants of the cells sharply as he and Miguel walked past. They stood passively, staring into space, their faces blank and hands idle at their sides. When he came closer to the High Lord, a couple of the guards moved between him and Calondir, while the rest of the circle moved back, not, he could tell, to allow him access to the screaming male that sat bound in a chair, but to move further away from him.

He bared his teeth at Calondir. Some foolish, naive creature might have called it a smile.

Calondir didn't even try to return a false response. Instead he said abruptly, "Those who were captured are all like you

see in the cells, and our healers cannot bring them back to themselves. This is the third person they've tried."

Dragos asked, "What happened to the other two?"

"The healers had to stop when their heartbeats became irregular."

He nodded. "Move," he said.

A couple stepped back timidly, but one stood stiffly defiant. Dragos regarded the Elf through lowered eyelids as the healer hissed, "My lord, we've barely begun to try. If you could only give us more time to experiment . . ."

"We don't have time," Calondir said bitterly. "Do as Cuelebre says. Move back and let him examine Threidyr."

Fortunately looks couldn't kill, and Dragos did not have a single finer feeling for the Elf to hurt. When the way had been cleared, he stepped forward and Miguel followed.

They had tied the male to a simple upright chair, his arms strapped to the wooden arms. Urine and vomit stained the Elf's clothes, although his screaming had faded when the healers had stopped doing whatever it was they had been trying to do to him. He stared dully into space, his face as slack and blank as all the others in the cells. Dragos noted that the bonds were carefully positioned to restrict but not injure. Their goal, then, was to recover the Elf, not to dig for information.

But his goal was not necessarily the same as the Elves'.

Careful to avoid the body liquids that smeared the stone floor, Dragos squatted in front of the Elf to examine him more closely. He took his time, and gradually the resentful muttering around him fell to silence. He ignored them, concentrating on the shards of Power in and around the male's aura. The dragon took note of the male's own Power first. Once he had identified it, he moved on to studying the rest.

The Elf's aura held a lingering taint of the Machine that was interwoven with another, third identity. Much as he was interested in locating the Machine itself, he was less interested in the aftereffects of its use. Instead, he filtered that out carefully until he could concentrate all his attention

on that last thread of Power. The dragon savored the taste of it like it was the blood of his prey.

And in a way it was.

That's who you are, he said silently. Amras Gaeleval, adept at persuasion and beguilement, and fire. It appears that we might have a few things in common, you and I. And no matter how you might change your looks, or where you go and what you do, I will know you again now.

Anywhere.

He could kill the Elf in the chair with the twist of his mind, and he could kill the others in the holding block too, quicker than they could do anything in retaliation but inflict incidental damage. He would not be who and what he was if he didn't at least consider the fact that he had unprecedented access, not only to Calondir but also to several key remaining Elves in this demesne.

And the unforgiving part of him that knew how to nurture a grudge wanted to. Oh, it wanted to.

Instead, he said, "I can try to remove the lingering beguilement from him and the others, but you must understand I can only try, not promise. Both Gaeleval's Power and the Machine he used are threaded into their core identities. Gaeleval had to go deep to establish the kind of control that would make them turn weapons on their own family and friends."

"What would happen if you can't remove it?" Calondir asked.

"Oh, I can remove it," Dragos said. He straightened lightly from his crouch and turned to the High Lord. "The question is whether or not it will break their minds if I did."

"My lord!" the healer exclaimed. "I beg of you, do not allow this. Give us more time to try!"

Dragos regarded the healer indifferently. Then he said to Calondir, "Personally, I do not care which you choose. But if you give your healers time to study this, they will only come to the same conclusion I just have. The beguilement cannot be completely removed without some risk to the victims." He met Calondir's sharp gaze. "You will lose more

people here. That is a fact, unless you want to leave them as they are, in which case you will have lost them all, for the only thing you have contained here are their bodies."

The Elves began to talk over each other and argue. Dragos turned away.

As he did so, the male bound in the chair whispered, "He knew you would come, Beast."

Dragos spun back around. He ignored the others' reactions as he stared at the Elf. The bound male's gaze was blank as ever, and a thin line of drool spilled from his slack lips. "Why does this not surprise me?" he murmured.

A woman's voice spoke from one of cells. "He saw you when he spoke his manifesto, just as you heard him."

Another woman, across from the first, said, "Then he saw your mate and unborn son."

At the mention of Pia and the baby, a fiery red haze obscured Dragos's sight. "Yes," he said between his teeth. "And Gaeleval tried to take them like he took the others."

Dead, he thought. You are *dead*.

Another male from down the hall said, "They would have been a worthy addition to his cause, their lights turned to new purpose and grand change."

"Grand change," he said.

Taliesin, the god of gods, was god of the Dance, of change. Dragos prowled down the hall, looking at the caged empty shells of the Elves' bodies. Someone who stood by Calondir was weeping. Dragos quoted softly to himself, " 'Lord Death himself has forgotten that he is but a part of this fractured whole.' " He pivoted and stalked back to the High Lord. "Calondir, which of the Deus Machinae did Numenlaur possess in the war?"

"Taliesin's," Calondir said. He was pale, his expression drawn stark. "Camthalion of Numenlaur was the one who insisted we rid ourselves of the Machinae. We all agreed to the pact then Numenlaur closed itself off from the world."

Threidyr, bound to the chair, whispered, "The guardian fulfilled his duty and barred the passage with a flaming sword so that none could enter. Thereafter he stood vigil at

the gate for an age, until the time came to pass that this all must pass."

"I think I'm hearing a little manifesto starting to creep back into the conversation again," said Dragos. He looked at Calondir. "At a wild guess I would say Numenlaur did not live up to their part in the pact."

Calondir said, "Camthalion was so persuasive and insistent, I always thought that of all of us, they would have been the ones to keep to their word."

Dragos rubbed his mouth as he considered Gaeleval's mouthpieces. It did not surprise him that Numenlaur might not have fulfilled their part in the pact. What was more surprising to him was the possibility that they might have held on to Taliesin's Machine successfully for all of this time.

Holding on to an item that belonged to the god of change would have been a challenging task. How would Taliesin's Power have affected the minds in Numenlaur over all these many centuries? What changes would it have caused physically? The longer it had been held in stasis, the more dangerous it would have become, and the more drastic would be the change it now induced.

"You know they're going to starve if you don't remove the beguilement," Dragos said. "They're shells right now, just mouthpieces. They won't remember to eat."

"Beast," hissed one of the women in the cells. "For the first time in your existence, you are truly vulnerable. Be careful what you meddle in. Nothing shines forever."

"Go home," three of them said.

Then others picked it up until the whole group spoke in eerie unison.

Go home, go home.

This time when rage took Dragos over, nothing would hold him back. Nobody threatened Pia and the baby and lived to tell of it. Nobody. He looked at all the empty shells of people in the cells. "That's it," he said. "You're done."

He began to whisper, picking the echo of it up with his Power. It reverberated off the walls, the ceiling and the floor,

slipped through the bars in the cells and soaked through the invisible bonds in each person's mind.

Someone in a cell halfway down the hallway laughed sharply. A few others sobbed. At first Calondir, his healers and the guards looked confused, but when a woman began shrieking and throwing herself violently against the wall, a few raced forward to stop her from hurting herself.

"My lord, stop him!"

"No," Calondir said. He told Dragos, "Break the beguilement."

Throughout it all, the dragon whispered, whispered, whispered. *Breathe on your own*, he told them. *Be who you were. Act, live. Separate.*

He spoke of freedom and remembrance as he tugged at the threads of Power from Taliesin's Machine. When he pulled out those threads, there was nothing left to sustain Gaeleval's spell.

Half were unconscious when he finished, and he knew that three were dead. Their bodies would be more fuel for those who hated and resented him.

As far as he was concerned, he had learned what he had come to learn. He gestured to Miguel and turned to leave the Elves to their chaotic reactions. As he did so, a runner came down to the block, bearing more news.

The Wyr had arrived.

⇒ THIRTEEN ⇐

Pia had slipped into a half doze, slumped against the arm of the couch, when running footsteps in the hall roused her. She jerked upright to a sitting position. Someone shouted in the distance, and the psychos rose to their feet.

"Don't tell me that's more bad news," she said, her voice blurred with sleep.

James strode to the window to look out. "It's good news this time. Our peeps have arrived. They had to have pushed hard to get here so fast."

She imagined they did push hard, as she could not personally recall ever hearing of Dragos himself summoning the Wyr to war. Granted, she was only in her twenties, but that was still a long enough period to cause people to take note.

She stood and moved to the window along with the others, and they all stared at the fantastic sight outside. A gryphon coasted in the air low over the river, wings outspread and steady as he headed for the torch-lit clearing. The golden feathers on his eagle's neck and the tawny fur on his gigantic lion's body were dark brown and deeply shadowed in the uncertain light. He carried three people on his broad, muscular back.

Behind him came another gryphon, similarly laden with passengers, his huge body seeming to float impossibly in the air. Then came a third. Pia smiled at the strangely beautiful, deadly sight.

Graydon, Bayne and Constantine were here, along with at least nine other Wyr.

A harpy flew in close after the third gryphon, her body and wings a study in grays darkening to black. She moved with powerful, confident assurance in the air, wheeling with precision to pass out of their line of sight and land in the clearing.

That was Aryal. Bleh, but okay. She had to admit it was far better to have that harpy with you than against you.

"Lookee there," said Eva. "Them's the big guns. They gonna smack that bad Elfie a good one."

Andrea and Miguel laughed, and Pia smiled.

"That mean we can take off for Atlantic City?" Johnny asked. He still chewed a bite of his meal. "I want to practice counting cards again."

Eva smacked Johnny on the back of his head although clearly there wasn't any real strength behind the blow. In the next moment Pia became too preoccupied to pay attention to any of the psychos' antics.

A large darkness sliced the night air. Like her experience with the Elven sculptures and the High Lord's home before fire had damaged it, at first she couldn't figure out what she was actually looking at. Then her perspective shifted and the scene became clear.

A pegasus soared over the river, his wingspread as wide as any of the gryphons. His wings and massive horse's body were pure, unrelieved black. A glimmer of torchlight rippled over him, highlighting a powerful chest and long sleek legs. She caught a glimpse of his proud, arched neck and a graceful equine head.

"Whoa," Eva whispered. "Now that's a fine sight you don't see every day."

Unlike the gryphons, the pegasus carried just one passenger, a tall figure that appeared to be male. Pia wasn't

sure, but she thought the rider might be Quentin, her old boss and current friend—and quite possibly one of Dragos's future sentinels. She still couldn't get over the fact that Quentin was part Wyr. Her heart twisted. If he was also part Elven as she had always guessed, then the devastation here would hit him very hard.

Close on the pegasus's heels came another gryphon.

A fourth one. Like the pegasus, this gryphon carried only one passenger.

Rune was here. His rider must be his mate, Carling Severan.

Did Dragos already know that Rune and Carling had come? Should she say something to warn him? Dragos had a huge telepathic range, but he had been silent for some time and she suspected that meant he was still busy with the beguiled Elves, and she didn't want to disturb his concentration. God only knew what he might be involved in.

Pia turned abruptly from the window. "Come on," she said. "Let's go."

She didn't wait but strode for the door, and the others sprang to assemble in a protective formation around her as she stepped out of the apartment. The halls were abandoned, everyone occupied elsewhere. She picked up speed as she reached the exit, and so did everyone else.

The clearing was a hive of activity. She paused to take it all in, and naturally her psychos all paused along with her. More torches had been set at regular intervals, and the whole area was well lit for the new arrivals.

Several Elves worked at the sad task of carrying out the covered bodies that lined one end of the clearing. Pia wasn't the only one affected by the sight. Andrea muttered a curse under her breath, and James shook his head, the corners of his mouth turned down.

Pia said, "I don't need all of you to stay with me, if you feel like helping."

"Go on, kids," Eva said. "I'll hang with her. Just stay close to hear any news. I expect we'll be heading out soon."

Johnny touched Pia's shoulder, gave her a small, grave smile and everyone but Eva took off.

A few Elves stood in the middle of the open clearing and waved their arms as they looked skyward. Pia glanced up as well. The smoke or fog had cleared, and parachutes dotted the clear, starlit night sky. Landing in a limited space at night was going to be tricky. She had a feeling more than a few of the arrivals were going to end up in the river.

Almost directly across from where she had paused, Graydon and Bayne talked with Ferion. Both gryphons were heavily armed and dressed in fatigues. Bayne rested his hands on his hips while Graydon rubbed the back of his neck as he looked around. All three of the males wore grim expressions.

Aryal stood nearby, arms crossed as she watched Wyr glide into the clearing. "Hurry up," she told them as they landed. As usual the harpy's dark hair was windswept and tangled, the angle of her high cheekbones accentuated by the flickering golden light. "Grab your chute and get out of the way. Move fast and keep moving."

Hugh and Johnny leaped to help the new arrivals bundle up their parachutes as they landed.

Aryal shot a scowling glance across the clearing. The look in the harpy's stormy gaze was sharp as a blade. Her glare was so intense, Pia found herself looking in the same direction to discover Quentin standing beside another male. Both men were tall, well formed and handsome, but that was the extent of their similarity. They were almost perfect in their contrast to each other.

Pia rubbed dry, irritated eyes and studied the male standing by Quentin. He was drop-dead gorgeous, with a lean, graceful body, a proud, strong face, mahogany skin, gleaming black hair and a brilliant dark gaze that took in everything around him. He was probably the pegasus that had flown in after the gryphons.

Then she turned her attention to Quentin. Like the gryphons, he was dressed in olive green fatigues and he was

armed. It was a huge difference from the casual suits and designer jeans he wore at his bar Elfie's. He used to have longer, dark blond hair that he kept bound back in a tight queue, but he had cut it for the Games. Now it was military short, which emphasized his spare, graceful features and piercing blue eyes. He looked almost like a stranger to Pia, even though she had known him ever since she had started work at Elfie's.

Quentin returned Aryal's stare, his own gaze glittering with such naked hostility that Pia had to blink. Whoa. Not that she blamed him in the slightest. Aryal could make a porcupine appear warm and cuddly, and the harpy was much more likely to make enemies than friends. As Pia watched, Quentin turned away to look around at the chaos in the clearing. His gaze was shadowed and his expression turned tight and bitter. Her heart squeezed. Whether or not he was part Elven himself was beside the point. She knew he'd had connections in the Elven demesne. He had lost friends here.

She wanted to walk over and hug him but resisted the impulse. He held himself in such a way that suggested physical overtures might not be welcome at the moment. Instead she turned her attention to the reason why she had hurried outside in the first place, and she looked for Rune and his Vampyre mate, Carling.

They stood together, well out of the way of those who were parachuting in. Rune was the most handsome of the four gryphons, with a tall, lean swordsman's body and even, tanned features. His mate Carling was also one of the oldest known Vampyres and one of the most beautiful women Pia had ever seen. The last time Pia had seen Carling, her dark hair had been chopped short. It had grown longer since last summer, and now it brushed the nape of her long, graceful neck.

Rune and Carling talked with a tall Elven woman. It took Pia a few moments to place her. Then she recognized Sidhiel, the Elder tribunal Councillor for the Elves. Sidhiel had been one of Carling's wardens when the Elder tribunal had placed her under quarantine. Neither Carling nor Rune

appeared to hold any grudges over that. As she watched, the Elven Councillor nodded to the other two and strode quickly toward the main building, her features set in a mask of grief.

Pia kept her focus on Rune and Carling as she walked around the edge of the clearing, Eva keeping pace at her side. Despite the activity and noise level, something attracted Rune's attention and he turned to watch her approach.

Even though she hadn't known him for long before he left, Rune seemed different from how she remembered him in New York. He looked a touch sharper, his expression darker. Or perhaps that was just his reaction to his surroundings. She gave him a wry smile as she reached him. "Heya, slick."

Rune's smile chased the darkness from his face. He pulled her into a brief, hard hug. "How are you doing?"

"I'm good, thanks." She hugged him back. "We got pretty warm for a little while, but it's cooled down some."

"I can see." Rune glanced around, his lion's gaze flaring with reflected torchlight.

Pia tapped him on the arm, and his attention came back to her. *I don't know who got in touch with you, but it's good to see you,* she told him.

He said, *Gray called me.*

She glanced at Graydon affectionately. God love him, Graydon really was true blue, right down to his bones. She turned back to Rune and said aloud, "I just wanted to tell you Dragos might snort and growl when he sees you, but don't pay any attention. He'll be glad to see you, no matter what he might say."

At least she was pretty sure that was true. Or maybe she was just hopeful. One thing about being in so far over your head that you couldn't see shore—you just had to strike out in some direction and hope for the best, because the surest way to drown was to tread water and stay where you were.

"I am not above saying I told you so," Carling murmured. "Neither one of you communicated with each other very well last summer, and you both need to get over it and move on."

Rune looked at his mate sourly. Carling raised her eyebrows and widened her eyes in response. Their nonverbal interaction was so like a married couple's that Pia had to smile. Whatever had added edges to Rune's expression, it didn't seem to have anything to do with his relationship with Carling.

Just then Pia's skin prickled, and the tiny hairs at the nape of her neck raised. She turned around as Dragos stepped out of the building.

Immediately his attention focused on them. His machete-edged features went still, and those gold, dangerous eyes of his reflected the lights from the nearby torches. He strode toward them, a natural juggernaut with a force of will that could move heaven and earth if he so desired. Both Wyr and Elves scrambled to get out of his path.

Nobody did expressionless quite like Dragos did, the muscles in his massive body coiled with intent. Even though she felt an intimacy with him that stemmed from some deep, instinctive recognition, in some ways he was the most unpredictable person she had ever met.

Then of course after whatever happened next, they had that whole war thing with Gaeleval to consider. Every day with Dragos turned into an adventure. She took a deep breath and braced herself for a bumpy ride.

Just after the runner had brought the news that the Wyr had arrived, Graydon said in Dragos's head, *We're here, all the sentinels except Grym, who got the short straw. We brought a hundred of our strongest Wyr just as you ordered. Some are regular army, and some are from the Games, plus there's two more.*

Dragos frowned. That meant Grym had stayed home to keep the peace in New York, which was standard protocol for the sentinels when something extraordinary called them away, but the last bit puzzled him. *Plus two?*

When I made the announcement to halt the Games, Rune

asked me what happened, so I told him, Graydon replied. *At least I told him what I knew. He and Carling came to help.*

Reaction pulsed through Dragos, every bit as complex as when he had first caught that faint whiff of Rune in the arena. He looked around the chaos in the Elven cell block. Those who had died had been discovered, and a frantic effort was being made to revive them with CPR. Unfortunately, it wouldn't work. Their spirits had already left their bodies, although he doubted anyone would appreciate it if he pointed that out.

He said to Calondir, "There is nothing else I can do here."

Distracted, Calondir nodded. "I will be up momentarily." The High Lord's gaze lifted to his. "We must not delay any longer."

"Agreed." He said to Graydon, *I'm on my way.*

An echo of his earlier thoughts ghosted through his head again as he walked outside, Miguel following close on his heels.

You should have said something earlier.

I should have listened better to you.

He stepped into the death-scented night, caught sight of Pia and Eva standing with Rune and Carling, and clenched his jaw as he strode toward them. Everyone else swirled away from him, like sparks shooting from the flames of the forest fire, each one a bright but ephemeral light. Even the Elves, who were so long-lived in comparison to many others, seemed ephemeral to him, and so easily extinguished.

He stopped and crossed his arms when he reached the quartet. His frowning gaze traveled from Pia, who stood side by side with her bodyguard, to Rune and at last to Carling, where his gaze lingered. The witch returned his regard with equanimity, her expression calm.

Whatever she and Rune had done when they had gotten together last summer, they had caused reality to shift so that the other gryphons felt it a continent away in New York. And they had done it not once, but three times—four if Dragos counted that last, strange ripple that had occurred

in the confrontation in the meadow at the Oracle's. The events were disturbing and mysterious, and Dragos did not like disturbing mysteries.

"I am surprised that you are still alive," he said to her.

Carling smiled. "No one is more surprised about that than I am."

The dragon took jealous note of the affectionate glance she gave Rune and that he returned.

Then Dragos relaxed and shook his head, and finally let it all go.

"I'm not sorry," he said to Rune. "We were overextended, I didn't know she was salvageable, and you were not expendable." He paused then added slowly, "But I should have listened when you asked me to."

Rune sucked a tooth, considering what Dragos said. Then he replied, "I think I was in denial about mating for a long time, and I should have said something sooner. But I'm not sorry either. You were pigheaded and autocratic."

There was that word again. Dragos sighed. Out of the corner of his eye he saw Carling put a casual hand over her mouth. Pia didn't even bother to hide her smile. "Do you know how much the blasted Games are costing me?" Dragos demanded. "I never would have bothered to hold them to replace just one sentinel."

Rune grinned. "I've seen Cuelebre Enterprises' bank accounts. You can afford it."

Dragos glowered at his former First. He asked telepathically, *Are you doing well—is she well?*

The gryphon sobered. *We're both very well, thank you. It's good to see you and Pia doing so well too.*

Dragos switched back to verbal conversation. "And what are you two doing? You've got a hell of a lot of talent gathering in Miami. It's making people nervous."

Rune and Carling exchanged another intimate, smiling glance.

Rune said, "We decided to collect underutilized resources. I like the consulting I've been doing for the Miami Police

Department. We're setting up a consulting agency, only we're going to expand and take it international."

"Consulting for what?" Dragos asked.

His mind shifted as he mulled over that piece of news. A "consulting agency" run by Rune and Carling would have almost limitless possibilities. It could be useful to contract out some things to an agency that was not officially connected to the Wyr demesne. And it would be very useful to have access to Rune's particular talents again, to . . . talk things over with him from time to time.

They might never be what they once were, but they could be something else, something new. And who the hell knew? Maybe it would even be something better. Something without him being the lord and Rune his servant. Something that was more simply and equitably friendship.

"Let's talk about it later," Rune told him. "We're still working on definitions."

He nodded and clapped Rune on the shoulder. The other man gave him a crooked smile.

Just then Graydon walked up, his hands in his pockets. Dragos watched from lowered eyelids as Pia threw her arms around the big man, who hugged her back.

Graydon told him, "It might not look like it at the moment, but we're actually pretty organized. The Elves are taking us in groups of ten to wait at the crossover passage. We're ready to go whenever they are."

"Calondir said he would be out momentarily." Speaking of which, Dragos turned to Pia. "I need to talk to you."

Rune gave him a nod, then he, Carling and Graydon backed away. Eva made as if to join them. "Don't go far," Pia said to her.

Eva smiled. "I won't. Just gonna hang a little out of the way."

Dragos waited until the bodyguard captain had stepped several feet away. Then he considered Pia's upturned face. It was impossible for him to feel more for her than he already did. She had been through so much last year, and

the thought of anything else happening to her made him more than a little crazy. He laid the tips of his fingers along the gorgeous, slender curve of her neck.

He said, *I want to see you in that harem outfit again, bells and all.*

Her eyes lit up, and a grin played around the corners of her mouth. *I wouldn't mind seeing you in that sheikh outfit again either. The half-bared chest is a good look on you.*

She looked so mischievous he had to smile, even as he clenched with the desire to kiss her senseless. He flashed to an image of bending her back over his arm as he ravished her mouth, and he could tell by her heavy-lidded expression that she had caught the drift of his thoughts.

He stroked along the delicate curve of her collarbone, relishing the satin softness of her skin. His callused fingers were so rough in comparison he made sure his touch was light and careful so that he did not mark her.

Then his smile faded, and as he grew serious, so did she. He said, *I want you to stay here when we cross over.*

She pursed her luscious lips as she studied his face thoughtfully. *I'm not going to do that, Dragos.*

His autocratic side fought to take control. He battered it into submission. *I really want you to change your mind,* he told her. *The gods only know what we're going to find on the other side of that crossover passage, but whether it happens directly on the other side or some distance away, we're going to see more bloodshed. It's going to get ugly and dangerous, and while you have many strengths that we have only just begun to explore, you are not a creature of war.*

She nodded slowly. *That's true, I'm not. But even though I do know things are going to get ugly, I'm still not going to stay behind.*

He pushed air out of his bared teeth as frustration clawed at him. He growled, "This decision does not make sense to me. You are going to hate it."

"That's also true," she said quietly. "I will. But you would

not stay behind while I crossed over to an Other land, would you?"

He glared at her. "The two scenarios do not compare."

She rubbed the back of her neck. "In a way they don't, but in a way they do too." She gave him a level look and said in an even softer tone of voice that nevertheless held an edge of inflexible steel. "As Eva said, you're Powerful as shit and older than dirt, but I will not stay behind when there may be any risk to you. That's not going to happen, Dragos. I'm pretty easygoing most of the time, and there aren't very many lines I feel the need to draw, but this is one of them. I know you're going to be in the thick of things, and I will be on hand if you need healing. I may also get involved if any of the sentinels are critically injured, or if there is anything I can do for Beluviel. She was kind, and that matters a lot to me. Other than that, I have no grand agenda nor do I have an ax to grind. I will be sensible, and I will keep my guards around me, and I am going. End of discussion."

"End of discussion?" he said, staring at her. He was fairly certain he had never heard anyone say such a thing to him before.

One corner of her mouth lifted. "Yup."

He bent over her until they were nose to nose. "Do not think for one minute that I have forgotten how you ordered me out of the room earlier," he whispered.

"Actually I had kind of forgotten about that." Her gaze widened. "I did, didn't I?"

"Yes, you did." He slid his own hand to the back of her neck, gripping her gently. "Do you know what I thought?"

She shook her head, staring at him mesmerized. "Huh-uh."

He growled, "I thought it was sexy as hell."

Her lovely, triangular features lit up. Surreptitiously she slipped her fingers into the edge of his black fatigues at his waist, and she tugged at the material gently. "I don't suppose we could put off this whole war thing until we got ten or twelve hours in the sack, could we? We could send a note to Gaeleval and ask him to take a day off."

Invisible fire danced along his skin. He bent to brush her lips with his. "If we had any chance of that succeeding, I would be all for it."

"It's been much too long," she whimpered.

He swallowed the tiny sound she made as the fire reached his brain. Before Pia, he had gone centuries between taking lovers, and he had never felt the lack. The women meant nothing. He had never remembered their names, and now he couldn't remember their faces.

He mouthed against her pouting lips, "We still haven't added manacles to any of the bedrooms. That's going to be the first thing we take care of when we get back home."

"Yeah, okay," she muttered, as her body trembled. He slipped an arm around her waist, holding her against him. Her head fell back and she looked at him with glazed, unfocused eyes. "Dragos?"

"Yes," he murmured. They were surrounded by people, but there was nobody else, anywhere, nobody at all.

"We're going to get married, right?"

He would have smiled at how dazed she looked, except he knew exactly how she felt. What they generated together was blinding. She was not only the most precious person in the universe to him, but she was also the most powerful. "I can't believe you framed that as a question."

She tried to scowl at him. "I was using the question as a conversation starter."

He licked at her lower lip. "And?"

She didn't sound like she could breathe right. "And I wanted to know if we were going to go on a honeymoon too. We haven't even gone on a date yet."

He lifted his head. Actually, he hadn't thought much beyond the big diamond ring and a lavish public display where the whole world watched as he claimed her. "Of course we are going on a honeymoon," he said. "What kind do you want?"

She heaved a big sigh. "No bodyguards," she said dreamily. "No urgent business calls, and no sentinels. No housecleaners or staff of any kind—and certainly that means no

Stanford, even though he'll claim to be heartbroken, of course. If you think he wouldn't dream of intruding on our honeymoon, think again. He would insist that I need a dresser, and I'm not talking about a piece of furniture."

She surprised him into snorting. He was loving the sound of a honeymoon more and more as she talked. "I'll swear there'll be no one but us," he promised. "Along with the peanut, of course, because he won't be born by then. We'll have our honeymoon as soon as I get the sentinels settled into place."

She looked at him from between her eyelashes. "That means a quick, quiet wedding, you know," she remarked casually. "There won't be time to set up anything else."

He frowned. "Wait a minute."

"I love the idea," she gushed. She threw her arms around his waist, hugging him tightly. "A quiet wedding and a quick getaway, and we'll be all alone. Do you realize we haven't even really been alone since we were kidnapped by Goblins, and we escaped and ran away? The only private time we get is when we close our bedroom door—and even then somebody may call or get in touch with you telepathically over some emergency or other."

He had to admit, she had a point. He scowled. "I was planning on a big wedding."

She gave him a coaxing smile. "I don't know why. You don't even like crowds, and you hate having your picture taken."

Apparently she was full of good points tonight. "We'll talk about this later. I can only give in so much, you know."

"I know," she said soothingly. "It's so hard being you."

"Well, it is," Dragos admitted. He grinned as she laughed. "You pretty much got everything you wanted in this conversation, didn't you?"

Her laughter died and she gave him a completely serious look. "I feel that is how every conversation should go."

He wrapped her up in his arms, crushing her to him. In the periphery of his vision, he could tell many others in the clearing stared at them both, but they counted as nothing to

him. "I will find you armor, and you will stay surrounded in the middle of the army."

"Whatever you say," she said meekly. "As long as you agree with me." She laid her head on his shoulder.

What a sneaky tyrant she was turning into. Actually, she wasn't all that sneaky. He was utterly enchanted with her bossiness.

Yes, for the first time in his existence, he was truly vulnerable. He cradled her close, savoring the weight and feel of her in his arms. He only lifted his head again when a stir passed through everyone in the area.

He turned to look and Pia did too, as Calondir exited his damaged home, along with a dozen Elven warriors. The High Lord was dressed in plate armor and armed with two crossed swords at his back.

He smiled at the sight. Who would have thought it? For once he and Calondir were going to fight on the same side.

While he had come to treasure the profound differences in nature between him and Pia, Dragos also would not be who and what he was if his blood didn't quicken at the possibility of an upcoming battle.

Payback and death weren't the dragon's only companions. He was on intimate terms with chaos and strife too.

≡ FOURTEEN ≡

Pia shivered and pulled her anorak closer around her torso as she watched Dragos stride over to Calondir. The chill wind felt much colder once he stepped away from her. He seemed to take away all the light and warmth with him.

The Elves around the High Lord bristled as Dragos approached. Their animosity had been entrenched for so many years that she didn't see that changing anytime soon, current alliance or not. Nobody was going to walk away friends from this interaction, not with so many years of conflict between Dragos and the Elves. The best she could hope for was that they achieve a guarded peace.

At worst . . . well, she didn't want to consider the worst.

She sensed someone coming up on her side and turned her head. Eva raised her eyebrows and held up a dirt-streaked crossbow. "Look at what one of the kids found. Does this look familiar to you, princess?"

Exasperated, she said, "Stop calling me princess."

Eva scratched her nose. "You prefer Tinker Bell?"

"Just use my name, dammit!" She snatched at the crossbow.

Eva held on for a second while Pia tugged uselessly on it. Then the other woman let go, and she staggered back a step. "You know," Eva said casually, and Pia tensed. She had learned to be wary of Eva's ultracasual tone of voice. "If you were in my unit, I'd be all over your ass for losing your weapon, and I wouldn't let up until I'd chewed off a good ten pounds or so of flesh."

Pia scowled as her face turned warm. "Well, I'm not in your unit, and in case you don't remember, I got grabbed and shoved around a lot in the dark. As I recall, you were the one who did most of the shoving."

Eva slanted a look at her. "That make it okay? You gonna drop your weapon whenever you sneeze too? Maybe when somebody gives you the stinkeye?"

"The *stinkeye*?" she said, her embarrassment and annoyance successfully diverted. She covered her mouth to muffle her snort. People had died tonight. Laughter wasn't appropriate. "All right, no matter how crowded, confused, dark or fiery it got, I should not have dropped my weapon."

"That's more like it. Sort of." Eva punched her in the shoulder, and she staggered again. "Stick with me, Tink. I'll get you sorted out."

"Well, isn't this too cute for fucking words," said an all-too-familiar voice. "Apparently you two got a little girl-bonding time in. How does that saying go? It isn't really cheating when there isn't any penis."

Both Pia and Eva turned to stare at Aryal, who stood a few feet away with her arms crossed, regarding them both with stormy gray eyes. The harpy wore her usual outfit of fighting leathers, but this time instead of holstered guns, she had two swords strapped to her back, along with long knives at her thighs. The harpy looked lean, muscled and all too eager for some kind of fight.

Aryal said to Pia, "You are the worst goddamn trouble magnet I have ever seen, and coming from a harpy, you know that's actually saying something."

Pia sighed and rubbed her eyes with thumb and forefinger. "Hello, Aryal." Nice to see you too. Not.

When she dropped her hand again, the world had shifted. Eva had moved to stand slightly in front of her instead of at her side. Eva was staring at Aryal with a cold expression on her bold features.

"Are you that insolent when you talk to Dragos?" Eva said between her teeth. "Because you sure as hell shouldn't be talking to his mate that way."

Wait, what? Pia did a double take at Captain Psycho. Eva was *defending* her to Aryal, and talking about respect?

The harpy laughed. "What did you do?" Aryal said to Pia. "Flick your perky cheerleader ponytail at her too? You're like some kind of insidious virus, but I thought you only infected people with the Y chromosome."

"Hey, look at me," Eva snapped. Fascinated, Pia did just that, her gaze bouncing back to Eva, whose hard, black eyes glittered in the torchlight. "I'm talking to you. She isn't."

Aryal smiled and said between her teeth, "Yeah, I think you may regret that."

"Yeah, I don't think so," said Eva. "I hear Tinker Bell here can kick your ass, and she's a nice person. I'm more like you. I'm not nice. Just think what she and I together could do to you."

Aryal's smile vanished. Oh-kay, that might not be a good sign.

"For God's sake, both of you," Pia hissed at both of them. "This isn't the time or the place."

Out of the corner of her eye, Pia saw both Johnny and Hugh circling closer. The two males were watching Eva alertly. When Pia looked around, Andrea, James and Miguel were not far behind.

Then the world changed again, as Quentin moved in, seemingly from nowhere. He shoved between Eva and Aryal, his body moving with liquid, lethal grace, and he didn't stop moving until he came nose to nose with the harpy, who shifted to face him. They were within a couple of inches of each other in height and glared at each other, their tall, lean bodies combat tense.

Quentin said in a low, bitter voice, "Pia's right, you demented bitch—this is not the time or the place for your made-up vendettas. Decent, innocent people have died here tonight, and their bodies aren't even cold in the ground."

"Don't pull that guilt-making crap on me," Aryal exclaimed. "Dead people are dead, and they don't know shit. And what happens between me and your special friend is none of your business, jackass."

"You think I don't know how long and hard you've tried to investigate me?" Quentin growled. "You've been trying to pin something on me for over two years now. And what have you found? Exactly nothing. So quit taking your resentment of me out on Pia."

Was *that* why Aryal didn't like her? Pia and Eva looked at each other. Eva raised her eyebrows, asking her silently, *What the fuck? You know anything about this?*

Pia shook her head and shrugged. For all she knew, it could be true.

The harpy's nose wrinkled as she stared at Quentin, and she coughed. "Oh gods," she said, staring at him with repugnance. "Are you a cat? You stink like a cat. That's just bloody fucking great. Not only is Quentin Caeravorn part Wyr, but he stinks like a cat." She threw up her hands. "Makes my whole fucking night to know this. If yet another Wyr with feline tendencies ends up as a sentinel, I'm going to slit somebody's wrists."

Quentin looked more out-of-control furious than Pia had ever seen him, his skin flushed dark and features clenched tight as a fist. Violence pulsed in the air. That was when the pegasus and all the gryphons arrived, even Rune, every tall male using his body like a battering ram to break the other two apart.

Graydon actually shoved Aryal by slapping the flat of his hands against her shoulders and making her stagger back a few paces. Normally he was so mild mannered and easygoing, Pia found it shocking to see him get violent. He demanded, "You realize what a line you've been walking this week, dipshit?"

"What?" Aryal snapped. "I'm not the criminal here!"

"Hell, you haven't even been trying to walk a line." Graydon stared at her with angry incredulity. "You've been staggering all over it like a drunk at a single's bar. Do you want to keep your job or not?"

Aryal snarled, "I will *win my job back* just like all you other sonsabitches—by hammering down any bastard that gets in my way."

"Is that so, Smurfette?" Quentin sneered at her from across a barrier made up of two gryphons and a pegasus. "And here I thought you were an example of affirmative action in the workplace."

Rage detonated in Aryal's expression. She flicked out both stiffened hands, and talons sprang out on all her fingers and thumbs. Then she plowed forward, only to be brought up short when Graydon came at her from behind and pinned her in a headlock.

"Smurfette," breathed Eva rapturously.

"Everybody has gone nuts," Pia muttered.

She looked from Eva to her other bodyguards, who had all come to surround her. And she had thought they were the psychos. They looked positively sane in comparison to the crazy pants developing between Quentin and Aryal.

Her gaze lingered on Eva's delighted face. Well, almost all of them looked sane.

She shoved her way through the bristling testosterone to reach Quentin, making sure he saw her before she put a hand on his bicep. The warm muscle beneath her fingertips felt rock hard with tension.

"Hey," she said softly. "Come on. Come talk to me."

At first he didn't respond, his blue eyes two ice chips of fury. He watched the harpy with a killer's face, a muscle leaping in his clenched jaw.

Once upon a time, that expression would have scared her spitless. Funny how things had changed. She tugged harder at his arm, injecting more authority into her voice. "Quentin, walk away with me right now."

Finally his attention snapped to her. She smiled at him,

197

and he jerked his head once in a nod. Still, she entwined one arm firmly with his as she led him to one side. When Eva made as if to join her, she sent the other woman a warning glance, and Eva responded by hanging back several steps.

At six-foot-two, Quentin stood half a head taller than she did. Even though she now knew that he had a strong enough Wyr side that he could change into his animal form, she still saw a strong resemblance to an Elven heritage in his graceful bone structure. Like Dragos, Quentin was broader in the shoulders than most Elves. His mixed race heritage had given him a spectacular combination of strength and beauty.

Before Dragos, she had enjoyed having a crush on her sexy boss. Now the crush had comfortably and quite irrevocably settled into friendship.

"Someday I'm going to fucking kill her," Quentin said between his teeth. "Just so you're warned. That harpy is *unendurable*."

"Okay," she said, soft and quiet. "You're not going to get any argument from me."

His gaze fully focused on her. "That looks like blood on your clothes. Are you all right? You weren't hurt?"

"I wasn't hurt," she told him. "The blood isn't mine."

"Well, that's something, at least." He put his arms around her with a deep sigh.

She hugged him tight. "Did I see you fly in on the pegasus?"

"Yeah, that's Alex," he said. "Going through the Games together has given us a chance to do some bonding. He's a really good guy. I hope he wins through to the end. I think the sentinels could use someone as even tempered as he is."

She glanced over her shoulder, noting that Alex had separated himself from the sentinels once Quentin had walked away. The pegasus stood nearby as well, watching the events in the clearing unfold, his hands on his hips.

She turned back to Quentin. "Are you okay?" she asked gently. "You've lost some people tonight, haven't you?"

"Yeah, I did," he whispered. His eyes were bloodshot. "But I'm not the only one. A lot of folks lost people tonight."

"Can I do anything for you?" She rubbed his back.

He shook his head and gave her a not-quite smile. "Other than keep yourself safe, no. Thanks." He looked around at the devastation, his expression turning grim once more. "I'm just glad Dragos did the decent thing and mustered the Wyr to help."

Quentin made no secret of the fact that he disliked Dragos, nor did Dragos hide the fact that he tolerated Quentin for Pia's sake. When Pia had asked Quentin about his decision to enter the Sentinel Games, he had told her, "I don't have to like Dragos in order to decide that I want to invest in my community. He may be Lord of the Wyr, but he's just one man, after all. The Wyr demesne is a lot bigger than he is."

Now her answering smile turned wry. "You sound surprised at the thought of Dragos doing something decent."

He searched her mild expression. She could tell he was looking to see if he had offended her. When he saw that he hadn't, he shrugged. "Yeah, what can I say," he said. "You're always going to be the best part of him."

"I think that might be the only thing you both agree on," she told him.

He took a deep breath and let it out slowly. "Thanks for the de-escalation. I'd better go see what I can do to help."

"Okay." She gave him another quick squeeze and let him go. "As long as you go in the opposite direction of Aryal. Just avoid her completely. Nobody needs any more strife right now, Quentin."

He glanced at where Aryal and Graydon were still arguing, and his face hardened, but he said, "Fair enough."

He kissed her cheek, then walked away to join Alex. She turned to find Eva, and as she did so, she looked around at everybody else in the clearing. Many people, both Elves and Wyr, were watching the sentinels.

Just as many Wyr, if not more, were watching her as well, their expressions closed and unfriendly. Jolted, she

looked from one person to the next. Each Wyr turned away when her gaze fell on him or her.

They didn't have to meet her eyes or say anything. She could see what they thought in their faces.

They thought she had started the whole thing.

She thought back to how everything had begun, a few minutes ago, then back to last year, and her mouth compressed into an unhappy line.

Maybe they were more right than she wanted to admit.

From that point on things seemed to move quickly. The sentinels took their squabbling elsewhere for a few minutes and returned in short order, each one wearing a tight face and the promise of imminent violence. Danger burned so hot in their auras, all the other Wyr turned subdued and quiet.

Still troubled, Pia settled on the corner of a nearby bench and concentrated on cleaning off her crossbow, while the last of the arriving Wyr fighters dried off and stowed their parachutes away, and last minute preparations were made. Eva and Johnny stayed with Pia, and they didn't talk much either.

Elven horses were brought out, only these weren't prettily saddled for a day's ride in the Wood. The horses wore head guards and neck plates, their bodies covered in blankets of protective chain mail. The animals had clearly been trained for war. They stamped the ground and blew through their nostrils, eager and restless.

After talking with Calondir, Dragos called Miguel over to him and sent him off with another Elf. Within ten minutes, Miguel returned, carrying exquisitely tooled leather armor suitable for a female of Pia's height and frame. Pia's slim runner's build was very compatible with an Elven body type, and the peanut bump wasn't obtrusive enough to cause a problem.

The armor was lined with a finely crafted, tough chain mail and padded with cotton, and it was heavier than it looked. Pia liked to think she recognized good sense when she saw it, though, and she didn't complain about the weight.

"It's a gift from the High Lord," Miguel said. His dark eyes were filled with admiration as he ran a hand down one piece. "This is really fine. It's got an aversion spell woven into the chain mail."

Pia stood, and Miguel and Eva helped to strap it into place on her, adjusting each buckle to make sure of the fit. She squatted when they asked, and twisted and turned. She said, "It doesn't feel as bad as I thought it would."

"It shouldn't," Eva told her. "You're wearing about fifty thousand dollars' worth of battle bling."

She almost fell over. "You're kidding."

"Nope. Elven armor is kinda like those wafers of wayfarer bread that you like so much—it's top-of-the-line and hard to come by. This stuff is not only resistant to sword cuts and knife throws, but it can block a bullet as long as it isn't an armor-piercing round fired point-blank at you. It's water repellant and lightweight too. With a little training in it, you shouldn't have any impairment in speed or stamina when you run." After tugging one last time on a shin plate, Eva slapped Pia's leg lightly and stood.

Pia felt a little like one of the horses that had just been saddled. She gave Eva a leery glance. "Training."

"Yep, and that's first on our agenda when we get back home."

"What are you talking about?"

Eva stood hipshot with her arms crossed as she looked over the clearing. She said, "Fact is, you need somebody on you, Tink, and it can't be the sentinels who take time off their regular work to do it piecemeal. It needs to be someone full time who has the ability to work with your schedule and needs, and who can coordinate the right staff for each occasion. So I put in a quick word with the Old Man earlier, about the possibility of a job transfer." Eva's gaze slid sideways to her. "If you would be amenable to working with me, that is."

Pia blinked rapidly. Evil Eva had asked for a job transfer to work with her? "I had no idea," she said inanely. "He never said anything."

Eva lifted one shoulder. "Well, we just barely had time for me to bring it up telepathically. Why don't you think about it, see how it sits? Nobody's deciding nuthin' without you."

"Why'd you ask?" The words burst out of her before she could stop it.

A small smile played around the edges of the captain's bold mouth. "First, I like you," Eva said bluntly. "I didn't want to, and I didn't expect it, but I do. Second, I've been doing the same thing for a while now. Sometimes you just need a change of pace, know what I mean?" Pia nodded as she watched the other woman's face. "Third, you're a challenge, and I need that too. You're always going to be facing something. You're always going to be in the public eye, and always going to be a target. Plus, you're gifted, and you're smart, but I gotta tell you, Tink, sometimes you're kind of stupid too."

She scowled. "I'm not stupid."

Eva said, "Crossbow."

"Fuck you."

Eva laughed softly, and after a moment she joined in. "Fourth," Eva said. "It may take me a while, because sometimes I'm kind of stupid too, but I recognize a top dog when I see one. And that's what you are. You surprised me with it, and I'm not talking about you kicking my ass, or Aryal's ass, or anything like that, because I haven't even seen you fight yet, so clearly I'm going on faith about that bit."

Pia toed a clump of grass. She muttered, "I can too kick your ass."

"Beside the point. Being an alpha is much more than kicking someone's ass." Eva grinned. "I watched you order the Lord of the Wyr—*the Old Man himself*—out of the room, and he went. You don't get more top dog than that. Shit, girl, I damn near genuflected, and I'm not even sure what that word means."

"If this is about Johnny, I don't want you to change careers because you feel like you might owe me something."

"I won't lie to you," Eva said quietly. "This is partly

about Johnny, but I wouldn't change careers because I feel like I owe you. I could always find some other way to repay you. It's everything, Pia. It's the total package."

A strange feeling pressed against her chest and made her eyes prickle. She whispered, "You figured it out, didn't you? What I am."

"I think so," Eva murmured in reply. "But in the end, that stuff don't matter. It's who you are, not what you are. That's what matters."

She nodded, thinking. "We could give it a trial basis," she said. "We should find out if you even like the change. If I talk to Dragos about it, I think he'd see to it that your old job was kept open until you were sure."

"If you asked him, I'm sure he would," Eva said, smiling. "Okay, that'd work. But I can tell you right now, I'll like the change. If you don't mind, I'd like to start talking to my crew about it. Some of them might be interested in making the switch with me, but most of them won't. I'll let you know what they have to say."

"Sounds good." She smiled. "Thank you, Eva."

"My pleasure. I'm glad you listened." Eva tugged at one of the side straps between the breast and the back plates, rather unnecessarily, she thought. "How's that feel? Think you could run in it?"

She looked down sourly at the thirty extra pounds tied onto her body. "I wouldn't want to," she said.

"But you *could* if you had to, right?" Eva stressed.

"I suppose," she grumbled.

"Now, here's the real question," Eva said. "Do you think you could run in it without dropping your crossbow?"

She rolled her eyes and threatened, "I'm not going to hire you if you keep bringing that up."

"Are you kidding?" Eva said. "That's totally why you're gonna hire me. I'm never gonna let you forget it, and someday that may just save your life."

A horn blew, the sharp blast of sound soaring over the snatches of conversation in the clearing, and Pia shivered. She turned, looking for Dragos, and found him watching

her with a frown. She pointed to the chest plate and gave him a thumbs-up. He just shook his head, his face grim.

Then he turned to look around the fighters in the clearing, who had all quieted. "Calondir and I have agreed to lead together," he said, his deep, powerful voice pitched to carry. "We will share command decisions and bring down Amras Gaeleval in partnership with each other. The heavier Wyr and all the avians will come after us. Then Wyr and Elves will follow together." As he looked at Pia, he added telepathically, *That's where you and your guards will be, in the middle. Do you understand?*

Of course, she said. *Don't waste your time worrying about me. Do what you have to do.*

He said to those nearby, "Stand back."

When everyone had retreated to give him sufficient room, he shimmered into a change, and expanded, until the massive bronze-and-black dragon appeared once again and dominated the clearing. The dragon arched his long, serpentine neck and looked down at Calondir, who stood in front of him.

"Now," Dragos told him.

The plate armor that Calondir wore didn't hamper him in the slightest as he leaped onto Dragos's back and settled into place at the base of his neck. The tall stern figure of the High Lord shone like bright silver against the dragon's duskier colors.

Pia stared, unable to look away or blink. Even considering how long she might live, she knew she was looking at a unique sight. A great roar welled up around her from the throats of Wyr and Elves alike. Dragos mantled, bared his teeth and roared back, the deep-chested, Powerful sound ripping the air, until every hair on her body raised and gooseflesh rippled along her skin.

Hell's bells, it almost made her want to bash somebody in the head.

She looked around. Many of the Wyr had changed into their animal forms too, including the harpy, the pegasus and all the gryphons. This time, like Dragos, the pegasus

and gryphons each carried one rider. As she had expected, Quentin rode the pegasus, and Carling was astride Rune. She wasn't familiar with the fighters that Bayne, Constantine and Graydon had chosen to carry, although Bayne's rider was a tall male with weather-beaten features and military-short white blond hair. He looked familiar enough that she thought she had seen him around the Tower once or twice.

As Pia glanced at her own psychos to see how they reacted to it all, she discovered half of them had shifted too. Eva, Miguel and Hugh remained in their human form, while Andrea, Johnny and James circled them. Johnny was a lean wolf with a shaggy pelt, while James looked more like a German shepherd mix, heavier in the chest and haunches. The biggest surprise, to Pia, was that Andrea in her Wyr form looked like an Irish wolfhound and stood taller than the other two. They all held their heads low to the ground, showing sharp, white fangs as their alert gazes roamed restlessly over the area.

Pia asked Eva, "Just out of curiosity, what do the rest of you look like?"

"I'm kinda like a Rottweiler," Eva said. "Miguel's another wolf. He's darker than Johnny."

"I look like a gargoyle," Hugh offered in a helpful tone. Pia laughed.

"Since the Elves and the Wyr are supposed to fall in together, do you mind if I stick with you guys?" a light, feminine voice asked. "Thought you might find it useful to have someone with you who knows what to expect on the other side."

Pia, Eva and the others turned to face Linwe. The Elf wore leather armor much like Pia's, only hers bore scrapes from obvious use. Like many of the other Elven warriors, she had a sword strapped to her back, along with a full quiver of arrows, and she carried a longbow that was as tall as she was.

Pia opened her mouth, but Eva spoke first. "I don't mind if you hang with us, as long as you know, we've got just one

agenda." The captain jerked her thumb at Pia. "And she's it. Don't get in our way, and we won't have any problems."

"I understand," Linwe said. Like so many other Elves, she still looked hollow-eyed from grief but otherwise was calm and alert.

"I'm glad you asked," Pia said to her, just as, out of the corner of her eye, the gigantic wall of bronze-and-black flesh that filled the clearing suddenly moved.

Pia's heart jerked as she looked up. Dragos strode out of the clearing, and all the larger Wyr followed.

Time was a funny thing, she thought. Instead of marching on in a measured pace, it seemed to flow like a river. Quiet days pooled together, languid with a sense of sameness, and events swirled and eddied, and time seemed to pick up its pace. Then there was the tumbling, dangerous rush of white water over rocks, and the heart-stopping terror of relentless inevitability as the water fell over the edge, and you knew that no matter what you might do or wish, you could not stop that flow from falling.

All you could do was surrender to the experience and flow with it.

When it came their turn to move, Pia and others fell into place and followed all the others to the crossover passageway that led to the Elven Other land.

When Dragos came to the Elven crossover passageway, he noticed for the first time how every inch of the floor and sides were carved, and he curled a lip in disgust. The passage was a symbol of everything he hated about the Elves, their arrogance and their Power to change the landscape around them. How like them to take something that already had so much natural Power and beauty and warp it into a vision of their own making.

He snapped his wings closed against his back, uncaring if he jostled the imperious gnat that he allowed to temporarily perch on his back, and he stalked through the passage. Frigid wind howled around his head and shoulders,

as the surrounding scene flickered and changed. The burned husk of night lightened into indeterminate day, and in another first experience, he came into the Elven Other land.

Metal scraped as Calondir drew his sword, and Dragos had to control his impulse to snatch the Elf off his back and fling him away. Tensed for battle he looked around, taking in details quickly.

Like the other end, the passageway on this side was surrounded by a cluster of trees, but these were snow laden. Evergreens sprinkled a white landscape that was broken with scattered rock. The temperature was well below freezing. The cold didn't bother Dragos in the slightest, and Wyr were, as a general rule, a hardy race with many natural defenses, but his thoughts winged to Pia and the baby anyway. Would they be warm enough? He should have made sure she had a lined cloak to go with the armor.

No one was in sight, and the acrid taint of smoke swirled on the biting wind, along with the scent of Elves. Had the smell blown over the passageway from Lirithriel Wood, or had something else burned here too? His gaze ran along the visible tree line, which was intact. The snow was trampled at the passageway entrance, which was no surprise, and footprints led away on a path that wound through a break in the trees.

Mindful of those behind him, Dragos kept moving. He nodded in the direction of the path. "Where does that go?"

"To my home here, just on the other side of the tree line. It overlooks a valley." Calondir shifted and said, his voice edged, "Can you tell if that smell is from Lirithriel or if something else has burned here?"

"Not yet," said Dragos. "We're too close to the passageway."

"I don't like this. It's too quiet."

"They're here," he told the High Lord. "And they've only had a few hours' start. We'll take to the air and find them."

"For now, we should make for the house and see if it is still intact," Calondir said. "Winter nights get bitter here, and we should make use of all the shelter we can get."

As Dragos strode down the path, he remembered his questions. "Where are the others that traveled with Gaeleval? What happened to the one who was wounded?"

"They're dead," Calondir said shortly. "Their bodies were found in the apartment where they and Gaeleval stayed."

That didn't surprise Dragos. They had fulfilled their function by leveraging a way into Calondir's home. Once Gaeleval had taken their will, he wouldn't have needed to actively wield the Machine, which was why none of Calondir's seers had sensed any issue. The seers would have had no cause to probe too deeply into anyone's mind.

"How did they travel to Lirithriel Wood?" he asked.

"What do you mean?"

He controlled his impatience. "I mean just what I said. Did they travel across this Other land, or did they travel on the other side, on Earth? Why did you host them in the Wood and not here?"

"They traveled here," Calondir said briefly. "And I had them brought over the crossover passageway to Lirithriel Wood. With your mate's impending visit, I didn't want to step out of sync with the time on Earth."

Just then a fresh gust of wind from the other side of the trees gusted in Dragos' face. It brought with it the smell of more wood smoke, and Elves.

A lot of Elves.

He sped up until he loped, sensing the gryphons pick up their pace behind them. "What is it?" Calondir demanded.

"Trouble."

He broke through the other side of the tree line and skidded to a halt at the edge of land. To his left, the path took an abrupt turn to follow the edge of a bluff up to the smoking ruins of what must have once been a long, gracious building at the top of a cliff.

The path along the bluff and the ruined building looked over a wide, snowy valley that would probably be beautiful in the springtime.

At the moment the valley was filled with an army.

Calondir whispered a shaken curse.

Dragos walked to the edge of the bluff and crouched like an enormous cat, gripping the rocks tight with his talons as he stared down at the thousands of Elves. Warriors and non-warriors. Men, women. *Children*. Some were better dressed than others. Some were barefoot in the snow. All of them looked ill fed. His snout wrinkled as he smelled the rarest of oddities for Elves—disease.

As he had reached the edge, all the Elves in the valley turned to look up at him.

All of them, all at the same time. Every single one of them cocked his or her head at exactly the same angle, in exactly the same way. His sharp raptor's gaze moved from blank face to blank face.

Wyr came up on either side of him, gryphons and the pegasus and the harpy, then other Wyr along with Elves. They stared down in silence.

The dragon chuckled. The low, bitter sound reverberated in the rock of the bluff on which he stood, and several Elves drew away from him in dismay.

"I think we just found the answer to one of my other questions," Dragos said. "What happened to all the Elves in Numenlaur?"

⇒ FIFTEEN ⇐

Every Elf in the valley smiled.

Dragos felt the Power of the God Machine pulse to life.

Shouts and screams came from behind him. *Fuck.* He whirled and lunged back through the trees, knocking people and horses aside in his rush to find Pia. Both Elves and Wyr dodged to get out of his way, horses plunging headlong off the path, while even more ran toward him from the direction of the passageway. He ignored all of them, looking for Pia and her bodyguards.

He saw a tower of flames through the trees.

Where was she?

In the next moment he saw her running toward him, surrounded by her guards, as she looked back over her shoulder at the blazing fire. He slowed to a stop, breathing hard, and waited for her to notice him.

She was the last of her group to do, looking away finally to discover him blocking the path. She skidded to a halt a few yards away.

Somehow Calondir had managed to avoid being dislodged from his back. Now the Elf Lord leaped to the ground

and raced back toward the passageway, along with several others. Dragos twitched his shoulders, glad to have Calondir's insignificant yet extremely annoying weight off of him.

"You," he said to Pia. "Forget everything I said about hanging back." She squeaked with surprise as he plucked her unceremoniously off the ground. He raised her up and held her to his shoulder until he felt her scramble onto him and perch at the base of his neck.

"All right," she muttered. "But I'm not riding like this if you're going to fly."

"Just stay put for now," he snapped. He looked down at her unit, three in canine form and three in human form, plus apparently Pia had managed to add the Elf girl with the blue hair to her collection. All seven stared up at him. "I don't know," he told them, answering their unspoken questions. "Figure out something to do with yourselves for now and get the hell out of my way."

They scrambled to either side of him, and he strode after Calondir and the others.

This time the trees weren't burning. The stone itself in the passageway was on fire, fueled by the Power in the God Machine. The flames roared thirty feet tall, and they threw off a ferocious heat. Of course the heat didn't bother him any more than the cold did, but mindful of Pia riding on his back, he took care to get no closer than Calondir and the others had.

Pia and her group had done just what he had told them to do. They had crossed over in the middle of the warriors.

It was a good thing they had. Those Wyr and the Elves who had been the last to cross over had been carried off to one side and were being triaged. Several suffered from burns. A few of them were severely injured and still screaming.

He sensed Pia's intention to go help those who were injured as she lifted one leg to sit sideways on him, preparatory to sliding down the outside of his front leg.

"No," he said to her.

But I can help them, she said. She didn't try to jump to the ground, although her telepathic voice throbbed with unhappiness.

You said you were prepared for how ugly this could get, he said ruthlessly. *Well, the ugliness has started. There will be too many people for you to help. There already are. Not only would you expose yourself but you would spread yourself too thin.*

Her breathing hitched, but after a moment she shifted back in place astride him.

Calondir approached. The Elf Lord looked incandescent with fury. He asked, "Can you put this fire out too?"

Dragos lowered his eyelids as he probed the magical blaze curiously. It was more resistant to him than the forest fire had been. "Probably," he said at last. "But I'm not going to waste time and energy doing it. Gaeleval wants to trap us on this side. Well, so be it. We don't want to leave. In the meantime, he has an entire army he has to control, and this fire is taking up more of his Power and concentration. There is a limit to what he can do. I say we help him reach it."

Calondir's chest moved as he sucked in a deep breath. The Elf glanced at the wounded, his face tight. He said between teeth, "Very well. Just see what you can do to keep something like this from happening again."

"You are mistaken about the purpose of my presence," said Dragos. "I am not here to do what you tell me to do, nor am I here to defend you. I'm here to attack him."

"Dragos," murmured Pia.

He twisted his head around so that he could scowl at her. She said nothing, just gave him a steady look.

He bared his teeth and growled at the High Lord, "But I'll see what I can do."

He had his sufferance rewarded, as she patted and stroked his neck. Calming down, he supposed it hadn't cost him all that much to promise to do what he could.

. . .

The temperature plummeted as the day began to fade.
Pia's armor had kept her comfortable earlier. After
the sun set, she was constantly on the tense side of a shiver,
and as a result, her muscles were tired and achy.

Dragos had relaxed enough to let her get down off his
back. He set the Wyr to setting up camp around the magical blaze, which continued to burn steadily, the stone of the
passageway glowing bright red.

"It's going to get cold tonight," he told them. "And Calondir's home on this side of the passage has been destroyed as
well. We should take advantage of the warmth Gaeleval is
giving us. Besides, if we're not going to engage him right
away, I'd better stay close so I can keep an eye on this and
make sure it doesn't spread."

Then he had returned to the cliff, along with Calondir,
Elven and Wyr mages, his sentinels, and Carling, to study
Gaeleval's "army."

Pia had gone with them but she hadn't stayed long. After
she took one long, horrified look at the tragedy in the valley below, she pivoted on her heel and walked away.

She understood now why Dragos had said there were
already too many people for her to help. A lack of attending to basic bodily needs, along with exposure and neglect,
had taken its toll on the enthralled Numenlaurians. She could
scent gangrene and other whiffs of disease on the wind,
and she didn't trust herself to control either her emotional
response or her impulse to vomit. Everybody was busy dealing with their own reactions. Nobody needed to be inflicted
with hers as well.

Already strained from the events of the night, the fighting spirit of the Elves had been broken. She could see it in
their faces. Calondir, Linwe, Ferion and all the others were
the walking wounded, the expression in their eyes heartsick.

*This whole nightmare leaves the Wyr in an even more
awkward position,* Dragos told Pia telepathically just before

she had walked away. *If the Elves themselves can't face the reality of fighting their own kin or possibly having to cut down an obviously sick Elven child that attacks them, they certainly aren't going to be able to handle it if the Wyr go alone into battle. When Calondir and I talked, he asked for my oath that we work in partnership on this, and I gave it to him. At the moment our goddamn hands are tied.*

They're in a terrible position, Pia said as she wiped her eyes. *I don't know how they can endure this. Something has to be done to break that maniac's hold.*

If I could locate Gaeleval, I might be able to stop him, but he has his army wrapped around him like a shield, Dragos said, his voice tense with frustration. *I can't just go hunting for him on my own. If the Wyr can't go alone into battle, I certainly can't kill any more Elves. Whatever we decide to do, Calondir and I have to stay united and do it together. Either that or we run the risk of becoming even worse enemies than we were before.*

Pia picked up her pace, reconnected with her guards and went back to the passageway with them to help construct a quick, rough camp along with the rest of the Wyr. They were basically water- and wind-resistant pup tents to give people a chance to shelter from the weather.

As the temperature turned bitter, more and more Elves joined them in tight silence, setting up their own shelters as near as they dared to the heat. They came just close enough for the fire to stave off the worst of the bitter night. Even though the fire had quickly melted the snow around in its immediate area until patches of grass showed, nobody wanted to get too close to that magical blaze. Thankfully, the screaming had stopped. There had been enough healers and healing potion to help the burn victims.

After the shelters were constructed, campfires were set to heat water for hot coffee and tea. Nobody wanted to try to use any part of the magical fire. Soon there came the smell of cooking food.

"We have to do something," James muttered. Those who had crossed over in their Wyr forms had since changed

back into their human forms to make use of their opposable thumbs and help set up camp. "We can't all just fucking sit here."

"You know better than that," Eva said. "More than half an army's time is spent waiting around. Take advantage of the downtime while we've got it. I expect we'll see action soon enough."

The group had gathered around their own campfire. Linwe had left them to wait for word and grieve with a few friends.

Looking spooked, Andrea said, "In the meantime, nobody better go to sleep, or that bastard might add more soldiers to his ranks."

Pia lifted her head. She was sitting on a sawed-off log, cradling a cup of tea in cold fingers as she stared into their fire and generally felt useless. Unused to wearing any kind of armor, no matter how lightweight, the molded leather plates had quickly come to feel heavy and restrictive, and she had relished the opportunity to loosen straps until the chest plate and the leg pieces simply hung in place. She would have removed them completely except that they helped to keep her warm.

She said, "If Dragos could break the enthrallment on the Elves, I bet he has the ability to cast protections on the camp. Besides, everybody is on guard now, and we have other magic users. Gaeleval won't catch people by surprise again."

"Truth," Miguel said. "If they're targeted right, aversion spells can work for more things than just physical weapons. But nobody should go to sleep until we get word that we have a plan of defense in place."

That plan better be set in place quickly, Pia thought, as she looked around at the other campfires. The Elves had been through more than enough. They were no longer juiced on adrenaline, and they were burdened by grief. They needed to rest and recover their motivation. She probably had less experience than almost anyone present, but she thought Calondir should think up something to do to help inspire his people.

Meanwhile, the Wyr had worked hard to reach South Carolina fast in response to Dragos's call. While they were fresher than the Elves and more battle ready, they could still use a few hour's downtime, and as Dragos had said, they couldn't go alone into any fight.

"Nothing's going to happen this evening," she said, surprising herself with the confidence she heard in her own voice. Everybody turned to look at her, and suddenly self-conscious, she shrugged. "I'm being logical," she told them. "I'm not offering you any kind of inside scoop. I don't think we've got a battle in us right now, not with the reality of what's waiting for us at the bottom of that bluff. Not unless Gaeleval does something else to provoke us or attacks us first."

Eva made a face. She said, "Another truth."

Not long after that, some second sense made Pia look up, and she saw Dragos striding toward their camp. Even though he was in his human form again, Elves still shied away from him or averted their eyes. Other than one quick, piercing look around, he ignored everybody else and focused on her.

The others stood as he reached their campfire. "Relax," he told them. He looked at Miguel. "Except you. Go report to Rune. Carling has agreed to coordinate the magic users on setting up defenses for the night."

Miguel nodded and slipped away. "Does that mean you will get the chance to rest tonight?" Pia asked as he bent to give her a swift, hard kiss. She relished the heat that poured off his skin.

"That remains to be seen," he said. "Carling thinks that our people can maintain an effective defense if Gaeleval tries something. He may be too overextended to do anything. He may not. If he does try something, the aversion spells they're going to cast over the camp may hold. They may not. This is all experimental."

"Have you had a chance to eat anything?" She stood.

"I had a couple sandwiches." He looked at her cup of tea and the dark slash of his eyebrows came together.

"I haven't had much of an appetite since I looked in the valley," she said. "Linwe gave me some wayfarer bread and I have more protein bars in the tent that I can nibble on when I get hungry. Don't fuss."

He gave her a hard look, his mouth held in a severe line. "It is too cold for you."

She said drily, "Well, not right here, it isn't. And the armor kept me warm enough earlier."

"I want to know why somebody hasn't found you a cloak by now. "

"Because I haven't asked anybody to," she said, exasperated.

He looked around at all the others with his jaw set.

Eva said to her unit, "Move."

As they scattered, Pia shook her head. "You didn't need to do that," she told her mate. "They worked hard to set up camp and they earned the right to relax for a bit. Besides, I am quite capable of looking after my own needs."

He didn't bother to reply. Instead he looked at the collection of tents. "Is one of these ours?"

"Yes." She pointed to the largest one.

He walked over, flicked open the flap and looked inside. The frame was tall enough to sit in but not stand upright. The lightweight, wind- and rain-resistant tarps had been stretched over a simple A wooden frame, and the bottoms of the tarps had been buried in snow to insulate the inside of the tent from the wind.

More wood had been roughly planked, tied together and set inside to provide an insulating barrier to the snowy ground. Each of the psychos' packs carried an emergency thermal sleeping bag that weighed a fraction of a pound and could retain up to ninety percent of one's body heat. With shelter from the weather, and a barrier against the cold, wet ground, the tents weren't comfortable, but they were quick to construct from materials that were either portable or easily harvested from the surrounding area, and they were sturdy enough to withstand a strong wind or even a snowstorm.

Pia and Dragos's tent was the Hilton of basic survival tents. It had been built large enough to contain the dimensions of his massive frame, and inside, along with two packages of emergency thermal sleeping bags, there were two real wool blankets folded on the planks.

Pia had set her pack inside, along with her canteen of water, and her stash of wayfarer bread and soy protein bars, and her crossbow and belt filled with bolts. A small LED flashlight dangled from the top post of the A-frame.

"Good enough," Dragos grunted.

He clicked on the flashlight, shook out one of the blankets over the planks and crawled into the tent, tucking Pia's pack underneath his head as a pillow. As soon as he was settled into place, he beckoned her with one outstretched hand, and she crawled inside too, tucking the flap shut behind her and trying to take care not to jab him too much with her elbows or knees.

When she was sitting beside him, she worked on getting the loosened armor off. He sat to help her, pulling the chest and back plates away while she wiggled out of the leg pieces. He threw off so much body heat that the interior of the tent was already warm by the time she was finished. She let out a deep sigh and sagged.

He lifted her hair gently and smoothed it over her shoulder. Then he put his warm, hard hands at the nape of her neck and began to massage her tired, sore muscles. Exhausted, she sagged further, leaning into his strength.

"It's so cold," she whispered. "And there are children out there."

"I know," he said. "I don't think they're aware of what is happening to them, if that's any consolation."

"It's not, much."

"I know," he said again, very low.

She twisted to face him. "You never had the chance to tell me what happened when you went to examine the enthralled Elves."

"When I removed the beguilement, three of them died," he said. He stroked his long, lean fingers through her hair.

"It was unavoidable, but still half of Calondir's advisors are calling for him to banish me from the Elven demesne again. Some bright soul put two and two together, and pointed out that I couldn't have responded so fast to the fire if I hadn't already broken their law and trespassed in their demesne again. That's why I can't go hunting Gaeleval on my own, and I can't kill any more Elves, at least not without an indisputable reason."

She groaned and dug the heels of her hands into her dry, tired eyes. "They can't banish you. They need us too much right now."

"I know." He paused. "Before I broke the beguilement, Gaeleval used the enthralled Elves as mouthpieces. I wanted to warn you in case he does that again here. It's pretty disturbing to watch."

She nodded as she took one of his hands in both of hers and held it in her lap. She stroked the broad back of his palm and laced her fingers through his. "Are you going to try to do the same thing here?"

"I don't know. Calondir asked what would happen if I did, and I told him that the death rate was going to be much higher. Gaeleval has controlled the ones in the valley for a lot longer than he did the ones in Lirithriel Wood. Aside from the fact that it will be harder to strip the beguilement from their identities, many of these Elves have sickened physically. It's possible his control is the only thing that still animates some of them." He shook his head, his mouth set in grim lines. "That's as far as we got. At that point he stopped the conversation."

It sounded like Dragos was describing zombie Elves. She shuddered. "Is there any real choice about trying to free them?"

"None at all. After we stop Gaeleval—and we *will* stop him—the beguilement will still need to be lifted from his victims. The ones who are too sick or weak will still die. It is possible though, that they may be able to save some of those who are sick, if proper medical attention is at hand. If we have to take the beguilement off in the middle of a

battle, we'll lose the ones that might otherwise have been saved."

The back of her nose prickled and her eyes grew damp.

He watched her face with a shadowed gaze. "It hurts to see things through your eyes sometimes," he said quietly.

She looked at him quickly. "Is it harder on you that I came?"

He took a deep breath. "I don't know. Maybe in some ways, yes. Gaeleval said through his mouthpieces that I'm vulnerable in ways I've never been before, and he's right. But in other ways, I'm stronger and better with you than without." He gave her a small smile. "And there's an added benefit. I don't have to miss you."

She couldn't smile back. "So I wasn't wrong to come?"

"No, Pia," he said. "I still don't like it that you're here, but you weren't wrong to come." He paused. "I suppose this is partnership."

"Yes," she said. "This is partnership."

She leaned forward then and kissed him, openmouthed, and he sank a hand underneath her hair to cup the back of her neck as he kissed her back. His breath ghosted over her as he licked the corner of her lips. "Dammit," he murmured. It was the barest thread of sound, yet it still carried the force of his frustration.

Her breasts felt heavy and full, and she throbbed with emptiness. "We could be really quiet," she breathed.

A corner of his sexy mouth lifted. "Well, I could be but I don't think you could. You tend to get a little noisy at times, lover. Not that I'm complaining in the slightest, as it speaks to your enthusiasm. I merely point out the fact."

She walked two fingers up his arm as she leaned forward. "We would just have to find a way to keep me muffled," she murmured against his ear. "Got any bright ideas?"

"You know I do," he told her. Then he lifted back his head to give her a serious look. "As long as you're sure. The conditions could hardly be any less ideal."

"I'm sure."

They were so lucky they could share stolen time together and draw comfort from each other in a warm, dry place. She was so incredibly lucky that she could relax against his inexhaustible strength and feel the two most luxurious things of all, love and safety. So many people would endure that night feeling neither love nor safety, and many of them might be in the valley. Dragos might not believe that the enthralled knew much about what was happening to them, but she wondered if something of their spirits knew. She had to wonder what Beluviel felt that night, or the children.

Dragos reached overhead and clicked off the flashlight, throwing their tent into darkness. A dim light from the camp-fires and the blazing passageway showed through the tarps. As her eyes adjusted, she saw the outline of his head and broad shoulders. He hugged her close, his big hands running down her back.

"My fingers are cold," she warned in a whisper.

"You know that doesn't matter." She could hear a smile in his murmur.

She gave into temptation and slipped her hands under his black silk sweater, and all the starch melted from her spine as she came in contact with his bare, hot skin. He sighed and shifted closer, slipping his hands under her own sweater to cup her breasts.

Are you warm enough? he asked, as he ran his fingers along the edge of her bra to the fastening at the back.

Mm. I'm plenty warm now. She reached over her head and pulled her sweater off as he unfastened her bra.

He bent his head, and she wondered what he saw, as he massaged her bare breasts gently. *I always thought I was a leg man,* he said, his voice filled with lazy sensuality. *Until I became acquainted with your truly outstanding breasts.*

Were they outstanding? She tucked her chin in and looked down at herself, but her body was just as shadowed as his was. She remarked, doubtfully, *I'm pretty sure they're just boobs.*

They're exquisite works of art, he told her. He pulled off

221

his own sweater and set it aside on top of hers. *And since you have the most remarkable legs I have ever seen, I get the best of both worlds.*

She smiled against the satin skin covering the hard muscles of his shoulder. She teased him about her changing body, partly in an effort to cover up how she occasionally felt self-conscious at her thickening waist and growing breasts, but he never left her in any doubt that he loved everything about how she looked, not only before the pregnancy started to show but at every stage since. She simply couldn't hold on to her self-consciousness for long.

Aren't you a lucky man, she said.

He bent his head further and licked along the swell of one breast. *I am a lucky man, and you know why? While I find everything about your body unutterably sexy, the most sexy thing of all is your mind. When you talk to me telepathically and I'm in a conference, sometimes I get a hard-on and I have to leave the room.*

Is that why you've shown up for a quickie when I thought you were busy? She scratched his flat, hard nipples lightly with the edge of her fingernails.

Of course. He hissed and grabbed her hands. *Dammit, woman, hurry up and get your jeans off.*

You say the prettiest things, she told him.

He exhaled a silent laugh as he helped her to wiggle out of her jeans. Then he tugged at the fastening of his fatigues. *Get over here,* he said. He coaxed her into sitting on his lap, facing him. *I'm not going to spend half the night pulling splinters out of your ass.*

Ooh, my hero, she crooned, full of sensuality and happiness. She raised her arms, lifting her hair off her neck as she arched her back, and she felt the breath leave him. He fitted his hands on her rib cage, and before she could stop him, he lifted her up to suckle at her nipples.

He must have forgotten the low tent ceiling. She cringed to avoid it, but she still smacked one of her raised elbows along with her head against the long pole that formed the top of the A-frame.

"Ow!"

"Shit," he snapped. He lowered her onto his lap immediately and hugged her.

She draped her arms around his neck and collapsed against him, dissolving into hiccups of laughter. *So much for trying to keep what we're doing quiet and private.*

"I'm sorry," he whispered, cupping the top of her head and rubbing at the spot where she had hit the pole.

Straddling him brought them into alignment, and the length of his cock pressed against her hypersensitive flesh. She lost her laughter as escalating hunger sank its claws deep into her flesh. "I'll let you make it up to me," she mouthed against his lips. At the same time she flexed her hips, rubbing herself along his hot, stiff penis.

"Gods, yes, let me make it up to you." He gripped her by the back of the neck, and as he kissed her hard and deep, he eased one hand between them and probed gently at the folds of her moist, sensitive skin until he found her clitoris.

A lightning bolt of pleasure jolted through her. As she moaned, he fisted his hand in her hair, held her in place and swallowed the sound with his mouth. She broke into a light sweat and started to shake as he stroked her, holding himself so tightly, the muscles in his chest and arms were rock hard.

She could feel the moisture of her arousal pouring out of her and coating his fingers. She rocked against his hand while she gripped his cock and fitted the thick, broad head against her entrance. *Come on, come on.*

Not yet, he said tensely in her head.

She growled, and he swallowed that sound too as he pierced her deeply with his hardened tongue, fucking her mouth with the same kind of rhythm he used as he stroked her. The lightning built, stronger and stronger, and she tried to twist, tried to impale herself on him, but he held her imprisoned with his fist in her hair and his hand between her legs. When she couldn't get what she wanted, she whined and clawed at his arms.

You're impossible. You make me crazy.

She didn't know if she just thought the words again, or if she actually said them telepathically. Her mind was glazed, her body filled with light. Just when she wanted to scream at him, the lightning peaked. She arched into her climax, gasping, and that was when he finally penetrated her. She was so ready for him by that point that his cock slid smooth as butter inside her, a liquid penetration that brought her pelvis hard against his and she peaked again, every muscle in her thighs shaking.

He clamped one arm around her hips and pumped up into her, once, twice, as he ground his mouth against hers. She gripped him with her inner muscles while the pleasure twisted her up and wrung her out, all their laughter and sexy talk burning away to rippling intensity.

Then it was his turn to make a sound, a quiet, shaken groan. She felt him climax deep inside of her, the outpouring of his pleasure beginning in the echoes of her own, and she wrapped her arms around him, holding him tightly as he rocked into her.

Breathing heavily, he loosened his grip in her hair at last. She pulled her mouth away from his to rest her head on his shoulder as he cradled her.

"My gods, you burn me up," he said against the skin of her neck. "I go up in flames every time."

"I do too," she whispered. Lucky, she was so, so lucky.

She felt limp as a dishrag as she draped on his chest, and he shook out one of the blankets to wrap it around her. She didn't even bother to move when he lay down on his back and tucked her pack behind his head; she just went down with him.

She wasn't exactly comfortable. Her pack felt rough and lumpy against her cheek, and she would probably have to move off of him soon. But she was so tired. She didn't think she could get more saturated with a sense of his presence or his vitality, and she didn't want to lose any shred of the comfort that it gave her.

Which made it even more of a pity that she couldn't take any of that comfort with her into sleep, or into her dreams.

═ SIXTEEN ═

The man had such compelling green eyes.

She didn't know how she could see the color when he sat in silhouette just outside their tent. Behind the man, the passageway blazed with black flames, while every living soul in the camp shone white as the stars. The man's outline was immaculately still.

"Won't you join me?" he asked gently. "Your soul has a light like no other. Together you and I could transform the world."

"You can't get in here," she told Amras Gaeleval. She peered out from underneath the flap at him. Somehow she had dragged her clothes on, but she didn't remember it. Dragos had to be in the tent with her. He was here the last time she looked. Cold sweat broke over her face. She did not dare take her eyes away from Gaeleval to check.

"No, I'm afraid I can't," the man said. "Your camp's defenses are not perfect although they are working somewhat. But I can ask you to come out here, Pia. That is what you like to call yourself, isn't it? Pia Giovanni."

Dread bled through her body. She gripped the edge of the tent flap tightly. "You can't compel me with that name."

"No, like all the Wyr, you have another Name, don't you? A true Name. Wouldn't you like to tell me what that is?"

She wanted to so badly. He was, after all, her closest and best-loved friend. Why, if she hadn't met Dragos first, he might even have become her mate. Maybe he could still become her mate. She and Dragos had, after all, only been together for seven months.

NO. Everything inside of her threw that concept out violently. She yanked her gaze away from him to look at the towering flames that shone so black they burned against her retinas.

She said coldly, "That was a mistake."

"I'm sorry you think so," Gaeleval said. "I could have meant it, you know. You are unlike anybody I have ever met. I believe you may be unique. I could even consider giving up all the others, if I could only have you."

She felt better once she looked at something other than him, and she realized that his eyes were a focus for his persuasion. Now if she could just find a way to get out of the dream. She had been so upset when she dreamed with Dragos that waking up had been easy.

"Do you know what I think is sad?" she heard herself asking.

"No, I don't. But I want you to tell me everything you think and feel."

She thought of the tall man she had seen so briefly in the apartment behind Beluviel, of his striking features and the autumnal spark of his chestnut hair, and how all the other Elves had looked to him. She thought of the sentinels, of even Aryal in her own abrasive, infuriating way, and how they all projected such unending strength.

"I think you must have been a good man once, a strong man," she said. "You were a Guardian of your people, and you were put in a position of trust and power. I know you're a gifted one, or you wouldn't have been able to do all that you've done."

As Gaeleval leaned forward, the small light from the

campfire fell on his beautiful face. He stared at her and whispered, "I have always done my duty."

Were there tears in his eyes? She didn't dare look too closely. He was too deadly.

"Calondir said you are an ancient and an adept," she said softly. "What makes me really sad is, I think you've become a monster, but I don't think you're evil. Numenlaur didn't honor the pact and cast out its God Machine, and the responsibility for that betrayal of trust lies on your Lord. That's not on you."

"Camthalion was convinced that we must be strong and hold to our original course," Gaeleval said. "All the other Elves had been mistaken, led astray by their lesser gods and inferior desires. Only Taliesin was worthy of grand purpose, and the god's message was clear in the shape of the crown that Camthalion held. So he convinced all the others to leave and he ordered the passageway barred so that they could never return."

"The God Machine was a crown?" she asked. If Camthalion had held a crown, how had Gaeleval gotten it? Had he taken it, or had Camthalion died? Was Gaeleval his heir? "You don't wear a crown."

His expression turned bittersweet. "I never wanted to rule," he said simply. "I only wanted to serve."

Her gaze fell to his hands. He was cupping something. He noticed the direction of her gaze and held open his fingers. The God Machine sat in his palms, an intensely burning black lotus of Power, eternally renewing itself. She had never seen anything so revolutionary. It was only a sliver of the god's Power yet it held an essence so pure it could birth solar systems and burn down empires. It was a piece of the engine that drove the universe.

The Machine no longer looked like a crown. It had taken another physical form that spilled out between Gaeleval's fingers. It took a moment for her to recognize what it was. When she did, her chest throbbed with a ferocious ache.

He held a string of plain, wooden prayer beads.

However he had gotten the God Machine, Dragos had said that the more he used it, the more it would work on him and affect his mind. The beads looked worn. She imagined him fingering the string. Perhaps he had prayed for guidance.

And the longer Taliesin's item had been held in check, the greater the change it would bring into the world.

"What happened to you?" she whispered.

She had not expected him to answer, but then he did.

"I was summoned to the palace and when I arrived, I found everybody dead," Gaeleval said softly. "All the attendants. Camthalion's children, along with their mother. They had been kneeling in the throne room and their throats had been slit. Camthalion was still burning when I got there. He had poured oil over his head and set himself on fire."

"My God," she breathed.

"When I looked for the crown, it had vanished. These were on the floor at Camthalion's feet." He looked down at the string of beads as he fingered them. "As soon as I saw them I knew they were meant for me. When I took them, I understood that Numenlaur could not continue the way it was. The Elves had been torn apart by ambition and war, and they had been scattered across the Earth on a lie. Camthalion was right, but he did not have the strength to see his vision through to the finish. Our time should have ended long ago. We just refused to see it. We must draw this age of brokenness to a close, unite together one last time and pass on."

So he intended both empire and destruction. He had such ruined nobility. Something tickled on her skin. She wiped her face, and only then did she realize that her cheeks had grown damp.

"Please, Amras," she said. "Please try to listen to me. No matter how much conviction or purpose you think you feel, you don't have to rule anybody. Camthalion was delusional, and now the Machine is affecting your mind too. It isn't too late for you, and it isn't too late for any of the others either. Let them go. Numenlaur has been cut off from

the rest of the world for too long, but we can help you adjust. Just give me those beads. Let me hold them for you for a little while."

"I am so tired of being a Guardian," he said, his voice worn and threadbare with age. His expression held a sadness that could break apart the world.

"You don't have to carry that burden any longer. You can let go and rest. Let me help you." She held out her hand.

If she could only get her hands on those beads for a few minutes. If she ran away from everyone and everything as far and as fast as she could go, she could fling them into the nearest ravine or river. It didn't matter where. Anywhere, anywhere, as long as the Machine was taken out of Gael-eval's hands and released.

There wasn't any way to stop the Machine, and she wouldn't try. She would let it go and it would work its way through the world, enacting the god's will according to its original purpose. She wouldn't even say anything to anybody. She could explain what had happened as soon as she got back.

She met Amras's gaze again. He gave her a small, grave smile and reached for her outstretched hand.

Dragos never knew what woke him.

It wasn't the influx of cold air into the tent. If he set his mind to it, he could sleep outside through a howling gale. It wasn't Pia shifting her weight off him or moving around. After sleeping in the same bed for seven months, they had grown used to each other's presence in every permutation and position imaginable.

For whatever reason, he stretched and opened his eyes.

The Power of the God Machine continued to blaze in the nearby passageway fire, in the stone that burned but never melted. He could also sense the interwoven defensive spells from the magic users in camp.

Pia was already dressed, her tangled hair knotted on

itself in a way that he never could understand. She put her hair up that way whenever she didn't have any other way to fasten it, and it always fell apart when he ran his fingers through it.

She knelt on the edge of their rough, makeshift floor, holding the flap open as she peered out. He couldn't see what held her attention. He yawned so widely, his jaws cracked.

"What are you looking at?" he asked, his voice gravelly from sleep.

She didn't respond to him, although he saw her lips move. She wiped her face. Was she crying? He sat up, angling his head to better look out the flap. That was when he heard her whisper, "Let me help you."

There was nobody outside. Nobody that Dragos could see, at any rate. There was only the wind and the fire, and the magic users' spells.

Along with the Power of the God Machine as Gaeleval wielded it.

Dragos roared and lunged at her, slamming his own Power down in a shield around her.

She shrieked, spun and kicked at him. "Stop it!"

He grabbed her shoulders and shook her, wild to yank her out of whatever she was experiencing. "You're dreaming," he said harshly. "Snap out of it."

"I know I was dreaming," she shouted. Her eyes swam with tears. She hit him in the chest with the back of her hand. "I almost had him. *Dammit*, why do you always assume that you've got to stomp in and save the day?"

He sat back on his heels, astonished by the violence in her reaction. "You were dreaming," he repeated. "And Gaeleval's using the Machine again. What did you mean, you *almost had him*?"

As they stared at each other, shouts came from the direction of the bluff. He hissed, grabbed her chin and looked deep into her eyes as he sent a spear of Power into her. Her back stiffened and she gritted her teeth, but evidently she recognized what he meant to do, for she bore

with it. As soon as he was convinced she wasn't controlled, he pulled out.

"Sorry," he muttered.

"Don't worry about it," she said, digging her thumb and forefinger into her eyes. "Just go."

The sound of running footsteps approached, along with a ripple of reaction through the camp. "Put your armor on," he told her. He rolled to the edge of the tent and planted his feet just outside the flap. Just before he shoved to his feet, she grabbed his arm and he paused.

"If you can, try not to kill him," she said quickly. She looked hard into his eyes. "Gaeleval is a victim too."

Bloody hell.

The reaction came closer as people shouted to each other. He gritted, "Pia, I don't know that we're going to have a choice."

"I know, *I know.* Just try." She searched his expression. "Trying is enough."

He nodded and expelled a breath. "I'll do my best."

"That's all I ask." She leaned over and kissed him quickly. "And I'm sorry too."

He hooked an arm around her shoulders and crushed her to him for an all-too-brief moment. Then he shoved out of the tent and rose to his feet.

Outside, the night had begun to pale, and the scene looked dirty and washed out. In contrast the light of the individual campfires, along with the larger fire still blazing in the passageway, looked garish and unsatisfying. The encampment had churned all the snow in the surrounding area to mud, and it had frozen into solid brown chunks of ice. If the temperature got over freezing that day, the ground would turn into a filthy soup.

Bayne walked toward him. Despite the sentinel's bulk, he was light on his feet and dodged nimbly around those who stood in his way. As soon as the gryphon laid eyes on him, Bayne said telepathically, *The Numenlaurians are starting to climb the bluff. Looks like Gaeleval has kept back the strongest and healthiest. He's sending in his battle*

fodder, and that includes the kids. There's too many to take prisoner, but I don't think any of us have the stomach to cut 'em down. They look bad, Chief.

Dragos wanted to spit fire. What a cluster fuck. Even if they took the enthralled Elves prisoner, they didn't have any place to hold them. *Get back to the bluff and issue a no-kill order,* he snapped. *If you can, focus on taking the kids and knock the rest of them back when they reach the top. Then if the falls kills anybody, it's on me.*

Bayne spun on his heel and loped away.

Dragos had to find Calondir. They could not continue to stay in this frozen state any longer. Whether Amras Gaeleval was a victim or not was beside the point. He was too dangerous, and he was causing too much damage. They had to stop him.

He strode to the heart of the Elven camp. "Get Calondir," he said to the first Elf that came toward him. The Elf took one wide-eyed look at him and spun away. Moments later, Calondir shoved out of a tent and hurried toward him, buckling on his sword as he approached and followed by Ferion and a few others.

Dragos told the Elf Lord in a preemptory tone, "Gaeleval slipped past our defenses. Somehow he got to Pia in a dream, and he might have gotten to others. Now he's sent Numenlaurians to scale the bluff. I've told my people to knock them back for now, but there's no more time to fuck around. We can't put this off any longer. We have to go after him, Calondir."

Calondir studied him with an inscrutable expression. Then the Elf Lord said abruptly, "I understand." He said to the others, "As heartsick as this makes all of us, we must find where he is keeping our people and concentrate our efforts on them. After that, we will help who we can of any Numenlaurians that survive."

"None of this is going to come easy," Dragos told him. "Bayne said Gaeleval's keeping the strongest back and sending out battle fodder to climb the bluff. Your people are the strongest. They're certainly the healthiest. That

means he's holding them close. They'll be wherever he is, because they are his best defense."

The hollows around Calondir's eyes grew deeper as his face tightened, but he nodded. "Above all else, we have to make him stop using the Machine. Will you allow me to ride with you once more, so that we can hunt him together?"

He ground his teeth. "Yes, of course, but we must do it now."

Calondir turned to Ferion. "Keep the fight defensive, and don't hesitate to do what you have to do to protect yourself."

"Yes, my lord," Ferion said. He said very low, eyes pleading, "But I would come with you."

"No, Ferion," Calondir said, just as quietly. "You are my heir. You know that we do not fight together."

Dragos had had enough. They were idiots if they hadn't already said everything they needed to say to each other before now. "Get out of the way," he said to those that hovered nearby. As soon as they were out of the way, he shifted and expanded. The dragon looked down at the Elf Lord. "Come."

Calondir leaped onto his back, and Dragos unfurled his wings. He took one moment to look over the encampment for one last glimpse of Pia. She was just outside their tent and tying on a cloak, and she paused as she caught sight of him. She looked calm.

She blew a kiss subtly, pressing the tips of her fingers to her lips and releasing them a few inches toward him.

The dragon smiled. Then he crouched and launched into the air. When he had cleared the trees, he wheeled and flew toward the Numenlaurian army in the valley.

Pia watched Dragos soar into the air. She fought the panicky compulsion to call out to him and try to coax him into returning. He wouldn't, nor should he. Talking to him now would only distract him from what he needed to do.

Eva and the psychos stood in a circle around her. She turned her attention to them. They watched her, ready for orders.

"I have no idea," she said irritably, unintentionally echoing what Dragos had said the night before. She looked at Hugh. "Except for you. You need to stay with me and be ready to shapeshift at a moment's notice. If Dragos or one of the sentinels gets hurt, and I tell you to take me to them, you will take me. No hesitation." Eva had started to protest, and Pia turned to stare the other woman down. "No arguments, no back talk."

Eva's face compressed. She looked ready to explode. "Jesus Christ and all his hairy-assed apostles," she hissed. "Hugh can only carry one person at a time." She turned to Johnny. "Find me another avian fighter who's strong enough to carry me, and make it snappy."

He looked from Eva to Pia, backed up a few steps and whirled to spring away.

Pia rubbed her face. Most of the camp had raced along the path to the bluff, and the noise level had increased from that direction. Shouts and curses echoed as sharp as gunshot reports against tree trunks. She pinched her nose. The sounds dug into her gut and strung out her nerves. It was even harder to listen to because she couldn't see what was happening.

"Crossbow," Eva said quietly.

She threw up her hands. *"Fuck you."*

Despite her reaction, she spun and reached into the tent for the crossbow and the bolts. Then she hesitated as she contemplated her pack. She hadn't been able to eat the night before and she hadn't eaten this morning either. Nerves might have her stomach tied in knots, but she also felt lightheaded and hollow.

She spat out another curse, snatched up her pack to find a protein bar, tore it open and jammed it into her mouth. With the way her luck had been going lately she was probably going to hork it all back up again, but she had to try to get some nutrition down.

When she turned around, Johnny jogged back on the path from the bluff. A large familiar figure ran beside him.

Graydon.

Another shock rippled through her as she caught sight of Graydon's expression. His face was set in such savage lines, she almost didn't recognize him. Pia broke through the circle and ran toward him, her heart in her throat. "Is everything all right?"

"I don't know rightly how to answer that, cupcake, because it's a hell of a mess." He hugged her tightly. "Numen-laurians are climbing the bluff, and we're shoving them back and trying to grab any kids that make it to the top. There's too many of them, and we're making plans to fall back. The High Lord's home might be burned, but the cliff is too steep to be scaled there, and that area is still the most defensible place around. Other than flying, the path is the only way you can get up there, and we can defend that in shifts." He cocked his head at her. "Heard you wanted to nail down a ride?"

She shook her head a little. "Only as a contingency. Can you be spared?"

"If you're needed," he said to her in a low voice as he squeezed her arm. "That will be the only thing that matters."

They exchanged a sober glance, then Pia turned to look at the others. She paused, struck by the frustration she saw in their faces. Miguel was still with the other magic users, but James, Andrea and Johnny all stood tensely, their gazes drifting in the direction of the bluff. Only Hugh and Eva kept their attention squarely fixed on her and Graydon.

Well, Eva had said most of them would not choose to make the switch with her into bodyguarding full time.

Graydon tapped her chin, and she looked at him. He was frowning. "We should be proactive and make the shift over to the cliff now. That way we'll be out of the way when the others fall back. Not only is it safer, it has a clear view of the valley. We can track events from up there."

She nodded. "Strike camp," she said to the others. "The

sooner you can haul our stuff up the path, the sooner you can be free to join the fighting." She said to Hugh, "Forget what I said earlier. Eva will stay with me, and Graydon can carry the both of us. You're free to do whatever you think is best."

Hugh said, "I'll help strike camp, then I'll come find you."

"Great." When she turned back to Graydon, he had already shifted. In his gryphon form, he was as big as an SUV, the tawny gold of his feathers and fur an oasis of warmth and color in the pallid cold day. He arched his graceful eagle's neck and fixed a keen gaze on her and Eva, who wasted no time and leaped up on his back.

Pia stared at Eva and Graydon in resignation. Oh man. She might have known that sooner or later she was going to have to ride on somebody's back without a seatbelt. Eva held out a hand. As soon as she took it, the other woman yanked her up.

"Giddyup, cowboy," Eva said, smacking Graydon on the shoulder.

"Wait, try to up easy . . ." Pia started to say, at the same time Graydon sprang into the air. *Shit!* She clamped her legs and held on to him as tightly as she could. Sitting behind her, Eva hooked an arm around her waist as he flew low over the trees.

Cold seared the skin on her hands and face and burned in her lungs. As unsettling as the passageway blaze had been, she had gotten used to the warmth that it threw into the surrounding area. She coughed and wheezed, struggling to adjust.

As soon as Graydon reached the bluff, he wheeled to follow the path as it wound up toward the burned shell of the building on the cliff. Pia forgot to worry about an unsettled stomach as, for the first time that morning, she caught sight of what happened below.

When they had first arrived, she had only taken one look into the valley before she had turned away. Now the sight struck her again like a blow.

Gaeleval's "army" was large enough that the valley floor

seemed to undulate with movement as Numenlaurians pushed forward to climb the bluff in a mindless wave. Working together, the Elves and the Wyr shoved away those who reached the top, striking them with the flat of their swords so that they fell back to the valley floor. They disappeared, trampled underfoot by more Numenlaurians who pressed forward to begin the climb.

As she watched, some of the Elves on the bluff lunged forward to grab at one of the smaller figures that reached the top. It kicked and fought as they dragged it away from the edge. They must be trying to save one of the children.

Over the brawling mass, the dragon flew, sleek and dangerous with his gigantic wings outspread. Calondir, the High Lord rode at the base of his neck, a bright, shining splinter of silver against the dragon's bronze hide. Dragos coasted a thermal, his triangular horned head lowered. He appeared to be searching for something. She guessed that they were hunting for Gaeleval.

Pia glanced back the way they had come, where the psychos had already grown small and antlike as they tore down pup tents. Beyond the camp, the inferno in the passageway towered above the trees.

Then the flames died down.

Just like that, from one moment to the next, the fire in the passageway disappeared as if it had never existed.

What did that mean? Had Gaeleval finally reached the limit of what he could do?

Even as she wondered, a hurricane of wind howled through the valley.

Out of nowhere, a colossal force slammed into them. Graydon coughed and clawed at the air as he struggled to remain upright. Pia screamed, clutching him with both arms and legs, as Eva grunted and slid down his back.

The wind was vicious, like a living creature. It tore at her hold on Graydon and raked at the skin of her face. Between her legs, she felt the gryphon's powerful body straining against a force that literally shoved him sideways. The ground tilted and raced up to meet them.

As Linwe had said, the most Powerful among the Elves could take an affinity to air and create a storm the size of Hurricane Rita.

And those ancients who were especially gifted had an affinity to more than one element that tended to be compatible with each other.

Like fire and air. That sort of thing.

Ancient and adept, Gaeleval was nothing if not gifted.

At the last moment, Graydon managed to yank up straight enough so that he took the brunt of the impact with the ground. He plowed into the rocky path, and as he struck, the landing knocked both Eva and Pia off his back.

It could be worse, it could be worse, it could be worse, Pia chanted in her head, even as she tumbled head over heels. She struck the trunk of a tree bruisingly along her left shoulder. It knocked the breath out of her, and her arm went numb. Cursing, Eva skidded on the ground beside her.

It could be worse.

Graydon had been cautious. He had flown low over the path. They hadn't been that high off the ground.

Not like Dragos and Calondir.

Pia dragged air back into her aching lungs and screamed again as she scrambled onto her hands and knees. She raked the sky with a frantic gaze.

A rotation of air had formed around the dragon, a visible dark funnel cloud constructed with hurricane force winds. Dragos's long body stretched, tail lashing as he fought to gain purchase.

Elsewhere, the gale had flattened everyone else. The bluff was cleared of any climbing Numenlaurians. Elven and Wyr fighters at the top of the bluff were crawling away from the edge. Sharp cracks of sound, like the percussion of modern artillery, sounded as trees snapped at the trunk.

Graydon lunged for Pia and covered her with his massive lion's body.

Are you all right? he asked telepathically.

Yes. She grabbed for Eva's arm and dragged the other

woman underneath the gryphon's protection. *Are you? Can you fly?*

Not in this, cupcake. None of us can get off the ground and hope to stay aloft.

She could feel Graydon's lungs working like bellows and the tension in his muscles as the gale threatened to send him crashing into the trees. On the high ground of the path, they were exposed to the worst of the wind that howled with an eerie sound like a thousand banshees. He crouched lower over the two women, his huge claws digging into the rocky ground for purchase.

Eyes streaming with tears, her terrified gaze went back to Dragos. This gods-damned gale threatened to flatten Graydon while he was on the ground. She couldn't imagine how Dragos had managed to stay in the air.

Even as she wondered, the funnel cloud took hold of the dragon and spun him in a circle.

A gleaming sliver of silver fell from his back. The dragon lunged to grab at it and missed. The bright silver streaked toward the earth like the fall of a god's tear.

Calondir.

She saw the very moment Dragos lost control. It looked as if an invisible hand lifted him up and flipped him over so that he turned completely upside down. He twisted in midair, like a gigantic cat trying to land on its feet.

One of his massive, powerful wings snapped like a twig. Suddenly he plunged downward in an escalating spiral.

Then the sound of the dragon's body as it struck the valley floor rolled through the air like thunder.

⇒ SEVENTEEN ⇐

No, nothing did shine forever.

Everything, even the universe itself, would end eventually.

The wind died down as suddenly as it had sprung up. It was no longer needed.

Dragos sprawled on the valley floor. Calondir lay nearby. The Elf Lord's head angled toward him, one arm flung out. The fingers of his hand curled over his palm as if he cupped something immeasurably precious. His face appeared young and peaceful, wiped clean of grief and stress. He looked like he had fallen asleep.

Dragos tried to move, and jagged pain tore through him. He felt as if someone had embedded shards of glass throughout his body. Mentally he assessed the damage. Broken neck and back, shattered ribs, and one broken wing.

It would take a lot more than a fall like that to kill him.

It would probably take all of the enthralled Elves who gathered around to gaze at him with empty eyes. He flexed the talons of one paw, but he lacked the ability to lift his front leg. His ribs had punctured one of his lungs, and he couldn't draw in a deep enough breath to spit fire. He needed

time to recover, time to whisper a beguilement to combat Gaeleval's control over the Elves that drew close. Time that he didn't have.

Beluviel walked into his line of sight. She was filthy and wore a torn, silken nightgown, and she carried a sword encrusted with dried blood. Barefoot, she left tracks of bright red in the snow, and long, tangled dark hair fell about her blank face like a shroud.

She knelt on one knee beside his head. "You should have listened to me when I warned you, Beast," she said. "I really am the Bringer of the End of Days." She stroked his snout gently, then braced one hand on him while she raised the sword over her head, angling the sharp tip toward one of his eyes.

A mountain fell out of the sky, and agony exploded as pieces of it landed on him. A second later, his mind processed what he had actually seen and spat out the information.

Graydon had plummeted with killing speed, shapeshifting into his human form even as he slammed into Beluviel and knocked her away from Dragos's head. The tip of her sword sliced the corner of Dragos's eyelid as it flew out of her hand. Pia and Eva, who had been riding on the gryphon's back, tumbled onto Dragos in an uncontrolled tangle of arms and legs.

A steaming trickle of blood from the cut slid down the side of his face. More agony, as Eva unceremoniously rolled off of him and leaped to the ground, drawing both swords that had been strapped to her back. She lunged to engage the Elves that crowded close, her dark features lit with ferocity.

Pia scrambled over the mound of his shoulder and slithered on her stomach headfirst to land in an awkward heap on the ground just under his chin. She wore her armor, he noticed with satisfaction, and she carried her crossbow slung over one shoulder along with a belt of bolts.

Dragging herself to her knees, she screamed at him, "Where are you hurt?"

He coughed, and that was agonizing too. He told her telepathically, *Neck, back, ribs, wing.*

"Goddammit," she said. "The only other two times I did this there was an actual wound."

What did she mean, the other two times? She had healed him once when they had run from the Goblin army. Who else had she healed?

I am actually wounded, he told her, bemused.

"That's not what I meant," she snarled. "I meant the wounds were on the surface and visible."

She looked and sounded demented. She yanked a crossbow bolt out of the belt and raked the tip of it down one of her forearms, from elbow to wrist. Blood and Power poured from the deep cut. Then she turned and jammed her entire arm into his mouth.

He gagged as her elbow hit the back of his tongue. *I am overwhelmed by your bedside manner.*

She glared at him, wild-eyed. "You're not in a bed, and it's all I can think of to do, *SO JUST SUCK IT UP, BABY.*"

It hurt too much to laugh. Besides, if he did he was afraid one of his long, razor sharp teeth would slice into her delicate flesh. As wetness trickled into his mouth, more mountains fell out of the sky to batter the ground around him.

The gryphons called to each other in their wild eagle voices as they lunged and struck at Gaeleval's army. Rune's mate Carling ran over to kneel on the other side of Dragos's head. The Vampyre wore a spell of protection against the light of day like an invisible cloak. She chanted one long, continuous incantation. As the words spilled from her mouth, hieroglyphs of Power hung in the air and glowed like lava in his mind's eye.

Others arrived. An enormous black panther coughed a hoarse scream as it leaped from the back of a pegasus that soared down. When the pegasus touched all four hooves to the ground, it transformed into a tall dark man who leaped to join the panther.

Then with a laugh Aryal winged into sight, and the

harpy whirled into action. She was at her most charming when she went into battle.

There was Grym too, hovering in the sky over all of the others, with his batlike wings and demonic face. Wait a minute, that couldn't be true. Grym had stayed behind in New York. This was the other gargoyle, from Pia's guards. Monroe. As Dragos watched, Monroe dove into the fight and then rose up again in the air almost immediately. In his arms he held a wriggling, filthy Elven child, and he wheeled to fly away.

The strange thing, Dragos noticed, was that Pia's blood didn't taste like blood. He had seen more than he had ever wanted to of her blood when she had been wounded last year. He certainly knew that it looked red enough, but the trickle that flowed down his throat did not have the heavy, rich taste of normal blood. Instead, it was like liquid moonlight.

Or maybe that was her Power flowing into his body. It cooled the hot agony that glazed his mind. He gasped as his shattered ribs eased back into place, and he was able to take in his first full breath since he had crashed. His neck fused into one long, sinuous unbroken line again, and his back straightened. The last thing to heal was his wing, partly because he had been lying on it. He rolled to pull it out from underneath his weight, and the bones and cartilage flared into seamless alignment. Rightness vibrated in his bones.

Most healing was just as messy as any wound or sickness, and healing spells and potions hurt like a bastard. *This* didn't. *This* was Pia gazing at him with eyes the color of midnight, as she laid cool fingers against his face and said, "I love you."

She was his best teacher, and the most Powerful force in his universe, and everything hinged on it, on her. Everything.

She watched him so worriedly. She still had her arm jammed in his mouth, which still made him want to laugh.

Her face was dirty and bruised, and the battle rang out all around them, but somehow the viciousness never touched them.

They existed somewhere else, somewhere sacred, apart from it all.

That was until Carling rapped on his snout with her knuckles. *Since you're getting better, you ought to know that my protection spell against the sun doesn't last as long as it used to,* said the witch. *I need to get out of the sun, and you need to take over this incantation. People are going to keep dying if we don't figure out how to make some headway against this.*

Dragos's attention snapped back to what was happening all around him.

Not ten feet away, Graydon had wrestled Beluviel to the ground. He held the Elven woman pinned from behind, his arms wrapped around her as he gripped her wrists. Her body strained convulsively to break his hold until the tendons in her arms and legs showed white like bone against her skin. All the while she stared blankly into space through the tangled curtain of her hair.

Even though violence churned all around them, Graydon talked to her. His voice was gentle as he said, "You're all right. You're going to be all right."

But while Monroe rescued children and Graydon held on to Beluviel, no one else had the luxury of picking just one person to save. He noticed that they tried to knock the Elves back without inflicting harm, but gradually they were both taking and inflicting damage as they were surrounded by an army that would not stop advancing.

Not until Gaeleval himself was stopped.

He focused on Carling's incantation. Analyzing, he realized that she was acting as a focal point for the other magic users. Her incantation took their individual spells and wove them together in a patchwork defense against Gaeleval and the God Machine.

They were holding together a bubble of shelter around the sentinels and other fighters who had managed to reach

him, while not twenty feet away, a hurricane force had picked up once again and battered against their shields. They were cut off from the rest of their troops, including Ferion and the other Wyr. Nobody else could fly in or out.

Even as he studied them, one of the magic users faltered and fell out of the pattern. Carling repaired the hole quickly by reweaving the other spells together, but Dragos could hear the strain in her voice. She wouldn't be able to hold the spells together for much longer, and when she lost control of the pattern, all the rest would fall apart.

Dragos gently pushed Pia's arm out of his mouth and shapeshifted, rolling onto his hands and knees. He straightened and put his hand on Pia's shoulder, squeezing, as he asked Carling, "Can you hold for a little while longer?"

Not far away, Rune glanced over his shoulder as he batted several Elves away with one wide swipe of his giant paw. Carling's face twisted but she nodded. The Vampyre wrapped her cloak tightly around her body and pulled the hood over her head, still chanting.

Pia said hoarsely, "I need to go to Calondir."

There was nothing anybody could do for Calondir, but he did not tell her that. Instead he let go of her shoulder and said, "Go."

Pia wobbled to her feet and, cradling her arm against her side, she limped toward the Elf Lord's still form. Eva noticed and pulled back from the fighting. As soon as those on either side of her filled the gap that she left, she jogged after Pia.

He could no longer act in partnership with a dead man. Freed from his oath to the High Lord, Dragos turned his attention back to the sole reason why he had come.

To Gaeleval, who couldn't seem to leave his mate alone, and who couldn't seem to go off and be a maniacal despot in a pocket of Other land somewhere else that had nothing to do with Dragos or the Wyr.

And Dragos could learn to give in sometimes, in some ways, but there really was only so far he could bend.

This was not going to be one of those times.

245

This was the time to make a real victim out of that son of a bitch.

Dragos cloaked himself with a spell so tight, not a mouse would have sensed his presence. Then he strode between Constantine and Aryal, into the howling gale, and he walked into the enthralled army.

As he hunted through the sea of hollowed eyes and empty faces, one by one he filtered everything out. Carling and the other magic users. The God Machine.

Everything but that last thread of Power, the blood of his prey.

When he located it, he did not try to push against it or fight it. Instead he followed it, tracing it back to its source.

Unlike Gaeleval, he did not have a God Machine to magnify his abilities. He needed to draw close to his target for what he meant to do.

When he had gotten close enough, he curled his own Power around that singular thread, and he began to whisper a beguilement that brought him into an almost perfect alignment with it. Then he slid his intention into it obliquely, as if by accident.

You are the bringer of the end of your days, he whispered. His enemy was very near, gathered behind a knot of strong Elven warriors. *This is the final note in your song. It was set in motion at your beginning. You have forgotten that Death himself is part of your whole. You have done your job well, and you can let go. Let go. What you wish for is here, your ending. Now you can fall into silence.*

Others like Gaeleval might share a talent for beguilement, but no one could beguile quite like the dragon, who could whisper death with such gentle purity that it marked the soul for which it was intended.

Even still, his prey could have fought him, and might even have had a chance against the beguilement if his survival instinct had been strong enough, except that Dragos used what Gaeleval wanted most against him.

The singular thread of Power dissolved. He almost imagined a sigh of relief as it dissipated.

His eardrums pounded as the howling gale died.

Gaeleval's army staggered to a halt.

Wyr shouted to each other and to him, while Ferion and others who had been left on the bluff raced toward them.

Several minutes later, searchers came upon Dragos standing over Amras Gaeleval, who was dead. The Elf sat in a lotus position, his empty hands in his lap. Like Calondir in the painting, Gaeleval looked as though he cupped something immeasurably precious.

Dragos stared at Gaeleval in silence for a long moment before he turned away.

Even as Pia and Eva had come close to the High Lord, Pia had known Calondir was gone.

Still, as she struggled to get past the restrictions of her leather armor and her stiff, sore body to kneel beside him, she knew she had to try. While Eva leaned over to shield her with her body, Pia slit her palm and let a few drops of her blood fall between the Elf Lord's parted lips. Of course nothing happened. Her blood could heal, but it couldn't bring back the dead.

She couldn't do anything else for him, so she sat with him until Ferion, Sidhiel, and others plunged into sight. When their faces broke apart into fresh grief, she held out her hand to Eva who helped hoist her to her feet. They walked away to give the Elves a measure of privacy.

After everything that had happened, the rest followed so fast it was disconcerting.

Dragos came to find her. "Gaeleval's dead," he told her. She merely nodded. She couldn't stop staring at the sea of catatonic people. He put his hands on her shoulders and tilted his head until he caught her attention. "Are you all right?"

She nodded and wiped at her eyes with the back of one hand. It was not quite a lie. "Did you find the prayer beads?"

He hesitated, then said, "There weren't any prayer beads, Pia."

She said dully, "I suppose that means the God Machine has turned into something else. I wonder where it has gone now."

Dragos took in a deep breath, then shook his head sharply. "We can talk about that later. Pia, listen to me. If I don't remove the beguilement soon, Gaeleval's entire army is going to die. When I do remove it, many of them will still die. The rest of this is going to be horrible and tedious. You are bruised all over, and you have to eat something. Now will you go home?"

"No," she said. She braced her aching back. "But I will eat something and go back to Lirithriel to help get in supplies of, well, everything. Medical supplies, food, clothing, shelter. Dragos, the survivors need to be sent back through the passageway as quickly as possible. It's too cold here. As many as you think might die when you take off the beguilement, we're going to lose more when the sun goes down."

He clenched his jaw, and she could see he hadn't had a chance to think that far ahead. "You're right," he said.

They parted with a quick, hard kiss.

Even though Carling kept deeply swaddled with her cloak, Rune was anxious to get her safely to shelter, either inside a building or under the cover of night. He flew Carling, Eva and Pia back through the passageway. They discovered that the time slippage between the Elven Other land and Lirithriel Wood had remained constant. Daytime in the Other land meant nighttime in South Carolina.

As soon as they cleared the passageway and the gryphon landed in the clearing, Carling drew back her hood and summoned Soren, the Demonkind Councillor and head of the Elder tribunal. Moments later, a cyclone whirled into the clearing and solidified into the tall figure of a white-haired Djinn with a roughly hewn face and starred eyes.

They told Soren quickly what had happened. He called in more Djinn to help. After they arrived, he blew away to inform the rest of the Elder tribunal. With dizzying swiftness, tribunal Peacekeepers began to arrive, along with doctors, other medical personnel, and all manner of supplies.

Pia had lost track a while ago of where her pack had gone. As soon as the first boxes of bottled water and emergency food supplies came in, she crammed an energy bar into her mouth, drank some water and threw herself into work. Eva never complained and never left her side, but worked alongside her, as did Rune and Carling. After a frantic explosion of activity, three large triage tents were set up and ready by the time the first of the injured Elves trickled through the passageway.

Pia was thrilled and relieved, and also incredibly saddened, when she saw that Beluviel was one of the first ones to come through. Graydon carried her close to his chest, his face drawn and jaw tight. The Elven woman, no longer the consort, was semiconscious and wrapped tightly in a cloak.

The trickle quickly became a deluge, and then word came back through the passageway along with the sick and injured. When the Lord of the Wyr had removed the last of the beguilement from the enthralled Elven army, over a third of the Numenlaurians had died. Everyone in the clearing fell into a stricken silence.

It was too much to take in. There were too many people coming over. There was too much to do. There was always some task right in front of her, until suddenly the next thing that stood in front of her was Dragos himself.

"Oh, hi," she said hoarsely. She had gone numb a long while back.

He looked at her grimly, his mouth set. Then he pulled her into his arms and said, "Enough."

Closing her eyes, she rested her head against his chest. She knew better than to argue with that tone of voice.

She was already half asleep when he picked her up in his arms, so she might have dreamed the next bit when Dragos called Soren over to him. Dragos said to the Djinn Councillor, "You have wanted to get me in your debt for some time. Now is your chance. Take us back to Cuelebre Tower, and I'll owe you a *small* favor."

Soren smiled, and his starred eyes turned calculating. "What a very precise bargain you offer."

"My jet is fueled and sitting on the tarmac at the Charleston airport," Dragos told him. "You are a convenience, not a necessity. *Small*, Soren."

Soren's smile widened. "You knew I couldn't resist."

"I was fairly certain," said Dragos.

Then a cyclone swept them up, and for the first time in too damn long, they went to bed together in their own bed. Pia was too tired to wash, and they were both filthy, and none of it mattered, because they were together, and they were home.

Dragos helped her strip out of her clothes and held the covers back for her as she crawled between the sheets. A few moments later he joined her. He pulled her into his arms, and she rested her head on his chest.

"The Freaky Deaky," she mumbled.

He lifted his head off the pillow to look at her. "The Freaky Deaky?"

"The Woo-Woo." She couldn't keep both eyes open at the same time, so she gave up and kept them closed. "You know, the Oracle's prophecy. It's all over now, right?"

He pressed his lips to her forehead. "Almost. There is one more thing to do."

Almost? What did that mean? What else needed to be done? And please God, could it wait until morning?

Before she could ask him, the questions melted into darkness and she plummeted deep into sleep.

D ragos made contact with Grym to let the sentinel know that he and Pia had returned. Telling the sentinel about what had happened in the Elven demesne could wait until later. It was too big of a story to share in a quick telepathic exchange.

As soon as Dragos was certain that Pia had fallen deeply asleep, he slid out of bed, dressed again in his dirty clothes and strode up a flight of stairs to the Tower's rooftop. The winter night was bitter cold, and lit with a massive spray of

colored lights. He could sense Soren's presence lingering, but he ignored the Djinn for now.

He reached into his pocket and pulled out the God Machine.

No longer a string of plain wooden prayer beads, the Machine looked like a perfect cut diamond, the largest and most sumptuous diamond Dragos had ever seen. It shone like a beacon in the darkness, the only true light in a world filled with uncertainty and shadows. Power burned in his hand, an eternal black lotus.

A perfect jewel, and Power.

They were his two most favorite things in the world, aside from Pia and the baby.

"No, you don't," he said to Taliesin's seductive Machine. "You cannot influence me that way."

He changed into the dragon, launched and flew out over the water. Past the New York harbor to open sea, and still further, flying strongly while the wind burned in his lungs and the stars overhead in the velvet night sky outshone everything on Earth.

Finally he reached a point where he was surrounded with nothing but dark ocean, sky and wind. The Djinn had wisely stayed back in New York, and he sensed no creature below the ocean's surface.

He threw the Machine as far as he could. The bright diamond/black lotus flashed in the night as it arced through the sky. It worked its magic on him even as he let it go and watched it fall. When it disappeared into the water, he yearned to dive after it.

But another lodestone drew him, the memory of Pia, soft and warm and sleeping in his bed, and his yearning for her was even stronger than the lure of the Machine. He didn't hesitate as he wheeled in the sky and flew back to the city, back home.

He landed on the roof and changed, more tired than he had been in a long time, and that was when the Djinn Soren chose to reappear, materializing in front of him in the

figure of that tall, white-haired man with a craggy face, and shining, starred eyes.

"Do not ask me for that favor right now," he growled at the Djinn.

"Are you sure?" asked Soren, with a bladelike smile. "It is a *small* favor, after all, quickly asked and granted, and then you will be debt free once more."

Dragos gritted his teeth at the bait the Djinn so adroitly dangled in front of him. He snapped, "Ask."

"Last year, my son Khalil told me the details of the Oracle's prophecy," Soren said. "He and I agreed that it posed some interesting questions."

Dragos's expression shuttered. He turned away from the Djinn's intensely curious gaze and stood with his hands on his hips, watching the New York skyline. "Careful, Soren. You get just one answer."

The Djinn walked over to stand by his side. "The prophecy talked about you along with the other primal Powers, not just as a beast but as Beast." Soren asked softly, "Why did you never cast a God Machine into the world?"

Dragos remained silent for a long time as he looked out over his city. New York was such a magnificent teeming brawl. As solitary as he was by nature, he still loved living right here, squarely immersed in the middle of all this rich, messy life.

He said, "I never felt the need."

≡ EIGHTEEN ≡

The next morning, the Sentinel Games resumed.

Pia was incredulous when she heard the news. Her head was under her pillow—her own pillow in her very own bed, rapture, joy, joy—and Dragos had just lifted up a corner of it to whisper good-bye to her. She grunted and lifted her head to peer at him, her rapture rudely interrupted.

He was showered, shaved and dressed in black jeans and a black T-shirt, and he looked so tired. He never looked tired. Their bedside clock read 6:42 A.M. She hooked her fingers into a belt loop of his jeans.

"Really?" she whined. "Nooo. I mean, *really*? Why?"

"Because when shit happens, it doesn't take a day off," he said. He sat on the edge of the bed and rubbed her back. "The relentless pace of the Games is as much a part of the weeding process as anything else. If someone doesn't like that, it's better that they back out now before they run into real trouble as a sentinel, trouble that won't slow down or go easy on them just because they're having a bad day."

Heh, yeah, she got that, but she didn't have to like it. "They didn't almost die," she whispered. "You did."

He bent his head and played with her fingers. She looked at the short black curl of his eyelashes against his cheeks, loving him so much that it twisted her into a pretzel. He said quietly, "That's all the more reason for me to be present."

She took in a quick breath, and suddenly she was wide-awake.

Because the problem is that people do talk.

As the Wyr had returned to New York throughout the night, word of Dragos's fall would have gotten around. It must have been clear to everyone that he had been critically injured. Not only did the Wyr demesne need to see proof that he was all right, but so did the other demesnes and countries throughout the world.

Hell, for that matter, so did Wall Street investors.

Remorse twinged. She sat up and said, "I'm sorry."

He gave her a hard hug. "Don't be," he said. "It's been a hellish goddamn week. After the Games are over tomorrow, you and I are spending the weekend in bed. In the meantime, you should eat and rest."

She smiled, a wry twist of the lips. "See you later."

He gave her a swift kiss and left.

An hour and fifteen minutes later, she had showered and dressed in jeans and a sweater. She had also put on makeup and eaten so many buckwheat pancakes that her stomach was full to bursting.

When she called for a driver, Eva and Hugh appeared. At her look of surprise, Eva gave her a small grin and told her, "Imma just keep turning up now like a bad penny."

Penny.

Pia doubled over and laughed uproariously, while the other two watched her with puzzled expressions. "I'll explain it someday," Pia told them. She cocked her head and smiled at Hugh. "It's good to see you. Are you here for the reason I hope you are?"

He returned her smile, his plain bony features creased with good humor. "Got my hat in hand and I'm looking for a job, if you'll have me."

"I'm delighted to have you," she told him. Not only did

she genuinely like Hugh, but he and Eva already knew how to work together. It was a good start.

Eva told her, "This kind of gig was too big a change of pace for the others, but no surprise there. Johnny's been waiting to have a word with you, though, if you can spare him a few minutes."

"All right," she said, resigned. "I need to get to the Garden, but I can take a few minutes right now."

"He's downstairs," Eva said. "I told him to grab a coffee at Starbucks." At her questioning look, the other woman added telepathically, *He don't know nuthin' about nuthin', Tink, but he's got questions.*

She nodded grimly and rode the elevator with Hugh and Eva down to the ground floor. Once they stepped into the Tower's main lobby, Eva said to Hugh, "Get a car and meet us out front."

"You got it," Hugh said. He disappeared, winding through the crowd at a deceptively sleepy pace.

Pia and Eva walked into Starbucks where Johnny sat at the window counter with an empty coffee cup in front of him. He hunched over his computer game. He looked up as Eva tapped him on the shoulder, then he switched off the game and shoved it into his back pocket as he stood.

Pia clasped her hands behind her back, twisting her fingers together hard as she gave him a smile. "Hey there," she said. "Thanks for everything you did on the trip. I'll want to tell the others in person later, myself, but for now, would you pass on my thanks to them too?"

"Sure, I'll tell them," Johnny said. It saddened her that he seemed ill at ease and uncertain. "Look, about that night? You know, when the shit hit the fan, and we were at the passageway where the Elves were fighting."

"I know which night you're talking about," she said quietly as she tensed.

He met her gaze shyly. "There for a while, I passed out, so I'm not sure what happened, but I know two things. I know I took a mean sumbitch wound. I even remember thinking, damn, I'm not gonna get over this one. Then when I woke

up, you and Evie were there. Now I've got no scar. I've got nothing but the memory of that sword going in, and—" He blinked rapidly as he looked from one to the other. "I don't know what you guys did or how you did it, but I wanted to say thank you."

Pia's face softened. She touched him on the shoulder. "We did what anybody would have done," she told him gently, as she chose her words with care. She'd gotten used to dancing around telling the whole truth. "We poured all the healing juice we could into you."

"That's just it," he said. "None of our healing potions were used."

She and Eva looked at each other. "I had healing potion in my pack," Pia said. That wasn't a lie either. She did carry a few, just in case.

"There's Hugh with the car," said Eva. "We gotta go, sport."

Eva and Johnny looked at each other. Moving as one, they stepped into a fierce hug. "It's not gonna be the same without you," he said, muffled.

"'Course it won't." She thumped him on the back. "You kids gonna have to worship my bitch-goddess self from afar."

He laughed, his arms loosening. "See you around, bitch."

"You know it." Eva slapped him on the cheek, an affectionate tap, and turned to Pia. "Ready, Tink."

She blew out a breath. "Let's go."

As they walked outside to the Cadillac idling at the curb, Eva said telepathically, *See, like I told you. He's confused and he don't really know anything.*

Pia didn't reply as she climbed into the backseat.

No, Johnny didn't know anything, she thought. But he knew enough to wonder about what really happened, and to question her story. Healing potion couldn't have healed him so completely, not that bad of a wound, and not without leaving a scar.

And people talk.

She told Hugh and Eva to wait outside, then she walked

256

into the Cuelebre supersuite at the Madison Square Arena. Dragos stood at the window that looked out over the arena. He had his head bent over a file while Kris talked to him. Both men turned as the door opened, and Dragos's eyebrows shot up in surprise. They lowered again immediately.

"What," he growled, "are you doing here?"

"I'm doing the same thing you are, so don't give me any lip about it," she said calmly. As he assessed her with a narrowed gaze, she walked over to kiss him. Then she looked out over the arena.

A smile hovered at the edges of his hard mouth as he bent his head again to read his file, and she could tell that he was really pleased. He murmured, "It's that whole partnership thing again, isn't it?"

"Yes," she said. She braced herself. "Dragos, in the spirit of partnership, we need to talk about something."

He lowered the file and brought his head up with a frown. "What'd I do this time?"

She shook her head at him. "Nothing. It's what I did."

"Kris," Dragos said without looking around at his assistant.

"Yeah, I got it," Kris said. "Go work somewhere else for a while."

As soon as the younger man left, Dragos threw his file on a chair and turned to her. "What happened?"

She told him about Johnny's injury and how she had healed him. When she had finished, she said, "He doesn't know what happened, but he's really puzzled."

"Ah," said Dragos. "That's the other healing you were talking about."

"What? When?"

The corners of his lips twitched. He told her, "When you stuck your elbow in my mouth."

She rubbed her temples. It wasn't even ten o'clock in the morning, and already a pressure headache was beginning to build behind her eyes.

"The thing is," she said, "Johnny's bound to talk about what happened. In fact, I'm sure he already has to his unit,

257

and who could blame him? Then there's what happened to you out on the battlefield, when, as you say, I stuck my elbow in your mouth. You were clearly down and not getting up on your own. People have got to know that I did something to heal you. And Dragos, you may not have noticed this, but I certainly have—people are starting to resent the fact that I haven't revealed my Wyr side."

His amusement had vaporized, leaving him taut with tension. He said, "Where are you going with all of this?"

She threw out her hand in a gesture of frustration. "I'm wondering if we should just throw my Wyr side out there and let the world know. I've thought before that this whole issue is like watching a slow-building train wreck—"

"No," he said. His gold eyes flared with incandescence. "We should not."

"I'm not sure that we're going to have any choice about it," she said.

"We have a choice, and I say no." His hands came down on her shoulders and he gripped her hard. "In fact," he said between his teeth, "I really want to forbid this. I want you to notice that I haven't."

She softened and rubbed his forearms. "I notice it, Dragos, and I'm very glad of it."

He studied her grimly, clearing thinking hard. "Speculation is not knowledge," he said. "Just like Johnny is confused about what happened to him, people cannot be sure about what happened in the valley. They don't know if you fed me healing potion, or if you threw a healing spell. Most of them were too far away. The only ones who were close by to see anything in detail are the sentinels."

"And Carling," she said. "And Quentin, and Alex, and Eva—and don't forget Hugh."

His dangerous gaze narrowed. "Eva."

"She won't say a word," Pia said hurriedly. "I believe that. She and Hugh came to work for me this morning. I only brought them up because they add to the total number of people who know something."

"Still, except for the gryphons, nobody knows anything

for sure," Dragos said. "And we should keep it that way. No, don't interrupt me—listen: I hear what you're saying. But in spite of everything that has happened, Pia, we've only seen a week go by, and you're suggesting we do something that we cannot take back once it is done. We haven't had time to consider all the consequences—especially for how it might affect the baby's life once the news gets out."

She sucked in a breath, her gaze turning stricken. "I hadn't even thought of that."

His fingers tightened. "People are going to speculate about you for the rest of your life. That's part of who you are now. Let them speculate about this too. It does no harm for them to think that you might be able to throw unusually effective healing spells."

"Yes." She sighed. He pulled her into his arms, and she rested her aching head on his chest. "Everything you said makes sense."

"Well, thank gods for that." He kissed her forehead. "I took Taliesin's Machine over the ocean last night and threw it in the water."

"*What*?" Her head snapped up so fast, she clipped him on the chin. "I thought you said you didn't see it!"

"Ouch!" He glowered at her and rubbed his chin. "You asked if I saw any prayer beads, and I hadn't. The Machine had taken the form of a perfect diamond. It was fucking gorgeous, Pia, and it was almost the size of my fist. So I put it in my pocket and cloaked it, and then we had a shitload of things to do, and when I knew that you were home, safe in bed, I threw it away."

She chewed her lip, her forehead wrinkled. "I don't suppose there was anything else to be done," she said at last.

"There wasn't. It can't be destroyed, and it was far too dangerous for us to hold on to. Eventually it will work its way back into the world. I just wanted you to know what I'd done."

She considered him for a long moment. Then she laid her head back on his chest. "You're going to make such a splendid husband."

His arms closed around her again, possessively. "I am, which is a good thing, because I'm the only husband you're ever going to get."

She closed her eyes, soaking up the sensation while she inhaled his masculine scent. "I can live with that."

The fighting in the arena that day was savage, and most of the contestants—except for Quentin again—got bloodied one way or another. Mostly Pia pretended to watch. She put on a good show, although more often than not her gaze rested on the Elven demesne's box that remained empty. At the end of the day, there were fourteen contestants left, including all five of the original sentinels. Again, Pia could tell that Dragos was pleased.

"They all want it," he said. "They're going to win through again."

She devoutly hoped that was a good thing, as she looked down on the top of Aryal's head.

The next day the rounds started early, and nobody could predict how long they would take. Pia joined Dragos at the window for the first half hour.

After she had put in a public appearance, she fled to one of the other rooms where she signed cards and wrapped presents for Beluviel and Linwe, and she wrote a letter of condolence to Ferion, the new High Lord.

Eva remained out by the window, and Dragos and Kris didn't even bother to pretend to work. They took turns calling out the name of the winner to Pia at the end of each fight.

Graydon.

Bayne.

Constantine.

Aryal.

Quentin.

At that, Pia had to sit down because her damn legs had turned shaky. She put her elbows on the table and her head in her hands. Quentin, who she knew disliked Dragos intensely. Aryal, who disliked her intensely.

And the gods knew, along with everybody else, how much they hated each other.

"What are we doing?" she whispered.

The last two names were almost an anticlimax. Almost, except compared to some of the others, they were a goddamn relief. Grym, quiet but always present, always reliable. And Alexander Elysias, the pegasus, who by all accounts was a peaceful man. She had a feeling they were going to need that peacefulness in the upcoming days.

She could hear the roar of the crowd through the sound system, and feel Dragos's charged energy moments before he strode into the room. He looked at her. "It's finally done. The Games are over. I'm going down to announce the new sentinels. Will you come?"

She stood immediately. "Of course."

He held out his hand to her, and she walked over to take it.

Somehow they would all have to figure out how to get along.

What are we doing? she thought. Why, we are doing what we must.

Dragos inclined his head to her.

She mouthed at him, "And then we get a weekend off."

He grinned, and together they strode out to their people.

═ NINETEEN ═

A couple of months later, a very large young man said to Pia, "Mom, you're just gonna have to trust me. I promise everything's going to be all right."

She bit back a smile. Now, where had she heard those words before? Like father, like son. "I trust you, baby," she told the young man as he lounged against the kitchen counter. "Of course everything's going to be all right."

She was in the middle of pouring birthday cake batter into a pan in a bright, airy kitchen with plenty of windows for natural light and a butcher-block island.

Then she stopped. Wait a minute. This wasn't the kitchen at the penthouse. Where the hell was she this time?

And why was she baking a birthday cake?

She set the batter bowl down carefully and turned to her son, who was killer gorgeous. He had to be nearly as tall as Dragos, broad shouldered and slim hipped, with long, strong legs encased in torn, faded jeans.

Every single one of the gods had to have been in a good mood when this boy was made. His features were not as rough-hewn as Dragos's, but the strong bone structure was

still there, and he had her dark violet eyes. A thatch of white blond hair tumbled down his forehead.

Killer. Gorgeous.

She felt punch-drunk. All she could think of was the robot from the old TV show *Lost in Space* whenever it waved its arms in alarm and shouted, "Danger, Will Robinson, danger."

She could see the future coming toward her, like the lights of an oncoming train. They couldn't take away his car keys. He had wings. They were going to have to institute a citywide curfew, maybe throughout the entire state. Eleven P.M. Lock up all your daughters, folks. No, better make the curfew ten P.M.

In the meantime, who was going to protect this beautiful boy from all the predators that were going to think he was their next tasty morsel? Oh geez, she and Dragos had their jobs cut out for them.

"I guess you learned this dream stuff a couple of months ago," she said. "Peanut, you are too precocious for your own good. You are a baby. You need to get back into my uterus and stay there for a while."

"I think my name is Liam," said the peanut. "At least I like it." He looked at her uncertainly. "Is that okay with you?"

Liam Cuelebre. Her eyes moistened. "It's more than okay. It's beautiful, and I love it. I love you. But why am I baking a birthday cake?"

He hooked a long finger into the batter and licked it. "Because it's my birthday, and I think I'm going to like cake. Don't worry, Mom. Everything is going to be fine. I'll make sure of it."

She pointed the spatula at him. "You are not supposed to say that to your mommy. Your mommy is supposed to say that to you."

The peanut gave her a sunny, innocent smile.

She plunged awake as the baby gave an especially robust kick, *pow*, right under her ribs, and as she put a hand over her swollen abdomen, she looked around at the deeply

shadowed room, disoriented. She was pretty sure she was awake, but this wasn't their bedroom in the penthouse either.

Dragos stretched out beside her on the bed, lying on his stomach, fast asleep. His long, powerful body was dark against the pale top sheet that had slipped to his waist, his broad shoulders relaxed. The king-sized bed—they couldn't sleep in anything but a king-sized bed—took up most of the room. A couple of dressers were against the wall, cosmetics strewn on one and cufflinks and a plain, masculine hairbrush on another. The door to a bathroom was half open, from which a dim night-light shone.

She rolled onto her side and peered over the edge of the bed. A pair of high-heeled ivory pumps lay on the floor, along with a tangled heap of a knee-length, pale chiffon maternity dress. It was her wedding dress from Target, and it had cost all of eighty-nine dollars.

Reality settled into place around her, and it looked a lot like a fat, contented cat.

That's right. They had gotten married that morning.

She held up her left hand to admire the simple, classic gold band that now nestled beside the outrageous, T. rex–sized diamond ring. Dragos had a gold band that matched hers. She grinned as she remembered how that particular conversation had gone.

It had been short and sweet, and to the point. They had been standing at a jewelry counter at Tiffany while an attendant showed them rings. Pia admired one particularly sleek, elegant set of his-and-hers wedding bands.

"But I collect jewelry," said Dragos with a frown. "I don't wear it."

She glanced at him. His frown was more bemusement than anything else. He stood very close to her, still dressed in a white shirt and dark suit from his day's work. He had removed his tie and unbuttoned the first couple of buttons on his shirt. His head was angled as he studied the rings in the black velvet tray, his gold eyes gleaming with acquisitive interest.

She recognized that look. She said telepathically to him, *We do not need this whole tray of rings.*

His gaze shifted to her. *Are you sure?*

I'm quite sure. Just beyond his shoulder, she caught sight of a woman standing some twenty feet away from them. The woman was model thin, sleek, intelligent-looking and immaculate. Her makeup, hair and polished nails were color coordinated, and her outfit and accessories hit around the ten-thousand mark. Thanks to Stanford, Pia was getting better at judging that sort of thing.

The woman stared fixedly at Dragos, not even bothering to disguise her naked hunger even though Pia stood right there with him, clearly pregnant, and together they were one of the world's most recognizable mated Wyr couples.

But neither mating nor marriage had necessarily anything to do with fidelity, and there would always be some sexual predator hoping to get her claws, even for a brief time, into the multibillionaire head of Cuelebre Enterprises.

None of them fazed Dragos for a moment. They were so unimportant to him that they didn't even register on his radar. Pia wished she could truly be that indifferent, but at best she could only fake it.

Pia turned her attention back to Dragos. She said, "Maybe you don't wear jewelry as a general rule, but you're going to wear this ring."

Amusement played at the edges of his hard, sexy mouth. "You know this because . . . ?"

"Because I get to have everything I want." And she wanted nothing more in that moment than to put her claim on him so that everybody could see it. Without bothering to lower her voice, she added, "And that includes having lots of fantastic sex whenever I like."

His smile deepened, and his eyes gleamed molten hot under lowered lids. "That you do." He bent his head to kiss her, while their attendant grinned and looked away.

Did she do it? Yes, yes, she did. While she sank one hand into Dragos's silken hair and tilted one foot up, she

held up her other hand behind his back, and she flipped up her middle finger as she kissed him. By the time they finished the kiss, the piranha had stalked off.

Dragos wore the ring.

And she *did* get everything she wanted.

She insisted that she plan the wedding. She told him that he could plan any kind of honeymoon he liked—as long as it was just as they had talked about, some kind of honeymoon where they were truly alone. No household staff, no sentinels, no psychos. No Stanford, no cell phones, no Kristoff "making this one exception" on some business emergency or other. Nobody but them and the peanut.

She could even cook if he wanted. Well, she amended that one pretty quickly. She could reheat any meat that somebody else had precooked for him, if all she had to do was to put a covered package in the oven and then leave the kitchen fast.

By that point, he was laughing at her, and she didn't blame him. But he agreed to take care of the honeymoon, and she got to plan the wedding of her dreams.

The justice of the peace came to the penthouse for a very simple ceremony. Pia wore the flirty maternity dress she had found at Target, which she loved, even though the sacrilege nearly put Stanford in the hospital. She felt fun and pretty, and she didn't worry for a minute about spilling anything down the front or ruining a piece of art that had cost a fortune. Dragos wore his best hand-stitched suit, with a silk shirt and platinum cuff links that, he informed her, were *not* jewelry but simply a necessary part of the suit ensemble.

Eva and Graydon stood as witnesses. Afterward, they had thirty people for breakfast, including the sentinels, Pia's friends from Elfie's, the other psychos, and Rune and Carling, who flew in from Miami. From Adriyel, Niniane and Tiago—well, Niniane, who also signed Tiago's name on the cards along with half a dozen *x*'s and *o*'s, and surrounded the signatures with a few hearts—sent a pile of handcrafted

presents, richly dyed textiles along with a stunning metal sculpture, all unique Dark Fae designs.

The only shadow that lay over her was knowing what a long, hard road to recovery lay in front of the Elves. Linwe had written her a small, sad note of thanks for all the gifts, and she passed on snippets of information. Beluviel had closed herself off from others and refused to speak of what happened. The Numenlaurian children that had survived were having difficulty with almost everything, and many of the adults were still in a vegetative state. Ferion never seemed to laugh any longer. He worked viciously long hours, and the Wood had not greened at all that spring.

Other than that sadness, Pia was happy, so happy. Nothing was hanging over her head. Dragos had promised her that if the sentinels didn't learn to get along, he was going to knock them around like bowling pins. The Freaky Deaky was over, the peanut was strong and growing fast, and she was head over heels in love with her new husband.

Even better, her husband was head over heels in love with her. She didn't have to have faith on that, or rely on the fact that they were mates. The evidence of how he felt lived in his eyes. He followed her with his gaze when she was across the room, frowned whenever she stepped away and watched for her return.

They ate from a sumptuous breakfast buffet and had a lightly flavored, lemon sponge wedding cake. Then for their honeymoon, they traveled by limousine upstate to Dragos's country estate just outside of Carthage.

Pia had fallen silent when she had looked at the gigantic mansion for the first time. Even though it was March and spring was fast approaching, the entire scene was blanketed in snow and looked like a winter wonderland. She could tell Dragos was watching her expression closely but she couldn't summon up any other reaction but a wide-eyed stare. She couldn't think of what to say.

The place was enormous. It had to have at least fifty rooms. If it went on the market, it would probably sell for

fifty million dollars and get a write-up in the *Wall Street Journal* or maybe the *New York Times*.

And she had offered to cook in there? She wasn't sure if she would be able to find the kitchen without a GPS.

She finally managed to say, "It's beautiful."

And it was, in a stunningly palatial, utterly uncomfortable, totally-not-what-she-had-envisioned-for-her-honeymoon way.

He rubbed her back, and when she was finally able to drag her gaze away from the sight, she found him biting back a smile. "We're not staying at the main house," he told her. "We're staying at the estate manager's house."

"Oh?" Her eyebrows rose hopefully.

"It has four bedrooms and four baths, and the family room has a fireplace along with a nice view of a private lake," he said. "That house is much cozier for a stay without any support staff, and I've already had the place stocked with food, along with recent releases in paperback and on DVD. There's Internet and the phones, but we can unplug the phones and choose not to get online, and the manager's already taken off for his own vacation. As soon as our limo driver leaves, there'll be no one else around but us for two hundred and fifty acres."

Somewhere in the middle of all that description, she began to smile. "That sounds like heaven," she confessed.

"It does, doesn't it?" He took a deep breath and let it out. She could almost see the longstanding tension that he carried coiled between his shoulders begin to drop away. "The last time I was in the manager's house was years ago. Let's go in and see what he's done with the place."

The limo took them on a well-plowed side drive to a charming house with a Cape Cod design. Beyond the house, a glimmer of the lake showed in a break between the trees. She said promptly, "I love it."

Dragos laughed. He would always be a hard-looking male, and he would always carry the blade of his personality in his face, but in that moment he looked happier than she had seen in a long time. He said, "Well, let's make sure the inside is all right. We can always leave and either stay

at the main house or go someplace else entirely, if you want to."

"I don't want to." She didn't wait for either Dragos or the driver to open her door. Instead she flung it open herself and hurried up the sidewalk. She hadn't wanted to change out of her fun dress for the trip, so she was careful with her high heels on the frigid pavement, even though it was immaculately clear of snow or ice. When she tried the handle, she found that the door was already unlocked.

Dragos followed at a slower pace, hands in his pockets. She waited just long enough for him to join her, then they went inside to explore the house, which was just as charming on the inside as it was on the outside.

There was large, comfortable furniture, sturdy enough for someone of Dragos's size to sprawl on comfortably, interesting prints and paintings, a kitchen filled with lots of windows, natural light and an island with a granite countertop, and a beautiful view of the lake from the family room. Their luggage had already been sent ahead. Everything was unpacked and waiting for them, along with more wedding cake and nonalcoholic champagne stored in the refrigerator.

She danced from room to room. The place was homey, warm and inviting, but she didn't feel like she and Dragos were intruding. They were all alone, and it couldn't be more perfect. She said, "I counted five TVs. There's one in each bedroom, and one in the family room. No wait, six—look, there's a little one here by the stove too!"

Dragos raised his eyebrows as he followed her into the kitchen. "Is this significant?"

"Yes," she sang out. "I want to turn on all the TVs, jump on the beds and raid the refrigerator."

He snagged her wrist as she pirouetted past him. "Stop for a few minutes and kiss your husband instead."

She did stop to stare at him. "Husband. What a strange word."

"It's my word now," he said.

She grinned. She might have known he would take

ownership of that as he took ownership of most things in his life. He yanked her, and she came up hard against his body, hands splayed on his chest as she stared up at him, wide-eyed. He tilted his head and looked down the length of her body, fingering the light, frothy material of her skirt. His breathing deepened, and she felt his erection press against her hip.

As always, just coming up against his body put her on a slow burn. She rubbed against his cock, watching as his lips pulled back in a silent hiss of reaction. "Can I coax you into jumping on some of the beds with me, big guy?"

"I'd rather eat something instead," he growled, his expression turning hard and hungry. As he kissed her, he bent to wrap an arm around her thighs and lift her up, and he carried her over to the island to perch her carefully on the edge of the counter.

Her slow burn escalated into a fast, hot flame. The peanut had put in a growth spurt over the last two months since January, and as a result, Dragos had become so very careful with her, it was driving her insane. She was as strong and healthy as a horse, just pregnant. Neither she nor the baby would break.

But he wouldn't listen, and it was only going to get worse as she grew bigger. "Someday, mister, you are not going to be able to use pregnancy as an excuse to slow me down," she panted against his gentle lips. "And I am going to ride you like a hungry cowgirl at her first rodeo."

He burst into a guffaw. Still laughing, he hugged her tightly. "You've been surprising me with the things you say ever since you left that note about the penny."

She clapped her hands over her ears. "My worst mistake ever. We should not talk about that penny any more, la la la."

He pulled her hands down. "We're never going to stop talking about it. That penny is one of my favorite memories."

Her mouth dropped open. "Liar! You only liked what came afterward. You *hated* having your penny stolen."

"True," he admitted. "But I loved the note you left me.

Maybe we could have found you with the Seven-Eleven security tape alone, but you really hanged yourself with that note."

Deciding that it was time to change the subject, she grumbled, "Just so you know, this granite countertop is cold to sit on, and it's putting a damper on my interest."

His attention shifted, just as she expected it would. "Well, we can't have that," he said. He swept her into his arms. "We'd better go eat in bed."

She settled against his chest with a happy sigh, stuck out a foot and admired one of her pretty wedding shoes as he carried her to the master bedroom. She could have walked. She could have insisted that she walked. But it was so much more fun when he exerted himself on her behalf.

In the bedroom, he eased her down onto the bed. She sat while he slipped her shoes off, first one then the other, and then he coaxed the dress over her head and unhooked her strapless bra until all she wore was a wisp of sheer panties.

"Wife," she said. "Husband."

His thoughtful look turned into a slight smile. "Mate," he said. "Partner."

He ran his fingers through her hair, freeing it from the loose topknot, and it tumbled about her shoulders. Again, without clothing, the changes to her body were even more pronounced, her breasts fuller and heavier, and the curve of her abdomen wider.

With a sigh, she stretched. "They're pretty words, but I wonder what they mean."

"With some patience and forgiveness, we'll find out," he said. "We'll teach each other."

She considered him from under lowered lids. "Do you think that dress made me look fat?"

For the merest moment outrage flashed across his face, and she almost giggled. Then he looked disgusted. "I can't believe you got me again."

"Patience and forgiveness," she reminded him.

"With a little discipline thrown in now and then, for good measure," he said. The late afternoon shadows were

271

deep across his hard, dark face as he looked at her, his humor darkening into intent. He yanked at his shirt buttons and jerked loose his tie.

She tried to laugh. It came out husky and breathless. "What—what kind of discipline?"

"The kind that comes with restraint," he said, his voice deepening.

Oh yay, he was going to tie her up? She loved that game. She almost clapped her hands, but then he stripped off his shirt and jacket, and the sight of his immense, muscled chest stole all of her IQ points again. Greedily she stroked her fingers over his hair-sprinkled skin, reveling in the taut, velvet-soft skin over iron muscles. They were so different from each other, so different, yet he pulled the deepest kind of responses out of her, and she wanted him all the time, so much so that it turned her inside out.

He eased her back down on the bed and came down beside her, his long, large body infinitely stronger than hers, a steady haven from all the ills that existed in the world.

His shadowed gold gaze flashed as he brought his mouth down to hers, touching her lips lightly. "I saw you standing in the middle of that forest fire with blood all over you, and the sight damn near pulled my heart out of my chest," he said roughly against her lips. "And when you were talking to Gaeleval in a fucking *dream*, the top of my head damn near came off. Pia, you might just make me one of the happiest men alive, if you don't kill me first."

There were times when it just wasn't possible to have a logical conversation. So instead of pointing out that none of those things were her fault, she said gently, "I'm sorry." She fingered his silken short hair and stroked his face. "I didn't mean to scare you."

"You always scare me, goddammit," he growled. "I've faced monsters and demons and nightmares that most people have never even heard of, but you have always scared me the most. We might make a list of pretty words that we can call each other or use for our relationship, but I don't

feel pretty things for you. I feel things for you that are volcanic and dangerous, and I'm not safe at the best of times."

She nestled her cheek against his bicep, watching his face as she listened. "What makes you think any of that might be bad?" she asked. "I didn't fall in love or mate with a safe man, because I didn't want to."

He fell silent and looked at her with narrowed eyes. "What are you talking about?"

She stroked his face. "Living this lifestyle with you goes against everything I have ever been taught. I had to fight my instincts every step of the way to get here, and the only way I had the courage to do that was because of you. Because you're the meanest, strongest, toughest son of a bitch I know, and if you decide to go after someone you are not going to stop until he's both sorry *and* dead, and I mean all of that as a total heartfelt compliment."

"I'll be sure to take it that way." He gave her a wry, sidelong look, but she could tell he was really listening.

She told him softly, "Sometimes the world is uncertain and it can be downright nasty, but I feel safe with you, and I trust you. And I do feel prettier things for you too—I love you, and I like you, and you make me laugh, and my God, the two of us generate so much heat together, somebody should slap a hazard warning on us."

His chest moved in a silent laugh. "Truth."

"But I think none of that would matter, if I couldn't feel safe." She tapped his nose until he lifted his head, and she could look deeply into his eyes. "That's my bedrock and my bottom line. I know that you will protect me and the peanut. I don't just have faith, and I don't hope that you will. I *know* it. Dragos, I don't think I knew what it felt like to be safe before I got together with you." She smiled sadly as she thought of Calondir and Beluviel's exquisite, soul-killing politeness toward each other then she eased them gently from her mind. "So all those volcanic and dangerous things you feel when you're around me? Bring 'em on, buddy. The absolute worst thing you could do is feel indifferent to me."

"That isn't ever going to happen," he whispered, circling her throat with one hand. "What I feel for you approaches the maniacal. There isn't a single shred of indifference in any part of what I feel for you."

"See why I'm such a happy girl?" she murmured. She wriggled against him, luxuriating in the sensation of his warm, bare chest. "Do we get to work on the discipline and restraint stuff now?"

"Absolutely," he whispered. "My discipline, my self-restraint."

Wait a minute. That wasn't how she thought this was going to go. She tried to sit up, but he wouldn't let her. Ooh, that was more like it.

He held her down by the neck, gently, gently, as he ran his hand along the sensitive curves and hollows of her body. Then he took her nipples in his mouth, one at a time, suckling at the plump, distended flesh, until flickers of invisible lightning danced across her body. Afterward, he nibbled his way all over her, biting at the tender flesh at the back of her knees, licking the base of her spine.

She couldn't lie still. Her legs shifted restlessly, as an urgent, empty pulse started between her legs. But he wouldn't touch her clitoris or come anywhere near the moist, fluted flesh of her sex. He touched her everywhere else instead, until she lost all self-control.

"Stop it," she panted. "Stop teasing me."

"No," he told her with a cruel smile, until she screamed in his face.

"Just fuck me, dammit!"

Then it was as if she had laid a whip across him, he reacted so violently. He reared back and yanked her up and around, until she was on her hands and knees, and she was there ahead of him, as she reached one hand between her legs and ripped her own panties off.

He froze for a moment, then muttered, "That's got to be one of the hottest things I've ever seen you do."

"Shut up," she sobbed, groping for his penis.

"Ease up, sugar," he whispered. "Let me do it."

She yanked a pillow to her and buried her face in it, trembling, as she felt his long, hard fingers probe at her tender, swollen flesh gently. He drew out more of her natural moisture, and there, there, she rocked against him as he rubbed the head of his cock against her, preparing her. Then he pressed into her, slick, hot and hard, hissing as she tightened her inner muscles around him. One final push and he was all the way home.

Her skin was damp, and she shivered all over. "You make me crazy," she whimpered, rocking back against him as she rubbed her teary face in the linen. She didn't know why making love often made her so weepy these days, unless it was her damn pregnancy hormones running amuck.

"Shh," he whispered. He lowered himself down so that he covered her as completely as possible as he rocked inside of her. He rubbed his whiskery cheek against her back and pressed his lips against her shoulder blade. "I love you."

She stilled and her head lifted. That was the second time he had said it, and instinctively, she knew that it wasn't going to be something he said very often. She tried to look at him over her shoulder, but her damn hair was everywhere, and she could only see when he brushed the mass of it to one side for her.

And there he was, looking into her eyes with a completely wide-open, unbarriered gaze as he moved inside of her. He was one of the hardest creatures she had ever met, and yet for her, he set all of his hardness aside. When her climax came, it didn't even feel physical it was so full of emotion.

I love you.

I love you, I love you.

After making love, they napped until the last of the afternoon melted away into evening.

When she woke up, she smiled as she curled her body along Dragos's warm body and remembered the details of the day.

And that strange, wonderful dream with the peanut!

Liam. She loved that name.

Her stomach growled. Maybe she would sneak out and raid the fridge after all. At nine months, she was nowhere near the size of full-term, human pregnancies, but she was definitely beginning to feel ungainly. She rocked a little to get some momentum going then rolled off the edge of the bed and onto her feet. She wanted another piece of that nomilicious lemon sponge cake.

Cake. Birthday.

She frowned.

Bam! The baby kicked again, harder than he had ever kicked before, and she doubled over as warm liquid gushed between her legs.

Bracing herself with one hand on the edge of the bed, she stared down at herself in bewilderment. Her legs, feet and the rug she was standing on were all soaked, and strangest of all, she felt more hugely swollen than she had ever felt before.

What had just happened?

She said, "Dragos?"

He took a deep breath and stretched. In a lazy, sleep gravelly voice, he asked, "What are you doing out of bed?"

She told him in a small voice, "I think I'm having the baby."

No matter how diffidently she said the words, they still rocketed through the room like a thunderclap. For one split second Dragos remained unmoving. Then he surged off the bed and stared at her, gold eyes blazing.

She stared back. She had never seen such a wild expression on his hard-edged face before.

"What did you just say?" he asked.

"My water just broke," she said.

"It can't do that," he told her. He sounded completely calm and looked entirely insane. "The baby isn't supposed to come for at least another year. He's too premature."

"Apparently he disagrees." A squeezing pain gripped

her, along with panic, and she sank to her knees. Oh God, oh God. She sobbed, "He told me his name is Liam."

Dragos crouched, and with an immense spring, he cleared the bed to land right beside her. Carefully he gathered her up in his arms and strode out of the room. "What do you mean, he told you his name was Liam?" he said. "He can't talk. He's a fetus. And there's no one around for fucking miles. No Wyr doctor, no nurse. No neighbors. *There's nobody here*, Pia."

She breathed through the vise that gripped her around the middle and said between her teeth, "Yeah, I got that."

He carried her to another bedroom, flipped the light on with his elbow and eased her gently down onto the bed. Then he leaned over her, stroking her hair back from her face. His hands were shaking. "I could call people and have them fly in," he said roughly. "But you need a hospital. I'll get you wrapped up and fly you out."

Finally the viselike grip in her abdomen eased and she sucked in a deep breath. "Wait a minute," she said, gripping him by the wrist. "We're panicking. We need to calm down and think about this." She looked down at herself and whimpered. "Why am I so big?"

He stared down at her, breathing heavily. Then he placed both his hands on her swollen belly and she gasped as he sent a spear of Power piercing into her. His gaze turned inward for a moment, and he said, "The baby's shapeshifted. He's in his human form now. I'm guessing he's around seven pounds."

She sagged back down against the pillows. "Oh, thank God."

"He feels strong and healthy." Dragos's gold eyes were red rimmed and worried. "Is that all right?"

Her mind whirled from one thought to the next. Since she had never expected to be able to come into her full Wyr form, she knew rather more about human babies than most Wyr did.

The baby was now in his human form, and she was nine months pregnant. Liam was much too small to be born as a

dragon baby, but in his human form, he appeared to be just right. And if she could give birth to him in his human form, it meant she didn't need to have a C-section. As long as he stayed in his human form he would be fine, until his dragon form had matured enough for him to maintain it independently.

Don't worry, Mom. Everything is going to be fine. I'll make sure of it.

"Seven pounds is a little on the small size, but for a human baby, it's good." Her own gaze dampened. "It's a really good size. It's normal. I think everything's going to be all right."

Dragos expelled a pent-up breath and hung his head. He stroked her belly with both hands. He still had not stopped shaking. "Okay. That's good. Do you want to get dressed before I take you to the hospital? I'll still wrap you in plenty of blankets."

She patted his shoulder as she calmed down. "We're not going to the hospital."

His head came up. "What?"

"I said we're not going to go to the hospital," she told him. She swung her legs over the side of the bed and pushed herself to a sitting position. Wow, oh wow, did she feel ungainly. How did human women go through an entire month like this? "I'm going to take a shower," she said. "And then I want to put on one of your T-shirts, and we're going to have the baby right here."

"Pia, no," he said.

"Dragos, yes," she told him. "Liam has surprised us, but he told me everything was going to be all right, and I believe him. Besides, I like it here. It's peaceful and quiet, and I want to look out at the lake."

"What do you mean, he told you, and you believe him?" Dragos roared, *"He's a fetus!"*

She pointed to the door. "All the big voices go outside now."

"PIA, GODDAMMIT!"

"I mean it, Dragos! It's my pregnancy and my body, and

I'm having the baby right here. Now, you can go outside and wait until it's done, and you've got two hundred and fifty acres that you can rip to shreds if you have to." She shook her finger at him. "But you do not come back inside until you can talk in a quiet voice. Do you hear me?"

He stared at her with his mouth open. Oh, she wished she had a photo of that look. Then his mouth snapped shut. "Okay," he said, and glory be, he sounded marginally calmer and much more quiet. "It's your pregnancy and your body, but you're my mate—my *wife*—and that's my son. I'm not going anywhere. Give me a few minutes to make a few phone calls, and then I'll help you with the shower. I don't want you to have one of those . . ." He rotated a hand at the wrist. ". . . One of those birthing spells . . ."

She raised her eyebrows. "Contractions?"

He snapped his fingers. ". . . Contractions, where you might run the risk of slipping and falling. You'll wait for me to get back, do you understand?"

She smiled. "Yes, I'll wait."

He rushed out of the room and leaped downstairs to the ground floor, and she did wait for him, sort of. She could hear him snorting and seething on the phone as she went into the bathroom off the master bedroom, where she washed her face and brushed her teeth. She had to put down the toilet lid and sit as she waited through another contraction. Was her hair all right? Yes, it was clean enough. She had washed it just that morning.

From the doorway of the bathroom, Dragos said, "Good gods, you're putting on makeup."

He hadn't bothered to get dressed yet. Even though she was in the middle of labor, his nude, muscled body was worth a moment of reverent silence.

"What?" she said, turning back to look at herself in the mirror and holding her lips stiff as she stroked on lipstick. "It's our son's birthday. I want to look nice."

"Makeup."

She noted that while he put emphasis on the word, he did not speak too loudly. She gave him a pointed look. "I

could hear what you did downstairs. How many phone calls did you make? I lost track at ten."

"Every one of those goddamn phone calls was necessary," he growled.

They were going to have to do something about his swearing, as little pitchers grew big ears. Actually, they were going to have to do something about her swearing too.

She shrugged. "My makeup is necessary too."

"Right."

Despite what he said, his hands were gentle and patient as he helped her into the shower. She had been planning to sluice off quickly from the neck down and was thankful for his help when another contraction hit in the middle of it. Gritting her teeth, she groaned and leaned on him, shaking, while warm water pattered against her back and swirled down her legs.

"Dr. Medina said to breathe into it," he whispered into her hair as he held her, rubbing her back. "Are you all right? Do you need to sit down?"

She shook her head silently, pressing her cheek against his damp, bare skin. She was glad he had stopped shouting. She didn't want to send him outside.

"Pia?" He angled his head, trying to look at her face. "Can you say something?"

"In a minute," she muttered. "I'm a little busy."

"Okay, darling," he said gently. "Take your time."

Two "I love yous" and one "darling." She smiled and decided she would start her own collection of priceless jewels, only hers would be memories of everything he had ever said to her.

The warm water seemed to help. As soon as the contraction was over with, she washed quickly. In a few minutes she was clean and dry, and wearing one of his T-shirts that fell down to her knees. He had taken a moment to throw on clothes too, dressing in worn, soft jeans and another T-shirt.

"How do I look?" she asked, her face tilted up to him.

For some reason the silly question seemed to hit him much harder than it should have. He took his time looking

at her, from her pinned-up hair and carefully made-up face to the voluminous T-shirt that gapped at the neck and arms. Then he gave her a slow smile that would never have the same kind of innocence in it that his son's smile had in the dream.

But this one smile of Dragos's had every bit as much of the brightness. Every bit as much, and it was all for her.

"You are the most beautiful thing in the world," he said deeply. "How would you like to go downstairs to the family room and look out at the lake?"

"I would really love that," she said, her face lighting up.

He carried her down the stairs and settled with her on the couch. She sat between his legs, with his arms wrapped around her. They looked out at the dark blue and silver moonlit lake.

In true keeping with the spirit of their honeymoon, Liam was born a short while later, a good fifteen minutes before the army of attendants, staff and medical personnel that Dragos had ordered arrived on the estate. Dr. Medina gave baby and mother a quick checkup and pronounced them both flawless.

Afterward, Dragos sent everybody away to stay at the main house. While his exhausted wife slept with her head in his lap, he cradled the miniscule miracle that was his son and watched the sun rise over the sparkling water.

He might be Powerful as shit and older than dirt, but no matter how many countless times he had seen the dawn before, somehow there had never been a newer, more perfect day.

Turn the page for a special preview of
the first book in a new series
by Thea Harrison

RISING
DARKNESS

Coming soon from Piatkus!

Terror was the color of crimson. It had a copper taste like arterial blood.

The criminal has escaped.

She stood beside her mate in a circle of seven. Their combined energies shone like a supernova. Dread darkened the group's colors. Their leader's grief and outrage was a smear of gray and black. The change in her mate was that of a warrior rousing from sleep. She felt her own energy resonate to his, ringing like strained crystal.

He has escaped and left our world. We have to stop him.

The circle said good-bye to their home. With power and arcane fire, their leader prepared a potion from which they drank to transform and travel to a strange world.

Her mate confronted his final moments with strength and courage. As his beautiful eyes closed, he vowed, *I will see you soon.*

They had fit together with such perfection. They had been born at the same moment and had journeyed together through life, contrast and confluence, two interlocking pieces that sustained and balanced each other. But no matter how connected they were in life, they each had to cross

that midnight bridge on their own. Her energy bled ribbons of bright red as she faced the final moments of the only life she had known.

She tried to reply but the poison had already disconnected her from her physical body. She sent him one last shining pulse of love and faith as darkness descended.

She had died such a long time ago.

Thousands of years ago.

Wait. No.

Mary flung out a hand and cracked her knuckles against something hard. Pain shot up her arm.

She surged upright. Shards of color surrounded her, like fractured pieces from the ruins of a chapel's stained-glass window. After several uncomprehending moments, she realized where she was. She was sprawled on her bed in a chaotic nest of comforter, pillows, clothes and scraps of material.

She wobbled where she sat. Her heart erupted into a congo drum medley then slowed to a more normal tempo. Her head, not so much. It pulsed with a steady throb of pain.

The bedside clock read six thirty A.M. For Christ's sake. She'd only gotten home five hours ago. Her ER shift had been twenty-six hours long. It had involved a five-car accident and two gunshot victims, one of whom, a seventeen-year-old single mother, had died.

Some people played golf in their downtime, or went hiking or took aerobic classes. She dreamed of glowing, rainbow-pulsing creatures that drank poison Kool-Aid in some kind of bizarre suicide pact. Was that better or worse than dreaming of the gunshot victims?

She thought of the dream-criminal the creatures had pursued. Sweat broke out as dread, mingled with a sense of unspeakable loss, ricocheted through her body with the intensity of a menopausal hot flash.

She sucked air into constricted lungs. Maybe she shouldn't try to answer that question right now.

Something stuck to her face. Her fingers quested across her skin. She pulled a scrap of cloth from her cheek and

stared at it. The cloth had a blue-and-green paisley design. A blurred memory surfaced, like the smear of color atop an oily roadside puddle. She had found the cloth a couple of days ago in a clearance bin at the fabric store, and she was planning to incorporate it into the pattern of her next quilt. She had been wound up from her overlong work shift when she had gotten home, so she had released some of the nervous energy by doing household chores. She had fallen asleep in the middle of folding laundry.

Adrenaline had destroyed any chance at getting back to sleep. She dragged herself off the rumpled bed and yanked at her wrinkled T-shirt and shorts. She attempted to finger-comb her hair, which crackled with electricity as she coaxed her fingers into blind alleys and dead ends. The shoulder-length tawny strands hinted at a mixed-race ancestry and were so thick and wavy they were layered by necessity. At present her hair seemed to have more energy than she did. She gave up trying to untangle the mess. It sprawled across her shoulders unconquered, a wild lion's mane.

Mary scooped up her house keys and sunglasses from the hall table, slipped on tennis shoes and grabbed a hooded sweatshirt. She was outside in the early warm spring morning in less than a minute. Bright sunshine stabbed at her before she slipped on her sunglasses.

She lived in an ivory tower near Witch Road. The ivory tower was a squat, crooked building in a wooded working-class neighborhood, located by the St. Joseph River in southeast Michigan. It was a shabby, unfashionable river dwelling, built almost a century ago, with a two-bedroom living area on the second floor over the garage that protected it from the river's periodic flooding. She had been renting it since her divorce five years ago.

The ivory had become dingy over the years, the aluminum siding loose at one corner. The outside concrete stairs to her dwelling were narrow and crooked. They were dangerous in an ice storm. Once, while she was at work, a heavy rain had turned to sleet. When she'd gotten home, she'd been forced to crawl up the icy stairs in order to get

inside. Still, the interior was warm, with old pine paneling and scarred but beautiful hardwood floors, and it had a brick-and-flagstone fireplace. The first time she had stepped inside, something seemed to flow over her, embracing her in an invisible hug. She fancied it was the spirit of the place, welcoming her. Despite its dirty condition and the many ways in which it was inconvenient, she had known she would live there the first time she'd seen it. Sometimes she wondered if she would die there.

For all its shabbiness the ivory tower embodied an ordinary yet powerful magic. In the view from the picture window, there was no sign of the street below or of the neighboring houses that dotted the dead-end road. It gave the generous illusion she was in a cabin in the woods, far away from anyone else. She could stare out the window for hours at the evergreens, oaks and sycamores, watching flurries of white snow swirling in a snowstorm, or shadows moving in the trees as daylight changed and faded.

Witch Road, as she had named it, was a nearby street in the same neighborhood, part of a loop she had mapped for a daily two-mile run. The route cut close by the nearby river and had gradually pulled her under its spell as she jogged it through the change of seasons.

Small houses were overpowered by tall, thick, deciduous trees whose bones were uncovered with the death of every year, from the ones with straight willowy lines to those that had a more arthritic beauty, with their gnarled joints and twisted limbs that shot in unexpected directions, ending in thousands of spidery-thin fingers grasping at air. The underbrush was secretive and tangled. Thick vines and fallen limbs discouraged trespass from outsiders. The trees met to whisper overhead in the ebb and flow of restless days, enclosing the narrow asphalt road in the summertime with a leafy green canopy.

She was too tired for her normal run. She walked the route instead.

The leafy canopy was fast returning with the warmer weather. On the other side of the green-edged lattice of tree

limbs, fluffy cumulous clouds traveled across the sky at such speed, they seemed to be running from some unseen menace. The trees shifted and rustled. Leaves and twigs, the detritus from the death of the forest last autumn and winter, danced in circles that followed her down the street.

The swirling circles whispered to each other in small voices.

She's not the one, stupid.

How do you know? She smells like blood.

She paused and turned to look behind her. What a thing to fantasize. She was imagining that, wasn't she? The only sounds in the silence were the murmurous trees, the distant report of a car door slamming, the sound of the wind tumbling sticks and leaves around like a child playing at jacks.

She shook her head, turned back around and resumed walking again.

You saw! She looked. Does that mean she heard us?

Normal people don't hear us.

She jerked to a halt and broke out in a fresh sweat.

I didn't just make that up.

I'm hearing voices.

I'm. Hearing. Voices.

An internal quake rattled her bones. She turned backward in a circle, staring around her with wide eyes. There was no one else close by. Down the street, two children with their school bags exploded out of the front door of a house.

A couple yards away twigs and pine needles tumbled in a tiny pagan dance.

Everything else had stopped. There was no wind, no lick of breeze against her skin. Even the trees overhead had gone silent, waiting.

There was nothing to cause that turbulence of air. It was wrong, impossible. The hair at the back of her neck raised and her teeth clenched. She stamped her foot at the dancing sticks and leaves, and hissed, "Stop it!"

The small voices burst into chatter.

Yes, she heard us. She did.

We must go!

As abruptly as they had started, the voices stopped. The leaves and twigs dropped to the ground.

Nothing else disturbed the stillness, just a few cars pulling out of driveways as people headed to work under the watchfulness of the looming forest, as some of the trees only tolerated the humans who had moved into their territory—

Where had that thought come from? Why would she think such a thing?

Panic clawed her. She was used to dreaming strange dreams. She'd done it her entire life. Hearing voices though, and seeing what she saw—seeing what she thought she just saw—that was psychosis.

She clamped down on that. No. She was just too tired. She wasn't fully awake yet. She was still half caught in a dream state where Escher's clock melted and stairways led on an endless loop to nowhere. Coffee would shake off this crazy fugue. She started back in the direction of her house, working to a lope as she rounded the corner.

Her ex-husband, Justin, stood on her deck at the bottom of the concrete stairs. His dark hair shone with glints of copper in the early morning sun, his narrow, clever face bisected by dark Ray-Ban sunglasses. He was dressed for the office in a functional yet elegant suit, the jacket unbuttoned in the unseasonal warmth of the spring morning.

She groaned and slowed as she saw him. Justin caught sight of her before she could pivot and jog away. Caught, she continued with obvious reluctance toward him and the house.

"Oh that's flattering," he said with a grin. "Good thing my ego is so preened and shiny. Good morning, and screw you too."

"You show up uninvited, you get what you get," Mary said. Her voice sounded rough. She cleared her throat. "For pity's sake, man. It's not even seven A.M. yet. I never talked to you this early when we lived together."

"Then why don't you answer your phone?" he said in exasperated reply. "If you'd pick up, I wouldn't have to stop by unannounced."

She squinted at him then jogged up the stairs to unlock the door as he followed. "Because it didn't ring."

"Is it even in the house?" he retorted. He peered past her at the riotous mess inside. "How can you tell? The hood of your car is cold but you weren't answering when I knocked. I was going to let myself in to make sure you were all right."

She sighed. "Don't make me regret giving you that key."

"You'll have to arm-wrestle me to get it back, and you know I cheat." Once inside, he looked at her again more closely. Something in his face changed, the humor dying away. "Are you okay? You look really pale."

"I'm fine." She removed her sunglasses and rubbed at her face. She could still feel creases on her cheek from the cloth she had slept on. The pounding in her head had gotten worse. She turned to walk to her kitchen and said over her shoulder, "I need coffee. Do you want a cup?"

"Yeah." Justin followed her. "Look, do me a favor. Make an appointment to see your doctor, okay?"

"What? No. I said I'm fine." Mary stopped in the middle of her kitchen and looked around in confusion. She knew exactly where she was but everything suddenly seemed alien.

She didn't belong here. Panic tried to clutch at her again, like a drowning victim being pulled underwater. She flung it off, shaking herself hard like a wet dog as she headed for the coffeepot.

"I don't think you're as fine as you say you are." Justin frowned at her.

"I just had a day from hell yesterday. My shift was twenty-six hours long. We had a multiple car accident and a couple of gunshot victims."

He shook his head. "That's rough. What happened?"

"The accident was a pileup on I-94. No fatalities. The shooting was a different story. Some girl found out her Baby Daddy had another Baby Mama. She borrowed her brother's nine millimeter and emptied the clip into them while they sat outside at Dairy Queen. Now she's in jail

facing murder charges. Baby Mama Two is dead and Baby Daddy is in ICU. He may or may not make it, and all the babies have been taken by child protective services, which, when you think about it, might be the best thing that's happened in their little lives."

Justin's voice turned hushed. "I heard about that on the news."

She yanked open a cupboard, pulled out the coffee and a filter. She said over her shoulder, "To top it all off, I got maybe four hours' sleep, so I look like shit. It's no big deal."

He sighed. "Look, I don't have time to argue with you. I've got twenty minutes to get to work—so just promise me you'll go get a checkup and shut up already."

She filled the coffeepot with water, poured it into the machine and started it. She slammed the pot onto the burner. "Seriously, Justin," she snapped. "Do I come over uninvited to your house and tell you and Tony what to do?"

"Honey, I'm sorry," he said in quick contrition. She startled as he put a gentle hand on her shoulder. "It's just—hell, even I know you're never supposed to talk to a woman about her weight but you've lost weight you couldn't afford to lose. You were always a little bit of a thing, the original five-foot-two-and-eyes-of-blue gal."

She gave him a grim smile as the pungent aroma of coffee filled the kitchen. "Don't start inflicting Dean Martin songs on me again at this time in the morning, or I swear I won't be responsible for my actions. I'll be sure to tell the police that when they arrive with the body bag."

He didn't smile back. Instead his handsome features took on a mulish expression. "I'm being serious here. You're not looking good, Mary. You're all bones and nerves. If you won't have a rational conversation about it, I'll have to make an appointment for you myself to go see Tony."

"The hell you will." Her smile turned to a glare.

He pulled out his cell phone, turned his back and ignored her. After a few moments he started to speak on the phone. He moved down the short hall to the living room.

Mary felt the urge to scream. Instead she blew air between her teeth, like steam escaping from a pressure cooker. She poured herself a cup of coffee and took it to the table. She shifted a stack of magazines and mail off a chair, which was when she discovered the cordless phone.

She clicked it on and listened. No dial tone. The battery had gone dead. She had a cell phone but she only used it for work, and Justin didn't have the number. She hung the phone to recharge and sat to put her elbows on the table, resting her forehead on the heels of her hands as she hunched over her coffee.

Her mind arrowed back to the dream. She was dreaming with more frequency and they were getting more vivid. This time the bodies of the seven in the circle were translucent. Ribbons of colored light had streamed from them, flowing and moving in the air as if the creatures were some kind of strange anemone. The poison had tasted bitter-sweet and smelled like cloves.

She had dreamed in color several times but she had never before dreamed a smell or a taste. Was that somehow connected to hearing voices and seeing impossible things?

She flinched as panic tried to grab hold again. Nope, don't go there right now. She pulled her hands down, stretched them in front of her and stared at her fingers. Slender and dexterous, they were an advantage in the OR, but they looked strange, as if they belonged to someone else.

Justin walked back into the kitchen with a brisk stride. He poured himself some coffee then came over to pat her on the back as he gulped hot liquid. "Tony moved some things around. He can see you this afternoon at three. And," he added, "I don't trust you to go on your own so I'm leaving the office early to take you myself."

"I was such a needy rabbit when I married you," she said. "But hey, pre-med plus law school equals the American Dream, right? Thank god those days are gone."

"What are you talking about, doctor girl?" Justin said. "What needy rabbit? You're the original Marlboro Man. Except for the cigarettes, the ten-gallon hat and the penis."

She raised an eyebrow at him.

"Well okay, you're quite a bit not like the Marlboro Man." He grinned. "But you've got this brooding silent hero thing going on, with a hint of something tragic in your past, except I know your past and it's as ordinary as dirt. It's very sexy. I'd always wanted to marry a doctor—and if you'd only had that penis . . ."

"Therapy has made you too cocky," she said.

"Which Tony appreciates," he told her.

She rolled her eyes. "Get out."

He sobered. "I'll be back this afternoon at two to pick you up. Be ready or I'll do the he-man thing and throw you over my shoulder."

"Quit being so damn patronizing. I'm not going." Her mug was empty. She stood and headed for the coffeepot.

"Whatever," Justin said, eyeing her. "I guess Tony isn't going to care if you haven't shaved your legs."

"For god's sake!" she exploded, turning on him. He scowled at her, looking as mutinous and adorable as a two-year-old. She tried to rein in her impatience. "Look, I appreciate your concern. It's sweet of you."

"Sweet." He snorted.

Her expression hardened. "But I'm warning you, I'm not putting up with your stubbornness and interference, and I am not going to go see Tony, of all people."

"But why not?"

"Because he's your partner and I socialize with him, dimwit! And today is my first day off in forever and I don't want to spend it in a doctor's waiting room," she snapped. "Besides, there's nothing wrong with me."

The lie reverberated in her throbbing head. She was cracked down to the middle to her foundation. Whatever her mysterious internal ailment was, it was getting worse. If she didn't figure out what was wrong she was going to break into pieces, deep inside where nobody could see but where the most vital part of her lived.

He ran a hand through his hair and glanced at his watch, looking hassled. "I don't have time to argue with you."

"Good," she retorted. A belated curiosity struck. "Why did you come over this morning anyway?"

"Oh. Yeah. I wanted to know if you could dog-sit Baxter again. I needed to know and you weren't answering your phone." He paused and she listened to nuances shift in the silence. "Tony and I got invited away for the weekend, but we don't have to go."

"I didn't answer my phone because the battery is dead. It didn't ring." She repeated it with as much patience as she could muster.

She remembered what she was doing and poured herself a second cup of coffee. She held it to her nose, closed her eyes and let the steam warm her chilled skin. Somehow Justin, Tony and that dog had become her entire social circle.

She would have to add that to her to-do list. Fix toilet. Fix lamp. Fix self.

She said, "Of course I'll watch Baxter for you. I love that dog."

"Thanks, I appreciate it." He glanced at his watch again. "I've got a deposition and I really have to run. But I'm coming back and we're going to duke this out later. I'll see you at two."

She felt the bones in her body compress with the urge to smack him over the head. She gritted her teeth instead. The quicker she stopped arguing with him, the quicker he would be out the door. "Hurry or you'll be late for work."

"Oh hell." He bent forward, kissed the air by her cheek and dashed out of the house.

Mary moved to the large living room window to watch with narrowed eyes as he drove away. She tapped a fingernail against the glass. "You can come," she whispered to his retreating car. "But I'm not going to be here."

She folded her laundry, put it away and straightened her bed. There was another load of colorful cloth scraps in the laundry room. She put the scraps in the washing machine and tidied the living room.

Since she lived alone and the two-bedroom house was more than big enough to suit her modest needs, she used the living room as one of her workrooms. She had four quilts in varying stages of completion. By far the most colorful was the patchwork crazy quilt. She fingered the cloth but the piece wasn't speaking to her. It seemed a lifeless fact, separate from her existence as though some stranger had left it in her house.

She moved down the hall to the second bedroom, which she had turned into a studio. There she spent two hours trying to capture on canvas something of the imagery from her dream, but it was hopeless.

Those creatures had shone from within. The colors that had shifted within their bodies and flowed outward in whorls of light were too delicate and strange for her to capture on paper. The colors seemed indicative of emotion or personality, as if the creatures had senses so different from humans, they could actually see the pheromones their bodies released. No matter how she tried, she couldn't convey the impression with paint or pencils, and she didn't have the illustrative skill of a commercial artist.

She had been plagued with strange dreams for as long as she could remember. The one she had labeled "the sacred poison dream" was only one of the ones that recurred on a regular basis. Sometimes the details of the sacred poison dream were vague, or just different. Several details remained constant. There were the seven people, or creatures, three pairs of whom were mates; an escaped criminal; the poison that they drank; and the terror and sense of appalling loss when she awakened.

She shook her head. Some people believed each person had a soul mate, but she didn't. The concept was too convenient, too romantic without real substance. People met other like-minded people because they shared things in common and engaged in similar activities. Birds of a feather really did flock together. Either that or they met by accident. She could never understand why that was a major recurring theme in her dreams.

At least she could be grateful that, no matter how violent or overwhelming the loss might feel in the dream's aftermath, it held her in its grip for only a brief time before fading away. No one could endure that kind of raw anguish for long, at least not that Mary had witnessed. People seemed to suffer intense grief in waves.

The dreams had not been so intense or vivid when she had been a child but they had always been unsettling. They had gained in color, detail and emotion as she had grown older. As a med student at Notre Dame University, she'd taken advantage of the counseling offered through the university in an attempt to put whatever demons existed inside her mind to rest. For over a year she and her counselor had explored her childhood and the possible symbolism involved in the dream imagery.

Justin was right. She had lived an almost entirely normal childhood. She had fallen out of trees, tripped and misspoke in school plays, made cupcakes for bake sales and had sleepovers with friends. She remembered her childhood with detailed clarity. There was simply nothing for her to be haunted about, other than the death of her parents when she was fourteen. Even then she had gone to live with a loving aunt who had been attentive to the needs of a grief-stricken child.

When she had graduated, she terminated the counseling sessions, and married and divorced Justin. Now she lived in her ivory tower. As far as she could tell the attempt at counseling had been a complete failure.

The painting she was trying to work on was a failure as well. She lifted it from the easel and set it against one wall to dry. Then she took up her sketchpad and pencils, hoping that the change in medium might help her convey some of the delicacy that she could see so clearly with her mind's eye.

As she worked, an old memory shook itself out of a dark recess in her mind. She paused to let it unfurl. She had always drawn as a child. As soon as her fingers were big enough to clutch a crayon she would draw, over and over again, people in cages. It had become an elaborate secret

project over the years. The people acquired names and personalities. They had rooms in their prisons. She would draw crude beds, chairs, bookcases, kitchens, all behind bars. They were her people, and she would never let them go.

Over time, she had stopped with that obsession but she had never spoken of it to anyone, and she'd always destroyed the pictures with a hot sense of shame. What kind of monster was she to daydream about caged people?

Seven. Her breathing hitched. She had always drawn seven people. How could she have forgotten that?

She sketched, her movements slow as she struggled past the adult's acquired finesse to approximate something of the child's crudity as she worked to recapture the details from years ago. A simple triangle of an ankle-length dress, the long sleeves, the curl of hair . . . She hesitated at the hem of the dress and her forehead wrinkled. If she remembered right, she had never drawn hands or feet.

Her college counselor would have had a field day with *that* imagery. She shut the sketchbook with a sharp slap.